HOMEPORT

ALSO BY NORA ROBERTS

Hot Ice
Sacred Sins
Brazen Virtues
Sweet Revenge
Public Secrets
Genuine Lies
Carnal Innocence
Divine Evil
Honest Illusions
Private Scandals
Hidden Riches
True Betrayals
Born in Fire
Born in Ice
Born in Shame
Montana Sky
Daring to Dream
Holding the Dream
Finding the Dream
Sanctuary

HOMEPORT

NORA ROBERTS

DOUBLEDAY DIRECT LARGE PRINT EDITION
G. P. Putnam's & Sons
New York

This Large Print Edition, prepared especially for Doubleday Direct, Inc., contains the complete unabridged text of the original Publisher's Edition.

G. P. Putnam's Sons
Publishers Since 1838
a member of
Penguin Putnam Inc.
200 Madison Avenue
New York, New York 10016

Published simultaneously in Canada.
1-56865-726-9

Printed in the United States of America

For Marianne and Ky,
with love and hope and admiration

HOMEPORT

PART ONE

HOMEPORT

Beauty is its own excuse for being.
—Emerson

CHAPTER ONE

THE DAMP, SNAPPING WIND ICED THE BONES THROUGH to the marrow. Snow from a storm earlier in the week was piled in irregular hills along the side of the road. The sky was bitter blue. Stern trees with black empty branches rose out of winter-browned grass and shook their limbs like fists against the cold.

That was March in Maine.

Miranda pumped the heater up to full, programmed her CD player to Puccini's *La Bohème* and drove with the music soaring.

She was coming home. After a ten-day lecture tour, bumping from hotel to college campus to airport and back to hotel, Miranda was more than ready for home.

Her relief might have had something to do with the fact that she hated giving lectures, suffered miserably every time she had to face those rows of eager faces. But shyness and stage fright weren't allowed to interfere with duty.

She was Dr. Miranda Jones, a Jones of Jones Point. And she was never permitted to forget it.

The city had been founded by the first Charles Jones to make his mark in the New World. The Joneses, Miranda knew, were required to make their marks, to maintain their position as the leading family of the Point, to contribute to society, to behave as expected of the Joneses of Jones Point, Maine.

Thrilled to put distance between herself and the airport, she turned onto the coast road and hit the gas. Driving fast was one of her small pleasures. She liked to move quickly, to get from one point to the next with a minimum of fuss and time. A woman who stood nearly six foot in her bare feet and had hair the color of a Tonka toy fire engine rarely went unnoticed. Even when she wasn't in charge, she looked as if she were.

And when she moved with the precision and purpose of a heat-seeking missile, the road ahead generally cleared.

She had a voice one infatuated man had compared to velvet wrapped in sandpaper. She compensated for what she considered an accident of fate by cultivating a brisk, clipped delivery that often bordered on prim.

But it got the job done.

Her body might have come down from some Celtic warrior ancestor, but her face was pure New England. Narrow and cool with a long straight nose, slightly pointed chin, and cheekbones that could have chipped ice. Her mouth was wide and most often set in a serious line. Her eyes were Fourth of July blue, and most often sober.

But now as she entertained herself with the long, winding drive that hugged the snow-laced cliffs, both her mouth and her eyes smiled. Beyond the cliffs, the sea was choppy and steel gray. She loved the moods of it, its power to soothe or thrill. As the road bent like a crooked finger, she heard the thunderous crash of water slapping against rock, then drawing back like a fist to strike again.

The thin sunlight sparkled on the snow, the wind blew fitful streams of it into the air, across the road. On the bay side, the naked trees were bent like old men, twisted by year after year of storms. When she was a child, and still fanciful, she'd imagined those trees muttering complaints to each other as they huddled against the wind.

Though she considered herself fanciful no longer, she still loved the look of them, gnarled and knotted, but lined up like old soldiers on the bluff.

The road climbed as the land narrowed, with the water creeping in on both sides. Sea and sound, both moody, often bleak, nibbled away at the shores with a perpetual hunger. The crooked spit of land rose, its topmost point humped like an arthritic knuckle and graced by the old Victorian house that looked over sea and land. Beyond it, where the ground tumbled down again toward the water, was the white spear of the lighthouse that guarded the coast.

The house had been her refuge and her joy as a child because of the woman who lived in it. Amelia Jones had bucked the Jones tradition and had lived as she chose, had said what she thought, and had always, always had a place in her heart for her two grandchildren.

Miranda had adored her. The only true grief she'd ever known was when Amelia had died—with no fuss or warning, in her sleep eight winters before.

She'd left the house, the tidy portfolio she'd cleverly put together over the years, and her art collection to Miranda and her brother. To her son, Miranda's father, she left her wishes that he be half the man she'd hoped before they met again. To her daughter-in-law, she left a strand of pearls because they were the only thing she could think of that Elizabeth had ever fully approved of.

It had been so like her, Miranda thought now. Those pithy little comments in the will. She'd stayed in the big stone house for years, living alone, having survived her husband by more than a decade.

Miranda thought of her grandmother as she reached the end of the coast road and turned into the long, curving drive.

The house that topped it had survived years and gales, the merciless cold of winter, the shocking and sudden heat of high summer. Now, Miranda thought with a little twist of guilt, it was surviving benign neglect.

Neither she nor Andrew seemed to find the time

to arrange for painters or lawn care. The house that had been a showplace when she was a child now displayed its sags and scars. Still, she thought it lovely, rather like an old woman not afraid to act her age. Rather than rambling, it stood in straight, soldierly angles, its gray stone dignified, its gables and turrets distinguished.

On the sound side a pergola offered charm and fancy. Wisteria tangled up its sides, buried its roof in blossoms in the spring. Miranda always meant to make time to sit on one of the marble benches under that fragrant canopy, to enjoy the scents, the shade, the quiet. But somehow spring ran into summer and summer into fall, and she never remembered her vow until winter, when the thick vines were bare.

Perhaps some of the boards on the wide front porch of the house needed replacing. Certainly the trim and shutters, faded from blue to gray, needed to be scraped and painted. The wisteria on the pergola probably needed to be pruned or fed or whatever you did with such things.

She would get to it. Sooner or later.

But the windows glinted, and the ferocious faces of the gargoyles crouched on the eaves grinned. Long terraces and narrow balconies offered views in every direction. The chimneys would puff smoke—when someone took the time to light a fire. Grand old oaks rose high, and a thick stand of pines broke the wind on the north side.

She and her brother shared the space compatibly enough—or had until Andrew's drinking became more habitual. But she wasn't going to think about that. She enjoyed having him close, liked as well as loved him, so that working with him, sharing a house with him, was a pleasure.

The wind blew her hair into her eyes the minute she stepped out of the car. Vaguely annoyed, she dragged it back, then leaned in to retrieve her laptop and briefcase. Shouldering both, humming the final strains of Puccini, she walked back to the trunk and popped it open.

Her hair blew into her face again, causing her to huff out an irritated breath. The half-sigh ended in a choked gasp as her hair was grabbed in one hard yank, used as a rope to snap her head back. Small white stars burst in front of her eyes as both pain and shock stabbed into her skull. And the point of a knife pressed cold and sharp against the pulse in her throat.

Fear screamed in her head, a primal burn that burst in the gut and shrieked toward the throat. Before she could release it, she was twisted around, shoved hard against the car so that the blossom of pain in her hip blurred her vision and turned her legs to jelly. The hand on her hair yanked again, jerking her head back like a doll's.

His face was hideous. Pasty white and scarred, its features blunted. It took her several seconds before the dry-mouthed terror allowed her to see it was a mask—rubber and paint twisted into deformity.

She didn't struggle, couldn't. There was nothing she feared as much as a knife with its deadly point, its smooth killing edge. The keen tip was pressed into the soft pad under her jaw so that each choked breath she took brought a searing jab of pain and terror.

He was big. Six-four or -five, she noted, struggling to pay attention, pay attention to details while her heart skittered into her throat where the blade pressed. Two hundred fifty or sixty pounds, wide at the shoulders, short at the neck.

Oh God.

Brown eyes, muddy brown. It was all she could see through the slits in the rubber fright mask he wore. And the eyes were flat as a shark's and just as dispassionate as he tipped the point of the knife, slid it over her throat to delicately slice the skin.

A small fire burned there while a thin line of blood trickled down to the collar of her coat.

"Please." The word bubbled out as she instinctively shoved at the wrist of his knife hand. Every rational thought clicked off into cold dread as he used the point to jerk up her head and expose the vulnerable line of her throat.

In her mind flashed the image of the knife slashing once, fast and silent, severing carotid artery, a gush of hot blood. And she would die on her feet, slaughtered like a lamb.

"Please don't. I have three hundred and fifty dollars in cash." Please let it be money he wants, she thought frantically. Let it just be money. If it was rape, she prayed she had the courage to fight, even knowing she couldn't win.

If it was blood, she hoped it would be quick.

"I'll give you the money," she began, then gasped in shock as he tossed her aside like a bundle of rags.

She fell hard on her hands and knees on the gravel drive, felt the burn of small, nasty cuts on her palms. She could hear herself whimpering, hated the helpless, numbing fear that made it impossible to do more than stare at him out of blurred eyes.

To stare at the knife that glinted in the thin sunlight. Even as her mind screamed to run, to fight, she hunched into herself, paralyzed.

He picked up her purse, her briefcase, turned the blade so that the sun shot off a spear of light into her eyes. Then he leaned down and jammed the point into the rear tire. When he yanked it free, took a step in her direction, she began to crawl toward the house.

She waited for him to strike again, to tear at her clothes, to plunge the knife into her back with the same careless force he'd used to stab it into the tire, but she kept crawling over the brittle winter grass.

When she reached the steps, she looked back with her eyes wheeling in her head, with small, hunted sounds bubbling through her lips.

And saw she was alone.

Short, rusty breaths scraped at her throat, burned in her lungs as she dragged herself up the steps. She had to get inside, get away. Lock the door. Before he came back, before he came back and used that knife on her.

Her hand slid off the knob once, twice before she managed to close her fingers around it. Locked. Of course it was locked. No one was home. No one was there to help.

For a moment, she simply curled there, outside the door, shivering with shock and the wind that whipped over the hill.

Move, she ordered herself. You have to move. Get the key, get inside, call the police.

Her eyes darted left and right, like a rabbit watching for wolves, and her teeth started to chatter. Using the knob for support, she pulled herself to her feet. Her legs threatened to buckle, her left knee was screaming, but she darted off the porch in a kind of drunken lope, searched frantically for her purse before she remembered he'd taken it.

She babbled out words, prayers, curses, pleas as she yanked open the car door and fumbled with the glove compartment. Even as her fingers closed over her spare keys a sound had her whirling around wildly, her hands coming up defensively.

There was nothing there but the wind sweeping through the bare black branches of trees, through the thorny canes of the climbing roses, over the brittle grass.

Breath whistling, she took off for the house in a limping run, jabbing frantically with the key at the lock, all but wailing with relief when it slid home.

She stumbled inside, slammed the door, turned the locks. When her back was against that solid wood, the keys slipped out of her fingers, landed with a musical crash. Her vision grayed, so she closed her eyes. Everything was numb now, mind, body. She needed to take the next step, to act, to cope, but she couldn't remember what step to take.

Her ears were ringing and nausea rose up in one long greasy wave. Gritting her teeth, she took one step forward, then another as the foyer seemed to tilt gently right and left.

She was nearly to the base of the stairs when she realized it wasn't her ears ringing, but the telephone. Mechanically, she walked through the haze into the parlor, where everything was so normal, so familiar, and picked up the phone.

"Hello?" Her voice sounded far away, hollow like a single beat in a wooden drum. Swaying a bit, she stared at the pattern the sun made as it slipped through the windows and onto the wide planks of the pine floor. "Yes. Yes, I understand. I'll be there. I have . . ." What? Shaking her head to clear it, Miranda struggled to remember what she needed to say. "I have some things . . . things to take care of first. No, I'll leave as soon as I can."

Then something bubbled up inside her she was too dazed to recognize as hysteria. "I'm already packed," she said, and laughed.

She was still laughing when she hung up the phone. Laughing when she slid bonelessly into a chair, and didn't realize when she tucked herself into a small, defensive ball that the laughter had turned to sobs.

She had both hands wrapped tight around a cup of hot tea, but she didn't drink it. She knew the cup would shake, but it was a comfort to hold it, to feel the heat pass through the cup and into her chilled fingers, soothe the abraded skin of her palms.

She'd been coherent—it was imperative to be coherent, to be clear and precise and calm when reporting a crime to the police.

Once she was able to think again, she'd made the proper calls, she'd spoken to the officers who had come to the house. But now that it was done and she was alone again, she couldn't seem to keep a single solid thought in her mind for more than ten seconds.

"Miranda!" The shout was followed by the cannon bang of the front door slamming. Andrew rushed in, took one horrified study of his sister's face. "Oh Jesus." He hurried to her, crouched at her feet and began to play his long fingers over her pale cheeks. "Oh, honey."

"I'm all right. Just some bruises." But the control she'd managed to build back into place trembled. "I was more scared than hurt."

He saw the tears in the knees of her trousers, the dried blood on the wool. "The son of a bitch." His eyes, a quieter blue than his sister's, abruptly went dark with horror. "Did he . . ." His hands lowered to hers so that they gripped the china cup together. "Did he rape you?"

"No. No. It was nothing like that. He just stole my purse. He just wanted money. I'm sorry I had the police call you. I should have done it myself."

"It's all right. Don't worry." He tightened his grip on her hands, then released them quickly when she winced. "Oh, baby." He took the cup from her hands, set it aside, then lifted her abraded palms. "I'm so sorry. Come on, I'll take you to the hospital."

"I don't need the hospital. It's just bumps and bruises." She drew a deep breath, finding it easier to do so now that he was here.

He could infuriate her, and he had disappointed her. But in all of her life, he'd been the only one to stick with her, to be there.

He picked up her cup of tea, pressed it into her hands again. "Drink a little," he ordered before he rose and paced off some of the fear and anger.

He had a thin, rather bony face that went well with the long, lanky build. His coloring was like his sister's, though his hair was a darker red, almost mahogany. Nerves had him patting his hand against his thigh as he moved.

"I wish I'd been here. Damn it, Miranda. I should have been here."

"You can't be everywhere, Andrew. No one could have predicted that I'd be mugged in our own front yard. I think—and the police think—that he was probably going to break into the house, rob us, and my coming home surprised him, changed his plans."

"They said he had a knife."

"Yeah." Gingerly she lifted a hand to the shallow cut on her throat. "And I can report that I haven't outgrown my knife phobia. One look at it, and my mind just froze."

Andrew's eyes went grim, but he spoke gently

as he came back to sit beside her. "What did he do? Can you tell me?"

"He just came out of nowhere. I was getting my things out of the trunk. He yanked me back by the hair, put the knife to my throat. I thought he was going to kill me, but he knocked me down, took my purse, my briefcase, slashed my tires, and left." She managed a wavering smile. "Not exactly the homecoming I was expecting."

"I should have been here," he said again.

"Andrew, don't." She leaned into him, closed her eyes. "You're here now." And that, it seemed, was enough to steady her. "Mother called."

"What?" He started to drape an arm around her shoulders, and now sat forward to look at her face.

"The phone was ringing when I got into the house. God, my mind's still fogged," she complained, and rubbed at her temple. "I have to go to Florence tomorrow."

"Don't be ridiculous. You just got home and you're hurt, you're shaken. Christ, how can she ask you to get on a plane right after you've been mugged?"

"I didn't tell her." She only shrugged. "I wasn't thinking. In any case, the summons was loud and clear. I have to book a flight."

"Miranda, you're going to bed."

"Oh yeah." She smiled again. "Very soon now."

"I'll call her." He sucked in his breath as a man might when faced with an ugly chore. "I'll explain."

"My hero." Loving him, she kissed his cheek. "No, I'll go. A hot bath, some aspirin, and I'll be fine. And after this little adventure, I could use a distraction. It seems she has a bronze she wants me to test." Because it had gone cold, she set the tea down again. "She wouldn't summon me to Standjo if it wasn't important. She wants an archeometrist, and she wants one quickly."

"She's got archeometrists on staff at Standjo."

"Exactly." This time Miranda's smile was thin and bright. "Standjo" stood for Standford-Jones. Elizabeth had made certain that not only her name but everything else on her agenda came first in the Florence operation. "So if she's sending for me, it's big. She wants to keep it in the family. Elizabeth Standford-Jones, director of Standjo, Florence, is sending for an expert on Italian Renaissance bronzes, and she wants one with the Jones name. I don't intend to disappoint her."

She didn't have any luck booking a flight for the following morning and had to settle for a seat on the evening flight to Rome with a transfer to Florence.

Nearly a full day's delay.

There would be hell to pay.

As she tried to soak out the aches in a hot tub, Miranda calculated the time difference and decided there was no point in calling her mother. Elizabeth would be at home, very likely in bed by now.

Nothing to be done about it tonight, she told herself. In the morning, she'd call Standjo. One day couldn't make that much difference, even to Elizabeth.

She'd hire a car to take her to the airport, because the way her knee was throbbing, driving could be a problem even if she could replace her tires quickly. All she had to do was . . .

She sat straight up in the tub, sloshing water to the rim.

Her passport. Her passport, her driver's license, her company IDs. He'd taken her briefcase and her purse—he'd taken all her identification documents.

"Oh hell," was the best she could do as she rubbed her hands over her face. That just made it all perfect.

She yanked the old-fashioned chain plug out of the drain of the claw-foot tub. She was steaming now, and the burst of angry energy had her getting to her feet, reaching for a towel, before her wrenched knee buckled under her. Biting back a yelp, she braced a hand against the wall and sat on the lip of the tub, the towel dropping in to slop in the water.

The tears wanted to come, from frustration, from the pain, from the sudden sharp fear that came stabbing back. She sat naked and shivering, her breath trembling out on little hitching gasps until she'd controlled them.

Tears wouldn't help her get back her papers, or soothe her bruises or get her to Florence. She sniffled them back and wrung out the towel. Carefully now, she used her hands to lift her legs out of the tub, one at a time. She gained her feet as clammy sweat popped out on her skin, causing the tears to swim close again. But she stood, clutching the sink for support, and took stock of herself in the full-length mirror on the back of the door.

There were bruises on her arms. She didn't remember him grabbing her there, but the marks were dark gray, so logically he had. Her hip was black-and-blue and stunningly painful. That, she remembered, was a result of being rammed back against the car.

Her knees were scraped and raw, the left one unattractively red and swollen. She must have taken the worst of the fall on it, twisted it. The heels of her hands burned from their rude meeting with the gravel of the drive.

But it was the long, shallow slice on her throat that had her head going light, her stomach rolling with fresh nausea. Fascinated and appalled, she lifted her fingers to it. Just a breath from the jugular, she thought. Just a breath from death.

If he'd wanted her to die, she would have died.

And that was worse than the bruising, the sick throbbing aches. A stranger had held her life in his hands.

"Never again." She turned away from the mirror, hobbled over to take her robe from the brass hook by the door. "I'm never going to let it happen again."

She was freezing, and wrapped herself as quickly as she could in the robe. As she was struggling to belt it, a movement outside the window had her head jerking up, her heart thundering.

He'd come back.

She wanted to run, to hide, to scream for Andrew, to curl herself into a ball behind a locked door. And with her teeth gritted, she eased closer to the window, looked out.

It was Andrew, she saw with a dizzying wave of relief. He was wearing the plaid lumberman's jacket he used when he split wood or hiked on the cliffs. He'd turned the floodlights on, and she could see something glinting in his hand, something he swung as he strode along over the yard.

Puzzled, she pressed her face against the window.

A golf club? What in the world was he doing outside marching across the snowy lawn with a golf club?

Then she knew, and love flooded into her, soothing her more than any painkiller.

He was guarding her. The tears came back. One spilled over. Then she saw him stop, pull something from his pocket, lift it.

And she watched him take a long swig from a bottle.

Oh, Andrew, she thought, as her eyes closed and her heart sank. What a mess we are.

It was the pain that woke her, bright pops of it that banged out of her knee. Miranda fumbled on the light, shook out pills from the bottle she'd put on her bedside table. Even as she swallowed them she realized she should have taken Andrew's advice and gone to the hospital, where some sympathetic doctor would have written her a prescription for some good, potent drugs.

She glanced at the luminous dial of her clock, saw it was after three. At least the cocktail of ibuprofen and aspirin she'd taken at midnight had given her three hours of relief. But she was awake now, and chasing the pain. Might as well finish it off, she decided, and face the music.

With the time difference, Elizabeth would be at her desk. Miranda picked up the phone and put the call through. Moaning a bit, she shifted her pillows against the curvy wrought-iron headboard and eased back against them.

"Miranda, I was about to call to leave a message at your hotel for your arrival tomorrow."

"I'm going to be delayed. I—"

"Delayed?" The word was like a single ice chip, frigid and sharp.

"I'm sorry."

"I thought I made it clear this project is priority. I've guaranteed the government that we would begin tests today."

"I'm going to send John Carter. I—"

"I didn't send for John Carter, I sent for you. Whatever other work you have can be delegated. I believe I made that clear as well."

"Yes, you did." No, she thought, the pills weren't going to help this time. But the cold anger beginning to stir inside her was bound to outdistance a little pain. "I had every intention of being there, as instructed."

"Then why aren't you?"

"My passport and other identification were stolen yesterday. I'll arrange to have them replaced as soon as possible and rebook my flight. This being Friday, I doubt I can have new documents before sometime next week."

She knew how bureaucracies worked, Miranda thought grimly. She'd been raised in one.

"Even in a relatively quiet place like Jones Point, it's foolishly careless not to lock your car."

"The documents weren't in my car, they were on me. I'll let you know as soon as they're replaced and I've rescheduled. I apologize for the delay. The project will have my full time and attention as soon as I arrive. Goodbye, Mother."

It gave her perverse satisfaction to hang up before Elizabeth could say another word.

In her elegant and spacious office three thousand miles away, Elizabeth stared at the phone with a mixture of annoyance and confusion.

"Is there a problem?"

Distracted, Elizabeth glanced over at her former daughter-in-law. Elise Warfield sat, a clipboard resting on her knee, her big green eyes puzzled, her soft, lush mouth curved slightly in an attentive smile.

The marriage between Elise and Andrew hadn't worked, which was a disappointment to Elizabeth. But her professional and personal relationship with Elise hadn't been damaged by the divorce.

"Yes. Miranda's been delayed."

"Delayed?" Elise lifted her brows so that they disappeared under the fringe of bangs that skimmed over her brow. "That's not like Miranda."

"Her passport and other identification were stolen."

"Oh, that's dreadful." Elise got to her feet. She stood just over five-two. Her body had lush feminine curves that managed to look delicate. With her sleek cap of ebony hair, her large, heavily lashed eyes and milky white skin, the deep red of her mouth, she resembled an efficient and sexy fairy. "She was robbed?"

"I didn't get the details." Elizabeth's lips tightened briefly. "She'll arrange to have them replaced and reschedule her flight. It may take several days."

Elise started to ask if Miranda had been hurt, then closed her mouth on the words. From the look in Elizabeth's eyes, either she didn't know, or it wasn't her major concern. "I know you want to begin testing today. It can certainly be arranged. I can shift some of my work and start them myself."

Considering, Elizabeth rose and turned to her window. She always thought more clearly when she looked out over the city. Florence was her home, had been her home since the first time she'd seen it. She'd been eighteen, a young college student with a desperate love for art and a secret thirst for adventure.

She'd fallen hopelessly in love with the city, with its red rooftops and majestic domes, its twisting streets and bustling piazzas.

And she'd fallen in love with a young sculptor who had charmingly lured her to bed, fed her pasta, and shown her her own heart.

Of course, he'd been unsuitable. Completely unsuitable. Poor and wildly passionate. Her parents had snapped her back to Boston the moment they'd learned of the affair.

And that, of course, had been the end of that.

She shook herself, annoyed that her mind had drifted there. She'd made her own choices, and they had been excellent ones.

Now she was the head of one of the largest and most respected research facilities for art in the world. Standjo might have been one of the arms of the Jones organization, but it was hers. Her name came first, and here, so did she.

She stood framed in the window, a trim, attractive woman of fifty-eight. Her hair was a quiet ash blond discreetly tinted by one of the top salons in Florence. Her impeccable taste was reflected in the perfectly cut Valentino suit she wore, the color a rich eggplant, with hammered-gold buttons. Her leather pumps matched the tone exactly.

Her complexion was clear, with good New England bone structure overcoming the few lines that dared show themselves. Her eyes were a sharp and ruthlessly intelligent blue. The image was one of a cool, fashionable, professional woman of wealth and position.

She would never have settled for less.

No, she thought, she would never settle for less than the absolute best.

"We'll wait for her," she said, and turned back to Elise. "It's her field, her specialty. I'll contact the minister personally and explain the short delay."

Elise smiled at her. "No one understands delays like the Italians."

"True enough. We'll go over those reports later today, Elise. I want to make this call now."

"You're the boss."

"Yes, I am. Oh, John Carter will be coming in tomorrow. He'll be working on Miranda's team. Feel free to assign him another project in the meantime. There's no point in having him twiddle his thumbs."

"John's coming? It'll be good to see him. We can always use him in the lab. I'll take care of it."

"Thank you, Elise."

When she was alone, Elizabeth sat at her desk again, studied the safe across the room. Considered what was inside.

Miranda would head the project. Her decision had been made the moment she'd seen the bronze. It would be a Standjo operation, with a Jones at the helm. That was what she had planned, what she expected.

And it was what she would have.

CHAPTER TWO

SHE WAS FIVE DAYS LATE, SO MIRANDA MOVED FAST, pushing through the towering medieval doors of Standjo, Florence, and striding across the floor so that the clicks of her practical pumps were like rapid gunshots on the gleaming white marble.

She clipped the Standjo ID Elizabeth's assistant had overnighted her to the lapel of her jacket as she rounded an excellent bronze reproduction of Cellini's figure of Perseus displaying Medusa's severed head.

Miranda had often wondered just what the choice of art in the entrance lobby said about her mother. Defeat all enemies, she supposed, with one swift stroke.

She stopped at the lobby counter, swiveling the logbook around and dashing off her name, noting the time on her watch, then adding it.

She'd dressed carefully, even strategically, for

the day, selecting a suit of royal-blue silk that was military and trim in style. Miranda considered it both dashing and powerful.

When you were to meet with the director of one of the top archeometry laboratories in the world, your appearance was vitally important. Even if that director was your mother.

Especially, Miranda thought with the faintest of sneers, if that director was your mother.

She punched the button on the elevator and waited, impatience shimmering. Nerves were jumping gleefully in her stomach, tickling in her throat, buzzing in her head. But she didn't let them show.

The minute she stepped into the elevator, she flipped open her compact and freshened her lipstick. A single tube of color could last her a year, sometimes more. She only bothered with such small annoyances when they couldn't be avoided.

Satisfied she'd done her best, she replaced the compact, and ran a hand over the sophisticated French twist that had taken her entirely too much time and trouble to create. She jammed a few loosened pins back firmly in place just as the doors opened again.

She stepped out into the quiet, elegant lobby of what she thought of as the inner sanctum. The pearl-gray carpet and ivory walls, the stern-backed antique chairs, suited her mother, she thought. Lovely, tasteful, and detached. The sleek console where the receptionist worked with its top-grade computer and phone system was also all Elizabeth. Efficient, brisk, and state-of-the-art.

"Buon giorno." Miranda approached the desk and stated her business briefly and in flawless Italian. *"Sono la Dottoressa Jones. Ho un appuntamento con la Signora Standford-Jones."*

"Sì, Dottoressa. Un momento."

In her head, Miranda shifted her feet, tugged at her jacket, rolled her shoulders. It sometimes helped her keep her body still and calm if she imagined twitching and shuffling. She was just finishing up some imaginary pacing when the receptionist smiled and gave her the go-ahead.

Miranda walked through the double glass doors to her left and down the cool white hallway that led to the office of the Signora Direttrice.

She knocked. One was always expected to knock on any door of Elizabeth's. The responding "*Entri*" came immediately.

Elizabeth was at her desk, an elegant satinwood Hepplewhite that suited her aristocratic New England looks perfectly. Framed in the window behind her was Florence, in all its sunny splendor.

They faced each other across the room, both appraising swiftly.

Elizabeth spoke first. "How was your trip?"

"Uneventful."

"Good."

"You look well."

"I am, quite well. And you?"

"Fine." Miranda imagined herself doing a wild tap dance around the perfectly appointed office, and stood straight as a cadet at inspection.

"Would you like some coffee? Something cold?"

"No, thank you." Miranda arched a brow. "You haven't asked about Andrew."

Elizabeth waved toward a chair. "How's your brother?"

Miserable, Miranda thought. Drinking too much. Angry, depressed, bitter. "He's fine. He sends his best." She lied without a qualm. "I assume you told Elise I was coming."

"Of course." Because Miranda had remained standing, Elizabeth rose. "All the department heads, and the appropriate staff members, are aware that you'll be working here temporarily. The Fiesole Bronze is a priority. Naturally you'll have full use of the labs and equipment, and the cooperation and assistance of any members of the team you choose."

"I spoke with John yesterday. You haven't started any tests yet."

"No. This delay has cost us time, and you'll be expected to begin immediately."

"That's why I'm here."

Elizabeth inclined her head. "What happened to your leg? You're limping a bit."

"I was mugged, remember?"

"You said you'd been robbed, you didn't say you'd been injured."

"You didn't ask."

Elizabeth let out what from anyone else Miranda would have considered a sigh. "You might have explained you'd been hurt during the incident."

"I might have. I didn't. The priority was, after all, the loss of my documents and the delay that caused." She inclined her head, in a mirror of Elizabeth's gesture. "That much was made very clear."

"I assumed—" Elizabeth cut herself off, flung her hand in a gesture that might have been annoyance or defeat. "Why don't you sit down while I give you some background?"

So, the matter was to be tabled. Miranda had expected it. She sat, crossed her legs.

"The man who discovered the bronze—"

"The plumber."

"Yes." For the first time Elizabeth smiled, a quick curving of lips that was more an acknowledgment of the absurdity than genuine amusement. "Carlo Rinaldi. Apparently he's an artist at heart, if not in deed. He's never been able to make a living from his painting and his wife's father owns a plumbing business, so . . ."

Miranda's quick eyebrow flick was a measure of mild surprise. "Does his background matter?"

"Only insofar as his connection to the piece. There appears to be none. He, from all accounts, literally stumbled over it. He claims to have found it hidden under a broken step in the cellar of the Villa della Donna Oscura. And that, as far as has been verified, seems to be the case."

"Was there some question of that? Is he suspected of fabricating the story—and the bronze?"

"If there was, the minister is satisfied with Rinaldi's story now."

Elizabeth folded her perfectly manicured hands on the edge of the desk. Her New England spine was straight as a ruler. Unconsciously, Miranda shifted ever so slightly to level her own.

"The fact that he found it," Elizabeth continued, "smuggled it out of the villa in his toolbox, then took his time reporting it through the proper channels caused some initial concern."

Troubled, Miranda folded her hands to keep her fingers from tapping on her knee. It didn't occur to her that she now exactly mirrored her mother's pose. "How long did he have it?"

"Five days."

"There was no damage? You've examined it?"

"I have. I'd rather not make any comments until you've seen it yourself."

"Well then." Miranda cocked her head. "Let's have a look."

In answer, Elizabeth walked over to a cabinet, and opening the door, revealed a small steel safe.

"You're keeping it in here?"

"My security is more than adequate. A number of people have access to the vaults in the labs, and I preferred to limit that access in this case. And I thought it would be less distracting for you to do an initial exam here."

With one coral-tipped finger, Elizabeth punched in a code, waited, then added another series of numbers. Opening the reinforced door, she took out a metal box. After setting it on her desk, she opened the lid and took out a bundle wrapped in faded velvet.

"We'll date the cloth as well, and the wood from the step."

"Naturally." Though her fingers itched, Miranda rose and stepped forward slowly when Elizabeth set the bundle on her spotless white blotter. "There are no documents, correct?"

"None, so far. You know the history of the villa."

"Yes, of course. It was once the home of Giulietta Buonadoni, a mistress of Lorenzo the Magnificent known as the Dark Lady. After his death she's believed to have become a companion of other Medicis. At one time or another every light of the Renaissance in or around Florence was welcomed into her home."

"So, you understand the possibilities."

"I don't deal in possibilities," Miranda said curtly.

"Exactly. That's why you're here."

Gently, Miranda brushed a finger over the tattered velvet. "Is it?"

"I wanted the best, and I'm in a position to access what I want. I also demand discretion. If news of this find leaks, the speculation will be wild. That is something Standjo can't and won't risk. The government wants no publicity, and no public speculation until the bronze is dated, and tests are complete."

"The plumber's probably already told all his drinking pals."

"I wouldn't think so." Again that small smile played around Elizabeth's mouth. "He took the bronze out of a government-owned building. He's quite aware, at this point, that if he doesn't do precisely what he's told, he could go to prison."

"Fear is often an efficient gag."

"Yes. But that isn't our concern. We've been commissioned to test the bronze, and to provide the government with all the information science can offer. We require an objective eye, someone who believes in facts, not romance."

"There's no room for romance in science," Miranda murmured, and carefully unwrapped the velvet.

Her heart gave one hard thud against her ribs when the bronze lay naked. Her skilled and experienced eye recognized the brilliance of the workmanship, the glory of it. But she frowned, instinctively burying admiration under skepticism.

"It's beautifully conceived and executed—certainly the style falls within the realm of the Renaissance." She slipped her glasses out of the case in her pocket, put them on before she lifted the bronze. She judged the weight, turning it slowly.

The proportions were perfect, the sensuality of the subject obvious. The smallest details—toenails, each tendril of hair, the definition of calf muscles—were stunningly depicted.

She was glorious, free, wonderfully aware of her own power. The long curvy body was arched back, the arms lifted up, not in prayer or supplication, Miranda noted. In triumph. The face wasn't delicate, but stunning, the eyes half closed as if in pleasure, the mouth curved slyly in enjoyment of that pleasure.

She was balanced on the balls of her feet, like a woman about to leap into a warm, scented pool. Or a lover's arms.

It was unashamedly sexual, and for one baffling instant, Miranda thought she could feel the heat of it. Like life.

The patina indicated age, but such things were deceiving, she knew. Patinas could be created. The style of the artist was unmistakable. But such a thing was all but impossible. Styles could be mimicked.

"It's the Dark Lady," she said. "Giulietta Buonadoni. There's no doubt about that. I've seen this face often enough in paintings and sculpture of the period. But I've never seen or heard of this bronze. I'll do some research on it, but I doubt I'd have missed it."

Elizabeth studied Miranda's face rather than the bronze. She'd seen that quick flicker of excitement, of delight, both of which had been quickly controlled. Exactly as she'd expected them to be.

"But you agree it is a bronze of Renaissance style."

"Yes. That hardly makes it a lost piece from the fifteenth century." Her eyes were narrowed as she slowly turned the bronze in her hands. "Any art student with a clever eye has sketched and copied her face over the years. I've done so myself." Idly, she scraped a bit at the blue-green patina with her thumbnail. The surface corrosion was visibly thick, but she needed more, much more.

"I'll start right away."

Vivaldi played lightly in the air of the lab. The walls were a pale hospital green, the floor a spotlessly white linoleum. Each station was militarily neat, fitted with microscopes, computer terminals, vials or tubes or sample bags. There were no personal items, no pretty framed family pictures, no mascots or souvenirs.

The men wore ties, the women skirts, and over all were the crisp white lab coats with the Standjo logo stitched in black on the breast pocket.

Conversation was muted and minimal, and equipment hummed like well-oiled clocks.

Elizabeth expected a tight ship, and her former daughter-in-law knew how to run one.

The house in Maine where Miranda had grown up had presented precisely the same atmosphere. It made for a cold home, Miranda thought as she scanned the area, but an efficient workplace.

"It's been some time since you were here," Elizabeth began. "But Elise will refresh your memory as to the setup. You'll have free access to all areas, of course. I have your security card and your codes."

"Fine." Miranda fixed a polite smile on her face as Elise turned from a microscope and started toward them.

"Miranda, welcome to Florence." Elise's voice was quiet, not quite breathy, but with the promise it could be if she were properly aroused.

"It's nice to be back. How are you?"

"Fine. Busy." She flashed a hundred-watt smile and took Miranda's hand. "How's Drew?"

"Not quite so fine—but busy." She lifted a brow when Elise squeezed her hand.

"I'm sorry."

"It's none of my business."

"I'm still sorry." She released Miranda's hand and turned to Elizabeth. "Will you head the tour, or shall I?"

"I don't need a tour," Miranda said before her mother could speak. "I need a lab coat, a microscope, a computer. I'll want to take photos, and X rays, of course."

"There you are." John Carter loped his way over. Miranda's lab manager looked endearingly rumpled in the midst of ruthless efficiency and style. His tie with silly grinning cows grazing was already askew. He'd snagged the pocket of his lab coat on something so that it flapped from loose threads. There was a nick on his chin where he'd cut himself shaving, a thumb-sized stub of a pencil behind his ear, and smudges on the lenses of his glasses.

He made Miranda feel cozily at home.

"You okay?" He patted her arm in three bouncing strokes, then: "How's the knee? Andrew told me the guy who mugged you tossed you around."

"Tossed you around?" Elise looked over quickly. "We didn't know you were hurt."

"Just shaken up. It's all right. I'm fine."

"He held a knife to her throat," Carter announced.

"A knife." Elise put a hand to her own throat. "That's horrible. It's—"

"It's all right," Miranda said again. "He just wanted money." She turned, meeting her mother's eyes. "And I think he's cost us enough valuable time."

For a moment Elizabeth said nothing. There was challenge in Miranda's gaze, and she decided the time for sympathy had passed.

"Then I'll let Elise set you up. Your ID and security cards are in here." Elizabeth handed Miranda an envelope. "Elise should be able to handle any of your questions or needs. Or you can contact me." She glanced at the slim watch on her wrist. "I have another meeting shortly, so I'll let you get started. I hope to have a preliminary report by end of day."

"You will," Miranda murmured as her mother walked away.

"She doesn't waste time." With another smile, Elise gestured. "I'm so sorry you had to go through such a terrible ordeal, but the work here should help you keep it off your mind. I have an office set up for you. The Fiesole Bronze is a top priority. You're authorized to pick your team from any of the A security staff."

"Miranda!" There was a wealth of pleasure in the word, and it was delivered with the heavy and exotic tones of Italy. Miranda felt herself smiling even before she turned and had her hands taken and lavishly kissed.

"Giovanni. You don't change." Indeed, the chemistry technician was as outrageously handsome as Miranda remembered. Dark and sleek, with eyes like melted chocolate and a smile that radiated charm. He stood an inch or so below her and still managed to make her feel feminine and tiny. He wore his glossy black hair in a ponytail—an affectation Elizabeth permitted only because besides being beautiful to look at, Giovanni Beredonno was a genius.

"But you change, *bella donna*. You're even more lovely. But what is this about being hurt?" He fluttered his fingers over her face.

"It's nothing, just a memory."

"Do you want me to go break someone in half for you?" He kissed her gently, one cheek, then the other.

"Can I get back to you on that?"

"Giovanni, Miranda has work."

"Yes, yes." He brushed off Elise's stiff and disapproving words with a careless gesture—another reason for Miranda to smile. "I know all about it. A big project, very hush-hush." He wiggled his expressive eyebrows. "When the *direttrice* sends to America for an expert, it is no small thing. So, *bellissima,* can you use me?"

"You're first on my list."

He tucked her hand through his arm, ignoring the tightening of Elise's lips. "When do we start?"

"Today," Miranda told him as Elise gestured toward a doorway. "I'll want tests run on the corrosion layers and the metal right away."

"I think Richard Hawthorne would be helpful to you." Elise tapped the shoulder of a man hunkered over the keyboard on a computer.

"Dr. Hawthorne." Miranda watched the balding man blink owlishly through his glasses, then fumble them off. There was something vaguely familiar about him, and she struggled to place him.

"Dr. Jones." He gave her a shy smile that added appeal to his face. His chin was short, his eyes a distracted and pale blue, but the smile was sweet as a boy's. "It's nice to see you again. We're, ah, happy to have you here. I read your paper on early Florentine humanism. It was quite brilliant."

"Thank you." Oh, yes, she remembered. He'd done a stint at the Institute a few years earlier. After a moment's hesitation, which Miranda knew came only because Elise had recommended him, she relented. "Elise has an office for me. Could you join us for a moment? I'd like to show you what I have."

"I'd be delighted." He fumbled with his glasses again, hit a series of keys that saved his work.

"It's not a large space." Elise began with an apology as she ushered Miranda through a door. "I've set it up with what I thought you'd need. Of course you can requisition anything you like."

Miranda took a quick scan. The computer station appeared efficient and neat. A wide white counter held microscopes, slides, and the small hand tools of her trade. A tape recorder had been provided for detailing notes. There was no window, only the one door, and with the four of them inside, barely room to turn around.

But there was a chair, a phone, and the pencils were sharpened. It would do, she thought, very well.

She set her briefcase on the counter, then the metal box. Carefully, she removed the wrapped bronze. "I'd like your opinion, Dr. Hawthorne. Just on a visual examination of the bronze."

"Of course, I'd be delighted."

"The project's been the hot topic around here for the last day or two," Giovanni put in as Miranda began to unwrap the velvet. "Ah." He let out a sigh as she set the undraped bronze on the counter. *"Bella, molto bella."*

"A fine execution." Richard pushed his glasses back into place and squinted at the bronze. "Simple. Fluid. Wonderful form and details. Perspective."

"Sensual," Giovanni said, bending to look closely. "The arrogance and the allure of the female."

Miranda cocked a brow at Giovanni before giving her attention back to Richard. "Do you recognize her?"

"It's the Dark Lady of the Medicis."

"That's my opinion as well. And the style?"

"Renaissance, unquestionably." Richard reached out with a tentative finger to stroke the left cheekbone. "I wouldn't say the model was used to represent a mythical or religious figure, but herself."

"Yes, the lady as the lady," Miranda agreed. "The artist portrayed her, I'd guess, as she was. From an artist's standpoint, I would say he knew her, personally. I'll need to do a search for documents. Your help would be invaluable there."

"I'd be happy to help. If this can be authenticated as a major piece from the Renaissance period, it will be quite a coup for Standjo. And for you, Dr. Jones."

She'd thought of it. Indeed, she'd thought of it. But she smiled coolly. "I don't count my chickens. If she spent any amount of time in the environment in which she was found—and it appears she did—the corrosion growth would have been affected. I'll want the results of that, of course," she added to Giovanni, "but I can't depend on it for true accuracy."

"You'll run relative comparisons, thermoluminescence."

"Yes." She smiled at Richard again. "We'll also be testing the cloth, and the wood from the stair tread. But the documentation will make it all the more conclusive."

Miranda leaned a hip on the corner of the small pickled-oak desk. "She was found in the cellar of the Villa della Donna Oscura, secreted under the bottom tread of the stairs. I'll have a report on the details we know at this point for the three of you. The three of you and Vincente only," she added. "Security is one of the director's top concerns. Whoever you require to assist you must have A-grade clearance, and the data you give them must be kept to a minimum until we've completed all tests."

"So, for now she's ours." Giovanni winked at her.

"She's mine," Miranda corrected with a slow, serious smile. "I need any and all information on the villa itself, on the woman. I want to know her."

Richard nodded. "I'll start right away."

Miranda turned back to the bronze. "Let's see what she's made of," she murmured.

A few hours later, Miranda rolled her shoulders and eased back in her chair. The bronze stood before her, smiling slyly. There were no signs of brass or silicon bronze, no platinum, none of the metals or materials that weren't used in the Renaissance in the sliver of patina and metal she'd extracted. The bronze had a clay core, just as a piece of that era should have. The early testing of the corrosion levels indicated late fifteenth century.

Don't be hasty, she ordered herself. Preliminary tests weren't enough. So far she was working in the negative. There was nothing out of place, no alloy that didn't belong, no sign of tool work that didn't jibe with the era in her visual exam, but she had yet to determine the positive.

Was the lady true or false?

She took time for one cup of coffee and some of the pretty crackers and cheese Elise had provided for her in lieu of lunch. Jet lag was threatening, and she refused to acknowledge it. The coffee, strong, black, and potent as only the Italians could brew, pumped through her system, providing a caffeine mask over fatigue. She'd crash eventually, Miranda knew, but not for a little while yet.

Placing her hands over the keyboard, she began hammering out the preliminary report for her mother. It was as strict and dry as a maiden aunt, thus far devoid of speculation and with very little personality. She may have thought of the bronze as a puzzle, a mystery to be solved, but none of the romance of that found its way into her report.

She sent the report via e-mail, saved it on the hard drive under her password, then took the bronze with her for the last test of the day.

The technician had little English and entirely too much awe for the daughter of the *direttrice* for Miranda to find comfortable. Miranda conjured up an errand, and sent her off for more coffee. Alone, she began the thermoluminescence process.

Ionizing radiation would trap electrons in higher-energy states in the clay core of a bronze. When heated, the crystals in the clay would give off bursts of light. Miranda set the equipment, taking quick notes on each step and result in a notebook. She took the measurements of those bursts, logging them in, adding them to her notes as well for backup. She increased the radiation, heated the clay again, to measure how susceptible it was to electron trapping. Those measurements were carefully logged in turn.

The next step was to test the radiation levels from the location where the bronze had been discovered. She tested both the dirt samples and the wood.

It was a matter of math now. Though the accuracy of the method was hardly foolproof, it was one more weight to add to the whole.

Late fifteenth century. She had no doubt of it.

Savonarola had been preaching against luxury and pagan art during that period, Miranda mused. The piece was a glorious kick in the ass to that narrow-minded view. The Medicis were in control of Florence, with the incompetent Piero the Unfortunate taking the helm for a short period before he was expelled from the city by King Charles VIII of France.

The Renaissance was moving from its early glory, when the architect Brunelleschi, the sculptor Donatello, and the painter Masaccio revolutionized the conception, and the functions, of art.

Coming from that, the next generation and the dawn of the sixteenth century—Leonardo, Michelangelo, Raphael, nonconformists searching for pure originality.

She knew the artist. Knew in her heart, her gut. There was nothing he had created that she hadn't studied as intensely and completely as a woman studies the face of her lover.

But the lab wasn't the place for heart, she reminded herself, or gut instinct. She would run all the tests again. And a third time. She would compare the known formula for bronzes of that era and check and recheck every ingredient and alloy in the statue. She would dog Richard Hawthorne for documentation.

And she'd find the answers.

CHAPTER THREE

SUNRISE OVER THE ROOFTOPS AND DOMES OF FLORence was a magnificent moment. It was art and glory. The same delicate light had shimmered over the city when men had conceived and constructed the grand domes and great towers, had faced them with marble mined from the hills and decorated them with the images of saints and gods.

The stars winked out as the sky turned from black velvet to pearl gray. The silhouettes of the long, slender pines that dotted the Tuscan hillsides blurred as the light shifted, wavered, then bloomed.

The city was quiet, as it was so rarely, while the sun inched upward, misting the air with hints of gold. The iron gates over the storefront newsstand rattled and clanged while the proprietor yawned and prepared for the day's business. Only a few lights shone in the many windows of the city. One of them was Miranda's.

She dressed quickly, facing away from the stunning canvas that was quietly painting itself outside her hotel room. Her mind was on work.

How much progress would she make that day? How much closer would she come to the answers? She dealt in facts, and would stick with facts, no matter how tempting it was to leap to the next level. Instincts couldn't always be trusted. Science could.

She bundled her hair back in a clip, then slipped on low-heeled pumps to go with her simple navy suit.

Her early arrival would guarantee her a couple of hours of working in solitude. Though she appreciated having experts at her disposal, *The Dark Lady* had already become hers. She intended for every step of the project to bear her stamp.

She held her ID up to the glass door for the heavy-eyed guard. He left his coffee and breakfast cakes reluctantly, and shuffled over to frown at the card, at her face, then back at the card. He seemed to sigh as he unlocked the door.

"You're very early, Dottoressa Jones."

"I have work."

Americans, as far as the guard was concerned, thought of little else. "You must sign the logbook."

"Of course." As she approached the counter, the scent of his coffee reached out and grabbed her by the throat. She did her best not to drool as she scrawled her name and noted the time of arrival in the log.

"Grazie."

"Prego," she murmured, then started toward the

elevator. So she'd make coffee first, she told herself. She could hardly expect to be sharp before she'd had at least one jolt of caffeine.

She used her key card to access the correct floor, then entered her code once she was at the security post outside the lab. When she hit the switches, banks of fluorescent lights blinked on. A quick glance told her everything was in place, that work in progress had been tidily stored at the end of the workday.

Her mother would expect that, she thought. She would tolerate nothing less than neat efficiency in her employees. And in her children. Miranda shrugged as if to shift the resentment off her shoulders.

Within moments she had coffee brewing, her computer booted, and was transcribing her notes from the evening before onto the hard drive.

If she moaned at the first taste of hot, rich coffee, there was no one to hear. If she leaned back in her chair, eyes closed, smile dreamy, there was no one to see. For five minutes she allowed herself to indulge, to be a woman lost in one of life's small pleasures. Her feet slipped out of her practical pumps, her sharp-boned face softened. She all but purred.

If the guard had seen her now, he would have approved completely.

Then she rose, poured a second cup, donned her lab coat, and got to work.

She retested the dirt from the site first, measuring the radiation, running figures. Once again she tested the clay that had been carefully extracted. She put a smear of each on a slide, then made a third with the scrapings of bronze and patina, and studied each under the microscope.

She was studying her computer screen when the first of the staff began to trickle in. It was there Giovanni hunted her down with a fresh cup of coffee and a delicately sugared roll.

"Tell me what you see," she demanded, and continued to study the colors and shapes on the screen.

"I see a woman who doesn't know how to relax." He laid his hands on her shoulders, rubbed gently. "Miranda, you've been here a week now, and haven't taken an hour to yourself."

"The imaging, Giovanni."

"Ah." Still massaging, he shifted so that their heads were close. "The primary decay process, corrosion. The white line there indicates the original surface of the bronze, *no*?"

"Yes."

"The corrosion is thick on the surface, and it grows downward, deep into the metal, which would be typical of a bronze of four hundred years."

"We need to pinpoint the rate of growth."

"Never easy," he said. "And she was in a damp basement. The corrosion would have grown quickly there."

"I'm taking that into account." She removed her glasses to pinch out the pressure in the bridge of her nose. "The temperature and the humidity. We can calculate an average there. I've never heard of corrosion levels like this being faked. They're there, Giovanni, inside her."

"The cloth is no more than a hundred years old. Less, I think by a decade or two."

"A hundred?" Irritated, Miranda turned to face him. "You're certain?"

"Yes. You'll run tests of your own, but you'll find I'm right. Eighty to a hundred years. No more."

She turned back to the computer. Her eyes saw what they saw, her brain knew what it knew. "All right. Then we're to believe that the bronze was wrapped in that cloth and in that cellar for eighty to a hundred years. But all tests indicate the bronze itself is a great deal older."

"Perhaps. Here, eat your breakfast."

"Um." She took the roll absently and bit in. "Eighty years ago—the early part of the century. World War One. Valuables are often hidden during wartime."

"True enough."

"But where was she before that? Why have we never heard of her? Hidden again," she murmured. "When Piero Medici was expelled from the city. During the Italian Wars perhaps. Hidden, yes, that could be accepted. But forgotten?" Dissatisfied, she shook her head. "This isn't the work of an amateur, Giovanni." She ordered the computer to print out the image. "It's the work of a master. There has to be some documentation, somewhere. I need to know more about that villa, more about the woman. Who did she leave her possessions to, who lived in the villa immediately after she died? Did she have children?"

"I'm a chemist," he said with a smile. "Not a historian. For this you want Richard."

"Is he in yet?"

"He is ever punctual. Wait." He laughed a little, taking her arm before she could hurry away. "Have dinner with me tonight."

"Giovanni." She gave his hand an affectionate squeeze, then drew hers away. "I appreciate the fact that you're worried about me, but I'm fine. I'm too busy to go out to dinner."

"You're working too hard, and not taking care of yourself. I'm your friend, so it's up to me."

"I promise, I'll order an enormous meal from room service while I work at the hotel tonight."

She touched her lips to his cheek just as the door opened. Elise lifted a brow, mouth tight in disapproval.

"I'm sorry to interrupt. Miranda, the director would like you to come to her office at four-thirty for a discussion of your progress."

"Of course. Elise, do you know if Richard's free for a moment?"

"We're all at your disposal."

"That's exactly what I was telling her." Obviously immune to frost, Giovanni grinned, then slipped out of the room.

"Miranda." After a brief hesitation, Elise stepped farther into the room and shut the door at her back. "I hope you won't be offended, but I feel I should warn you that Giovanni . . ."

Darkly amused by Elise's obvious discomfort, Miranda merely smiled blandly. "Giovanni?"

"He's brilliant at his work, a valuable asset to Standjo. But on a personal level, he's a womanizer."

"I wouldn't say so." Head angled, Miranda slipped on her glasses, tipping them down to look over the copper tops. "A womanizer uses. Giovanni gives."

"That may be true, but the fact is he flirts with every female on staff."

"Including you?"

Elise's well-arched brows drew together. "On occasion, and I can tolerate that as part of his personality. Still, the lab isn't the place for flirtations and stolen kisses."

"God, you sound like my mother." And nothing could have irritated Miranda more. "But I'll keep that in mind, Elise, the next time Giovanni and I toy with having wild sex in the chem lab."

"I have offended you." Elise sighed, lifted her hands helplessly. "I only wanted to . . . It's just that he can be so charming. I nearly fell for it myself when I first transferred here. I was feeling so low, and unhappy."

"Were you?"

The ice in Miranda's tone had Elise straightening her slim shoulders. "Divorcing your brother didn't make me jump for joy, Miranda. It was a painful and difficult decision, and I can only hope it was the right one. I loved Drew, but he . . ." Her voice broke, and she shook her head fiercely. "I can only say it wasn't enough for either of us."

The gleam of moisture in Elise's eyes brought Miranda a hard tug of shame. "I'm sorry," she murmured. "It happened so quickly. I didn't think you gave a damn."

"I did. I still do." She sighed, then blinked back the threatening tears. "I wish it had been different, but the fact is that it wasn't, and isn't different. I have to live my life."

"Yes, you do." Miranda shrugged. "Andrew's been so miserable, and it was easier for me to blame you. I don't imagine the breakup of a marriage is ever one person's fault."

"I don't think either of us was very good at marriage. It seemed cleaner and even kinder to end it than to go on pretending."

"Like my parents?"

Elise's eyes widened. "Oh, Miranda, I didn't mean—"

"It's all right. I agree with you. My parents haven't lived under the same roof in more than twenty-five years, but neither of them bothers to end it, cleanly or kindly. Andrew may be hurt, but all in all I prefer your way."

It was, she admitted, the route she would have taken herself—if she'd ever made the mistake of getting married in the first place. Divorce, she decided, was a more humane alternative to the pale illusion of marriage.

"Shall I apologize for all the nasty thoughts I've had about you in the last year or so?"

Elise's lips curved. "Not necessary. I understand your loyalty to Drew. I admire it and always have. I know how close the two of you are."

"United we stand, divided we rush to therapy."

"We never really managed to be friends. We were colleagues, then relatives, but never really made it to friends even with all we have in common. Maybe we can't, but I'd like to think we could at least be friendly."

"I don't have many friends." Too much of an intimacy risk, Miranda thought with a hint of self-disgust. "It would be foolish of me to refuse the offer of one."

Elise opened the door again. "I don't have many friends either," she said quietly. "It's nice to have you."

Touched, Miranda stared after her, then gathered her printouts and samples to lock them in the safe.

She snagged Carter briefly, assigning him to check all sources for bronze formulas of the appropriate era—though she'd already done so herself, and would do so again.

She found Richard nearly buried in computer printouts and books. His nose all but scraped along the pages like a bloodhound's on the scent.

"Find anything I can use?" Miranda asked him.

"Huh?" He blinked at the page, but didn't look up. "The villa was completed in 1489. Lorenzo de' Medici commissioned the architect, but the deed was held by Giulietta Buonadoni."

"She was a powerful woman." Miranda pulled up

a chair, pushing at papers. "It wouldn't have been usual for a mistress to own such valuable property. She cut quite a deal."

"Women of great beauty already hold great power," he muttered. "The clever ones know how to use it. History indicates she was clever."

Intrigued, Miranda took a photo of the bronze out of her file. "You can see in her face this was a woman who knew her own worth. What else can you tell me about her?"

"Her name comes up from time to time. But there's not much detail. Her lineage, for instance, is buried in time. I can't find anything. The first mentions of her I've found so far begin in 1487. Indications are she was a member of the Medici household, potentially a young cousin of Clarice Orsini."

"So, going with that, Lorenzo took his wife's cousin for his mistress. Keeping it in the family," she said with a smile. Richard only nodded soberly.

"It would explain how she caught his eye. Though another source indicates she may have been the illegitimate daughter of one of the members of Lorenzo's Neoplatonic Academy. That would also have put her into his line of sight. However they met, he moved her into the villa in 1489. By all accounts she was as devoted to the arts as he, and used her power and influence to gather the stars of the era under her roof. She died in 1530, during the siege of Florence."

"Interesting." Again, she thought, a time when valuables might have been secreted away. Leaning back, she swung her glasses by the earpiece. "So she died before it was certain the Medicis would remain in power."

"So it appears."

"Children?"

"I haven't found anything on children."

"Give me a few of those books," she decided. "I'll help you look."

Vincente Morelli was the closest thing to an uncle Miranda could claim. He'd known her parents since before she was born and for several years had handled the publicity and promotions and events for the Institute in Maine.

When his first wife had taken ill, he'd brought her home to Florence, and had buried her there twelve years ago. He'd grieved for three years, then to everyone's surprise, had abruptly married a marginally successful actress. The fact that Gina was two years younger than his eldest daughter had caused some consternation in his family, and some smirking grins among his associates.

Vincente was round as a barrel with a Pavarotti chest and legs like tree stumps, while his wife resembled a young Sophia Loren, lush and lusty and gorgeous. She was rarely seen without several pounds of Italian gold and winking gems clasped around her throat and wrist or at her ears.

They were both boisterous, loud, and occasionally crude. Miranda was fond of both of them, but often wondered how such an extroverted couple managed to remain in close association with her mother.

"I've sent copies of the reports upstairs," Miranda told Vincente as he filled her small office with his bulk and personality. "I thought you'd want to see the progress, and that way when the time comes for an announcement to the media, you'll have been able to extrapolate data for the statement."

"Yes, yes. The facts are simple enough to write, but tell me what you think, *cara*. Give me some color."

"My thoughts are we've still got work to do."

"Miranda." He said it slowly, with a persuasive smile, as he leaned back in the chair that creaked alarmingly under his weight. "Your beautiful mother has tied my hands until all—what is it?—*t*'s are crossed. So, when I'm able to take this story to the press, it must have impact and passion and romance."

"If the bronze proves to be genuine, you'll have impact."

"Yes, yes, but more. The lovely and talented daughter of the *direttrice* comes across the sea. One lady to another. What do you think of her? What do you feel from her?"

Miranda arched a brow and tapped her pencil against the edge of her desk. "I think the Fiesole bronze is ninety point four centimeters in height, twenty-four point sixty-eight kilograms in weight. It's a bronze nude, female," she continued, holding back a smile as Vincente rolled his eyes to the ceiling, "crafted in the Renaissance style. Testing so far indicates it was cast in the last decade of the fifteenth century."

"You are too like your mama."

"You won't get anywhere with me with insults," Miranda warned, and they grinned at each other.

"You make my job difficult, *cara*." When the time was right, he thought, he'd take his own angles on the press release.

Elizabeth scanned the paperwork with sharp eyes. Miranda had been very careful with the facts, with numbers, with formulas, with every step and stage of every test. But it was still possible to see where she was leaning, and where she believed she would end.

"You believe it's genuine."

"Every test indicates its age is between four hundred and fifty and five hundred years. You have copies of the computer-generated photos, the chemicals tests."

"Who took them?"

"I did."

"And the thermoluminescence process. Who conducted it?"

"I did."

"And the dating by style is also yours. The bulk of the documentation is from your own research. You supervised the chemical tests, testing the patina and metal personally, did the formula comparisons."

"Isn't that why you brought me here?"

"Yes, but I also provided you with a team of experts. I expected you to make more use of them."

"If I run the tests myself, I have more control," Miranda said curtly. "There's less possibility of error. This is my field. I've authenticated five pieces from this era, three of them bronzes, one of them a Cellini."

"The Cellini had unassaultable documentation, and excavation records."

"Regardless," Miranda said with bubbling resentment. Though she imagined herself flinging up her hands, shaking her fists, she kept her arms quietly by her sides. "I ran precisely the same tests on that piece as I have on this one in order to rule out forgery. I've consulted with the Louvre, the Smithsonian, the Bargello. I believe my credentials are in order."

Wearily Elizabeth leaned back. "No one is questioning your credentials, or your skill. I would hardly have called you in on this project if I doubted either."

"Then why are you questioning them now that I've done the work?"

"I'm commenting on your lack of teamwork, Miranda, and I'm concerned that you formed your opinion the moment you saw the bronze."

"I recognized the style, the era, and the artist." As did you, Miranda thought furiously. Damn you, as did you. "However," she continued coolly, "I conducted every standard test, then retested, and documented the procedure and the results. From these I can form an opinion, and a belief that the bronze currently locked in the safe is a depiction of Giulietta Buonadoni, cast circa late fifteenth century, and the work of a young Michelangelo Buonarroti."

"I will agree that the style is of the school of Michelangelo."

"The bronze is too early a work to be of his school. He was barely twenty. And only genius can duplicate genius."

"To my knowledge there is no documentation of a bronze of this artist that supports this piece as his work."

"Then the documentation has yet to be found, or it never existed. We have documentation of many of his pieces that are lost. Why not have a piece and not the documentation? The cartoon for the fresco for the Battle of Cascina. Lost. His bronze of Julius the Second, destroyed and melted down, many of his drawings apparently burned by his own hand shortly before his death."

"However, we know they existed."

"*The Dark Lady* exists. The age is right, the style is right, particularly in his early work. He would have been about eighteen when this was cast. He'd already carved *Madonna of the Stairs, Battle of the Lapiths and Centaurs*. He had already shown genius."

Considering herself a patient woman, Elizabeth merely nodded. "There is no argument that the bronze is superior work and of his style. This does not, however, prove it is his work."

"He lived in the Medici Palace, was treated like

Lorenzo's son. He knew her. There *is* documentation that they were acquainted. She was often used as a model. It would be more unusual if he hadn't used her. You knew this possibility existed when you sent for me."

"Possibility and fact are different issues, Miranda." Elizabeth folded her hands. "As you said on your first day here, you don't deal in possibilities."

"I'm giving you fact. The formula of the bronze is correct, exactly correct, X rays verify that the tool work is authentic for the era. The clay core and scrapings have been dated. The tests reveal the deep downward corrosion growth. The patina is correct. The bronze is late-fifteenth-century. Most likely the last decade."

She held up a hand before her mother could speak. "As an expert in the field, and after a careful and objective study of the piece, it's my conclusion that the bronze is the work of Michelangelo. All that's missing is his signature. And he didn't sign his pieces, with the exception of the *Pietà* in Rome."

"I won't argue with the results of your testing." Elizabeth angled her head. "With your conclusions, however, I hold reservations. We can't afford to let your enthusiasm weigh on either side. You're to say nothing of this to any of the staff at this point. And I must insist you say nothing at all outside the lab. If any rumors leak to the press, it would be disastrous."

"I'm hardly going to call the newspapers and announce I've authenticated a lost Michelangelo. But

I have." She placed her hands on the desk and leaned forward. "I know it. And sooner or later, you'll have to admit it."

"Nothing would please me more, I promise you. But in the meantime, this must be kept quiet."

"I'm not in this for glory." Though she could taste it, on the tip of her tongue. She could feel it, tingling in the tips of her fingers.

"We're all in this for glory," Elizabeth corrected with a small smile. "Why pretend otherwise? If your theory proves out, you'll have plenty of it. If it doesn't, and you're premature in your statement, you'll damage your reputation. And mine, and that of this facility. That, Miranda, I won't allow. Continue the document search."

"I intend to." Miranda turned on her heel and stalked out. She would gather up a pile of books, take them back to the hotel, and by God, she told herself, she'd find the link.

At three A.M., when the phone rang, she was sitting up in bed, surrounded by books and papers. The two-toned shrill jerked her out of some colorful dream of sunny hillsides and cool marble courtyards, musical fountains and harpsong.

Disoriented, she blinked against the glare of the lights she'd left burning and groped for the phone.

"*Pronto*. Dr. Jones. Hello?"

"Miranda, I need you to come to my house as soon as possible."

"What? Mother?" She stared bleary-eyed at the bedside clock. "It's three in the morning."

"I'm perfectly aware of the time. As is the assistant minister who was awakened some twenty minutes ago by a reporter who demanded to know the details of the lost bronze by Michelangelo."

"What? But—"

"I don't choose to discuss this over the phone." Elizabeth's voice vibrated with cold and barely suppressed fury. "Do you remember how to get here?"

"Yes, of course."

"I'll expect you within thirty minutes," she said, seconds before the phone clicked.

Miranda made it in twenty.

Elizabeth's home was small and elegant, a two-story dwelling typical of Florence, with its yellowed ivory walls and red-tiled roof. Flowers spilled out of pots and window boxes, and were cared for religiously by the maid.

In the dark, the windows gleamed, bright stripes of light leaking through the louvered blinds. It was roomy, as Miranda recalled, an attractive arena for entertaining. It would have occurred to neither mother nor daughter to share the space while Miranda was in Florence.

The door was wrenched open before she could knock. Elizabeth stood, neatly groomed and perfectly presented in a peach-colored robe.

"What happened?" Miranda demanded.

"That's precisely my question." Strict control was all that prevented Elizabeth from slamming the door. "If this was your way of proving your point, of exerting your expertise, or of causing me professional embarrassment, all you accomplished was the last."

"I don't know what you're talking about." Miranda hadn't taken time to tame her hair, and scooped an impatient hand through it to shove it out of her eyes. "You said a reporter called—"

"That's correct."

Straight as a general, Elizabeth turned and strode into the front parlor. A fire was laid, but had yet to be lighted. Lamps blazed, shooting shine from polished wood. There was a vase of white roses on the mantel, and nothing else. The colors were all soft, all pale.

Part of Miranda's mind registered what it always did when she stepped inside this, or any, room in the house. It was more showcase than home, and just as cool.

"The reporter, of course, refused to reveal his source. But he had quite a bit of information."

"Vincente would never have gone to the press prematurely."

"No," Elizabeth agreed coolly. "Vincente would not."

"Could the plumber—what was his name—have talked to a reporter?"

"The plumber couldn't have provided him with photos of the bronze, with test results."

"Test results." Because her knees were suddenly loose, Miranda sat. "My tests?"

"Standjo's tests," Elizabeth said between her teeth. "Despite the fact that you conducted them, it remains the responsibility of my lab. And it's the security of that lab that has been breached."

"But how . . ." It hit home then, the tone, the look in her mother's eyes. She rose slowly. "You think I called a reporter and fed him information? Secured photos and test results?"

Elizabeth merely studied Miranda's furious face. "Did you?"

"No, I did not. Even if we hadn't discussed the ramifications, I would never undermine a project this way. It's my reputation on the line as well."

"And it's your reputation that could very well be made."

Miranda looked into Elizabeth's eyes and saw the opinion had already been formed. "You can go to hell."

"The reporter quoted from your report."

"Straight to hell, and take your precious lab with you. It's always meant more to you than your own flesh and blood."

"My precious lab has provided you with training and employment, and with the potential for reaching the top of your field. Now, because of haste and stubbornness and ego, my professional integrity is in question, and your reputation may very well be ruined. The bronze is being transferred to another facility today."

"Transferred?"

"We've been fired," Elizabeth snapped, then snatched up the phone that rang on a table beside her. Her lips thinned, and her breath hissed through them once. "No comment," she said in Italian, and hung up. "Another reporter. The third who's reached me on my private number."

"It doesn't matter." Though her stomach was jumping, Miranda spoke calmly. "Let them transfer her. Any reputable lab will only verify my findings."

"That's precisely the kind of arrogance that put us in this position." Her eyes fired such icy temper that Miranda didn't notice the strain or dark circles under them. "I've worked for years to reach this point, to build and maintain a facility that is without question among the finest in the world."

"This won't change that. Leaks happen even in the finest facilities."

"They don't happen at Standjo." The silk of Elizabeth's robe swirled as she paced. The matching slippers made no sound as they trampled the pink roses blooming on the carpet. "I'll begin repairing the damage immediately. I expect you to avoid the press, and take the first available flight back to Maine."

"I'm not leaving until this is finished."

"It is finished, for you. Your services are no longer required at Standjo, Florence." She turned back to her daughter, her face set, her tired eyes chilly and direct. "Your security clearance will be voided."

"I see. A quick execution without a trial. I shouldn't be surprised," she said half to herself. "Why am I?"

"This isn't the time to indulge in drama."

Because her nerves were raw, Elizabeth indulged herself and moved to a cabinet for the brandy. There was a dull drumming at the base of her skull that caused her more irritation than pain.

"It's going to take quite a bit of work to put Standjo back on an even keel after this. And there will be questions, a lot of questions." With her back to Miranda, Elizabeth splashed two inches of brandy into a snifter. "It would be better for you if you aren't in the country when they're asked."

"I'm not afraid of questions." The panic was creeping in now, sneaking slyly up her spine. She was to be sent away, *The Dark Lady* taken from her. Her work questioned, her integrity shadowed. "I didn't do anything illegal or unethical. And I'll stand by my authentication of the bronze. Because it's right. Because it's real."

"For your sake, I hope so. The press has your name, Miranda." Elizabeth lifted her brandy in unconscious toast. "Believe me, they'll use it."

"Let them."

"Arrogance." Elizabeth hissed out a breath. "Obviously you haven't taken account that your actions will reflect on me, personally and professionally."

"You thought of it," Miranda shot back, "when you brought me here to verify and corroborate your own suspicions. You may head Standjo, but you don't have the qualifications for this kind of work. You wanted the glory." Miranda's heart hammered painfully in her throat as she stepped closer. "You sent for me because I share part of your name, and your blood, however much we both regret that."

Elizabeth's eyes narrowed. The accusation wasn't inaccurate, but neither was it complete. "I gave you the opportunity of a lifetime, because of your qualifications, and yes, because you're a Jones. You've damaged that opportunity, and my organization in the process."

"I've done nothing but what I was brought here to do. I've spoken to no one outside the organization, and to no one in the organization who didn't meet with your clearance specifications."

Elizabeth drew a calming breath. Her decision had already been made, she reminded herself. There was no point in discussing it further. "You will leave Italy today. You will not return to the lab, or contact anyone who works there. If you don't agree, I'll be forced to terminate your position at the museum."

"You don't run the Institute anymore, and neither does Father. Andrew and I do."

"If you want that situation to continue, you'll do what I say. Whether you believe it or not, I'm trying to save you embarrassment."

"Don't do me any favors, Mother. We wouldn't want to spoil your record." Banished, was all she could think. Cut off from the most exciting work of her life, and sent away as powerlessly as a child ordered to her room.

"I've given you your choice, Miranda. If you stay, you'll do so alone. And you will no longer be welcome at any Standjo facility, including the New England Institute of Art History."

Miranda could feel herself begin to shake, from both fear and rage. Even as she heard the inner screams of that fear and rage echo in her head, she spoke quietly. "I'll never forgive you for this. Not ever. But I'll go, because the Institute's important to me. And because, when this is over, you'll have to apologize, and I'll tell you to go to hell. Those will be the last words I ever speak to you."

She took the snifter out of her mother's hand. *"Salute,"* she said, and tossed back the brandy defiantly. Setting the snifter down with a crack of glass against wood, she turned and walked out. She didn't look back.

CHAPTER FOUR

ANDREW JONES WAS THINKING OF MARRIAGE AND failure as he sipped Jack Daniel's Black, straight up, from a short glass. He was well aware that everyone who knew him thought it was long past time for him to turn the page on his divorce and move on.

But he didn't feel like moving on. Not when it was so comforting to wallow.

Marriage had been an enormous step for him, and one he'd considered carefully even though he'd been wildly in love. Making that commitment, turning an emotion into a legal document, had given him many sleepless nights. No one on the Jones side of the family had ever made a successful run at marriage.

He and Miranda called it the Jones curse.

His grandmother had outlived her husband by more than a decade and had never—at least in her grandson's hearing—had a good word to say about the man she'd lived with for thirty-odd years.

It was hard to blame her, as the late and unlamented Andrew Jones had been infamous for his affection for young blondes and Jack Daniel's Black.

His namesake was well aware that the old man had been a bastard, clever and successful, but a bastard nonetheless.

Andrew's father preferred digs to home fires, and had spent most of his son's childhood away from home, brushing ancient dirt from ancient bones. When he was in residence, he'd agreed with everything his wife said, blinked owlishly at his children as if he'd forgotten how they came to be in his line of sight, and locked himself for hours at a time in his office.

It hadn't been women and whiskey for Charles Jones. He'd committed his adultery and neglect with science.

Not that the great Dr. Elizabeth Standford-Jones had given a shit, Andrew thought as he brooded over what he'd intended to be one friendly drink at Annie's Place. She'd left the child-rearing to servants, run the household like a Nazi general, and ignored her husband as sublimely as he had ignored her.

It always made Andrew shudder to imagine that at least twice, these cold-blooded, self-absorbed people had tangled in bed long enough to conceive a couple of children.

When he was a boy, Andrew had often fantasized that Charles and Elizabeth had purchased him and his sister from some poor couple who'd wept copiously when they traded their children for rent money.

When he was older, he'd enjoyed imagining that he and Miranda had been created in a lab, experiments conceived out of science rather than sex.

But the sad fact was that there was too much Jones in him for it not to have come down naturally.

Yeah, he thought, and lifted his glass, old Charles and Elizabeth had tangoed one night thirty-three years ago and conceived the next generation of assholes.

But he'd tried, Andrew told himself, letting the whiskey slide down his throat in a hot caress. He'd done his best to make his marriage work, to make Elise happy, to be the kind of husband she wanted and break the Jones curse.

And had failed all around.

"I'll take another, Annie."

"No, you won't."

Andrew shifted on his stool, sighed gustily. He'd known Annie McLean most of his life, and knew how to get around her.

In the sweet summer when they were seventeen, they'd tumbled together onto a rough blanket over rougher sand and had made love by the crashing waves of the Atlantic.

He supposed the stumbling sex—which had turned out to be a first for both of them—had as much to do with the beer they'd consumed, the night itself, and the foolishness of youth as the licks of heat they'd sparked off each other.

And neither of them could have known what that one night, those few hot hours by the sea, would do to both of them.

"Come on, Annie, let me have another drink."

"You've already had two."

"So one more won't hurt."

Annie finished drawing a beer, slid the mug gracefully down the length of the cherrywood bar toward the waiting customer. Briskly, she wiped her narrow hands on her bar apron.

At five-six and a hundred thirty well-toned pounds, Annie McLean gave the impression of no-nonsense competence.

A select few—including a two-timing cheat of an ex-husband—knew there was a delicate-winged blue butterfly on her butt.

Her wheat-colored hair was worn short and spiky to frame a face more interesting than pretty. Her chin was pointed, her nose listed slightly to the left and was splattered with freckles. Her voice was pure Down East and tended to flatten vowels.

She could, and had, tossed grown men out of her bar with her own work-roughened hands.

Annie's Place was hers because she'd made it hers. She'd sunk every penny of her savings from her days of cocktail waitressing into the bar—every penny her slick-talking ex hadn't run off with—and had begged and borrowed the rest. She'd worked day and night transforming what had been little more than a cellar into a comfortable neighborhood bar.

She ran a clean place, knew her regulars, their families, their troubles. She knew when to draw another draft, when to switch to coffee, and when to demand car keys and call cabs.

She looked at Andrew and shook her head. He'd drink himself blind if she let him.

"Andrew, go home. Make yourself a meal."

"I'm not hungry." He smiled, knowing how to put his dimples to work. "It's cold and rainy out, Annie. I just want a little something to warm the blood."

"Fine." She turned to the coffee station and filled a mug from the pot. "This is hot and fresh."

"Christ. I can go right down the street and get a goddamn drink without the hassle."

She merely lifted her eyebrows. "Drink your coffee and stop whining." With this, she began to work her way down the bar.

The rain was keeping most of her customers home. But those who had braved the storm were glued to their seats, sipping beer, watching the sports channel on TV, huddled in conversations.

There was a pretty fire burning in the little stone hearth and someone had plugged in quarters and Ella Fitzgerald on the juke.

It was her kind of night. Warm, friendly, easy. This was the reason she'd been willing to risk every dime, to work her hands raw and lie awake in bed worrying night after night. Not many had believed she could succeed, a twenty-six-year-old woman whose only business experience had come from serving mugs of beer and counting tips.

Seven years later, and Annie's Place was a Jones Point standard.

Andrew had believed, she remembered with a tug of guilt as she saw him stomp out of the bar. He'd lent her money when the banks wouldn't. He'd come by with sandwiches when she'd been painting walls and staining wood. He'd listened to her dreams when others had ignored them.

He figured he owed her, she thought now. And he was a decent man who paid his debts.

But he couldn't erase the night sixteen years before when, lost in love with him, she'd given him her innocence, taken his. He couldn't make her forget that in doing so they'd created a life, one that had flickered only briefly.

He couldn't make her forget the look on his face when, with joy leaping under terror, she'd told him she was pregnant. His face had gone blank, his body stiff as he sat on the rock on the long stretch of beach and stared out to sea.

And his voice had been flat, cool, impersonal when he offered to marry her.

Paying a debt, she thought now. Nothing more, nothing less. And by offering to do what most would consider the honorable thing, he'd broken her heart.

Losing the baby only two weeks later was fate, she supposed. It had spared both of them overwhelming decisions. But she'd loved what had been growing inside her, just as she'd loved Andrew.

Once she accepted the baby was gone, she'd stopped loving. That, she knew, had been as much a relief to Andrew as it had been to her.

The hum of friendship, she thought, was a lot easier to dance to than the pluck of heartstrings.

Damn women were the bane of his existence, Andrew decided as he unlocked his car and climbed behind the wheel. Always telling you what to do, how to do it, and most of all how you were doing it wrong.

He was glad he was done with them.

He was better off burying himself in work at the Institute by day and blurring the edges with whiskey at night. Nobody got hurt that way. Especially him.

Now he was much too sober, and the night ahead was much too long.

He drove through the rain, wondering what it would be like to just keep driving. To go until he just ran out of gas and start fresh wherever that might be. He could change his name, get a job in construction. He had a strong back and good hands. Maybe hard, manual labor was the answer.

No one would know him, or expect anything of him.

But he knew he wouldn't. He would never leave the Institute. It was, as nothing else had ever been, home. He needed it every bit as much as it needed him.

Well, he had a bottle or two at the house. There was no reason he couldn't have a couple drinks in front of his own fire to lull him to sleep.

But he saw the lights winking through the rain as he drove up the winding lane. Miranda. He hadn't expected his sister home, not for days yet. His fingers tightened on the wheel as he thought of her in Florence, with Elise. It took him several minutes after he'd stopped the car before he was able to relax them.

The wind whipped at him as he shoved the car door open. Rain slapped at his face and streamed down his collar. Directly over the peaks and gables of the house, the sky exploded with sharp forks of lightning.

A wild night. He imagined Miranda was inside enjoying it. She loved a good storm. For himself, he would take peace, quiet, and oblivion.

He dashed toward the door, then shook himself like a dog the minute he was inside the foyer. He hung his wet coat on the old oak hallrack, dragged a hand through his hair without glancing in the antique mirror. He could hear the funereal tones of Mozart's Requiem coming from the parlor.

If Miranda was playing that, he knew the trip hadn't gone well.

He found her curled up in a chair in front of the fire, bundled into her favored gray cashmere robe, sipping tea from their grandmother's best china.

All of her comfort tools, he noted, neatly in place.

"You're back early."

"Looks that way." She studied him. She was

sure he'd been drinking, but his eyes were clear, his color normal. At least he was still marginally sober.

Though he wanted a drink, he sat down across from her. It was easy to spot the signs of simmering temper. But he knew her better than anyone, and could also see the misery under it. "So, what's the deal?"

"She had a project for me." Because she'd hoped he would come home before she went to bed, Miranda had brought two cups. She poured tea into the second now and pretended she didn't see Andrew's wince of distaste.

She knew very well he'd prefer a glass of whiskey.

"An incredible project," Miranda continued, holding out the cup and saucer. "A bronze was discovered in the cellar of the Villa della Donna Oscura. Do you know the history of the place?"

"Refresh me."

"Giulietta Buonadoni."

"Okay, got it. The Dark Lady, a mistress of one of the Medicis."

"Lorenzo the Magnificent—at least he was her first protector," Miranda specified, grateful that Andrew's knowledge of the era was thorough enough. It would save time. "The bronze was of the lady herself, no mistaking that face. She wanted me to do the tests, the dating."

He waited a beat. "Elise could have handled it."

"Elise's field is broader than mine." There was a hint of annoyance in Miranda's tone. "Renaissance is my era, bronzes my specialty. Elizabeth wanted the best."

"She always does. So, you ran the tests?"

"I ran them. I ran them again. I had top members of the staff assisting me. I did everything, personally, step by step. Then I went back and did it all again."

"And?"

"It was genuine, Andrew." Some of the excitement leaked through as she leaned forward. "Late fifteenth century."

"That's incredible. Wonderful. Why aren't you celebrating?"

"There's more." She had to take a breath, steady herself. "It's a Michelangelo."

"Jesus." He set his cup aside hurriedly. "Are you sure? I don't remember anything about a lost bronze."

A stubborn line dug its way between her eyebrows. "I'd stake my reputation on it. It's an early work, brilliantly executed—it's a gorgeous piece, echoing the sensual style of his drunken *Bacchus*. I was still working on documentation when I left, but there's enough to support it."

"The bronze wasn't documented?"

Miranda began to tap her foot in irritation. "Giulietta probably hid it, or at least kept it to herself. Politics. It fits," she insisted. "I'd have proven it without a doubt if she'd given me more time."

"Why didn't she?"

Unable to sit, Miranda unfolded her legs and got up to jab at the fire with a poker. "Someone leaked it to the press. We weren't nearly ready for an official announcement, and the government got nervous. They fired Standjo, and she fired me. She accused me of leaking it." Furious, she whirled back. "Of wanting the glory so badly I'd have risked the project to get it. I would never have done that."

"No, of course not." He could brush that aside without a thought. "They fired her." Though it was small of him, he couldn't quite stop the grin. "I bet that set her off."

"She was livid. Under other circumstances, I might get some satisfaction out of that. But now I've lost the project. Not only won't I get credit, but the only way I'll see that piece again is in a museum. Damn it, Andrew, I was so close."

"You can bet that when the bronze is authenticated and announced, she'll find a way to get Standjo's name in it." He arched a brow at his sister. "And when she does, you'll just have to make sure yours isn't left out."

"It's not the same." She took it away from me, was all Miranda could think.

"Take what you can get." He rose as well, wandering over to the liquor cabinet. Because he would have to ask. "You saw Elise?"

"Yes." Miranda slid her hands into the pockets of her robe. Because she would have to answer. "She looks fine. I think she's well suited to managing the lab there. She asked how you were."

"And you told her I was just dandy."

Miranda watched him pour the first drink. "I didn't

think you wanted me to tell her you were turning into a brooding, self-destructive drunk."

"I've always brooded," he said, saluting her. "All of us do, so that doesn't count. Is she seeing anyone?"

"I don't know. We never got around to discussing our sex lives. Andrew, you have to stop this."

"Why?"

"Because it's a waste and it's stupid. And frankly, though I like her, she's not worth it." She lifted her shoulders. "No one's worth it."

"I loved her," he murmured, watching the liquor swirl before he drank. "I gave her the best I had."

"Did you ever consider that maybe she didn't give her best? Maybe she was the one who didn't measure up?"

He studied Miranda over the rim of his glass. "No."

"Maybe you should. Or maybe you should consider that the best you had and the best she had didn't equal the best together. Marriages fail all the time. People get over it."

He studied the liquor, watching the light flicker through the glass. "Maybe if they didn't get over it so easily, marriages wouldn't fail so often."

"And maybe if people didn't pretend love makes the world go round, they'd pick their partners with more care."

"Love does make the world go round, Miranda. That's why the world's so fucked up."

He lifted his glass and drank deeply.

CHAPTER FIVE

THE SKY SHIMMERED WITH A COLD, GRAY, ANGRY dawn. Restless, dark, and full of sound, the sea hammered against the rocks and rose up to punch its white fists into the raw and bitter air. Spring would have a fight on its hands before it could beat back winter.

Nothing could have pleased Miranda more.

She stood on the bluff, her mood as fitful as the churning water below. She watched it spew up from the rocks, ice-edged and mean, and drew in the ancient violence of its scent.

She'd slept poorly, tangled in dreams she blamed on temper as much as travel fatigue. She wasn't one for dreaming. It was still dark when she'd given up on sleep, and had dressed in a thick green sweater and dun-colored slacks of soft wool. She'd scraped out the last of the coffee—Andrew wasn't going to be pleased when he awoke—and had brewed herself half a pot.

Now she sipped that coffee, strong and black, out of a big white mug and watched dawn claw its way to life in the unhappy eastern sky.

The rain had stopped, but it would come back, she thought. And as the temperatures had dropped sharply through the night, it would likely come back as snow and sleet. That was fine, that was dandy.

That was Maine.

Florence, with its white, flashing sun and warm, dry wind, was an ocean away. But inside her, in her angry heart, it was close.

The Dark Lady had been her ticket to glory. Elizabeth was right about that at least. Glory was always the goal. But by God, she had worked for it. She'd studied, pushing herself brutally to learn, to absorb, to remember, when her contemporaries had jumped from party to party and relationship to relationship.

There'd been no wild rebellious period in her life, no thumbing her nose at rules and traditions while in college, no mad, heart-wrenching affairs. Repressed, one roommate had called her. Boring as dirt had been the opinion of another. Because some secret part of her had agreed, she had solved that problem by moving off campus and into a small apartment of her own.

She'd been better off, Miranda always thought. She had no skill for social interactions. Beneath the armor of composure and the starch of training she was miserably shy with people, and so much more comfortable with information.

So she had read, written, closed herself into other centuries with a discipline fired by the hot light of ambition.

That ambition had one focus. To be the best. And by being the best, to see her parents look at her with pride, with stunned delight, with respect. Oh, it galled her to know that motivation was buried inside her still, but she'd never been able to dig it out and dispose of it.

She was nearly thirty, had her doctorate, her position at the Institute, a solid reputation in archeometry. And a pitiful need to hear her parents applaud her act. Well, she would just have to get over it.

Before long, she thought, her findings would be proven. Then she would make certain that she gained the credit she deserved. She would write a paper on *The Dark Lady*, and her own involvement in its testing and authentication. And she would never, never forgive Elizabeth for taking the control and the joy out of her hands. Or for having the power to do so.

The wind rose, sneaking under her sweater like hands grabbing at flesh. The first thin, wet flakes began to swirl. Miranda turned from the sea, her boots clattering on rock as she climbed down the cliff.

The steady beam of the great light continued to circle atop the white tower, shooting out over the water and rock though there were no ships within its range. From dusk to dawn, year after year, she thought, it never failed. Some would look and see romance, but when Miranda studied the sturdy whitewashed tower, she saw reliability.

More, she thought now, than was usually found in people.

In the distance the house was still dark and sleepy, a fanciful silhouette from another time etched against an unforgiving sky.

The grass was a sickly winter brown and crunched under her heels from frost. The scar of her grandmother's once lovely garden seemed to scold her.

This year, Miranda promised herself when she passed the blackened leaves and brittle sticks of stems, she would give it some time and attention. She would make gardening her hobby—she was always promising herself a hobby.

In the kitchen, she poured the last of the coffee from the pot into her mug. After a final glance outside at the fast-falling snow, she decided to drive to the Institute early, before the roads were covered.

From the warm comfort of his rented Mercedes, he watched the Land Rover glide effortlessly over the thin layer of snow on the street, then turn into the parking lot beside the New England Institute of Art History. It looked like a vehicle that should have been driven by a general during an elegant little war.

She made quite a picture herself, he mused,

watching her climb out. About six feet of female in her boots, he judged, and most of it wrapped in a steel-gray coat that owed more to warmth than fashion. Her hair was a sexy stoplight red that escaped in untidy curls from a black ski cap. She carried a thick briefcase that bulged a bit with its contents, and she moved with a precision and purpose that would have made that wartime general proud.

But beneath that long-legged stride was the arrogant and unwitting sexuality of a woman who believed herself a step beyond the physical need for men. It was a swinging, aloof gait.

Even in the dim light, he recognized her. She was, he thought with a slow smile, a hard woman not to notice.

He'd been sitting there for nearly an hour now, entertaining himself with various arias from *Carmen, La Bohème, The Marriage of Figaro*. Really, he had all he needed for now, and had done what he needed to do, but he was grateful he'd loitered long enough to see her arrive.

An early riser, he decided, a woman who liked her work well enough to face it on a cold, snowy morning before most of the city stirred. He appreciated a person who enjoyed their work. God knew, he loved his.

But what to do about Dr. Miranda Jones? he wondered. He imagined she was using the side entrance, even now sliding her key card through the slot, adding her code on the number pad. No doubt she would carefully reset the security alarms once she was inside.

All reports indicated she was a practical and careful woman. He appreciated practical women. It was such a joy to corrupt them.

He could work around her, or he could use her. Either way, he would get the job done. But using her would be so much more . . . entertaining. Since this would be his last job, it seemed only fair it include some entertainment in addition to the thrill and the profit.

He thought it would be worth his while to get to know Miranda Jones, to indulge himself with her. Before he stole from her.

He saw the light flick on in a window on the third floor of the sprawling granite building. Straight to work, he mused, smiling again as he caught the shadow of movement behind the window.

It was about time he got to work himself. He started the car, pulled away from the curve, and drove off to dress for the next part of his day.

The New England Institute of Art History had been built by Miranda's great-grandfather. But it was her grandfather, Andrew Jones, who had expanded it to its full potential. He'd always had a keen interest in the arts, and had even fancied himself a painter. He'd been at least good enough to convince a number of healthy young models to take off their clothes and pose for him.

He'd enjoyed socializing with artists, entertaining them, acting as patron when one—particularly an attractive female one—caught his eye. A ladies' man and enthusiastic drinker he might have been, but he'd also been generous, imaginative, and had never been afraid to put his money where his heart lay.

The building was a strong gray granite, spreading over a full block, with its towering columns, its wings and squared-off archways. The original structure had been a museum with carefully tended grounds, huge old shade trees, and a quiet, rather stern-faced dignity.

Andrew had wanted more. He'd seen the Institute as a showcase for art and for artists, as an arena where art was displayed, restored, taught, and analyzed. So he had cut down the trees, slabbed over the grounds, and erected the graceful and somewhat fanciful additions to the original structure.

There were classrooms with high light-filled windows, carefully designed laboratories, lofty storerooms, and a beehive of offices. Gallery space had been more than tripled.

Students who wished to study there were taken on merit. Those who could afford to pay paid dearly for the privilege. Those who couldn't, and were deemed worthy, were subsidized.

Art was holy at the Institute, and science was its deity.

Carved in a stone lintel above the main entrance were the words of Longfellow.

ART IS LONG, AND TIME IS FLEETING

Studying, preserving, and displaying that art was how the Institute spent its time.

It remained basically true to Andrew's conception fifty years later with his grandchildren at the helm.

The museum galleries it held were arguably the finest in Maine, and the work represented there had been carefully chosen and acquired over the years, beginning with Charles's and then Andrew's own collections.

The public areas swept the main floor, gallery spilling into gallery through wide archways. Classrooms and studios jammed the second level, with the restoration area separated from them by a small lobby where visitors with the correct passes could tour the work spaces.

The labs occupied the lower level and shot off into all wings. They were, despite the grand galleries and educational facilities, the foundation.

The labs, Miranda often thought, were her foundation as well.

Setting her briefcase aside, she moved to the Federal library table under her window to brew coffee. As she switched the pot on, her fax line rang. After opening her blinds, she moved to the machine and took out the page.

Welcome home, Miranda. Did you enjoy Florence? Too bad your trip was cut so rudely short. Where do you think you made your mistake? Have you thought about it? Or are you so sure you're right?

Prepare for the fall. It's going to be a hard jolt.

I've waited so long. I've watched so patiently.

I'm watching still, and the wait's almost over.

Miranda caught herself rubbing a hand up and down her arm to warm it as she read the message. Though she made herself stop, the chill remained.

There was no name, no return number.

It read like a sly chuckle, she thought. The tone taunting and eerily threatening. But why, and who?

Her mother? It shamed her that Elizabeth's name was the first to form in her mind. But surely a woman of Elizabeth's power, personality, and position wouldn't stoop to cryptic and anonymous messages.

She'd already hurt Miranda in the most direct way possible.

It was more likely a disgruntled employee at either Standjo or the Institute, someone who felt she'd been unfair in her policy or work assignments.

Of course, that was it, she decided and tried to breathe cleanly again. A technician she'd reprimanded or a student who was unhappy with a grade. This was only meant to unsettle her, and she wouldn't allow it to work.

But rather than discarding it, she slipped it into her bottom drawer and turned the key in the lock.

Putting it out of her mind, she sat to outline her day on paper. By the time she'd completed the first tasks on her list—reading her mail and memos, organizing her phone messages—the sun was up and streaming in bands through the slats of her blinds.

"Miranda?" A quick rap on the door jolted her.

"Yes, come in." She glanced at the clock, noting her assistant was punctual, as always.

"I saw your car in the lot. Didn't know you were coming back today."

"No, it was . . . unscheduled."

"So how was Florence?" Lori moved briskly around the room, checking for messages, adjusting the slant of the blinds.

"Warm, sunny."

"Sounds wonderful." Satisfied all was in its proper place, Lori sat and perched her notebook on her knee. She was a pretty blonde with a Kewpie doll mouth, a voice like Betty Boop, and an edge of efficiency sharp as a honed razor. "It's nice to have you back," she said with a smile.

"Thanks." Because the welcome was sincere, Miranda smiled in return. "It's nice to *be* back. I've got a lot to catch up on. Right now I need updates on the Carbello *Nude* and the Bronzino restoration."

The routine was soothing, so much so that Miranda forgot everything but the matters at hand for the next two hours. Leaving Lori to set up appointments and meetings, she headed out to check in with the lab.

Because she was thinking of Andrew, Miranda decided to detour by his office before heading down. His domain was in the opposite wing, closer to the public areas. The galleries, acquisitions, and displays were his province, while Miranda preferred working mainly behind the scenes.

She strode down the corridors, her practical

boots treading over marble. Here and there the wide square windows allowed streams of pale light to streak over the floor, offered the muffled sound of street traffic, glimpses of buildings and bare trees.

Office doors were discreetly closed. The occasional sound of phones or the whine of faxes echoed dully. A secretary carried a ream of paper out of the supply room and shot Miranda a startled-rabbit look, before murmuring a "Good morning, Dr. Jones," then scurrying on.

Was she that intimidating? Miranda thought. That unfriendly? Because it made her think of the fax, she narrowed her eyes at the woman's back as she scooted through a door and closed it behind her.

Maybe she wasn't outgoing, maybe the staff didn't have the same easy affection for her that they seemed to have for Andrew, but she wasn't . . . hard. Was she?

It disturbed her to think so, to wonder if her innate reserve was perceived as coldness.

Like her mother.

No, she didn't want to believe that. Those who knew her wouldn't think so. She had a solid relationship with Lori, an easy camaraderie with John Carter. She didn't run the lab here like a boot camp where no one could speak their mind or tell a joke.

Though no one joked with her, she thought.

She was in charge, she reminded herself. What else could she expect?

Deliberately she relaxed her shoulders again.

She couldn't let one timid secretary set her off on a tangent of self-analysis.

Because, happily, she had no appointments or public meetings scheduled, she wore the same sweater and trousers she'd slipped into that morning to watch the dawn. Her hair was bundled back in an excuse for a braid and curls were already escaping from the messy plait.

She was thinking that it was past midday in Italy, and the bronze would be in intense testing. It made her shoulders knot up again.

She stepped through the door of her brother's outer office. Inside was a sturdy Victorian desk, two viciously straight-backed chairs, filing cabinets in no-nonsense gray, and the woman who guarded it all.

"Good morning, Ms. Purdue."

Andrew's assistant was somewhere on the downside of fifty, tidy as a nun and just as strict. She wore her streaky salt-and-pepper hair in an identical knot every day, year in, year out, and was never without a starched blouse and dark blazer and skirt.

She was always Ms. Purdue.

She nodded, removed her busy fingers from her keyboard and folded them neatly. "Good morning, Dr. Jones. I didn't know you were back from Italy."

"I got back yesterday." She tried a smile, thinking it was as good a time as any to be more personable with the staff. "It's a bit of a shock coming back to this cold." When Ms. Purdue responded only with a brisk nod, Miranda gave up on the idea—gratefully—of a chat. "Is my brother in?"

"Dr. Jones just stepped downstairs to greet a guest. He should be back momentarily. Would you care to wait, or shall I take a message?"

"No, it's nothing. I'll see him later." She turned when she heard male voices echo up the stairs. If Ms. Purdue's critical eyes hadn't been on her, Miranda would have made a dash for cover rather than risk the possibility of socializing with Andrew's guest.

She wouldn't be stuck if she'd gone straight to the lab, she thought, and briskly brushed the hair out of her eyes and fixed on a polite smile.

Her smile wavered when Andrew and his companion reached the top of the stairs.

"Miranda, this is handy." Andrew beamed at her—and a quick survey showed Miranda no sign of a night of drinking. "Saves me from calling your office. I'd like you to meet Ryan Boldari, of the Boldari Gallery."

He stepped forward, took Miranda's hand and brought it smoothly to his lips. "How nice to meet you, finally."

He had a face that could have been reproduced with rich bold strokes on one of the Institute's paintings. The dark, wild good looks were only marginally tamed by an impeccably cut gray suit and perfectly knotted silk tie. His hair was thick, black as ink, and gloriously wavy. His skin was dusky gold, taut over strong bones and marred intriguingly by a small crescent-shaped scar at the far tip of his left eyebrow.

His eyes held hers and were a dark, rich brown that took little drifts of gold from the light. His mouth might have been sculpted by a master and was curved in a smile designed to make a woman wonder how it would feel against hers. And sigh.

She heard a ping—a single and cheerful snapping sound inside her head—as her heart bumped twice.

"Welcome to the Institute, Mr. Boldari."

"I'm delighted to be here." He kept her hand in his because it appeared to fluster her. However politely she smiled, there was a faint line of annoyance between her brows.

She debated giving her hand one good tug, then decided it would seem entirely too female a move.

"Why don't we step into my office?" Oblivious to whatever games were being played under his nose, Andrew gestured toward his office door. "Miranda, got a minute?"

"Actually, I was just—"

"I'd appreciate a few moments of your time, Dr. Jones." Ryan flashed that smile at her as he shifted his hand from hers to her elbow. "I have a proposition for your brother I believe you'll be interested in. Your main field of study is Renaissance, isn't it?"

Trapped, she allowed herself to be guided into Andrew's office. "That's right."

"A brilliant era, so rich in beauty and energy. You know the work of Giorgio Vasari?"

"Of course, Late Renaissance, a Mannerist, one whose style typified the movement toward elegance."

"Ryan has three Vasaris." Andrew gestured toward chairs that, thanks to Ms. Purdue, weren't covered with books and papers as they normally were.

"Really?" Miranda took a seat and fixed on another smile. Andrew's office was a great deal smaller than hers, because he preferred it that way. It was also cluttered, colorful, and full of the trinkets he liked to surround himself with. Old bones, shards of pottery, bits of glass. She would have preferred to hold this unexpected meeting in the acerbic formality of her own territory.

Because she was nervous, she imagined herself drumming her fingers, wiggling her foot.

"Yes." Ryan gave his slacks a casual hitch to preserve the crease as he settled himself into a narrow leather-backed chair. "Don't you find his work a bit self-conscious? Overripe?"

"That too is typical of Mannerism," Miranda countered. "Vasari is an important artist of that time and style."

"Agreed." Ryan merely smiled. "On a personal level I prefer the style of the Early and High Renaissance, but business is business." He waved a hand—he had strong, graceful hands, Miranda noted. Wide of palm, long of finger.

It irritated her to notice, embarrassed her to have—for a second or two—imagined the feel of them on her skin. Like a teenager faced with a rock star, she thought, amazed at herself.

When she deliberately shifted her gaze from his hands, it collided with his. He smiled again, with a definite gleam in his eyes.

In defense her voice turned chilly. "And what business do you have with the Institute?"

Fascinating woman, he thought. The body of a goddess, the manner of a prude, the fashion sense of a refugee, and a very appealing hint of shyness around those hot blue eyes.

He kept his eyes locked on hers, delighted when faint and flattering color bloomed in her cheeks. In his opinion, women didn't blush nearly often enough these days.

He wondered how she looked in those wire-framed glasses that were hooked in the neck of her sweater.

Scholarly sexy.

"I met your brother a few months ago when we were both in D.C. for the Women in the Arts benefit. I believe he went in your stead."

"Yes, I couldn't get away."

"Miranda was hip-deep in the lab." Andrew grinned. "I'm more easily dispensable." He leaned back in his own chair. "Ryan's interested in our Cellini Madonna."

Miranda arched a brow. "It's one of our prizes."

"Yes, I've just seen it. Glorious. Your brother and I discussed a trade."

"The Cellini." Her gaze whipped to her brother. "Andrew."

"Not permanent," Ryan said quickly, and didn't bother to disguise the chuckle at her quick distress. "A three-month exchange—to our mutual benefit. I'm planning on doing a Cellini exhibit in our New York gallery, and the loan of your Madonna would be a coup for me. In exchange, I'm willing to lend the Institute all three of my Vasaris for the same span of time."

"You could do the three-styles-of-the-Renaissance exhibit you've muttered about for years," Andrew pointed out.

It was one of her dreams, a full-scale exhibit showcasing the full scope of her field of interest. Art, artifacts, history, documents, all on display, precisely as she chose.

She kept her hands neatly folded to stop herself from pumping a triumphant fist in the air.

"Yes, I suppose I could." She felt the quick churn of excitement in her gut, but turned placidly to Ryan. "The Vasaris have been authenticated."

Ryan inclined his head, and both of them pretended not to hear Andrew's low moan. "Yes, of course. I'll see that you get copies of the documents before we draft the agreement. And you'll do the same for me, on the Cellini."

"I can have them for you today. My assistant can have them messengered to your hotel."

"Good. I'd appreciate it."

"Well, I'll leave you to work out the details."

But when she rose, he rose with her, and took her hand again. "I wonder if I can impose on you to show me around a bit. Andrew tells me that the labs and restoration facilities are your milieu. I'd very much like to see them."

"I—"

Before she could excuse herself, Andrew was up and giving her a none too subtle jab in the ribs. "You couldn't be in better hands. I'll see you back here in a couple hours, Ryan. Then we'll check out that clam chowder I promised you."

"Looking forward to it. . . . My galleries are for the display of art," he began, keeping Miranda's hand casually in his as she strode down the corridor to the next wing. "I know next to nothing about the science of it. Do you ever find yourself at odds merging the two?"

"No, without one there wouldn't be the other." Realizing her answer had been abrupt, she drew a careful breath. The man made her nervous, nervous enough to show. That would never do. "The Institute was built to house both, you might say celebrate both. As a scientist who studies art, I appreciate that."

"I was a miserable student of science," he said, with such a charming smile her lips curved in response.

"I'm sure you had other strong points."

"I like to think so."

He was an observant man, and noted carefully the flow of space between wings, the position of the stairs, offices, storerooms, windows. And of course, the security cameras. It was exactly as his information had indicated. Still, he would transcribe the observations into detailed notes later. But for now he simply filed them neatly in his mind while he enjoyed the subtle fragrance of Miranda's perfume.

Nothing overt for Dr. Jones, he thought. Nothing obviously female. And the woodsy scent he imagined came from soap rather than a delicate bottle suited her, he decided, perfectly.

At the end of a corridor, she turned right, then stopped to slide her key card into a slot beside a gray metal door. A buzzer sounded, locks clicked. Ryan flicked a mild glance upward at the camera.

"Our internal security is tight," she began. "No one passes into this department without a key or an escort. We often do independent testing for individuals and for other museums."

She led him into an area much like Standjo, Florence, though on a smaller scale. Technicians worked at computers and microscopes or walked briskly into anterooms with a flap of their lab coat.

She noted a staff member working with a crusted pot, and guided Ryan toward it. "Stanley, what can you tell us about this?"

The tech scratched at his blond moustache, sucked air in through slightly bucked teeth. "Your father sent it from the dig in Utah, along with several other artifacts. This is probably Anasazi, twelfth century, and was used as a cooking vessel."

He cleared his throat, shooting Miranda a quick glance, and at her nod continued. "The beauty is it's nearly intact, with only this small chip on the lip."

"Why a cooking vessel?" Ryan wanted to know, and Stanley blinked.

"The shape, size, thickness."

"Thank you, Stanley." Miranda turned back to Ryan, nearly bumped into him, as he'd moved closer when her back was turned. She shifted aside immediately, but not before noting that he had a good two inches on her in height. And that glint in his eyes of amused awareness took his face a step beyond sensual and straight into sexy.

She heard the damn ping again.

"We're primarily an institute for art, but as my father's interests are in archaeology, we have a section for artifact display, and do quite a bit of testing and dating in that area. It's not my field. Now this . . ."

She walked over to a cabinet, opened a drawer, and flipped through until she found a small brown bag. She transferred the tiny bits of paint inside onto a slide, then loaded it onto an unoccupied microscope.

"Take a look," she invited. "Tell me what you see."

He bent over, adjusted his focus. "Color, shape, interesting in its way—rather like a Pollock painting." He straightened and fixed those brandy-colored eyes on hers. "What am I looking at, Dr. Jones?"

"A scraping from a Bronzino we're restoring. The paint is unquestionably sixteenth century. We take a sample for security both before we begin the work and after the work is completed. In this way there's no doubt we've received an authentic work, and no doubt we return the same work to its owners upon completion."

"How do you know this is sixteenth-century paint?"

"Do you want a science lesson, Mr. Boldari?"

"Ryan—then I can say your name. Miranda's such a lovely name." His voice was like warm cream over whiskey and made her itchy. "And I might actually enjoy that science lesson with the right teacher."

"You'll have to sign up for a class."

"Poor students do better with one-on-ones. Have dinner with me tonight."

"I'm a mediocre teacher."

"Have dinner with me anyway. We can discuss art and science, and I can tell you about the Vasaris." He had an urge to lift his hand and play with the messy curls escaping their confinement. She'd jump like a rabbit, he decided. "We'll call it business if it makes you more at ease."

"I'm not ill at ease."

"Well then. I'll pick you up at seven. You know," he continued, slipping his hand over hers again. "I'd love to see that Bronzino. I admire the formal purity in his work."

Before she could calculate how to free her hand, he'd tucked it comfortably through his arm and headed for the door.

CHAPTER SIX

SHE DIDN'T KNOW WHY SHE'D AGREED TO DINNER. Although, when she thought back over the conversation, she hadn't actually agreed. Which didn't explain why she was getting dressed to go out.

He was an associate, she reminded herself. The Boldari Gallery had a glossy reputation for elegance and exclusivity. The single time she'd managed to carve out an hour when in New York to visit it, she'd been impressed with the understated grandeur of the building almost as much as the art itself.

It would hardly hurt the Institute for her to help forge a relationship between one of the most glamorous galleries in the country and the Jones organization.

He wanted to have dinner to discuss business. She'd make sure it stayed in the business arena.

Even if that smile of his sent little sparks of undiluted lust straight to her gut.

If he wanted to flirt with her, fine. Ping or no ping, flirting didn't affect her. She wasn't some impressionable mush brain, after all. Men who looked like Ryan Boldari were born with fully developed flirtation skills.

She liked to think she'd been born with an innate immunity to such shallow talents.

He had the most incredible eyes. Eyes that looked at you as if everything but you had simply melted away.

When she realized she'd sighed and closed her own, she muttered under her breath and yanked up the zipper in the back of her dress.

It was only a matter of pride and professional courtesy that she chose to be particular about her appearance this evening. The first time she saw him she'd resembled a scruffy student. Tonight he would see she was a mature, sophisticated woman who'd have no problem handling a man over a meal.

She'd selected a black dress in thin, soft wool scooped low at the bodice, low enough so that the swell of her breasts rose firmly over the straight-edge neckline. The sleeves were long and snug, the skirt narrow and fluid to the ankles. She added an excellent, and unquestionably sexy, reproduction of a Byzantine cross. Its ornate vertical stem rested cozily at the hollow of her breasts.

She yanked her hair up, jamming in pins at random. The result was, if she said so herself, carelessly sexy.

It was a good look, she decided, a confident look, and a far cry from the too tall, socially inept nerd she'd been all through college. No one who glanced at this woman would realize she had nerves in her stomach over a simple business dinner, or that she worried she'd run out of intelligent conversation before the appetizers were served.

They would see poise and style, she thought. They—and he—would see exactly what she wanted to be seen.

She grabbed her purse, craned her neck to study her butt in the mirror and assure herself the dress didn't make it look too big, then headed downstairs.

Andrew was in the front parlor, already into his second whiskey. He lowered the glass when she walked in, and raised his eyebrows high.

"Well. Wow."

"Andrew, you're such a poet. Do I look fat in this?"

"There's never a correct answer to that question. Or if there is, no man has ever found it. Therefore . . ." He raised his glass in toast. "I abstain."

"Coward." And because her stomach was far too jittery, she poured herself half a glass of white wine.

"Aren't you a little slicked up for a business dinner?"

She sipped, let the wine cruise down to dampen some of the butterfly wings. "Aren't you the one who lectured me for twenty minutes this afternoon on how beneficial a relationship with the Boldari Gallery could be to us?"

"Yeah." But he narrowed his eyes. Though Andrew didn't often see his sister as a woman, he was seeing her now. She looked, he thought uncomfortably, staggering. "Did he hit on you?"

"Get a grip on yourself."

"Did he?"

"No. Not exactly," she amended. "And if he did, or does, I'm a grown woman who knows how to block the blow or hit back, as the choice may be."

"Where are you going?"

"I didn't ask."

"The roads are still pretty crappy."

"It's March in Maine—of course the roads are crappy. Don't go big brother on me, Andrew." She patted his cheek when she said it, more relaxed now because he wasn't. "That must be Ryan," she added when the doorbell rang. "Behave."

"For three Vasaris, I'll behave," he muttered, but his brow creased as he watched Miranda walk out. Sometimes he forgot how outrageous she could look if she took a little time on it. The fact that she'd obviously taken the time gave him an itch between the shoulder blades.

The itch might have become a burn if he'd seen the way Ryan's eyes flashed, the way the heat in them simmered, when Miranda opened the door and stood framed in it.

It was a solid punch to the gut, Ryan thought, and one he should have been better prepared for.

"You look like something Titian would have painted." He took her hand, but this time stepped in and brushed his lips over her cheeks—one, then the other, European-style.

"Thank you." She closed the door and resisted the urge to lean back against it to catch her balance. There was something powerful and unnerving about the way her heeled boots made them of a height so that their eyes and mouths were lined up. As they would be, she thought, in bed.

"Andrew's in the parlor," she told him. "Would you like to come in for a moment?"

"Yes, I would. You have a fabulous home." He scanned the foyer, flicked a glance at the staircase as he followed her toward the parlor. "Dramatic and comfortable at the same time. You should commission someone to paint it."

"My grandfather did an oil of it. It's not very good, but we're fond of it. Can I get you a drink?"

"No, nothing. Hello, Andrew." He offered his hand. "I'm stealing your sister away for the evening, unless you'd like to join us."

Ryan had played the odds all of his life, but he cursed himself now as he saw Andrew consider the invitation. Though he was unaware that Miranda was making narrow-eyed, threatening faces behind his back, Ryan was relieved when Andrew shook his head.

"I appreciate it, but I've got some plans. You two enjoy yourselves."

"I'll just get my coat."

Andrew saw them off, then dragged his own coat

out of the closet. His plans had changed. He no longer felt like drinking alone. He preferred getting drunk in company.

Miranda pursed her lips as she slid into the back of the limo. "Do you always travel this way?"

"No." Ryan slipped in beside her, took a single white rose out of a bud vase and offered it. "But I had a yen for champagne I couldn't indulge if I was driving." To prove it, he lifted an already opened bottle of Cristal from an ice bucket and poured her a flute.

"Business dinners rarely start with roses and champagne."

"They should." He poured his own glass, tapped it to hers. "When they include women with arresting looks. To the beginning of an entertaining relationship."

"Association," she corrected, and sipped. "I've been in your New York gallery."

"Really? And what did you think of it?"

"Intimate. Glamorous. A small polished jewel with art as the facets."

"I'm flattered. Our gallery in San Francisco is airier, more light and space. We focus on contemporary and modern art there. My brother Michael has an eye and an affection for it. I prefer the classic . . . and the intimate."

His voice rippled softly over her skin. A telling sign and, Miranda thought, a dangerous one. "So Boldari is a family enterprise."

"Yes, like yours."

"I doubt it," she muttered, then moved her shoulders. Make conversation, she reminded herself. She was a confident woman. She could make conversation. "How did you become involved with art?"

"My parents are artists. For the most part they teach, but my mother's watercolors are glorious. My father sculpts, complicated metal structures no one but Michael seems to understand. But it feeds his soul."

He kept his eyes on hers as he spoke, directly on hers with a quiet intensity that had insistent sexual jolts dancing over her skin. "And do you paint or sculpt?" she asked.

"No, I haven't the hands for it, or the soul. It was a huge disappointment to my parents that none of their six children had a talent for creating art."

"Six." Miranda blinked as he topped off her glass. "Six children."

"My mother's Irish, my father Italian." He grinned, quick and charming. "What else could they do? I have two brothers, three sisters, and I'm the oldest of the lot. You have the most fascinating hair," he murmured, twirling a loose lock around his finger. He was right. She jumped. "How do you keep your hands off it?"

"It's red and unmanageable and if I wouldn't look like a six-foot azalea, I'd chop it off short."

"It was the first thing I noticed about you." His gaze slid down, locked on hers again. "Then it was your eyes. You're made up of bold colors and shapes."

She struggled to repress the fascinating image of grabbing his lapels and simply yanking their bodies together until they were a tangle of limbs on the backseat. And despite her fight for control, she fidgeted. "Like modern art?"

He chuckled. "No, too much classic practicality for that. I like your looks," he said when the limo pulled to the curb and stopped. When the door opened, he took her hand to help her out. His mouth nearly grazed her ear. "Let's see if we like each other's company."

She couldn't say when she started to relax. Perhaps it was sometime during her third glass of champagne. She had to admit he was smooth—maybe just a tad too smooth—but it worked. It was a long time since she'd sat across a candlelit table from a man, and when the man had a face that belonged on a Renaissance portrait, it was impossible not to appreciate the moment.

And he listened. He might claim to have been a poor student of science, but he certainly asked questions and appeared interested in the answers. Perhaps he was simply putting her at ease by steering the conversation onto professional ground, but she was grateful for the results.

She couldn't remember the last time she'd spent an evening talking about her work, and talking of it, she remembered why she loved it.

"It's the discovery," she told him. "The study of a piece of art, and finding its history, its individuality, its personality, I suppose."

"Dissecting it?"

"In a way, yes." It was so pleasant to sit like this, in the cozy warmth of the restaurant with a fire blazing nearby and the cold dark sea just outside the window. "The paint itself, then the brushstrokes, the subject, the purpose. All the parts of it that can be studied and analyzed to give the answers."

"And you don't feel, in the end, the answer is simply the art itself?"

"Without the history, and the analysis, it's just a painting."

"When something's beautiful, it's enough. If I was to analyze your face, I'd take your eyes, the bold summer blue of them, the intelligence in them, the hint of sadness. And the suspicion," he added with a smile. "Your mouth, soft, wide, reluctant to smile. Your cheekbones, sharp, aristocratic. Your nose, slim, elegant. Separate the features, study, analyze, I'd still come to the conclusion that you're a stunning woman. And I can do that by just sitting back and appreciating the whole."

She toyed with her scrod, struggling not to be overly flattered or charmed. "That was clever."

"I'm a clever man, and you don't trust me."

Her gaze lifted to his again. "I don't know you."

"What else can I tell you? I come from a big, loud, ethnic family, grew up in New York, studied, without a great deal of enthusiasm, at Columbia. Then because I'm not artistic, shifted into the business of art. I've never married, which displeases my mother—enough that I once considered it seriously, and briefly."

She arched a brow. "And rejected it?"

"At that particular time, with that particular woman. We lacked a spark." He leaned closer, for the pleasure of her, and because he enjoyed the cautious awareness that came into her eyes when he did. "Do you believe in sparks, Miranda?"

Sparks, she imagined, were cousins to pings. "I believe they fuel initial attraction, but sparks die out and aren't enough for the long haul."

"You're cynical," he decided. "I'm a romantic. You analyze and I appreciate. That's an interesting combination, don't you think?"

She moved her shoulder, discovering she wasn't quite so relaxed any longer. He had her hand again, just playing with her fingers on the table. He had a habit of touching she wasn't used to, and one that made her all too aware of sparks.

Sparks, she reminded herself, made a pretty light. But they could also burn.

Being this quickly, and outrageously, attracted to him was dangerous, and it was illogical. It had everything to do with glands and nothing to do with intellect.

Therefore, she concluded, it could and would be controlled.

"I don't understand romantics. They make decisions based on feelings rather than fact." Andrew was a romantic, she thought, and hurt for him. "Then they're surprised when those decisions turn out to be mistakes."

"But we have so much more fun than cynics." And he, he realized, was much more attracted to her than he'd anticipated. Not just her looks, he decided as their plates were cleared. It was that leading edge of practicality, of pragmatism. One he found it hard to resist buffing away.

And yes, the big sad eyes.

"Dessert?" he asked her.

"No, I couldn't. It was a lovely meal."

"Coffee?"

"It's too late for coffee."

He grinned, absolutely charmed. "You're an orderly woman, Miranda. I like that about you." Still watching her, he signaled for the bill. "Why don't we take a walk? You can show me the waterfront."

"Jones Point's a safe city," she began when they strolled in the icy wind that whipped off the water. The limo followed them at a crawl, a fact that both amused and staggered her. However much wealth she'd come from, no Jones would ever hire a limo to pace them as they walked. "It's very walkable. There are several parks. They're gorgeous in the spring and summer. Shade trees, banks of flowers. You've never been here before?"

"No. Your family's lived here for generations?"

"Yes. There have always been Joneses in Jones Point."

"Is that why you live here?" His gloved fingers tangled with hers, leather sliding over leather. "Because it's expected?"

"No. It's where I come from, where I am." It was difficult to explain, even to herself, how deep her roots were sunk in that rocky New England soil. "I enjoy traveling, but this is where I want to be when it's time to come home."

"Then tell me about Jones Point."

"It's quiet and settled. The city itself grew from a fishing village into a community with emphasis on culture and tourism. A number of residents still make their living from the sea. What we call the waterfront is actually along Commercial Street. Lobstering is profitable—the packing plant ships all over the world."

"Have you ever done it?"

"What?"

"Gone lobstering."

"No." She smiled a little. "I can see the boats and buoys from the cliffs behind the house. I like to watch them."

Observe rather than participate, he thought.

"This area is Old Port," she continued. "You'll find a lot of galleries in this part of town. You might be interested in visiting some of them before you leave."

"I might."

"The city shows best in the spring, when you can make use of the parks and beaches. There are some beautiful stretches of marsh and sand, views of Miracle Bay and the islands. But in dead winter, it can be a postcard. The pond freezes in Atlantic Park, and people come to ice-skate."

"Do you?" He slipped an arm around her shoulder to block her from the edge of the wind. Their bodies bumped. "Skate."

"Yes." Her blood simmered; her throat went dry. "It's excellent exercise."

He laughed, and just beyond the circle of light tossed out by a streetlamp, turned her to him. Now his hands were on her shoulders, and the wind at his back streamed through his hair. "So it's for the exercise, not for the fun."

"I enjoy it. It's too late in the year for skating now."

He could feel her nerves, the shimmer of them under his hands. Intrigued by them, he drew her a little closer. "And how do you get your exercise this late in the year?"

"I walk a lot. Swim when I can." Her pulse was beginning to jump, a sensation she knew she couldn't trust. "It's too cold to stand."

"Then why don't we consider this an exercise in sharing body heat." He hadn't intended to kiss her—eventually yes, of course—but not this soon. Still, he hadn't lied when he told her he was a romantic. And the moment simply called for it.

He brushed his lips over hers, testing, his eyes open as hers were. The wariness in hers caused his lips to curve as he tasted her a second time. He was a man who believed in practicing until he was skilled in a matter he enjoyed. He was very skilled in the matter of women and patiently warmed her lips with his until hers softened, parted, until her lashes fluttered down and she sighed quietly into his mouth.

Maybe it was foolish, but what could it hurt? The little war of reason in her head faded to whispers as sensation layered over. His mouth was firm and persuasive, his body long and hard. He tasted faintly of the wine they'd shared and was just as arousingly foreign and rich.

She found herself leaning into him, her hands clutching at his coat at the waist. And her mind went blank with pleasure.

Suddenly his hands were cupping her face, the cold, smooth leather of his gloves a shock to her dreaming brain. Her eyes opened to find his narrowed on her face, with an intensity burning in them the easy kiss didn't warrant.

"Let's try that again."

This time his mouth was rough and hot, plundering hers until her head roared with sounds like the sea below the cliffs of her home. There was demand here, and the arrogant certainty it would be answered. Even as her mind lurched back, bent on refusing, her mouth answered.

He knew what it was to want. He'd wanted a great deal in his life, and had made it his business to see his desires were met. Wanting her was acceptable, even expected. But wanting her now, this forcibly, was dangerous. Even a man who gambled by choice knew to avoid unwinnable risks.

Still, he lingered long enough to be certain he would spend a very uncomfortable night, alone. He couldn't afford to seduce her, to take her back to his bed. There was work to be done, and the timing was already set. Most of all, he couldn't afford to care for her. Growing attached to a pawn was a certain way to lose the game.

He never lost.

He held her away, skimming his gaze over her face. Her cheeks were flushed, from the cold and the heat. Her eyes were clouded still with a passion he imagined had surprised her as much as him. She shivered as he stroked his hands down to her shoulders again. And she said nothing.

"I should take you home." However much he cursed himself, his smile was smooth and easy.

"Yes." She wanted to sit, to steady herself. To think again. "It's getting late."

"Another minute," he murmured, "it would have been too late." Taking her hand, he led her to the waiting limo. "Do you get to New York often?"

"Now and again." The heat seemed to be centered in a ball in her gut. The rest of her was cold, viciously cold.

"You'll let me know when your plans take you there. And I'll adjust mine."

"All right," she heard herself say, and didn't feel foolish at all.

She sang in the shower. It was something she never did. She didn't have to be told she had a dreadful voice, when she could hear it for herself. But this morning she belted out "Making Whoopee." She had no idea why that tune was lodged in her head—had no idea she even knew the lyrics—but she gurgled them as water sluiced over her head.

She was still humming when she dried off.

Bending from the waist, she wrapped a towel

around her mass of hair, swinging her hips as she did so. She was no better at dancing, though she knew all the proper steps. The members of the art council who had guided her through her rigid waltzes would have been shocked to see the cool Dr. Jones bumping and grinding around her efficient bathroom.

She giggled at the thought of it, a sound so unprecedented she had to stop and catch her breath. She realized with a kind of jolt that she was happy. Really happy. That too was a rare thing. Content she often was, involved, satisfied, or challenged. But she knew simple happiness often eluded her.

It was marvelous to feel it now.

And why shouldn't she? She slipped into a practical terry robe and smoothed her arms and legs with quietly scented body cream. She was interested in a very appealing man, and he was interested in her. He enjoyed her company, appreciated her work, found her attractive on both a physical and an intellectual plane.

He wasn't intimidated, as so many were, by her position or her personality. He was charming, successful—to say nothing of gorgeous—and he'd been civilized enough not to press an obvious advantage and attempt to lure her into bed.

Would she have gone? Miranda wondered as she briskly dried off the foggy mirror. Normally the answer would have been a firm no. She didn't indulge in reckless affairs with men she barely knew. She didn't indulge in affairs period for that matter. It had been over two years since she'd had a lover, and that had ended so miserably she'd resolved to avoid even casual relationships.

But last night . . . Yes, she thought she could have been persuaded. Against her better judgment she could have been swayed. But he had respected her enough not to ask.

She continued to hum as she dressed for the day, choosing a wool suit with a short skirt and long jacket in a flattering shade of steel blue. She took care with her makeup, then let her hair tumble as it chose. In a last act of female defiance against the elements, she slipped into impractical heels.

She left for work in the chilly dark, and was still singing.

Andrew awoke with the mother of all hangovers. Not being able to stand his own whimpering, he tried to smother himself with pillows. Survival was stronger than misery, and he burst up, gasping for air and grabbing his head to keep it from falling off his shoulders.

Then he let go, praying it would.

He inched out of bed. As a scientist he knew it wasn't possible for his bones to actually shatter, but he was afraid they might defy the laws of physics and do just that.

It was Annie's fault, he decided. She'd gotten just annoyed enough with him the night before to let him drink himself blind. He'd counted on her to cut him off, as she usually did. But no, she kept slapping those drinks in front of him, every time he called for one.

He dimly remembered her shoving him into a cab and saying something pithy about hoping he was sick as three dogs.

She'd gotten her wish, he thought as he stumbled downstairs. If he felt any worse, he'd be dead.

When he saw there was already coffee, brewed and waiting, he nearly wept with love and gratitude for his sister. With hands that fumbled and trembled, he shook out four extra-strength Excedrin and washed them down with coffee that scalded his mouth.

Never again, he promised himself, pressing his fingers to his throbbing, bloodshot eyes. He would never drink to excess again. Even as he vowed, the slick longing for just one glass shuddered through him. Just one glass to steady his hands, to settle his stomach.

He refused it, telling himself there was a difference between overindulging and alcoholism. If he took a drink at seven A.M., he'd be an alcoholic. At seven P.M. now, it was fine. He could wait. He would wait. Twelve hours.

The ringing of the doorbell split through his skull like a keen-edged blade. He very nearly screamed. Instead of answering, he sat at the long trestle table there in the kitchen, laid his head down, and prayed for oblivion.

He'd nearly dozed off when the back door opened, letting in a frigid blast of air and an angry woman.

"I thought you'd be curled up somewhere feeling sorry for yourself." Annie set a grocery bag on the counter, slapped her hands on her hips, and scowled at him. "Look at you, Andrew. A pitiful mess. Half naked, unshaven, bloodshot, and smelly. Go take a shower."

He lifted his head to blink at her. "I don't wanna."

"Go take a shower while I fix your breakfast." When he tried to lower his head again, she simply took a handful of his hair and dragged it up again. "You're getting just what you deserve."

"Jesus, Annie, you're going to yank my head off."

"And you'd feel considerably better if I could. You get your skinny butt out of that chair and go clean up—and use some industrial-strength mouthwash. You need it."

"Christ Almighty. What the hell are you doing here?" He hadn't thought there was room for embarrassment in the rage of the hangover, but he'd been wrong. He could feel the flush—a curse of his coloring—work up his bare chest toward his face. "Go away."

"I sold you the liquor." She let his hair go, and his head fell back onto the table with a thunk that made him howl. "You made me mad, so I let you keep drinking. So I'm going to fix you a decent breakfast, see that you get yourself cleaned up and go to work. Now go take a shower, or I'll take you up and toss you in the tub myself."

"Okay, okay." Anything was better than having her nag at him. With what dignity he could muster in his boxer shorts, he rose. "I don't want anything to eat."

"You'll eat what I fix you." She turned to the counter and began unloading the bag. "Now get out of here. You smell like the floor of a second-class bar."

She waited until she heard him shuffle away, then closed her eyes and leaned on the counter.

Oh, he'd looked so pathetic. So sad and sick and silly. She'd wanted to cuddle him, to soothe, to stroke all those poisons out of him. Poisons, she thought guiltily, she'd sold him because she was angry.

It wasn't the liquor, not really, she thought. It was his heart, and she just didn't know how to reach it.

She wondered if she could if she only cared about him a little less.

She heard the pipes clunk as he ran the shower, and it made her smile. He was so much like this house, she thought. A little threadbare, a little damaged, but surprisingly sturdy under it all.

He just couldn't see that Elise, for all her brains and beauty, hadn't been right for him. They'd made a stunning couple, bright and brilliant, but that was all surface. She hadn't understood his foundation, his need for sweetness, and the ache in his heart that came from not believing himself worthy of love.

He needed tending.

That she could do, Annie decided, pushing up her sleeves. If nothing else, she could bully him into finding his feet again.

Friends, she told herself, stood by friends.

The kitchen was full of homey scents when he came back. If it had been anyone but Annie, he might have locked himself in his room. The shower had helped, and the pills had shoved the worst of the hangover away. The edges of it were still churning in his stomach and rolling in his head, but he thought he could manage now.

He cleared his throat, worked up a smile. "Smells great."

"Sit down," she told him without turning.

"Okay. I'm sorry, Annie."

"No need to apologize to me. You should apologize to yourself. That's who's being hurt here."

"I'm sorry anyway." He looked down at the bowl she put in front of him. "Oatmeal?"

"It'll stick to you, coat your stomach."

"Mrs. Patch used to make me eat oatmeal," he said, thinking of the sharp stick of a woman who'd cooked for them when he was a boy. "Every day before school, fall, winter, and spring."

"Mrs. Patch knew what was good for you."

"She used to put a little maple syrup in it."

Feeling her lips twitch, Annie reached into a cupboard. She knew his kitchen as well as her own. She set the bottle of syrup in front of him, and added a plate of hot toasted bread. "Eat."

"Yes, ma'am." He took the first bite cautiously, uncertain anything would stay down. "It's good. Thanks."

When she saw he was making headway, and his color was no longer sickly gray, she sat across from him. Friends stood by friends, she thought again. And they were honest with each other.

"Andrew, you've got to stop doing this to yourself."

"I know. I shouldn't have had so much to drink."

She reached out, touched his hand. "If you take one drink, you're going to take the next, and the next."

Annoyed, he jerked his shoulders. "Nothing wrong with a drink now and then. Nothing wrong with getting drunk now and then."

"There is when you're an alcoholic."

"I'm not."

She sat back. "I run a bar and I was married to a drunk. I know the signs. There's a difference between someone who has a couple too many and someone who can't stop."

"I can stop." He picked up the coffee she'd poured him. "I'm not drinking now, am I? I don't drink at work—and I don't let it affect my work. I don't get drunk every night."

"But you drink every night."

"So does half the goddamn world. What's the difference between a couple glasses of wine with dinner and a shot or two in the evening?"

"You'll have to figure that out for yourself. The way I did. We were both half drunk the night we . . ." It hurt to say it. She thought she'd been ready, but it hurt and she couldn't say it after all.

"Christ, Annie." Remembering had him raking a hand through his hair, wishing the ball of shame and guilt hadn't just dropped into his gut. "We were just kids."

"We were old enough to make a baby between

us. Temporarily." She pressed her lips together. No matter what it cost she would get at least part of it out. "We were stupid, and we were innocent, and we were irresponsible. I've accepted that." Oh God, she tried to accept that. "But it taught me what you can lose, what it can do if you don't stay in control. You're not in control, Andrew."

"One night fifteen years ago doesn't have anything to do with now." The minute the words were out, the minute he saw the way her body jerked back, he regretted it. "I didn't mean it like that, Annie. Not that it didn't matter. I just—"

"Don't." Her voice was cool now and distant. "Just don't. We're better off when we pretend it never happened. I only brought it up because you can't seem to see the difference. You were only seventeen, but you already had a drinking problem. I didn't. I don't. You've managed to get through most of your life without letting it take over. Now you've crossed the line. It's starting to rule you, Andrew, and you have to take back the controls. I'm telling you this as a friend." She rose, cupped his face in her hands. "Don't come in my place anymore. I won't serve you."

"Come on, Annie—"

"You can come for conversation, but don't come for a drink because I won't give it to you."

She turned, picked up her coat, and hurried out.

CHAPTER SEVEN

RYAN WANDERED THE SOUTH GALLERY, ADMIRING THE use of light, the flow of space. The Joneses knew their business, he mused. The displays were elegantly arranged, the educational plaques discreet and informative.

He listened with half an ear as a blue-haired woman with a sharp Down East accent led a small tour to one of Raphael's magnificent Madonnas.

Another tour, a bit larger and quite a bit noisier, was composed of schoolchildren and led by a perky brunette. They were heading off to the Impressionists, much to Ryan's relief.

Not that he didn't like children. The fact was his nieces and nephews were a great source of delight and amusement for him. He took pleasure in spoiling them outrageously as often as possible. But children tended to be a distraction during work hours. Ryan was very much at work.

The guards were unobtrusive, but there were plenty of them. He noted their stations, and judged by one uniform's surreptitious glance at his watch that they were nearing change of shift.

He appeared to wander aimlessly, stopping here and there to study a painting, a sculpture, or a display of artifacts. In his mind he counted off paces. From the doorway to the camera in the southwest corner, from the camera to the archway, from the archway to the next camera, and from there to his goal.

He lingered no longer in front of the display case than any art lover might when studying the rare beauty of a fifteenth-century bronze. The bronze *David* was a small jewel, young, cocky, slender, his sling whipped back at that historic moment of truth.

Though the artist was unknown, the style was Leonardo's. And as the plaque indicated, it was assumed to be the work of one of his students.

Ryan's client was a particular fan of Leonardo's, and had commissioned for this particular piece after seeing it in the Institute six months before.

Ryan thought his client would be very happy, and sooner rather than later. He'd decided to move up his own schedule. It was, he thought, wiser to move along, and away before he made a mistake with Miranda. He was already feeling a little sorry that he would cause her some inconvenience and annoyance.

But, after all, she was insured. And the bronze was hardly the best piece the Institute possessed.

If he was choosing for himself, he'd have taken

the Cellini, or perhaps the Titian woman who reminded him of Miranda. But the pocket-sized bronze was his client's choice. And it would be an easier job than either the Cellini or the Titian.

Due to his own unplanned reaction to Miranda, he'd spent a productive hour or two, after taking her home and changing out of his dinner suit, in the tube-sized crawl space beneath the Institute. There, as he'd already known, was the wiring for the building's security system. Alarms, cameras, sensors.

All he'd needed was his laptop and a little time to reset the main to his personal specifications. He hadn't diddled with much. Most of the work would be done in a few hours, but a few judicious changes would make his job easier in the long run.

He completed his measurements, then, following his schedule, executed the first test. He smiled at the blue-haired lady, edging just past her group. With his hands in his pockets, he studied a shadowy painting of the Annunciation. Once he had the small mechanism in hand, he ran his thumb over the controls until he felt the proper button. The camera was directly to his right.

He smiled at the Virgin when he saw, out of the corner of his eye, the tiny red light on the camera blink out.

God, he loved technology.

In his other pocket, he depressed the stem of a stopwatch. And waited.

He judged nearly two minutes passed before the nearest guard's walkie-talkie beeped. Ryan clicked the stopwatch again, unjammed the camera with his other hand, and strolled over to study the sad and baffled face of Saint Sebastian.

More than satisfied, Ryan walked out of the gallery and stepped outside to use his cell phone.

"Dr. Jones's office. May I help you?"

"I hope you can." The wifty little voice of Miranda's assistant made him grin. "Is Dr. Jones available? Ryan Boldari calling."

"One moment, Mr. Boldari."

Ryan stepped back out of the wind while he waited. He liked the look of downtown, he decided, the variety of architecture, the granite and the brick. He'd passed a dignified statue of Longfellow in his wanderings, and found that it and the other statues and monuments added to an interesting city.

Perhaps he preferred New York, the pace and the demand there. But he didn't think he'd mind spending a bit more time right here. Some other time, of course. It was never wise to linger long after a job was completed.

"Ryan?" Her voice sounded slightly breathless. "Sorry I kept you waiting."

"I don't mind. I've just taken a busman's holiday and wandered through your galleries." Best that she know, as it was likely they'd be reviewing tapes the following day.

"Oh. I wish you'd told me you were coming. I'd have taken you around myself."

"I didn't want to keep you from your work. But I wanted to tell you I believe my Vasaris are going to have a wonderful temporary home. You should come to New York and see where your Cellini will be staying."

He hadn't meant to say that. Damn it. He shifted the phone to his other hand, reminding himself some distance would be required for a time.

"I might do that. Would you like to come up? I can have you cleared."

"I would but I have some appointments I couldn't reschedule. I'd hoped to take you to lunch, but I can't blow these meetings off. I'm going to be tied up the rest of the day, but wondered if you'd have lunch with me tomorrow."

"I'm sure I can schedule it in. What time works for you?"

"The sooner the better. I want to see you, Miranda." He could imagine her sitting in her office, perhaps wearing a lab coat over some bulky sweater. Oh yes, he wanted to see her, a great deal of her. "How about noon?"

He heard papers rustle. Checking her calendar, he thought, and for some reason found that delightful. "Yes, noon's fine. Um, the documentation on your Vasaris just came across my desk. You work quickly."

"Beautiful women shouldn't have to wait. I'll see you tomorrow. I'll think of you tonight."

He broke the connection and suffered a very rare sensation. He recognized it as guilt only because he couldn't actually recall experiencing it before. Certainly not when it came to women or work.

"Can't be helped," he said softly, and replaced his cell phone. As he strode toward the parking lot, he took out his stopwatch. One hundred and ten seconds.

Time enough. More than time enough.

He glanced up toward the window where he knew Miranda's office to be. There'd be time for that too. Eventually. But professional obligations came first. He was sure a woman of her practical nature would agree.

Ryan spent the next several hours locked in his suite. He'd ordered up a quick lunch, turned the stereo on to a classical station, and spread out his notes for review.

He had the blueprints for the Institute anchored on the conference table with the salt and pepper shakers and the tiny bottles of mustard and ketchup that had come on his room service tray.

The schematics of the security system were on the screen of his laptop. He nibbled on a french fry, sipped Evian, and studied.

The blueprints had been easy enough to access. Contacts and cash could access nearly everything. He was also very handy with a computer. It was a skill he'd developed and honed while still in high school.

His mother had insisted he learn how to type—because you just never knew—but he'd had more interesting things to do with a keyboard than hammer out correspondence.

He'd built the laptop he carried with him himself, and had added a number of bonuses that weren't strictly legal. Then again, neither was his profession.

The Boldari Galleries were completely aboveboard, and were now self-financed and earned a nice, comfortable profit. But they had been built on funds he'd accumulated over the years, beginning as a nimble-fingered, fast-thinking boy on the streets of New York.

Some people were born artists, others were born accountants. Ryan had been born a thief.

Initially he'd picked pockets and lifted trinkets because money was tight. After all, art teachers weren't raking in dough, and there were a lot of mouths to feed in the Boldari household.

Later, he shifted into second-story work because, well, he was good at it, and it was exciting. He could still remember his first foray into a dark, sleeping home. The quiet, the tension, the thrill of being somewhere he had no business being, the initial edginess that swam up with the possibility of being caught had added to the kick of it all.

Like having sex in some odd public place, in broad daylight. With another man's wife.

Since he had a strict code against adultery, he limited that wired sensation to stealing.

Nearly twenty years later, he would feel that same thrill each time he lifted a lock and slipped into a secured building.

He fined his craft down and for more than a decade had specialized in art. He had a feel for art, a love of it, and in his heart considered it public domain. If he slipped a painting out of the Smithsonian—and he had—he was simply providing a service to an individual for which he was well paid.

And with his fee he acquired more art to put on display at his galleries for public view and enjoyment.

It seemed to balance things out nicely.

Since he had a flair for electronics and gadgets, why shouldn't he put them to use along with his God-given gift for larceny?

Turning to his laptop, he logged in the measurements he'd taken in the South Gallery, and brought up the three-dimensional floor plan on-screen. Camera positions were highlighted in red. With a few keystrokes, he requested the machine to calculate the angles, the distance and best approach.

He was, he thought, a long way from his cat burglar days when he would case a home, climb through a window, and creep around stuffing glitters in a bag. That aspect of the profession was for the young, the reckless, or the foolish. And in these unsettled times, too many people had guns in their homes and shot at anything that moved in the night.

He preferred avoiding trigger-happy homeowners.

Better to put the age of technology to use, do the job quick, clean, and tidy, and move on.

As a matter of habit, he checked the batteries in his pocket jammer. It was of his own design, and fashioned of parts cannibalized from a TV remote control, a cell phone, and a pager.

Once he studied the security system of a mark—

which Andrew had been kind enough to show him—he could easily adjust the range and frequency to apply after he'd jury-rigged the system at its source. His test late that morning had proven he'd been successful in that area.

Gaining entrance had been more problematic. If he worked with a partner, one could work the computer in the crawl space to bypass locks. He worked alone, and needed the jammer for the cameras.

Locks were a relatively simple matter. He'd accessed the schematics of the security system weeks ago, and had finally cracked it. After spending two nights on the scene, he'd earmarked the side door and had forged a key card.

The security code itself had again come courtesy of Andrew. It was amazing to Ryan what information people carried around in their wallets. The numbers and sequence had been written neatly on a folded piece of paper tucked behind Andrew's driver's license. It had taken Ryan seconds to lift the wallet, moments to flip through, find the numbers and memorize them, and nothing more than a friendly pat on the back to slide the wallet back into Andrew's pocket.

Ryan figured the job had taken him approximately seventy-two hours of work to prep; adding the hour it would take to execute, and deducting his outlay and expenses, he would see a profit of eighty-five thousand.

Nice work if you can get it, he thought, and tried not to regret that this was his last adventure. He'd given his word on that, and he never went back on a promise. Not to family.

He checked the time, noted he had eight hours before curtain. He spent the first of them dealing with any evidence, burning the blueprints in the cheerful fireplace his suite provided, locking all of his electronics in a reinforced case, then adding additional paths and passwords to his computer work to tuck it away safely.

That left him time for a workout, a steam, a swim, and a short nap. He believed in being alert in mind and body before breaking and entering.

Just past six, Miranda sat alone in her office to compose a letter she preferred typing herself. Though she and Andrew essentially ran the Institute, it was still standard procedure for both of their parents to be informed of, and to approve, any loan or transfer of art.

She intended to make the letter crisp and businesslike and was willing to work on it word by word until it was as stringent as vinegar, just as unfriendly, but viciously professional.

She thought the vinegar would go very well with the crow her mother would soon be sampling.

She'd completed the first draft and was beginning the refinements when the phone rang.

"New England Institute, Dr. Jones."

"Miranda, thank God I caught you."

"Excuse me." Annoyed at the clicking, she shifted the phone and tugged off her earring. "Who's calling?"

"It's Giovanni."

"Giovanni?" She scanned her desk clock, calculated time. "It's after midnight there. Is something wrong?"

"Everything's wrong. It's a disaster. I didn't dare call you earlier, but I felt you had to know, as soon as possible, before . . . before morning."

Her heart jerked once, brutally hard, and the earring she'd removed fell to bounce musically on her desk. "My mother? Has something happened to my mother?"

"Yes—no. She's well, she's not hurt. I'm sorry. I'm upset."

"It's all right." To calm herself she closed her eyes, took deep, quiet breaths. "Just tell me what's happened."

"The bronze, the Fiesole bronze. It's a fake."

"That's ridiculous." She sat straight up, her voice snapping out. "Of course it's not a fake. Who says so?"

"The results came back earlier today from the tests taken in Rome. Arcana-Jasper Laboratories. Dr. Ponti oversaw the testing. You know his work?"

"Yes, of course. You have bad information, Giovanni."

"I tell you, I saw the results myself. Dr. Standford-Jones called me in, along with Richard and Elise, as we were on the original team. She even raked Vincente. She's furious, Miranda, and humiliated and not a little sick. The bronze is fake. It was probably cast no more than months ago, if that. The formula was right for the metal, even the patina was perfect, and could have been mistaken."

"I didn't mistake anything," she insisted, but could feel crab claws of panic crawling up her spine.

"The corrosion levels were wrong, all wrong. I don't know how we missed it, Miranda, but they were wrong. Some attempt had been made to create them in the metal, but it wasn't successful."

"You saw the results, the computer photos, the X rays."

"I know it. I told your mother this, but . . ."

"But what, Giovanni?"

"She asked me who took the X rays, who programmed the computer. Who ran the radiation tests. *Cara,* I'm sorry."

"I understand." She was numb now, her mind clouding. "It's my responsibility. I took the tests, I wrote the reports."

"If it hadn't been for the leak to the press, we could have swept this under the rug, at least part of it."

"Ponti could be wrong." She rubbed her hand over her mouth. "He could be wrong. I didn't miss something as basic as corrosion levels. I need to think about this, Giovanni. I appreciate you telling me."

"I hate to ask, Miranda, but I must if I hope to keep my position. Your mother can't know I spoke with you about this, spoke with you at all. I believe she intends to contact you in the morning herself."

"Don't worry, I won't mention your name. I can't talk now. I need to think."

"All right. I'm sorry, so sorry."

Slowly, deliberately, she replaced the receiver and sat, still as a stone, staring at nothing. She struggled to bring all the data back into her mind, to make order of it, to see it again as clearly as she had in Florence. But there was nothing but a buzzing that made her give in and drop her head between her knees.

A fake? It couldn't be. It wasn't possible. Her breath came short, making it impossible to fill her lungs. Then her fingertips began to tingle as the numbness passed and the shaking began.

She'd been careful, she assured herself. She'd been thorough. She'd been accurate. Her heart thudded so painfully she pressed the heel of her hand against her sternum.

Oh God, she hadn't been careful enough, thorough enough, accurate enough.

Had her mother been right? Despite all her claims to the contrary, had she made up her mind about the bronze the moment she'd seen it?

Wanted it, she admitted, and lifted her head to lean back in the chair in the slow, deliberate movement of the aged or ill. She'd wanted it to be real, wanted to know that she'd held something that important, that precious and rare in her hands.

Arrogance, Elizabeth had called it. Her arrogance and her ambition. Had she let that cockiness, that wanting, that thirst for approval cloud her judgment and affect her work?

No, no, no. She fisted her hands, pressed them against her eyes. She'd seen the pictures, the radiation results, the chemical tests. Studied them. They were fact, and fact didn't lie. Every test had proven her belief. There had to be a mistake, but she hadn't made it.

Because if she had, she thought, and lowered her fists to the desk, it was worse than failure. No one would trust her again. She wouldn't even trust herself.

She closed her eyes, laid her head back.

That was how Andrew found her twenty minutes later.

"I saw your light. I was working late myself, and . . ." He trailed off, pausing at the doorway. She was pale as water, and when she opened her eyes they were too dark, too bright, and too blank. "Hey, are you sick?"

Though illness made him nervous, he crossed the room to lay a palm to her brow. "You're cold." Instinctively he took her hands between his and began to rub. "You've got a chill or something. I'll take you home. You should lie down."

"Andrew . . ." She was going to have to say it, say it out loud. And her throat was raw on the words. "*The Dark Lady*. It's fake."

"What?" He'd begun to pat her head. Now his hand froze there. "The bronze? In Florence?"

"The retesting. The results are in. The corrosion growth is wrong, the radiation figures are wrong. Ponti, in Rome. He supervised the tests himself."

He sat on the edge of the desk, knowing brotherly head pats were not going to soothe this sickness away. "How do you know?"

"Giovanni—he just called. He wasn't supposed to. If Mother finds out she could fire him for it."

"Okay." Giovanni wasn't his concern at the moment. "Are you sure his information's accurate?"

"I don't want to think so." She crossed her arms over her chest, digging her fingers into her biceps. Squeezing, releasing, squeezing, releasing. "He wouldn't have contacted me otherwise. Mother called him and Elise and Richard Hawthorne in to tell them. Vincente too. I imagine she blasted them. They're going to say I screwed up." Her voice broke, causing her to shake her head fiercely as if to deny the emotion. "Just as she predicted."

"Did you?"

She opened her mouth to deny that too, just as fiercely. But closed it again, pressing her lips together. Control, she ordered herself. At the very least she needed control. "I don't see how. I ran the tests. I followed procedure. I documented the results. But I wanted it, Andrew, maybe I wanted it too much."

"I've never known you to let what you want get in the way of what is." He couldn't stand to see her look so stricken. Of the two of them, she'd always been the stronger. Both of them had counted on it. "Could there have been some technical glitch, faulty equipment?"

She nearly laughed. "We're talking about Elizabeth's pride and joy here, Andrew."

"Machines break down."

"Or the people inputting data into those machines make mistakes. Ponti's team could have made one." She pushed away from the desk now, and though her legs trembled, began to pace. "It's no more far-fetched than my making one. I need to see my data again, and the results. I need to see his. I need to see *The Dark Lady*."

"You'll need to talk to her."

"I know." She stopped, turned to the window, but saw only the dark. "I'd call her now if it wouldn't damage Giovanni's confidence. I'd rather get it over with than wait until she contacts me."

"You were always one to take your medicine in one gulp. I'm a big believer in putting off forever what you don't want to face today."

"There's no avoiding it. When the results are made public, it's going to ripple down. I'll be either a fool or a fraud, and one's as bad as the other. Vincente will find some spin to put on it, but it won't stop the press. She was right about that. It'll affect Standjo, her, me." She turned back to face him. "It's going to affect the Institute."

"We can handle it."

"This is my mess, Andrew. Not yours."

He walked over, put his hands on her shoulder. "No." He said it simply, and had tears burning the backs of her eyes. "We'll stand together, just like always."

She let out a breath, leaned into him and let herself be comforted. But she thought their mother might give her no choice. If it came down to the Institute or her daughter, there was no doubt in Miranda's mind which would take precedence.

CHAPTER EIGHT

THE MIDNIGHT WIND WAS BITTER AS A SCORNED woman and just as bad-tempered. Ryan didn't mind it. He found it invigorating as he walked the three crosstown blocks from where he'd parked his car.

Everything he needed was under his coat in pouches and pockets or in the small briefcase he carried. If the cops stopped him for some reason, and took a look, he'd be in a cage before he could exercise his civil right for a phone call. But that was just part of the thrill.

God, he would miss it, he thought, and strode along with the eager step of a man hurrying to meet a lover. The planning stage was over, and so was that aspect of his life. Now the execution was approaching, his last. He wanted to file every detail in his mind so that when he was a very old man with grandchildren at his feet, he could bring back this young and vital feeling of power.

He scanned the streets. The trees were bare and shivering in the wind, the traffic was spotty, the moon faded to a hint of shape by the city lights and the drifting clouds. He passed a bar where a blue neon martini glass winked in the window, and smiled. He might just slip in for a drink after work. A small toast to the end of an era seemed appropriate.

He crossed the street at the light, a law-abiding citizen who wouldn't dream of jaywalking. At least not when he was in possession of burglary tools.

He saw the Institute up ahead, a majestic silhouette of good Yankee granite. It pleased him that his last job would be to break into such a proud and dignified old building.

The windows were dark but for the glow of security lights in the lobby. He thought it was odd, and really rather sweet, that people left on lights to keep thieves at bay. A good one could steal in broad daylight as easily as under the cover of dark.

And he was very good.

His gaze swept up and down the street before he checked his watch. His stakeouts had given him the pattern of police cruisers in the area. Unless there was a call for one, he had a good fifteen minutes before a black-and-white would pass this way.

He crossed to the south side of the building, keeping his gait brisk but unhurried. His long coat gave him the illusion of bulk, the snappy fedora shadowed his face, and the hair beneath it was now a dignified and rather dapper steel gray.

Anyone taking notice of him would see a middle-aged businessman, slightly overweight.

He was still two yards from the door, and out of range of the camera, when he took his jammer out of his pocket and aimed it. He saw the red light blink off, and moved quickly.

His forged key card took some finesse, but the slot accepted and read it on the third try. Recalling the code from memory, he logged it in, and was inside the anteroom within forty-five seconds. He reset the camera—there was no use having some gung-ho guard come out to check—then closed the door, relocked it.

He took off his coat and hung it neatly beside the staff's soft-drink and snack machines. His black doeskin gloves went into the pocket. Beneath them he wore thin surgical gloves any honest man could buy by the box from a medical supply store. He covered his silver hair with a black cap.

Efficiently, he checked his tools one last time.

It was only then that he let himself pause, just for a moment, and enjoy.

He stood in the dark listening to the silence that wasn't really silence at all. Buildings had their language, and this one hummed and creaked. He could hear the whirl of the heat through the vents, the sighs of the wind pressing at the door behind him.

The guard and security rooms were a level

above, and the floors were thick. He heard nothing from them, and they, he knew, heard nothing from him. With his eyes adjusted to the dark, he moved to the next door. It had a good police lock that required his picks, his penlight, which he clamped between his teeth, and approximately thirty seconds of his time to deal with.

He smiled at the music of tumblers clicking, then slipped through and into the hallway.

The first camera was at the end of the corridor where it split left and right. It didn't overly concern him. He was a shadow among shadows here, and the camera was aimed toward the gallery. He slid along the wall beneath it, out of range, and took the left fork.

Aladdin's Cave, he thought when he crouched just outside the South Gallery. The Tower of London, Blackbeard's Treasure, Wonderland. Such a place was all the fairy tales he'd read and been read as a child.

Glorious anticipation shimmered along his skin, tightened his muscles, churned like desire in his gut. His for the taking. It made him think how easily a professional could succumb to greed—and disaster.

Once more he checked his watch. The Yankee sensibility in such a place would mean guards still did rounds, though the cameras and sensors should have sufficed. Of course, he was proof they didn't, and if he was in charge of security, he'd have employed twice as many guards and doubled their rounds.

But that wasn't his job.

He didn't use his light now, and didn't need it. Even the pinhole glow would set off the sensors. Using his measurements and excellent night vision, he moved to the corner of the gallery, aimed his jammer, and shut down the bothersome camera.

In one part of his brain he counted off seconds. The rest of him moved fast. By the time he crouched in front of the display, his glass cutter was in hand. He made a neat circle, slightly larger than his fist, suctioned it off with barely a tickle of sound, and set it neatly on the top of the cabinet.

He worked quickly, but with a smooth economy of motion that was as innate as the color of his eyes. He wasted no time in admiring his take, or considering the delight of taking more than what he'd come for. That was for amateurs. He simply reached in, picked up the bronze, and tucked it into the pouch on his belt.

Because he appreciated order, and irony, he fitted the circle of glass back into place, then catfooted it back to the corner. He turned the camera on again, and started back the way he came.

By his count it had taken him seventy-five seconds.

When he reached the anteroom, he transferred the bronze to the briefcase, snuggling it between two thick slabs of foam. He switched hats, stripped off the surgical gloves and rolled them neatly into his pocket.

He bundled into his coat, keyed himself out, locked up tidily behind him, and was a block away in less than ten minutes from the time he'd entered the building.

Smooth, slick, and neat, he thought. A good way to end a career. He eyed the bar again, nearly went inside. At the last minute he decided he'd go back to the hotel and order up a bottle of champagne instead.

Some toasts were private matters.

At six A.M., after a sleepless night, Miranda was shocked out of her first real doze by the ringing of the phone. Headachy, disoriented, she fumbled for the receiver.

"Dr. Jones. *Pronto*." No, not Italy. Maine. Home. "Hello?"

"Dr. Jones, this is Ken Scutter, security."

"Mr. Scutter." She got no image from the name and was too bleary to try for one. "What is it?"

"Wc'vc had an incident."

"An incident?" As her mind began to clear she pushed herself up in bed. The sheets and blankets were tangled around her like wrappings on a mummy, and she cursed under her breath as she fought her way free. "What sort of incident?"

"It wasn't noticed until the change of shifts, moments ago, but I wanted to contact you immediately. We've had a break-in."

"A break-in." She bolted up fully awake, the blood rushing into her head in a flood. "At the Institute?"

"Yes, ma'am. I thought you'd want to come right over."

"Was there damage? Was something stolen?"

"No real damage, Dr. Jones. One item is missing from the South Gallery display. Cataloguing indicates it's a fifteenth-century bronze, artist unknown, of David."

A bronze, she thought. She was suddenly plagued by bronzes. "I'm on my way."

She bolted out of bed, and without bothering with her robe, raced in her blue flannel pajamas to Andrew's room. She burst in, shot toward the mound in the bed, and shook viciously.

"Andrew, wake up. There's been a break-in."

"Huh? What?" He shoved at her hand, ran a tongue around his teeth, started to yawn. His jaw cracked as he shot up in bed. "What? Where? When?"

"At the Institute. There's a bronze missing from the South Gallery. Get dressed, let's move."

"A bronze?" He rubbed a hand over his face. "Miranda, were you dreaming?"

"Scutter from security just phoned," she snapped out. "I don't dream. Ten minutes, Andrew," she said over her shoulder as she hurried out.

Within forty, she was standing beside her brother in the South Gallery, staring down at the perfect circle in the glass, and the empty space behind it. Miranda's stomach rolled once, then dropped to her knees.

"Call the police, Mr. Scutter."

"Yes, ma'am." He signaled to one of his men. "I

ordered a sweep of the building—it's still under way—but so far we've found nothing out of place, and nothing else missing."

Andrew nodded. "I'll want to review the security tapes for the last twenty-four hours."

"Yes, sir." Scutter heaved a sigh. "Dr. Jones, the night chief reported a small problem with two of the cameras."

"Problem." Miranda turned. She remembered Scutter now. He was a short, barrel-shaped man, a former cop who'd decided to trade the streets for private security. His record was spotless. Andrew had interviewed and hired him personally.

"This camera." Scutter shifted, gestured up. "It blanked for about ninety seconds yesterday morning. No one thought much of it, though the standard diagnostic was run. Last night, at about midnight, the exterior camera on the south entrance failed for just under a minute. There were high winds, and the glitch was attributed to weather. This interior camera also went off, for about eighty seconds between midnight and one. The exact times will be stamped on the tapes."

"I see." Andrew stuck his hands in his pockets and balled them into fists. "Opinion, Mr. Scutter?"

"My take would be the burglar's a pro, with a knowledge of security and electronics. He got in through the south side, bypassed the alarm, and the camera. He knew what he was after, didn't piss around—excuse me, Dr. Jones," he muttered with an apologetic nod toward Miranda. "It tells me he knows the museum, the setup."

"And he waltzes in," Miranda said with barely suppressed fury, "takes what he wants, then waltzes out—despite a complex and expensive security system, and half a dozen armed guards."

"Yes, ma'am." Scutter's lips thinned as he pressed them together. "That pretty much sums it up."

"Thank you. Will you go out in the lobby and wait for the police, please?" She waited until his footsteps receded; then because she was alone with Andrew, she allowed the steam to show.

"Son of a bitch. Son of a bitch, Andrew." She stalked in a straight line to the camera in question, scowled at it, then stalked back. "That man wants us to believe that someone can override the security, slide in here, and steal one specific piece of art in less than ten minutes."

"That's the most likely theory, unless you think the guards have a conspiracy going, and the lot of them suddenly developed an obsession for small, naked Italian boys cast in bronze."

He was sick inside. He'd loved that piece, the vitality and the pure arrogance of it. "It could have been a hell of a lot worse, Miranda."

"Our security failed, our property was taken. How could it be worse?"

"From the looks of it, this guy could have loaded up a Santa sack and cleaned out half this area."

"One piece or a dozen, we've still been violated. God." She covered her face with her hands. "Nothing's been taken from the Institute since the six paintings in the fifties, and four of them were recovered."

"Then maybe we were due," he said wearily.

"Bullshit." She spun on her heel. "We protected our property, sparing no expense with security."

"No motion detectors," he murmured.

"You wanted them."

"The system I wanted would have meant taking up the floor." He looked down at the thick and lovely marble. "The brass wouldn't go for it."

By brass he meant their parents. His father had been appalled at the idea of destroying the floor, and nearly as appalled by the estimated cost of the proposed system.

"Probably wouldn't have mattered," he said with a shrug. "Just as likely he'd have found a way to get past that too. Damn it, Miranda, security's my responsibility."

"This is not your fault."

He sighed and desperately, viciously, wanted a drink. "It's always somebody's fault. I'll have to tell them. I don't even know how to contact the old man in Utah."

"She'll know, but let's not move too fast. Let me think a minute." She closed her eyes and stood still. "As you said, it could have been much worse. We only lost one piece—and we may very well recover it. Meanwhile, it's insured and the police are on their way. Everything's being done. We have to let the police do their job."

"I have to do mine, Miranda. I have to call Florence." He worked up a weak smile. "Look at it this way—our little incident might push your problem with her to the back burner for a while."

She snorted. "If I thought that would happen, I might have stolen the damn thing myself."

"Dr. Jones." A man stepped into the room, his cheeks red with cold, his eyes of pale green narrowly focused under heavy graying brows. "And Dr. Jones. Detective Cook." He held up a gold shield. "Word is you've lost something."

By nine, Miranda's head was pounding violently enough for her to give in and lay it down on her desk. She had her door closed, had barely resisted the urge to lock it, and was allowing herself ten minutes to indulge in despair and self-pity.

She'd only managed five when her intercom buzzed. "Miranda, I'm sorry." There was both concern and hesitation in Lori's voice. "Dr. Standford-Jones is on line one. Do you want me to tell her you're unavailable?"

Oh, it was tempting. But she drew a deep breath, straightened her spine. "No, I'll take it. Thank you, Lori." Because her voice sounded rusty, she cleared it, then punched line one. "Hello, Mother."

"The testing on the Fiesole Bronze has been completed," Elizabeth said without preamble.

"I see."

"Your findings were inaccurate."

"I don't believe they were."

"Whatever you insist on believing, they have been disproved. The bronze is nothing more than a clever and well-executed attempt to mimic Renaissance style and materials. The authorities are investigating Carlo Rinaldi, the man who claimed to have found the piece."

"I want to see the results of the second test."

"That is not an option."

"You can arrange it. I'm entitled to—"

"You're entitled to nothing, Miranda. Let's understand each other. My priority at this point is to prevent this damage from spreading. We've already had two government projects canceled. Your reputation, and as a result, my own, is under attack. There are some who believe you purposely doctored tests and results in order to take credit for a find."

With slow care, Miranda wiped away the ring of moisture that a teacup had left on her desk. "Is that what you believe?"

The hesitation spoke more clearly than the words that followed it. "I believe you allowed ambition, haste, and enthusiasm to cloud judgment, logic, and efficiency. I take the responsibility, as I involved you."

"I'm responsible for myself. Thank you for your support."

"Sarcasm is unbecoming. I'm sure the media will attempt to contact you over the next few days. You'll be unavailable for comment."

"I have plenty of comments."

"Which you'll keep to yourself. It would be best if you took a leave of absence."

"Would it?" Her hand was starting to tremble, so she balled it into a fist. "That's a passive admission of guilt, and I won't do it. I want to see those results. If I made a mistake, at least I need to know where and how."

"It's out of my hands."

"Fine. I'll find a way around you." She glanced over in irritation as her fax rang and whined. "I'll contact Ponti myself."

"I've already spoken to him. He has no interest in you. The matter is closed. Transfer me to Andrew's office."

"Oh, I'll be delighted to. He has some news for you." Furious, she jabbed the hold button and buzzed Lori. "Transfer this call to Andrew," she ordered, then shoved away from her desk.

She took a deep breath first. She would give Andrew a few moments, then go in to him. She would be calm when she did. Calm and supportive. To manage that, she had to push her own problem aside for a while, and concentrate on the break-in.

To distract herself, she walked over and snagged the page from the fax tray.

And her blood iced over.

You were so sure, weren't you? It appears you were wrong. How will you explain it?

What's left for you now, Miranda, now that your reputation is in tatters? Nothing. That's all you were, a reputation, a name, a chestful of degrees.

Now you're just pitiful. Now you have nothing.

Now I have everything.

How does it feel, Miranda, to be exposed as a fraud, to be found incompetent? To be a failure?

She clutched one hand between her breasts as she read it through. Her ragged, rapid breathing made her head go light so that she staggered back, leaned heavily on the desk to steady herself.

"Who are you?" Anger leaked through, balancing her again. "Who the hell are you?"

It doesn't matter, she told herself. She wouldn't let these mean, petty messages affect her. They meant nothing.

But she slipped the fax into the drawer with the other, and locked it.

She'd find out eventually. There was always a way to find out. Putting her hands to her cheeks, she pressed to bring the blood back into her face. And when she found out, she promised herself, she would deal with it.

Now wasn't the time to concern herself with nasty little taunts. She drew in air, exhaled, rubbed her hands together until they were warm again.

Andrew needed her. The Institute needed her. Her eyes squeezed tightly shut as the pressure in her chest built into pain. She wasn't just a name, a collection of degrees.

She was more than that. She intended to prove it.

Squaring her shoulders, she marched out of her office with the intention of marching into Andrew's.

At least two members of the family would stand by each other.

Detective Cook stood by Lori's desk. "Another moment of your time, Dr. Jones."

"Of course." Even as her stomach dipped, she

composed her features and gestured. "Please come in and sit down. Lori, hold my calls please. Can I get you coffee, Detective?"

"No, thanks. I'm cutting back. Caffeine and tobacco, they're real killers." He settled into a chair, took out his notebook. "Dr. Jones—Dr. Andrew Jones tells me that the piece that was taken was insured."

"The Institute is fully insured against theft, and fire."

"Five hundred thousand dollars. Isn't that a lot for a little piece like that? It wasn't signed or anything either, is that right?"

"The artist was unknown, but believed to be a student of Leonardo da Vinci." She longed to nurse the nagging ache in her temple, but kept her hands still. "It was an excellent study of David, circa 1524."

She'd tested it herself, she thought sourly. And no one had questioned her findings.

"Five hundred thousand is well within the range should the piece have been auctioned or sold to a collector," she added.

"You do that kind of thing here?" Cook pursed his lips. "Sell off?"

"Occasionally. We also acquire. It's part of our purpose."

He let his gaze skim around her office. Efficient, neat, with high-end equipment and a desk that was probably worth a small fortune as well. "It takes a lot of money to run a place like this."

"Yes, it does. The fees we generate for classes,

consulting work, and admissions cover a large part of it. There's also a trust fund set up by my grandfather. In addition patrons often donate funds or collections." Though it flickered through her mind that it might be wise to call their lawyer, she leaned forward. "Detective Cook, we don't need five hundred thousand dollars in insurance money to run the Institute."

"I guess it's a drop in the bucket. Of course, for some people it's a nice chunk of change. Especially if they gamble or have debts, or just want to buy a fancy car."

However tight her neck and shoulders were now, she met his gaze levelly. "I don't gamble, I don't have any difficult debts, and I have a car."

"If you'll excuse me saying so, Dr. Jones, you don't seem particularly upset about this loss."

"Is my being upset going to help you recover the bronze?"

He clucked his tongue. "You got a point. Your brother now, he's pretty shaken up."

Because her eyes clouded, she dropped her gaze and stared into the remains of her tea. "He feels responsible. He takes things to heart."

"And you don't?"

"Feel responsible, or take things to heart?" she countered, then lifted her hands a few inches off the desk. "In this case, neither."

"Just for my notes, would you mind going over your evening for me?"

"All right." Her muscles had bunched up again, but she spoke calmly. "Andrew and I both worked until around seven. I sent my assistant home just after six. I had a long-distance call shortly after."

"From?"

"Florence, Italy. An associate of mine." Distress burned under her breastbone like an ulcer. "I imagine we were on the phone for ten minutes, maybe a little less. Andrew dropped by here a bit after that. We had a discussion, and left together right around seven."

"Do you usually come and go to work together?"

"No, we don't. Our hours don't always coincide. I wasn't feeling well last night, so he took me home. We share the house our grandmother left us. We had a little dinner. I went upstairs around nine."

"And stayed in the rest of the night?"

"Yes, as I said, I wasn't feeling very well."

"And your brother was at home all night."

She had no idea. "Yes, he was. I woke him right after I got the call from Mr. Scutter in security, just after six this morning. We came in together, assessed the situation, and ordered Mr. Scutter to call the police."

"That little bronze . . ." Cook rested his pad on his knee. "You've got pieces in that gallery worth a lot more, I'd guess. Funny he only took that piece—only one piece after he'd gone to all the trouble to get inside."

"Yes," she said evenly. "I thought the same myself. How would you explain that, Detective?"

He had to smile. It was a good comeback. "I'd have to say he wanted it. There's nothing else missing?"

"The gallery spaces are being checked thoroughly. Nothing else appears to be missing. I don't know what else I can tell you."

"That should do it for now." He rose, tucked his notebook away. "We'll be interviewing your staff, and it's likely I'll need to talk to you again."

"We're more than willing to cooperate." She rose as well. She wanted him out. "You can contact me here, or at home," she continued as she walked to the door. When she opened it, she saw Ryan pacing the outer office.

"Miranda." He came straight to her, took both of her hands. "I just heard."

For some reason tears swam close again, and were battled back. "Bad day," she managed.

"I'm so sorry. How much was taken? Do the police have any leads?"

"I—Ryan, this is Detective Cook. He's in charge. Detective, this is Ryan Boldari, an associate."

"Detective." Ryan could have spotted him as a cop from six blocks at a dead run in the opposite direction.

"Mr. Boldari. You work here?"

"No, I own galleries in New York and San Francisco. I'm here on business for a few days. Miranda, what can I do to help?"

"There's nothing. I don't know." It hit her again, like a wave, and made her hands tremble in his.

"You should sit down, you're upset."

"Mr. Boldari?" Cook held up a finger as Ryan turned to nudge Miranda back into her office. "What are the names of your galleries?"

"Boldari," he said with an arch of brow. "The Boldari Gallery." He slipped out a hammered-silver case and removed a business card. "The addresses for both are there. Excuse me, Detective. Dr. Jones needs a moment."

It gave him a quiet satisfaction to shut the door in Cook's face. "Sit down, Miranda. Tell me what happened."

She did as he asked, grateful now for the firm grip of his hand on hers.

"Only one piece," Ryan said when she'd finished. "Odd."

"He had to be a stupid thief," she said with some spirit. "He could have cleaned out that display without much more time and no more effort."

Ryan tucked his tongue in his cheek and reminded himself not to be offended. "Apparently he was selective, but stupid? Difficult to believe a stupid man—or woman for that matter—could get past your security with such apparent ease and speed."

"Well, he might know electronics, but he doesn't know art." Unable to sit, she rose and flipped on her coffeepot. "The *David* was a lovely little piece, but hardly the best we have. Oh it doesn't matter," she muttered, dragging a hand through her hair. "I sound as though I'm annoyed he didn't take more or choose better. I'm just so angry that he got in at all."

"As I would be." He walked over to kiss the top of her head. "I'm sure the police will find him, and *David*. Cook struck me as an efficient type."

"I suppose—once he eliminates Andrew and me from his list of suspects and can concentrate on finding the real thief."

"That would be typical, I'd imagine." The little worm of guilt wriggled again as he turned her to face him. "You're not worried about that part, are you?"

"No, not really. Annoyed, but not worried. I appreciate you coming by, Ryan, I— Oh, lunch," she remembered. "I'm not going to be able to make it."

"Don't give it a thought. We'll reschedule when I make my next trip in."

"Next trip?"

"I have to leave this evening. I'd hoped to stay another day or two . . . for personal reasons. But I need to get back tonight."

"Oh." She hadn't thought it possible to be any more unhappy.

He lifted her hands to his lips. Sad eyes, he thought, were so compelling. "It wouldn't hurt to miss me. It might help take your mind off all this."

"I have a feeling I'm going to be busy for the next few days. But I'm sorry you can't stay longer. This won't— This problem isn't going to change your mind about the exchange, is it?"

"Miranda." He enjoyed the moment, playing the stalwart and supporting hero. "Don't be foolish. The Vasaris will be in your hands within the month."

"Thank you. After the morning I've had, I appreciate the confidence more than I can tell you."

"And you'll miss me."

Her lips curved. "I think I will."

"Now say goodbye."

She began to, but he stopped her mouth with his. Indulged himself by taking it deep, sliding past her initial surprise, her initial resistance, like the thief he was.

It would be, he knew, a considerable amount of time before he saw her again—if he ever did. Their lives separated here, but he wanted to take something with him.

So he took the sweetness he'd just begun to sense under the strength, and the passion he'd just begun to stir under the control.

He eased her back, studied her face, let his hands stroke once up her arms, down again until the touch lingered just on fingertips.

"Goodbye, Miranda," he said, with more regret than was comfortable. And left her, certain she would deal with the small inconvenience he'd caused in her life.

CHAPTER NINE

BY THE TIME ANDREW GOT OFF THE PHONE WITH HIS mother, he would have betrayed his country for three fingers of Jack Daniel's. It hung on him. He accepted that. The day-to-day running of the Institute was his responsibility, and security was first priority.

His mother had pointed that out—in short, declarative sentences.

It would have done no good to counter that since that security had been breached, they should be kicking up their heels that only one item had been lost. To Elizabeth the break-in was a personal insult, and the loss of the small bronze *David* was as bitter as a wholesale clearing of the galleries.

He could accept that too. He could and would shoulder the responsibility of dealing with the police, the insurance company, the staff, the press. But what he couldn't accept, what made him wish he had access to a bottle, was her complete lack of support or sympathy.

But he didn't have access to a bottle. Keeping one in his office was a line he hadn't crossed, and one that allowed him to shrug off any suggestion that he had a drinking problem.

He drank at home, at bars, at social events. He didn't drink during business hours. Therefore, he was in control.

Fantasizing about slipping out to the nearest liquor store and getting a little something to help him through a long, hard day wasn't the same as doing it.

He depressed the intercom button on his phone. "Ms. Purdue."

"Yes, Dr. Jones?"

Run down to Freedom Liquors, would you, Ms. Purdue darling, and pick me up a fifth of Jack Daniel's Black. It's a family tradition.

"Could you come in, please?"

"Right away, sir."

Andrew pushed away from the desk and turned to the window. His hands were steady, weren't they? His stomach might have been rolling in greasy waves, his spine might have been damp with clammy sweat, but his hands were still steady. He was in control.

He heard her come in, shut the door quietly.

"The insurance investigator will be here at eleven," he said without turning. "Make sure my calendar's clear."

"I've canceled all but essential appointments for the day, Dr. Jones."

"Good, thank you. Ah . . ." He pinched the bridge of his nose, hoping to relieve some pressure. "We'll need to schedule a staff meeting, department heads only. As early in the afternoon as possible."

"One o'clock, Dr. Jones."

"Fine. Send a memo to my sister. I'd like her to work with publicity on a statement. Inform any and all reporters who call that we'll be issuing a statement by end of day and have no comment at this time."

"Yes, sir. Dr. Jones, Detective Cook would like to speak with you again as soon as possible. He's downstairs."

"I'll go down shortly. We need to draft a letter to Dr. Standford-Jones and Dr. Charles Jones, detailing this incident and its current status. They—" He broke off at the knock on the door, then turned when Miranda stepped in.

"I'm sorry, Andrew. I can come back if you're busy."

"That's all right. We'll save Ms. Purdue a memo. Can you work with publicity on a statement?"

"I'll get right on it." She could see the strain around his eyes. "You talked to Florence."

He smiled thinly. "Florence talked to me. I'm going to draft a letter, telling the sad tale, and copy her and Father."

"Why don't *I* do that?" The shadows under his eyes were too dark, she thought, the lines around his mouth too deep. "Save you a little time and trouble."

"I'd appreciate it. The insurance investigator will be here shortly, and Cook wants me again."

"Oh." She linked her hands together to keep them still. "Ms. Purdue, would you give us a moment?"

"Of course. I'll set up the staff meeting, Dr. Jones."

"Department heads," Andrew told Miranda when the door closed again. "One o'clock."

"All right. Andrew, about Cook. He's going to want to know about last night. Where you were, what you were doing, who you were with. I told him we left here together about seven, and that both of us were home all night."

"Fine."

Her fingers twisted. "Were you?"

"What? Home? Yes." He angled his head, eyes narrowing. "Why?"

"I didn't know if you'd gone out or not." Unlinking her fingers, she rubbed her hands over her face. "I just thought it best to say you hadn't."

"You don't have to protect me, Miranda. I haven't done anything—which according to our mother is the problem."

"I know you haven't. I didn't mean that." She reached out, touched a hand to his arm. "It just seemed less complicated to say you'd been home all night. Then I started thinking, what if you had gone out, and you'd been seen . . ."

"Bellied up to a bar?" Bitter resentment coated his voice. "Or skulking around the building?"

"Oh, Andrew." Miserable, she lowered herself to the arm of a chair. "Let's not snipe at each other. It's just that Cook makes me nervous, and I started to worry that if he caught me in a lie, however harmless, it would just make it all worse."

With a sigh, he dropped into the chair. "Looks like we're in shit up to our knees."

"I'm up to my waist," she muttered. "She ordered me to take a leave of absence. I refused."

"Are you standing up for yourself, or just kicking at her?"

Miranda frowned and studied her nails. *How does it feel to be a failure?* No, she wouldn't give in to that. "I can do both."

"Be careful you don't fall on your butt. Last night I would have agreed with her—not for the same reason, but I'd have agreed. Today changes things. I need you here."

"I'm not going anywhere."

He patted her knee before he rose. "I'll go talk to Cook. Send me a copy of the press release, and the letter. Oh, she gave me Father's address in Utah." He tore a piece of notepaper from the pad on his desk and handed it to her. "Overnight the letters. The sooner they have it in writing, the better."

"I'll see you at one, then. Oh, Andrew, Ryan said to tell you goodbye."

He stopped with his hand on the doorknob. "Goodbye?"

"He had to get back to New York tonight."

"He was here? Damn it. He knows about this mess already? The Vasaris?"

"He's completely supportive. He assured me this problem wouldn't affect the trade. I'm, ah, thinking about going down to New York in a couple of weeks." In fact, she'd just thought of it. "To . . . expedite the loan."

Distracted, he nodded. "Good, that's fine. We'll talk about that later. A new exhibit's just what we need to offset this mess."

He started downstairs, glancing at his watch. It amazed him it was barely ten. It felt as if he'd been running on this particular wheel for days.

Cops, both uniformed and plainclothes, swarmed the main floor. What he assumed was fingerprint powder was smeared over the display cabinet. The little circle of glass was gone. Tucked away in some evidence bag, he figured.

Andrew questioned one of the uniformed officers and was told he'd find Detective Cook at the south entrance.

Andrew traveled the route, trying to imagine the thief doing the same. Dressed in black, he imagined, a man with a hard face. Maybe a scar sliced down the cheek. Had he carried a gun? A knife? A knife, Andrew decided. He would have wanted to kill quietly and quickly should it become necessary.

He thought of how many nights Miranda worked late in the lab or her office, and cursed violently.

Fresh fury was bubbling under his skin as he

pushed into the anteroom and found Cook perusing the offerings of the snack machine.

"Is this how you find this son of a bitch?" Andrew demanded. "By munching on potato chips?"

"Actually, I'm going for the pretzels." Calmly, Cook pushed the proper buttons. "I'm cutting down on fat grams." The bag thunked against the metal tray. Cook pushed through the slot, nipped it out.

"Great. A health-conscious cop."

"You got your health," Cook claimed as he ripped open the bag, "you got everything."

"I want to know what you're doing to find the bastard who broke into my building."

"My job, Dr. Jones. Why don't we sit down here?" He gestured to one of the little cafe tables. "You look like you could use some coffee."

Andrew's eyes flashed, the sudden brilliant blue of temper that turned his aesthetic face into something tough and potentially mean. The quick change had Cook reconsidering the man.

"I don't want to sit down," Andrew shot back, "and I don't want any coffee." He would have killed for some. "My sister works late, Detective. She often works late, alone, in this building. If she hadn't been ill last night, she might have been here when he broke in. I might have lost something a great deal more valuable to me than a bronze."

"I understand your concern."

"No, you couldn't possibly."

"I got family myself." Despite Andrew's refusal, Cook counted out coins and turned to the coffee machine. "How do you take it?"

"I said—Black," Andrew muttered. "Just black."

"I used to drink it the same way. Still miss it." Cook breathed in deep as the coffee began to spurt into the insulated cup. "Let me relieve your mind a bit, Dr. Jones. Typically a B-and-E man—especially a smart one—isn't looking to hurt anyone. Fact is he'll back off a job before he'll get into that kind of tangle. He won't even carry a weapon, because if he does that adds years onto his time if he's caught."

He set the coffee on the table, sat, waited. After a moment Andrew relented and joined him. As the hot edge of temper faded from his eyes, his narrow face smoothed out, his shoulders slipped back into their slight hunch. "Maybe this guy wasn't typical."

"I'd say he wasn't—but if he's as smart as I think, he'd have followed that rule. No weapons, no contact with people. In and out. If your sister had been here, he'd have avoided her."

"You don't know my sister." The coffee made him feel slightly more human.

"A strong lady, your sister?"

"She's had to be. But she was mugged recently, right in front of our house. The guy had a knife—she's terrified of knives. There was nothing she could do."

Cook pursed his lips. "When was this?"

"A couple of weeks ago, I guess." He dug fingers through his hair. "He knocked her down, took her purse, her briefcase." He trailed off, took another breath, another sip of coffee. "It shook her, shook us both. And thinking that she might have been here when this guy broke in—"

"This type of thief, it's not his style to knock women around and grab their purses."

"Maybe not. But they never caught him. He terrified her, took her things, then he walked. Miranda's had enough—between that and the problems in Florence." Andrew caught himself, realizing he was relaxing, and chatting about Miranda, for God's sake. "This isn't what you wanted to talk to me about."

"Actually, it's helpful, Dr. Jones." A mugging and a burglary in less than a month. Same victim? It was, Cook decided, interesting. "You say your sister wasn't well last night. What was wrong with her?"

"A problem in Florence," he said briefly. "Some difficulty with our mother. It upset her."

"Your mother's in Italy?"

"She lives there. She works there. She heads Standjo. It's a laboratory for testing art and artifacts. It's part of the family business. An offshoot of the Institute."

"So there's some friction between your mother and your sister?"

Andrew took another sip of coffee to steady himself and watched Cook over the rim. His eyes went hard again. "My family relationships aren't police business."

"Just trying to get the whole picture. This is a family organization, after all. There's no sign of forced entry."

Andrew's hand jerked, nearly spilling his coffee as he tried to make the sharp turn. "Excuse me?"

"There's no overt sign of forced entry on either of these doors." Cook wagged a finger to the exterior and interior doors. "Both were locked. Outside, you need a key card and a code, correct?"

"Yes. Only department heads can use this entrance. This area is used as a staff lounge. There's another lounge for general staff on level three."

"I'll need a list of department heads."

"Of course. You think it's someone who works here?"

"I don't think anything. Biggest mistake is to come onto a scene with an idea." He smiled a little. "It's just procedure."

The break-in at the Institute was the lead story on the local eleven o'clock news. In New York, it earned thirty seconds in the lower half of the hour. Stretched out on the sofa in his apartment on Central Park South, Ryan sipped a brandy, enjoyed the tang of a slim Cuban cigar, and noted the details.

There weren't many. Then New York had plenty of its own crime and scandals to fill the time. If the Institute hadn't been a landmark and the Joneses quite such a prominent New England family, the burglary wouldn't have merited so much as a blip outside of Maine.

Police were investigating. Ryan grinned around the cigar as he thought of Cook. He knew the type. Dogged, thorough, with a solid record of closing cases. It was satisfying to have a good cop investigating his last job. Rounded off his career nicely.

Pursuing several leads. Well, that was bullshit. There were no leads, but they would have to say there were and save face.

He sat up as he caught a glimpse of Miranda leaving the building. Her hair was smoothed back in a twist. She'd done that for the cameras, he thought, remembering how it had been loose and tangled when he'd kissed her good-bye. Her face was calm, composed. Cold, he decided. The lady had quite a cold streak, which inspired him to melt her. Which he would have done, he thought, if there'd been a bit more time.

Still, he was pleased to see she was handling the situation well. She was a tough one. Even with those pockets of shyness and sadness, she was tough. Another day or two, he calculated, and her life would slip back into routine. The little bump he'd put into it would smooth out, the insurance would kick in, and the cops would file the case and forget it.

And he, Ryan thought as he blew cheerful smoke rings at the ceiling, had a satisfied client, a perfect record, and some leisure time coming.

Maybe, just maybe, he'd bend the rules in this case and take Miranda to the West Indies for a couple of weeks. Sun, sand, and sex. It would do her good, he decided.

And it sure as hell wouldn't hurt him any.

* * *

Annie McLean's apartment would have fit into Ryan's living room, but she did have a view of the park. If she leaned far enough out her bedroom window, twisted her neck until it ached, and strained her eyes. But that was good enough for her.

Maybe the furniture was secondhand, but she had bright colors. The rug might have come from a garage sale, but it had shampooed up just fine. And she liked the overblown cabbage roses around the border.

She'd put the shelves together herself, painted them a deep dark green, and crammed them with books she bought when the library held its annual sale.

Classics for the most part. Books she'd neglected to read in school and longed to explore now. She did so whenever she had a free hour or two, bundling under the cheerful blue-and-green-striped throw her mother had crocheted and diving into Hemingway or Steinbeck or Fitzgerald.

Her CD player had been an indulgent Christmas present to herself two years before. Deliberately, she'd collected a wide range of music—eclectic, she liked to think of it.

She'd been too busy working to develop a wide range of tastes in books and music when she was in her teens and early twenties. A pregnancy, miscarriage, and broken heart all before her eighteenth birthday had changed her direction. She'd been determined to make something of herself, to have something for herself.

Then she'd let herself be charmed by slick-talking, high-living, no-good son-of-a-bitching Buster.

Hormones, she thought, and a need to make a home, to build her own family, had blinded her to the impossibility of marriage with a mostly unemployed mechanic with a taste for Coors and blondes.

She'd wanted a child, she thought now. Maybe, Lord help her, to make up for the one she'd lost.

Live and learn, she often told herself. She'd done both. Now she was an independent woman with a solid business, one who was taking the time and making the effort to improve her mind.

She liked to listen to her customers, their opinions and views, and measure them against her own. She was broadening her outlook, and calculated that in the seven years she'd had Annie's Place, she'd learned more about politics, religion, sex, and the economy than any college graduate.

If there were some nights when, slipping into bed alone, she longed for someone to listen to her, to hold her, to laugh with her when she spoke of her day, it was a small price to pay for independence.

In her experience, men didn't want to listen to what you had to say, they just wanted to do a little bitching and scratch their butts. Then yank off your nightgown and fuck.

She was much better off on her own.

One day, she thought, she might buy a house, with a yard. She wouldn't mind having a dog. She would cut back on her hours, hire a bar manager, maybe take a vacation. Ireland first, naturally. She wanted to see the hills—and the pubs, of course.

But she'd suffered the humiliation of not having enough money, of having doors shut in her face when she asked for a loan, of being told she was a bad risk.

She never intended to go through that again.

So her profits were fed back into her business, and what she sliced off of them was tucked into conservative stocks and bonds. She didn't need to be rich, but she would never be poor again.

Her parents had skirted the slippery edge of poor all of Annie's life. They'd done what they could for her, but her father—bless him—had held on to money as a man holds a handful of water. It had continually trickled through his fingers.

When they moved to Florida three winters before, Annie had kissed them both goodbye, cried a little, and slipped her mother five hundred dollars. It had been hard-earned, but she knew her mother could make it stretch through several of her father's get-rich-quick schemes.

She called them every week, on Sunday afternoons when the rates were down, and sent her mother another check every three months. She promised to visit often, but had managed only two short trips in three years.

Annie thought of them now as she watched the end of the late news and closed the book she'd been struggling to read. Her parents adored Andrew. Of course, they'd never known about that night on the beach, about the baby she'd conceived, then lost.

With a shake of her head she put it all out of her mind. She switched off the television, picked up the mug of tea she'd let go cold, and took it into the closet her landlord claimed was a kitchen.

She was reaching to switch off the light when someone knocked at her door. Annie glanced at the Louisville Slugger she kept by the door—the twin of one she kept behind the bar at work. Though she'd never had occasion to use either, they made her feel secure.

"Who is it?"

"It's Andrew. Let me in, will you? Your landlord keeps these halls in a deep freeze."

Though she wasn't particularly pleased to find him on her doorstep, Annie slipped off the chain, released the dead bolt and thumb lock, and opened the door. "It's late, Andrew."

"You're telling me," he said, though she wore a plaid robe and thick black socks. "I saw your light under the door. Come on, Annie, be a pal and let me in."

"I'm not giving you a drink."

"That's okay." Once he was inside, he reached under his coat and pulled out a bottle. "I brought my own. It's been a long, miserable day, Annie." He gave her a hound dog look that wrenched at her heart. "I didn't want to be home."

"Fine." Annoyed, she stalked to the kitchen and got out a short glass. "You're a grown man, you'll drink if you want."

"I want." He poured, lifted his glass in a half-salute. "Thanks. I guess you've heard the news."

"Yes, I'm sorry." She sat on the couch and slipped the copy of *Moby Dick* out of sight between the cushions, though she couldn't have explained why it would embarrass her to have him see it.

"Cops think it was an inside job." He drank, laughed a little. "I never thought I'd use that phrase in a sentence. They're taking a hard look at Miranda and me first."

"Why in the world would they think you'd steal from yourself?"

"People do, all the time. Insurance company's investigating. We're being thoroughly studied."

"It's just routine." Concerned now, she reached up to take his hand and draw him down beside her.

"Yeah. Routine sucks. I loved that bronze."

"What? The one that was taken?"

"It said something to me. The young David taking on the giant, willing to pit a stone against a sword. Courage. The kind I've never had."

"Why do you do that to yourself?" Irritation rang in her voice as she shoved against him.

"I never take on the giants," he said, and reached for the bottle again. "I just roll with the flow and follow orders. My parents say, It's time you took over the running of the Institute, Andrew. And I say, When do you want me to start?"

"You love the Institute."

"A happy coincidence. If they'd told me to go to Borneo and study native habits . . . I bet I'd have a hell of a tan by now. Elise says, It's time we got married; I say, Set the date. She says, I want a divorce; I say, Gee, honey, do you want me to pay for the lawyer?"

I tell you I'm pregnant, Annie thought, and you ask if I want to get married.

He studied the liquor in his glass, watched the way the light from her floor lamp slipped through the amber. "I never bucked the system, because it never seemed to matter enough to make the effort. And that doesn't say much for Andrew Jones."

"So you drink because it's easier than seeing if it matters?"

"Maybe." But he set the glass down to see if he could, to see how it felt to say what else was on his mind without the crutch. "I didn't do the right thing by you, Annie, didn't really stand by you the way I should have all those years ago, because I was terrified of what they'd do."

"I don't want to talk about that."

"We never have, mostly because I didn't think you wanted to. But you brought it up the other day."

"I shouldn't have." A little finger of panic curled in her stomach at the thought of it. "It's old business."

"It's our business, Annie." He said it gently because he heard a trace of that panic.

"Let it alone." She drew away from him, folded her arms defensively.

"All right." Why scratch at old wounds, he decided, when you had fresh juicy ones? "We'll just move along through the life and times of Andrew

Jones. At this point in it I'm waiting patiently for the cops to tell me I don't have to go to prison."

This time when he reached for the bottle, she grabbed it, stood up, and walking into the kitchen, poured the contents down the sink.

"Goddamn it, Annie."

"You don't need whiskey to make yourself miserable, Andrew. You do fine all on your own. Your parents didn't love you enough. That's rough." Temper she hadn't known crouched inside her sprang free. "Mine loved me plenty, but I'm still sitting alone at night with memories and regrets that rip at my heart. Your wife didn't love you enough either. Tough break. My husband would get himself oiled up on a couple of six-packs and love me whether I wanted him to or not."

"Annie. Christ." He hadn't known that, hadn't imagined that. "I'm sorry."

"Don't tell me you're sorry," she fired back. "I got through. I got through you and I got through him by realizing I'd made a mistake and fixing it."

"Don't do that." Out of nowhere his own anger spurted up. A dangerous light glinted in his eyes, hardening them as he got to his feet. "Don't compare what we had with what you had with him."

"Then don't you use what we had the same way you use what you had with Elise."

"I wasn't. It's not the same."

"Damn right, because she was beautiful, and she was brilliant." Annie jabbed a finger into his chest hard enough to make him take a step back. "And maybe you didn't love her enough. If you had you'd still have her. Because I've never known you to go without what you really want. You may not pick up a stone and go to war for it, but you get it."

"She wanted out." He shouted it. "You can't make someone love you."

She leaned on the tiny counter, closed her eyes, and to his surprise, began to laugh. "You sure as hell can't." She wiped at the tears the fit of laughter had brought to her eyes. "You may have a Ph.D., Dr. Jones, but you're stupid. You're a stupid man, and I'm tired. I'm going to bed. You can let yourself out."

She stormed by him, half hoping she'd made him angry enough to grab her. But he didn't, and she walked into the bedroom alone. When she heard him go out, heard the door click behind him, she curled onto the bed and indulged herself in a good, hard cry.

CHAPTER TEN

TECHNOLOGY NEVER FAILED TO DELIGHT AND AMAZE Cook. When he started out as a beat cop twenty-three years before, he'd seen that a detective's job involved hours of phone calls, paperwork, and door-to-doors. Not as exciting as Hollywood liked, nor as he—young and eager—had intended to settle for once he joined the ranks.

He'd planned to spend this particular Sunday afternoon doing some fishing in Miracle Bay, as the weather had turned calm and the temperatures had crept into the sixties. But he'd detoured by the station house on a whim. He believed in following whims, which he considered a short step down from hunches.

There on his desk, stacked among the files cluttering his in box, was the computer-generated report from pretty young officer Mary Chaney.

For himself, Cook approached the computer with

the caution and respect of a street cop approaching a junkie in a dark alley. You had to deal with it, you had to do the job, but you knew damn well anything could go wrong if you missed a step.

The Jones case was a priority because the Joneses were rich and the governor knew them personally. As the case was on his mind, he'd asked Mary to run a computer check, searching for like crimes.

Such information as he had in his hands would have taken weeks, if he'd ever been able to gather it, in his early days at this desk. Now he had a pattern in front of him that made his fishing plans slide out of his mind as he tipped back in his chair and studied it.

He had six likes over a period of ten years, and twice that many other hits similar enough to warrant a mention.

New York, Chicago, San Francisco, Boston, Kansas City, Atlanta. A museum or gallery in each of those cities had reported a break-in and the loss of one item in the past decade. The value of each item ranged from a hundred thousand to just over a cool million. No damage to the property, no mess, no alarm sounded. Each piece had been covered by insurance, and no arrest had been made.

Slick, he thought. The guy was slick.

In the dozen that followed, there were some variations. Two or more pieces had been taken, and in one case a guard's coffee had been drugged and the security system was simply shut off for a period of thirty minutes. In another an arrest had been made. A guard had attempted to pawn a fifteenth century cameo. He was arrested and confessed, but claimed that he'd taken the cameo after the break-in. The Renoir landscape and the Manet portrait that had also been stolen were never recovered.

Interesting, Cook thought again. The profile that was forming in his mind of his quarry didn't include sloppy trips to pawnshops. Could be he enlisted a guard as an inside source. It was something to check out.

And it wouldn't hurt to see where the Joneses had been during the dates of the other thefts. It was, after all, just another kind of fishing.

The first thing on Miranda's mind when she opened her eyes on Sunday morning was *The Dark Lady*. She had to see it again, examine it again. How else would she know how she had been so completely mistaken?

For as the days passed, she had come to the painful conclusion that she'd been wrong. What other explanation was there? She knew her mother too well. To save Standjo's reputation, Elizabeth would have questioned every detail of the second testing. She would have insisted on, and received, absolute proof of its accuracy.

She would never have settled for less.

The practical thing to do was to accept it, to salvage her pride by saying nothing more on the matter until the situation cooled. Stirring the pot could accomplish nothing positive because the damage had already been done.

Deciding she could make better use of her time than brooding, she changed into sweats. A couple hours at the health club might sweat some of the depression out of her.

Two hours later, she returned to the house to find Andrew stumbling around nursing a hangover. She was just about to go upstairs when the doorbell chimed.

"Let me take your jacket, Detective Cook," she heard Andrew say.

Cook? On a Sunday afternoon? Miranda pushed her hands at her hair, cleared her throat, and sat down.

As Andrew led Cook in, Miranda offered him a polite smile. "Do you have news for us?"

"Nothing solid, Dr. Jones. Just a loose end or two."

"Please sit down."

"Great house." Cop's eyes below their bushy gray brows scanned the room as he walked to a chair. "Really makes a statement up here on the cliffs." Old money, he thought, it had its own smell, its own look. Here it was beeswax and lemon oil. It was heirloom furniture and faded wallpaper and floor-to-ceiling windows framed in a burgundy waterfall of what was probably silk.

Class and privilege, and just enough clutter to make it a home.

"What can we do for you, Detective?"

"I've got a little angle I'm working on. I wonder if you could tell me where you were, where both of you were, last November. First week."

"Last November." It was such an odd question. Andrew scratched his head over it. "I was here in Jones Point. I didn't do any traveling last fall. Did I?" he asked Miranda.

"Not that I recall. Why is that important, Detective?"

"Just clearing up some details. Were you here as well, Dr. Jones?"

"I was in D.C. for a few days in early November. Some consult work at the Smithsonian. I'd have to get my desk calendar to be sure."

"Would you mind?" He smiled apologetically. "Just so I can tidy this up."

"All right." She couldn't see the point, but she couldn't see the harm either. "It's up in my office."

"Yes, sir," Cook continued when she left the room. "This is quite a place. Must be a bear to heat."

"We go through a lot of firewood," Andrew muttered.

"You do much traveling, Dr. Jones?"

"The Institute keeps me pretty close to home. Miranda's the frequent flier. She does a lot of consulting, the occasional lecture." He tapped his fingers on his knee, and noted that Cook's gaze had shifted to linger on the bottle of Jack Daniel's on the table beside the sofa. His shoulders hunched defensively. "What does last November have to do with our break-in?"

"I'm not sure it does, just tugging on a line. You do any fishing?"

"No, I get seasick."

"Too bad."

"According to my records," Miranda said as she came back in, "I was in Washington from November third through the seventh."

And the burglary in San Francisco had occurred in the early hours of the fifth, Cook recalled. "I guess you flew down there."

"Yes, into National." She checked her book. "USAir flight four-one-oh-eight, departing Jones Point at ten-fifty, arriving National at twelve fifty-nine. I stayed at The Four Seasons. Is that specific enough for you?"

"Sure is. Being a scientist, you'd keep good records."

"Yes, I do." She walked over to Andrew's chair, sat on the arm beside him. They became a unit. "What's this about?"

"Just getting things ordered in my head. Would you have where you were in June in that book? Say the third week."

"Of course." Steadied by Andrew's hand on her knee, she flipped back to June. "I was at the Institute the entire month of June. Lab work, some summer classes. You taught a couple yourself, didn't you, Andrew, when Jack Goldbloom's allergies kicked up and he took a few days off?"

"Yeah." He closed his eyes to help him think back. "That was toward the end of June. Oriental Art of the Twelfth Century." He opened his eyes again and grinned at her. "You wouldn't touch it, and I had to cram. We can easily get the exact dates for you, Detective," he continued. "We keep excellent records at the Institute as well."

"Fine. Appreciate it."

"We'll cooperate." Miranda's voice was brisk and stern. "And we expect you to do the same. It was our property taken, Detective. I think we have the right to know what avenues you're investigating."

"No problem." He rested his hands on his knees. "I'm checking out a series of burglaries that match the profile of yours. Maybe you heard something, seeing as you're in the same line, about a theft up in Boston last June."

"The Harvard University art museum." A shudder climbed up Miranda's spine. "The *kuang*. Chinese tomb piece, thought to be late thirteenth to early twelfth century B.C. Another bronze."

"You've got a good memory for detail."

"Yes, I do. It was a huge loss. It's one of the most beautifully preserved pieces of Chinese bronze ever recovered, and worth a great deal more than our David."

"November it was San Francisco, a painting that time."

Not a bronze, she thought, and for some reason all but trembled with relief. "It was the M. H. de Young Memorial Museum."

"That's right."

"American art," Andrew put in. "Colonial period. Where's the connection?"

"I didn't say there was, but I think there is." Cook

rose. "Could be we've got a thief with what you could call an eclectic taste in art. Me, I like that Georgia O'Keeffe stuff. It's bright, looks like what it is. I appreciate your time." He turned away, turned back. "I wonder if I could borrow that datebook of yours, Dr. Jones. And if the two of you would have written records of the year before. Just to help me put it all in order."

Miranda hesitated, again thought of lawyers. But pride had her standing and holding the slim leather book out to him. "You're welcome to it, and I have calendars for the last three years stored at my office at the Institute."

"Appreciate it. I'll just give you a receipt for this." He tucked her book away and took out his own to scrawl the information and his signature.

Andrew rose as well. "I'll have mine messengered over to you."

"That would be a blg help."

"It's difficult not to be insulted by this, Detective."

Cook raised his eyebrows at Miranda. "I'm sorry about that, Dr. Jones. I'm just trying to do my job."

"I imagine you are, and once you put my brother and me off your list of suspects, you'll be able to do it with more speed and efficiency. Which is why we're willing to tolerate this sort of treatment. I'll show you out."

Cook nodded at Andrew and followed her into the foyer. "Didn't mean to put your back up, Dr. Jones."

"Oh yes you did, Detective." She wrenched open the door. "Good afternoon."

"Ma'am." A quarter-century on the force hadn't made him immune to the sharp tongue of an angry woman. He ducked his head and grimaced a bit when the door shut loudly at his back.

"The man thinks we're thieves." Fuming, she stalked back into the parlor. It annoyed her, but didn't surprise her, to see Andrew pouring himself a drink. "He thinks we're bouncing around the country breaking into museums."

"Would be kind of fun, wouldn't it?"

"What?"

"Just trying to relieve the tension." He lifted his glass. "One way or the other."

"This isn't a game, Andrew, and I don't care to be smeared on a slide under a police microscope."

"There's nothing for him to find but the truth."

"It's not the end that worries me, it's the means. We're under investigation. The press is bound to get ahold of some of this."

"Miranda." He spoke softly and added an affectionate smile. "You're sounding dangerously close to Mother."

"There's no reason to insult me."

"I'm sorry—you're right."

"I'm going to make a pot roast," Miranda announced as she walked toward the kitchen.

"A pot roast." His mood lifted dramatically. "With the little potatoes and carrots?"

"You peel the potatoes. Keep me company, Andrew." She asked as much for herself as to get him away from the bottle. "I don't want to be alone."

"Sure." He set the glass down. It was empty anyway. And slipped an arm over her shoulders.

The meal helped, as did the preparation of it. She enjoyed cooking, and considered it another science. It was Mrs. Patch who had taught her, pleased that the young girl had shown an interest in kitchen work. It had been the warmth of that kitchen, and the company, that drew Miranda. The rest of the house had been so cold, so regimented. But Mrs. Patch had ruled in the kitchen. Even Elizabeth hadn't dared to intrude.

More likely she hadn't cared to, Miranda thought as she prepared for bed. She'd never known her mother to fix a meal, and that simple fact made learning how herself more appealing.

She would not be a mirror of Elizabeth.

The pot roast had done its work, she thought now. Good solid meat and potatoes, drop biscuits she'd made from scratch, conversation with Andrew. Maybe he'd had more wine with dinner than she liked, but at least he hadn't been alone.

It had been almost a happy time. They'd tacitically agreed not to discuss the Institute, or the trouble in Florence. It was much more relaxing to argue over their diverse views on music and books.

They'd always argued about them, she remembered as she tugged on her pajamas. They'd always shared views and thoughts and hopes. She doubted she would have survived childhood intact without him. They'd been each other's anchor in a chilly sea for as long as she could remember.

She only wished she could do more to steady him now and convince him to seek help. But whenever she touched on the subject of his drinking, he only closed up. And drank more. All she could do was watch, and stand with him until he fell off the edge of the cliff he was so tenuously poised on. Then she would do what she could to help him pick up the pieces.

She climbed into bed, arranging her pillows to support her back, then picked up her volume of bedtime reading. Some might say rereading Homer wasn't a particularly relaxing occupation. But it worked for her.

By midnight, her mind was full of Greek battles and betrayals and clear of worries. She marked her place, set the book aside, and turned off her light. In moments she was dreamlessly asleep.

Deeply enough that she didn't hear the door open, close again. She didn't hear the lock click smoothly into place, or the footsteps cross the room toward the bed.

She awoke with a jolt, a gloved hand hard over her mouth, another clamped firmly at her throat, and a man's voice softly threatening in her ear.

"I could strangle you."

PART TWO

THE THIEF

All men love to appropriate the belongings of others. It is a universal desire; only the manner of doing it differs.

—Alain René Lesage

CHAPTER ELEVEN

HER MIND SIMPLY FROZE. THE KNIFE. FOR A HIDEOUS moment she would have sworn she felt the prick of a blade at her throat rather than the smooth grip of hands, and her body went lax with terror.

Dreaming, she must be dreaming. But she could smell leather and man, she could feel the pressure on her throat that forced her to dig deep for air, and the hand that covered her mouth to block any sound. She could see a faint outline, the shape of a head, the breadth of shoulders.

All of that blipped into her stunned brain and was processed in seconds that seemed like hours.

Not again, she promised herself. Never again.

In instinctive reaction, her right hand balled into a fist, and came off the mattress in a snap of movement. He was either faster, or a mind reader, as he shifted an instant before the blow landed. Her fist bounced harmlessly off his biceps.

"Lie still and keep quiet." He hissed the order and added a convincing little shake. "However much I'd like to hurt you, I won't. Your brother's snoring at the other end of the house, so it's unlikely he'll hear you if you scream. Besides, you won't scream, will you?" His fingers gentled on her throat, with a shivering caress of thumb. "It'd bruise your Yankee pride."

She muttered something against his gloved hand. He removed it, but kept the other on her throat. "What do you want?"

"I want to kick your excellent ass from here to Chicago. Damn it, Dr. Jones, you fucked up."

"I don't know what you're talking about." It was hard to keep her breathing under control, but she managed it. That too was pride. "Let go of me. I won't scream."

She wouldn't because Andrew might hear, and might come roaring in. And whoever was currently pinning her to the bed was probably armed.

Well, she thought, this time so was she. If she could manage to get into her nightstand drawer and grab her gun.

In response, he sat on the bed beside her, and still holding her in place, reached out for the switch on the bedside lamp. She blinked rapidly against the flash of light, then stared wide-eyed, slack-jawed.

"Ryan?"

"How could you make such a stupid, sloppy, unprofessional mistake?"

He was dressed in black, snug jeans, boots, a

turtleneck and bomber jacket. His face was as strikingly handsome as ever, but his eyes weren't warm and appealing as she remembered. They were hot, impatient, and unmistakably dangerous.

"Ryan," she managed again. "What are you doing here?"

"Trying to clean up the mess you made."

"I see." Perhaps he'd had some sort of . . . breakdown. It was vital to remain calm, she reminded herself, and not to alarm him. Slowly, she put a hand on his wrist and nudged his hand away from her throat. She sat up instinctively, and primly, tugging at the collar of her pajamas.

"Ryan." She even worked up what she thought was a soothing smile. "You're in my bedroom, in the middle of the night. How did you get in?"

"The way I usually get into houses that aren't my own. I picked your locks. You really ought to have better."

"You picked the locks." She blinked, blinked again. He simply didn't look like a man in the middle of a mental crisis, but one who was simmering with barely suppressed temper. "You broke into my house?" And the phrase had a ridiculous notion popping into her head. "You broke in," she repeated.

"That's right." He toyed with the hair that tumbled over her shoulder. He was absolutely crazy about her hair. "It's what I do."

"But you're a businessman, you're an art patron. You're—why, you're not Ryan Boldari at all, are you?"

"I certainly am." For the first time that wicked smile flashed, reaching his eyes, turning them gold and amused. "And have been since my sainted mother named me thirty-two years ago in Brooklyn. And up to my association with you, that name has stood for something." The smile vanished into a snarl. "Reliability, perfection. The goddamn bronze was a fake."

"The bronze?" The blood simply drained out of her face. She felt it go, drop by drop. "How do you know about the bronze?"

"I know about it because I stole the worthless piece of shit." And cocked his head. "Or maybe you're thinking of the bronze in Florence, the other one you screwed up. I got wind of that yesterday—after my client reamed me out for passing him a forgery. A forgery, for sweet Christ's sake."

Too incensed to sit, he sprang off the bed and began to pace the room. "Over twenty years without a blemish, and now this. And all because I trusted you."

"Trusted me." She shoved up to her knees, teeth clenched. There was no room for fear or anxiety when temper percolated so hard and fast through the bloodstream. "You stole from me, you son of a bitch."

"So what? What I took's worth maybe a hundred bucks as a paperweight." He stepped closer again, annoyed that he found the hot gleam in her eyes and the angry color in her cheeks so appealing. "How many other pieces are you passing off in that museum of yours?"

She didn't think, she acted. She was off the bed like a bullet, launching herself at him. At five-eleven, she was no flyweight, and Ryan got the full impact of her well-toned body and well-oiled temper. It was an innate affection for women that had him shifting his body to break her fall—a gesture he instantly regretted as they hit the floor. To spare both of them, he rolled over and pinned her flat.

"You stole from me." She bucked, wriggled, and didn't budge him an inch. "You used me. You son of a bitch, you came on to me." Oh, and that was the worst of it. He'd flattered, romanced, and had her on the edge of slipping into temptation.

"The last was a side benefit." He clamped her wrists with his hands to keep her from pounding his face. "You're very attractive. It was no trouble at all."

"You're a thief. You're nothing but a common thief."

"If you think that insults me, you're off target. I'm a really good thief. Now we can sit down and work this out, or we can lie here and keep wrestling. But I'm going to warn you that even in those incredibly ugly pajamas, you're an appealing handful. Up to you, Miranda."

She went very still, and he watched with reluctant admiration as her eyes went from fire to frost. "Get off me. Get the hell off me."

"Okay." He eased off, then nimbly rocked up to his feet. Though he offered her a hand, she slapped it away, and pushed herself up.

"If you've hurt Andrew—"

"Why the hell should I hurt Andrew? You're the one who documented the bronze."

"And you're the one who stole it." She snatched her robe from the foot of the bed. "What are you going to do now? Shoot me, then clean out the house?"

"I don't shoot people. I'm a thief, not a thug."

"Then you're remarkably stupid. What do you think I'm going to do the moment you're gone?" She tossed that over her shoulder as she tugged on the robe. "I'm going to pick up that phone, call Detective Cook, and tell him just who broke into the Institute."

He merely hooked his thumbs in the front pockets of his jeans. The robe, he decided, was as amazingly unattractive as the pajamas. There was absolutely no reason why he should have to block an urge to start nibbling his way through all that flannel.

"If you call the cops, you'll look like a fool. First, because no one would believe you. I'm not even here, Miranda. I'm in New York." His smile spread, cocky and sure. "And there are several people who'll be more than happy to swear to it."

"Criminals."

"That's no way to talk about my friends and family. Especially when you haven't met them. Second," he continued while she ground her teeth, "you'd have to explain to the police why the stolen item was insured for six figures and was worth pocket change."

"You're lying. I authenticated that piece myself. It's sixteenth century."

"Yeah, and the Fiesole bronze was cast by Michelangelo." He smirked at her. "That shut you up. Now sit down, and I'll tell you just how we're going to handle this."

"I want you out of here." She tossed up her chin. "I want you to leave this house immediately."

"Or what?"

It was impulse, a wild one, but for once she followed the primal instinct. She made a dive, had the drawer open, and the gun at her fingertips. His hand closed over her wrist, and he cursed lightly as he yanked the gun free. With his other hand he shoved her back onto the bed.

"Do you know how many accidental shootings happen in the home because people keep loaded guns?"

He was stronger than she'd estimated. And faster. "This wouldn't have been an accident."

"You could hurt yourself," he muttered, and neatly removed the clip. He pocketed it and tossed the gun back in her drawer. "Now—"

She made a move to get up and he placed his spread hand on her face and pushed her back.

"Sit. Stay. Listen. You owe me, Miranda."

"I—" She almost choked. "I *owe* you?"

"I had a spotless record. Every time I took on a job, I satisfied the client. And this was my last one, damn it. I can't believe I'd get to the end and have some brainy redhead sully my reputation. I had to give my client a piece out of my private collection, and refund his fee in order to satisfy our contract."

"Record? Client? Contract?" She barely resisted tearing at her hair and screaming. "You're a thief, for God's sake, not an art dealer."

"I'm not going to argue semantics with you." He spoke calmly, a man totally in charge. "I want the little Venus, the Donatello."

"Excuse me, you want what?"

"The small Venus that was in the display with your forged David. I could go back and take it, but that wouldn't square the deal. I want you to get it, give it to me, and if it's authentic, we'll consider this matter closed."

No amount of willpower could stop her from gaping. "You're out of your mind."

"If you don't, I'll arrange for the David to find its way on the market again. When the insurance company recovers it—and has it tested, as is routine—your incompetence will be uncovered." He angled his head and saw by the way her brow creased that she was following the path very well. "That, on top of your recent disaster in Florence, would put a snug, and unattractive, cap on your career, Dr. Jones. I'd like to spare you that embarrassment, though I have no idea why."

"Don't do me any favors. You're not blackmailing me into giving you a Donatello, or anything else. The bronze is not a fake, and you're going to prison."

"Just can't admit you made a mistake, can you?"

You were so sure, weren't you? It appears you

were wrong. How will you explain it? She shuddered once before she could control it. "When I make one, I will."

"The way you did in Florence?" he countered, and watched her eyes flicker. "News of that blunder's trickling through the art world. Opinions are about fifty-fifty as to whether you doctored the tests or were just incompetent."

"I don't care what the opinions are." But the statement was weak and she began to rub her arms for warmth.

"If I'd heard about it a few days earlier, I wouldn't have risked lifting something you'd authenticated."

"I couldn't have made a mistake." She closed her eyes because suddenly the thought of that was worse, much worse, than knowing he'd used her to steal. "Not that kind of a mistake. I couldn't have."

The quiet despair in her voice had him tucking his hands in his pockets. She looked fragile suddenly, and unbearably weary.

"Everybody makes them, Miranda. It's part of the human condition."

"Not in my work." There were tears in her throat as she opened her eyes to stare at him. "I don't make them in my work. I'm too careful. I don't jump to conclusions. I follow procedure. I . . ." Her voice began to hitch, her chest to heave. She pressed her crossed hands between her breasts to try to control the hot tears that rose inside her like a tide.

"Okay, hold on. Let's not get emotional."

"I'm not going to cry. I'm not going to cry." She repeated it over and over, like a mantra.

"There's good news. This is business, Miranda." Those big blue eyes were wet and brilliant. And distracting. "Let's keep it on that level, and we'll both be happier."

"Business." She rubbed the back of her hand over her mouth, relieved that the absurdity of the statement had stemmed the tide of tears. "All right, Mr. Boldari. Business. You say the bronze is a fake. I say it's not. You say I won't report this to the police. I say I will. What are you going to do about it?"

He studied her a moment. In his line of work—both of them—he had to be a quick and accurate judge of people. It was easy to see that she would stand by her testing, and that she'd call the police. The second part didn't worry him overmuch, but it would cause some inconvenience.

"Okay, get dressed."

"Why?"

"We'll go to the lab—you can test it again, in front of me, satisfy the first level of business."

"It's two in the morning."

"So we won't be interrupted. Unless you want to go in your pajamas, get some clothes on."

"I can't test what I don't have."

"I have it." He gestured toward the leather bag he'd set just inside the door. "I brought it with me, with the idea of ramming it down your throat. But reason prevailed. Dress warm," he suggested, and sat comfortably in her armchair. "The temperature's dropped."

"I'm not taking you into the Institute."

"You're a logical woman. Be logical. I have the bronze and your reputation in my hands. You want a chance of getting the first back and salvaging the second. I'm giving it to you." He waited a moment to let that sink in. "I'll give you the time to test it, but I'm going to be right there, breathing down your neck when you do. That's the deal, Dr. Jones. Be smart. Take the deal."

She needed to know, didn't she? To be sure. And once she was sure, she would toss him to the police before he could blink those pretty eyes of his.

She could handle him, she decided. The fact was, her pride demanded she take the opportunity to do just that. "I'm not going to change clothes in front of you."

"Dr. Jones, if I had sex on my mind, we'd have dealt with that when we were on the floor. Business," he said again. "And you're not getting out of my sight until we've concluded it."

"I really hate you." She said it with such loathing he saw no cause to doubt her word. But he smiled to himself as she shut herself into the closet and hangers began to rattle.

She was a scientist, an educated woman with unimpeachable breeding and an unblemished reputation. She had had papers published in a dozen important science and art journals. *Newsweek* had done an article on her. She'd lectured at Harvard and had spent three months as a guest professor at Oxford.

It wasn't possible that she was driving through the chilly Maine night with a thief, intending to break into her own lab and conduct clandestine tests on a stolen bronze.

She hit the brakes and swung her car to the shoulder of the road. "I can't do this. It's ridiculous, not to mention illegal. I'm calling the police."

"Fine." Ryan merely shrugged as she reached for her car phone. "You do that, sweetheart. And you explain to them what you're doing with a worthless hunk of metal you tried to pass off as a work of art. Then you can explain to the insurance company—you've already made a claim, haven't you?—how it happens you expected them to pay you five hundred grand for a fake. One you authenticated, personally."

"It's not a fake," she said between her teeth, but she didn't punch in 911.

"Prove it." His grin flashed in the dark. "To me, Dr. Jones, and to yourself. If you do . . . we'll negotiate."

"Negotiate, my ass. You're going to jail," she told him, and shifted in her seat so they were face-to-face. "I'm going to see to it."

"First things first." Amused, he reached out and gave her chin a friendly pinch. "Call your security. Tell them you and your brother are coming in to do some work in the lab."

"I'm not involving Andrew."

"Andrew's already involved. Just make the call. Use whatever excuse you like. You couldn't sleep, so you decided to get some work done while it's quiet. Go on, Miranda. You want to know the truth, don't you?"

"I know the truth. You wouldn't know it if it jumped up and bit you."

"You lose a little of that high-society cool when you're pissed off." He leaned forward, kissed her lightly before she could shove him back. "I like it."

"Keep your hands off me."

"That wasn't my hands." He took her shoulders, caressed. "Those were my hands. Make the call."

She elbowed him aside, and jabbed in the number. The cameras would be on, she thought. He'd never pass as Andrew, so they were finished before they began. Her security chief, if he had any sense at all, would call the police. All she'd have to do was tell her story, and Ryan Boldari would be cuffed and penned and out of her life.

"This is Dr. Miranda Jones." She slapped out as Ryan patted her knee in approval. "My brother and I are on our way in. Yes, to work. With all the confusion of the last few days, I'm behind in my lab work. We should be there in about ten minutes. We'll use the main door. Thank you."

She disconnected, sniffed. She had him now, she decided, and he'd turned the key himself. "They're expecting me, and will switch off the alarm when I get there."

"Fine." He stretched out his legs as she pulled onto the road again. "I'm doing this for you, you know."

"I can't tell you how much I appreciate it."

"No thanks necessary." He waved them away,

grinning while she snarled. "Really. Despite all the trouble you've caused me, I like you."

"Why, I'm all aflutter."

"See? You've got style—not to mention a mouth that just begs to be savored over long hours in the dark. I really regretted not having more time with that mouth of yours."

Her hands tightened on the wheel. The hitch in her breathing was fury. She wouldn't allow it to be anything else. "You'll have more time, Ryan," she said sweetly. "This mouth of mine is going to chew you up and spit you out before we're done."

"I look forward to it. This is a nice area." He made the comment conversationally as she followed the coast road into town. "Windswept, dramatic, lonely, but with culture and civilization close at hand. It suits you. The house came down through your family, I take it."

She didn't answer. However ludicrous her actions, she wasn't about to add to them by holding a conversation with him.

"It's enviable," he continued, unoffended. "The heritage, and the money, of course. But beyond the privilege it's the name, you know? The Joneses of Maine. Just reeks of class."

"Unlike the Boldaris of Brooklyn," she muttered, but that only made him laugh.

"Oh, we reek of other things. You'd like my family. It's impossible not to. And what, I wonder, would they make of you, Dr. Jones?"

"Perhaps we'll meet at your trial."

"Still determined to bring me to justice." He appreciated her profile almost as much as the shadows of ragged rocks, the quick glimpses of dark sea. "I've been in this game for twenty years, darling. I've no intention of making a misstep on the eve of my retirement."

"Once a thief, always a thief."

"Oh, in the heart, I agree with you. But in deed. . . ." He sighed. "Once I clear my record, I'm done. If you hadn't messed things up, I'd be taking a well-deserved vacation on St. Bart's right now."

"How tragic for you."

"Yeah, well." He moved his shoulders again. "I can still salvage a few days." He unhooked his seat belt, and turned to reach into the backseat for the bag he'd tossed there.

"What are you doing?"

"Nearly there." He whistled lightly as he took out a ski cap and pulled it down low over his head until his hair was concealed. Next came a long black scarf of cashmere that he wrapped around his neck and over the lower part of his face.

"You can try to alert the guards," he began, flipping down the visor to check the result in the vanity mirror. "But if you do you won't see the bronze, or me again. You play it straight, go in, head to the lab just like you would normally, and we'll be fine. Andrew's a little taller than I am," he considered as he unrolled a long, dark coat. "Shouldn't matter. They'll see what they expect to see. People always do."

When she pulled into the parking lot, she had to admit he was right. He was so anonymous in the cold weather gear that no one would look twice at him. More, when they got out of the car and started toward the main entrance, she realized she might have taken him for Andrew herself.

The body language, the gait, the slight hunch in the shoulders were perfect.

She yanked her card through the slot with one irritable flick of the wrist. After a pause, she punched in her code. She imagined herself making wild faces at the camera, tackling Ryan and pounding her fists into his smug face while the guards scrambled. Instead, she tapped her key card lightly against her palm and waited for the buzzer to sound and the locks to open.

Ryan opened the doors himself, laying one brotherly hand on her shoulder. He kept his head down, muttering to her as they walked in. "No detours, Dr. Jones. You don't really want the trouble, or the publicity."

"What I want is the bronze."

"You're about to get it. Temporarily at least."

He kept his hand on her shoulder, guiding her down the corridors, down the stairs, to the lab doors. Again, she keyed them in. "You won't be walking out of here with my property."

He turned on the lights. "Run your tests," he suggested, peeling out of his coat. "You're wasting time." He kept his gloves on to take out the bronze and hand it to her. "I do know something about authenticating, Dr. Jones, and I'll be watching you closely."

And this, he told himself, was one of the biggest

risks of his long career. Coming here, with her. He'd boxed himself in, and was damned if he could rationalize the reason. Oh, coming back was one thing, he thought as he watched her take a pair of wire-rim glasses out of a drawer and slip them on.

He'd been right about that, he mused. The sexy scholar. Tucking that thought away, he made himself comfortable while she took the bronze to a work station for an extraction.

His reputation, his pride—which were one and the same—were at stake.

The job, which should have been a nice, tidy, and uneventful close to his career, had ended up costing him a great deal of trouble, money, and loss of face.

But what he should have done, and had intended to do, was confront her, threaten her, blackmail her into offsetting his losses, and walk away.

He hadn't been able to resist outwitting her. He had no doubt in his mind she intended to slant the tests in her favor, to try to convince him that the bronze was genuine. And when she did, it was going to cost her.

He thought the Cellini would be fair payment for his indulgence. The Institute, he decided, slipping his hands in his pockets as he watched her work, was about to make a generous donation to the Boldari Gallery.

It was going to kill her.

Her brows were knit as she straightened from the microscope. There was a twist in her stomach that no longer had anything to do with anger or with irritated arousal. She didn't speak at all, but made notes in a steady hand.

She took another scraping from the bronze, both the patina and the metal now, put it on a slide and studied that in turn. Her face was pale and set as she placed the bronze on a scale, took additional notes.

"I need to test the corrosion level, take X rays for the tool work."

"Fine. Let's go." He moved through the lab with her, imagining just where he would display the Cellini. The little bronze Venus she would give him would go into his own collection, but the Cellini was for the gallery, for the public, and would add a nice splash of prestige to his business.

He pulled a slim cigar out of his pocket, reached for his lighter.

"No smoking in here," she snapped.

He merely clamped it between his teeth and lighted it. "Call a cop," he suggested. "How about some coffee?"

"Leave me alone. Be quiet."

The twist in her stomach was sharper now, and spread like acid as the minutes ticked away. She followed procedure to the letter. But she already knew.

She heated the clay, waiting, praying for the flash of light from the crystals. And had to bite her lip to hold back the gasp. She wouldn't give him the satisfaction.

But when she held the X ray up, saw her instincts confirmed, her fingers were icy cold.

"Well?" He arched a brow, and waited for the con.

"This bronze is a forgery." Because her legs were weak, she sat on a stool and missed the flicker of surprise in his eyes. "The formula, as far as I can tell with preliminary tests, is correct. The patina, however, has been recently applied, and the corrosion levels are inconsistent with those of a bronze of the sixteenth century. The tool work is wrong. It's well done," she continued, with one hand unconsciously pressed hard against her churning stomach. "But it's not authentic."

"Well, well, Dr. Jones," he murmured, "you surprise me."

"This is not the bronze I authenticated three years ago."

He tucked his thumbs in his pockets and rocked back on his heels. "You screwed up, Miranda. You're going to have to face it."

"This is not the bronze," she repeated, and her spine snapped straight as she pushed off the stool. "I don't know what you thought you could prove, bringing me this forgery, taking us through this ridiculous charade."

"That's the bronze I took from the South Gallery," he said evenly, "and one I took on your reputation, Doctor. So let's cut the bullshit, and deal."

"I'm not dealing with you." She snatched up the bronze and shoved it at him. "You think you can break in my home, then try to pass this obvious fake off as my property so that I'll give you something else? You're a lunatic."

"I stole this bronze in good faith."

"Oh for God's sake—I'm calling security."

He grabbed her arm, shoved her roughly against the counter. "Look, sweetheart. I went through this little game against my better judgment. Now it's done. Maybe you weren't trying to pass anything off. Maybe it was an honest mistake, but—"

"I didn't make a mistake. I don't make mistakes."

"Does the name Fiesole ring a bell?"

The angry flush died out of her cheeks. Her eyes unfocused, went glassy. For a moment he thought she'd slip through his hold like water. If she was feigning distress, he realized he'd underestimated her.

"I didn't make a mistake," she repeated, but now her voice shook. "I can prove it. I have the records, my notes, the X rays and results for the tests on the original bronze."

The vulnerability got to him, enough for him to let her go as she twisted. He shook his head and followed her into a room lined with file cabinets.

"The weight was wrong," she said quickly, as she fumbled with keys to unlock a drawer. "The scraping I took didn't jibe, but the weight—I knew it was wrong as soon as I picked it up. It was too heavy but—Where the hell is the file?"

"Miranda—"

"It was too heavy, just slightly too heavy, and the patina, it's close but it's not right. It's just not right. Even if you'd miss that, you couldn't possibly mistake the corrosion levels. You can't mistake them."

Babbling now, she slammed the drawer shut, unlocked another, then another.

"It's not here. The files aren't here. They're missing." Fighting for calm, she closed the drawer. "The pictures, the notes, the reports, everything on the bronze David is missing. You took them."

"To what purpose?" he asked, with what he considered saintly patience. "Look, if I could get in here and take a fake, I could have taken anything I wanted. What would be the point in going through this routine, Miranda?"

"I have to think. Just be quiet. I have to think." She pressed her hands to her mouth and paced. Logical, be logical, she ordered herself. Deal with the facts.

He'd stolen the bronze, and the bronze was fake. What was the point in stealing a fake, then bringing it back? None, none at all. If it had been genuine, why would he be here? He wouldn't. Therefore, the story he'd told her, however absurd, was true.

She'd tested it, and agreed with his conclusions.

Had she made a mistake? Oh God, had she made a mistake?

No. Logic, not emotion, she reminded herself. She made herself stop her erratic movements and stand perfectly still.

Logic, when properly applied, was amazingly simple.

"Someone beat you to it," she said quietly. "Someone beat you to it and replaced it with a forgery."

She turned to him, seeing by the considering

look on his face that he was likely reaching the same conclusion.

"Well, Dr. Jones, it looks like we've both gotten that kick in the ass." He angled his head to study her. "What are we going to do about it?"

CHAPTER TWELVE

MIRANDA DECIDED TO ACCEPT THAT IT WAS A DAY FOR abnormal behavior when she found herself sitting in a truck stop off Route 1 at six A.M.

Their waitress brought them a pot of coffee, two thick brown mugs, and a pair of laminated menus.

"What are we doing here?"

Ryan poured, sniffed, sipped, then sighed. "Now that's coffee."

"Boldari, what are we doing here?"

"Having breakfast." He kicked back and studied the menu.

She took a deep breath. "It's six o'clock in the morning. I've had a difficult night, and I'm tired. I have some serious thinking to do and I don't have time to sit in some truck stop trading witticisms with a thief."

"So far you haven't been that witty. But as you

said, you've had a difficult night. Are you going to run into anyone you know here?"

"Of course not."

"Exactly. We need to eat, and we need to talk." He set his menu down and shot a smile at their waitress when she came over, pad in hand. "I'll go for the half-stack of hotcakes, eggs over easy, and side of bacon, please."

"You got it, cap'n. How 'bout you, honey?"

"I . . ." Resigned, Miranda squinted and scanned the menu in search of something nonlethal. "Just the, um, oatmeal. Do you have skim milk for that?"

"I'll see what I can do, and be back to you in a jiff."

"Okay, let's outline our situation," Ryan continued. "Three years ago you acquired a small bronze statue of David. My research indicates this came through your father, from a private dig outside of Rome."

"Your research is correct. The majority of the finds were donated to the National Museum in Rome. He brought the David home for the Institute. For study and authentication, and display."

"And you studied it, you authenticated it."

"Yes."

"Who worked with you?"

"Without my notes I can't be sure."

"Just try to picture it."

"It was three years ago." Because her mind was fuzzy, she tried the coffee. It was like sipping lightning. "Andrew, of course," she began. "He was very fond of that piece. It appealed to him. I think he might have done sketches of it. My father was in and out of the lab, checking the progress of the testing. He was pleased with the results. John Carter," she added, rubbing an ache in the center of her forehead. "He's lab manager."

"So he'd have had access to it. Who else?"

"Almost anyone working in the lab during that period. It wasn't a priority project."

"How many work in the lab?"

"Anywhere from twelve to fifteen, depending."

"All of them have access to the files?"

"No." She paused as their breakfasts were served. "Not all the assistants and techs would have keys."

"Trust me, Miranda. Keys are overrated." He flashed that smile again as he topped off their coffee. "We'll assume that anyone who worked in the lab had access to the files. You'll need to get a list of names from personnel."

"Will I really?"

"You want to find it? You've got a three-year time span," he explained. "From the time you authenticated the piece until I relieved you of the forgery. Whoever replaced it had to have access to the original to make the copy. The smartest, simplest way to do that would be to make a silicon mold, a wax reproduction from that."

"I imagine you know all about forgeries," she said with a sniff, as she spooned up oatmeal.

"Only what a man in my field—fields—needs to know. You'd need the original to make the mold," he continued, so obviously unoffended she wondered why she bothered to snipe at him. "The most efficient way to do that would be to make it while the bronze was still in the lab. Once it's displayed, you've got to get around security—and yours is pretty good."

"Thank you so much. This isn't skim milk," she complained, frowning at the little pitcher the waitress had brought with the oatmeal.

"Live dangerously." He dashed salt on his eggs. "Here's how I see it. Someone in the lab at that time saw the way your tests were leaning. It's a nice little piece, one a collector would pay a fair price for. So this person, maybe he has debts or he's pissed off at you or your family, maybe he's just decided to try his luck. He makes the mold some night. It's not a complicated process, and he's already in a lab. Nothing easier. If he doesn't know how to cast it himself, he certainly knows someone who does. More, he knows how to make the bronze appear to be, on the surface, several centuries old. When it's done, he switches the pieces—likely just before it's moved to display. Nobody's the wiser."

"It couldn't have been done on impulse. It takes time, it takes planning."

"I'm not saying it was impulse. But it wouldn't have taken that much time, either. How long was the bronze in the lab?"

"I don't know for sure. Two weeks, maybe three."

"More than enough." Ryan gestured with a slice

of bacon before biting it. "If I were you, I'd run tests on some of my other pieces."

"Others?" She didn't know why it hadn't occurred to her, not when it hit her now with such force. "Oh God."

"He did it once, and did it well enough to pull it off. Why not do it again? Don't look so devastated, darling. I'm going to help you."

"Help me." She pressed her fingers to her gritty eyes. "Why?"

"Because I want that bronze. After all, I guaranteed it to my client."

She dropped her hands. "You're going to help me get it back so you can steal it again?"

"I've got a vested interest. Finish your breakfast. We've got work to do." He picked up his coffee and grinned at her. "Partner."

Partner. The word made her shudder. Perhaps she was too tired to think clearly, but at the moment she couldn't see her way to recovering her property without him.

He'd used her, she remembered as she unlocked the front door of her house. Now, she would use him. Then she would see that he spent the next twenty years of his life taking group showers in a federal installation.

"You expecting anyone today? Housekeeper, cable guy, appliance repairman?"

"No. The cleaning company comes on Tuesdays and Fridays."

"Cleaning company." He took off his jacket.

"You won't get homey casseroles and sage advice from cleaning companies. You need a housekeeper named Mabel who wears a white bib apron and sensible shoes."

"The cleaning company is efficient, and unobtrusive."

"Too bad. Andrew's left for work by now." He noted by his watch it was eight-fifteen. "What time does your assistant get in?"

"Lori gets in by nine, usually a bit before."

"You'll need to call her—got her home number?"

"Yes, but—"

"Give her a call, tell her you're not going to make it in today."

"Of course I'm going in. I have meetings."

"She'll cancel them." He moved into the parlor and made himself at home by stacking kindling for a fire. "Tell her to get copies of personnel records for the lab, going back three years. It's the best place to start. Have her shoot them to your computer here."

He lighted the starter and within seconds the kindling was crackling. She said nothing as he chose two logs from the woodbox, and placed them on the flaming kindling with the efficiency of an Eagle Scout.

When he rose, turned, her smile was as sharp and unfriendly as an unsheathed blade. "Is there anything else I can do?"

"Honey, you're going to have to take orders a bit more cheerfully. Somebody's got to be in charge, you know."

"And you're in charge."

"That's right." He crossed over to her, took her by the shoulders. "I know a lot more about larceny than you do."

"Most people wouldn't consider that an attribute for leadership."

"Most people aren't trying to catch a thief." His gaze roamed down, lingered on her mouth.

"Don't even think about it."

"I never censor my thoughts. It gives you ulcers. We could enjoy this . . . association a lot more if you were a little friendlier."

"Friendlier?"

"More flexible." He drew her closer. "In certain areas."

She let her body bump lightly against his, allowed her lashes to flutter. "Such as?"

"Well, for starters . . ." He lowered his head, drew in her scent, anticipated that first taste. And his breath whooshed out in a pained rush as her fist plowed into his stomach.

"I told you to keep your hands off of me."

"So you did." With a slow nod, he rubbed his gut. Another few inches to the south, he thought, and her fist would have unmanned him. "You've got a good, solid punch, Dr. Jones."

"Be grateful I pulled it, Boldari." Though she hadn't, not by an inch. "Or you'd be on your hands and knees whistling for air. I take it we understand each other on this point."

"Perfectly. Make the call, Miranda. And let's get to work."

She did what he asked because it made sense. The only way to proceed was to begin, and to begin you needed a starting point.

By nine-thirty, she was in her home office, calling up data on her desktop.

The room was as efficient as her office at the Institute, if slightly cozier. Ryan had lighted a fire there as well, though she didn't consider it cold enough to indulge in one. Flames crackled cheerfully in the stone hearth; the late-winter sun beamed through the curtains he'd swept back.

They sat hip to hip at her desk, scanning names.

"Looks like you had an unusually large turnover about eighteen months ago," he pointed out.

"Yes. My mother revamped her lab in Florence. Several staff members transferred there, or moved from there to the Institute."

"I'm surprised you didn't jump at it."

"At what?"

"A move to Florence."

She shot the file to the printer. A hard copy would mean she didn't have to sit next to him. "It wasn't an option. Andrew and I run the Institute. My mother runs Standjo."

"I see." And he thought he did. "Some friction between you and Mama?"

"My family relationships are none of your concern."

"More than some friction, I'd say. How about your father?"

"I beg your pardon?"

"Are you Daddy's little girl?"

She laughed before she could stop herself, then rose to retrieve the printout. "I've never been anyone's little girl."

"That's too bad," he said, and meant it.

"My family isn't the issue here." She sat on the raspberry-colored love seat and tried to concentrate on the names that kept blurring in front of her tired eyes.

"They could be. Yours is a family-run business. Maybe someone took a shot at your family by taking the bronze."

"Your Italian's showing," she said dryly, and made him smile.

"The Irish are every bit as interested in revenge, darling. Tell me about the people on the list."

"John Carter. Lab manager. Got his doctorate from Duke. He's worked at the Institute for sixteen years. Oriental art is his primary interest."

"No, get personal. Is he married? Does he pay alimony? Gamble, drink his lunch, dress in women's clothes on Saturday night?"

"Don't be ridiculous." She tried to sit up straight, then gave in and curled up her legs. "He's married, no divorces. Two children. I think the oldest just started college."

"Takes a lot of money to raise kids, send them to college." He scanned across, noted the annual salary. "He makes a decent living, but decent doesn't satisfy everyone."

"His wife's a lawyer, and likely makes more than he does. Money isn't a problem for them."

"Money's always a problem. What kind of car does he drive?"

"I don't have any idea."

"How does he dress?"

She started to sigh, but thought she saw what he was getting at. "Old jackets and silly ties," she began, closing her eyes to try to bring her lab manager into focus. "No flash—though his wife bought him a Rolex for their twentieth anniversary." She stifled a yawn and snuggled down a little farther into the cushions. "He wears the same shoes every day. Hush Puppies. When they're ready to fall off his feet, he buys another pair."

"Take a nap, Miranda."

"I'm all right. Who's next?" She forced her eyes open. "Oh, Elise. My brother's ex-wife."

"Ugly divorce?"

"I don't imagine they're ever pretty, but she was very gentle with him. She was John's assistant here, then transferred to Florence. She's lab manager for my mother. She and Andrew met at the Institute—in fact, I introduced them. He fell like a tree. They were married six months later." She yawned again, and didn't bother to stifle it.

"How long did it last?"

"A couple of years. They seemed very happy for most of it, then it just started to fall apart."

"What did she want? Snazzy clothes, European vacations, a big, fancy house?"

"She wanted his attention," Miranda mumbled, and pillowed her head on her hands. "She wanted him to stay sober and focused on their marriage.

It's the Jones curse. We just can't do it. We're relationship-jinxed. I have to rest my eyes a minute."

"Sure, go ahead."

He went back to studying the list. Right now they were just names on a page to him. He intended for them to be a great deal more. Before it was done, he would know the intimate details. Bank balances. Vices. Habits.

And to that list he added three names: Andrew Jones, Charles Jones, and Elizabeth Standford-Jones.

He rose, then bent down to slip her glasses off, lay them on the table beside her. She didn't look like an innocent young girl in sleep, he decided. But like an exhausted woman.

Moving quietly, he took the chenille throw from the back of the love seat and tossed it over her. He'd let her sleep an hour or two, recharge her mind and her body.

Somewhere inside her were the answers, he was sure of it. She was the link.

While she slept he made a call to New York. There was no point in having a brother who was a genius with computers if you didn't use him once in a while.

"Patrick? It's Ryan." He eased back in the chair and watched Miranda sleep. "I've got several things on my plate here, and a little hacker job I don't have time to deal with. Interested?" He laughed. "Yeah, it pays."

* * *

Church bells were ringing. The music of them echoed over the red-tiled roofs and out to the distant hills. The air was warm, the sky as blue as the inside of a wish.

But in the dank basement of the villa, the shadows were thick. She shivered once as she pried off the stair tread. It was there, she knew it was there.

Waiting for her.

Wood splintered as she hacked at it. *Hurry. Hurry.* Her breath began to wheeze in her lungs, sweat dripped nastily down her back. And her hands trembled as she reached for it, drew it out of the dark and played her flashlight over the features.

Uplifted arms, generous breasts, a seductive tumble of hair. The bronze was glossy, without the blue-green patina of age. She could trace her fingers over it and feel the chill of the metal.

Then there was harpsong and the light laughter of a woman. The eyes of the statue took on life and luster, the bronze mouth smiled and said her name.

Miranda.

She awoke with a jolt, her heart galloping. For a moment she would have sworn she smelled perfume—floral and strong. And could hear the faint echo of harp strings.

But it was the buzzer on the front door that sounded, repeatedly and with some impatience. Shaken, Miranda tossed back the throw and hurried out of the room.

It was surprising enough to see Ryan at the open

front door. But it was a shock to the heart to see her father standing on the doorstep.

"Father." She cleared the sleep out of her voice and tried again. "Hello. I didn't know you were coming to Maine."

"Just got in." He was a tall man, trim, browned by the sun. His hair was full and thick and shiny as polished steel. It matched his trim beard and moustache and suited his narrow face.

His eyes—the same deep blue as his daughter's—peered out of the lenses of wire-rim glasses and studied Ryan.

"I see you have company. I hope I'm not intruding."

Sizing up the situation quickly, Ryan offered a hand. "Dr. Jones, what a pleasure. Rodney J. Pettebone. I'm an associate of your daughter's—and a friend, I hope. Just in from London," he continued, stepping back and drawing Charles neatly inside. He glanced toward the stairs where Miranda continued to stand, staring at him as if he'd grown two heads.

"Miranda's been kind enough to give me a bit of her time while I'm here. Miranda dear." He held out a hand and a ridiculously adoring smile.

She wasn't sure which baffled her more, the puppy dog smile or the upper-crust British accent that was rolling off his tongue as if he'd been born a royal.

"Pettebone?" Charles frowned as Miranda stood stiff and still as one of her bronzes. "Roger's boy."

"No, he's my uncle."

"Uncle? I didn't realize Roger had siblings."

"Half brother, Clarence. My father. Can I take your coat, Dr. Jones?"

"Yes, thank you. Miranda, I was just at the Institute. I was told you weren't feeling well today."

"I was—A headache. Nothing . . ."

"We've been caught, darling." Ryan moved up the stairs to take her hand, squeezing it hard enough to rub bone. "I'm sure your father will understand."

"No," Miranda said, definitely, "he won't."

"It's completely my fault, Dr. Jones. I only have a few days in the country." He accented this by kissing Miranda's fingers lovingly. "I'm afraid I persuaded your daughter to take the day off. She's helping me with my research on Flemish art of the seventeenth century. I'd be nowhere without her."

"I see." Obvious disapproval flickered in Charles's eyes. "I'm afraid—"

"I was about to make some tea." Miranda interrupted neatly. She needed a moment to realign her thoughts. "If you'll excuse us, Father. Why don't you wait in the parlor? It won't take long. Rodney, you'll give me a hand, won't you?"

"Love to." He beamed a smile when she returned the vise squeeze on his hand.

"Have you lost your mind?" she hissed as she slammed through the kitchen door. "Rodney J. Pettebone? Who the hell is that?"

"At the moment, I am. I'm not here, remember?" He pinched her chin.

"You gave my father the impression we were

playing hooky, for God's sake." She grabbed the kettle from the stove and took it to the sink. "Not only that, but that we were spending the day playing patty-cake."

"Patty-cake." He just couldn't resist it, and wrapped his arms around her back to hug. He didn't even mind the elbow in the ribs. "You're so cute, Miranda."

"I am not cute, and I am not happy with this ridiculous lie."

"Well, I suppose I could have told him I'm the one who stole the bronze. Then we could explain to him how it's a forgery and the Institute is now hip-deep in insurance fraud. Somehow I think the fact that you're playing patty-cake with some British twit is more palatable."

Teeth clenched, she warmed the teapot. "Why a British twit, for God's sake?"

"Just came to me. I thought he might be your type." He smiled engagingly when she sent a withering look over her shoulder. "The point is, Miranda, your father's here, he's been to the Institute, he obviously wants some answers. You have to figure out just which answers to give him."

"You don't think I know that? Do I look stupid?"

"Not at all, but I'd say you're an inherently honest person. Lying takes skill. What you have to do here is give him everything you knew up until the point where I joined you in bed this morning."

"I could have figured that out for myself, Rodney." But her stomach was already busy tying itself into knots over the lie.

"You've had less than three hours' sleep. You're sluggish. Where are your cups?" He reached into a cupboard.

"No, don't use the everyday." She waved an absent hand. "Get the good china out of the breakfront in the dining room."

He lifted his brows. Good china was for company, not for family. It gave him another insight into Miranda Jones. "I'll get two. I believe Rodney perceives your father wants to have a private chat with you."

"Coward," she muttered.

She arranged the pot, the cups, the saucers meticulously on the tray, and tried not to be annoyed that Ryan had gone up the back steps and left her to deal with it alone. She squared her shoulders, lifted the tray, and carried it out to the parlor, where her father stood in front of the fireplace, reading from a small leather notebook.

He was so handsome, was all she could think. Tall and straight and tanned, his hair shining. When she was very young, she'd thought he looked like a picture out of a fairy tale. Not a prince or a knight, but a wizard. So wise and dignified.

She'd so desperately wanted him to love her. To give her piggyback rides and cuddle her in his lap, to tuck the blankets around her at night and tell her foolish stories.

Instead, she'd had to settle for a mild and often absent kind of affection. No one had ever given her piggyback rides or told her foolish stories.

She sighed the sorrow of that away and continued into the room. "I asked Rodney to give us a few minutes alone," she began. "I imagine you want to talk to me about the burglary."

"Yes, I do. It's very upsetting, Miranda."

"Yes, we're all very upset." She set the tray down, settled into a chair, and poured out as she had been taught. "The police are investigating. We have hopes to recover the bronze."

"In the meantime, the publicity is damaging for the Institute. Your mother is distressed, and I've had to leave my project at a very key time to come here."

"There was no reason for you to come." Hands steady, she held out his cup. "Everything's being done that can be done."

"Obviously our security is not at an acceptable level. Your brother is responsible for that."

"This isn't Andrew's fault."

"We put the Institute in his hands, and yours," he reminded her, and idly sipped his tea.

"He's doing a marvelous job. Class attendance is up ten percent, gate receipts have increased. The quality of our acquisitions over the past five years has been astonishing."

Oh, and it galled so to have to defend and justify when the man across from her had walked away from the responsibilities of the Institute as easily as he had the responsibilities of family.

"The Institute was never one of your priorities." She said it mildly, knowing he would only tune out anger. "You preferred fieldwork. Andrew and I have put all our time and energy into it."

"And now we have our first theft in more than a generation. It can't be overlooked, Miranda."

"No, but the time and sweat and work and the improvements we've made, they can be overlooked."

"No one's faulting your enthusiasm." He waved it aside. "However, this must be dealt with. And with the negative publicity from your misstep in Florence added to it, it leaves us in a difficult position."

"My misstep," she murmured. How like him to use some limp euphemism for a crisis. "I did everything I was required to do in Florence. Everything." When she felt the emotion spurting up, she swallowed it and met him on the dispassionate level he expected. "If I could see the results of the retesting, I could analyze my own results and determine where the mistakes were made."

"That's something you have to take up with your mother. Though I can tell you, she's very displeased. If the press hadn't been notified—"

"I never talked to the press." She rose now, unable to sit, unable to pretend she was calm. "I *never* discussed *The Dark Lady* with anyone outside of the lab. Damn it, why would I?"

He paused a moment, set his teacup aside. He hated confrontations, disliked messy emotions that interfered with smooth production. He was well aware that there were floods of those messy emotions simmering inside his daughter. He'd never been able to understand where they came from.

"I believe you."

"And to be accused—What?"

"I believe you. While you may be headstrong and often wrong-minded in my opinion, I've never known you to be dishonest. If you tell me you didn't speak to the press about this matter, then I believe you."

"I—" The back of her throat burned. "Thank you."

"It hardly changes the situation, however. The publicity must be downplayed. Through circumstances, you're at the center of the storm, so to speak. Your mother and I believe it would be best if you took an extended leave."

The tears that had swum into her eyes dried up. "I've already discussed that with her. And I've told her I won't hide from this. I've done nothing."

"What you've done or haven't done isn't the issue. Until both of these matters are resolved, your presence at the Institute is detrimental."

He brushed off the knees of his slacks, then stood. "Starting today, you're to take a month personal leave. If necessary, you may go in, clear up any pending business, but it would be best if you do that from here, within the next forty-eight hours."

"You might as well paint a G for guilty on my forehead."

"You're overreacting, as usual."

"And you're walking away, as usual. Well, I know where I stand. Alone." Though it was humiliating, she tried one last time. "Once, just once, couldn't you take my side?"

"This isn't a matter of sides, Miranda. And it's

not a personal attack. This is what's best for everyone involved, and for both the Institute and Standjo."

"It hurts me."

He cleared his throat, and avoided her eyes. "I'm sure once you have time to think it through, you'll agree this is the most logical course to take. I'll be at the Regency until tomorrow if you need to reach me."

"I've never been able to reach you," she said quietly. "I'll get your coat."

Because he felt some regret, he followed her into the foyer. "You should take this time, do a little traveling. Get some sun. Perhaps your, ah, young man would join you."

"My what?" She took his coat out of the closet, then glanced up the stairs. And began to laugh. "Oh sure." She had to wipe at her eyes, even as she recognized the jittery onset of hysteria. "I bet old Rodney would just love to go traveling with me."

She waved her father out of the house, then sat on the bottom step and laughed like a loon—until she started to weep.

CHAPTER THIRTEEN

A MAN WHO HAD THREE SISTERS KNEW ALL ABOUT women's tears. There were the slow, rather lovely ones that could slide down a female cheek like small, liquid diamonds and reduce a man to begging. There were hot, angry ones that spurted out of a woman's eyes like clear fire and induced a wise man to run for cover.

And there were those that were hidden so deep in the heart that when they broke loose and stormed free they were a deluge of pain beyond any man's comfort.

So he let her be, let her curl into herself on the bottom step while those heart-born tears raged. He knew that the hurt that spawned such a flood closed her off. All he could do was give her privacy, and wait.

When those harsh, ripping sobs quieted, he walked down the hall, opened the closet, and pushed through until he found a jacket. "Here." He held it out to her. "Let's get some air."

She stared at him out of swollen and confused eyes. She'd simply forgotten he was there. "What?"

"Let's get some air," he repeated, and because she was still largely helpless, he pulled her to her feet. He slid the jacket over her arms, turned her, and efficiently fastened the buttons.

"I'd prefer to be alone." She tried for coolness, but her throat was still raw, and she fell far short.

"You've been alone long enough." He grabbed his own jacket, shrugged it on, then pulled her out the front door.

The air was bracing, the sun strong enough to sting her sore eyes. Humiliation was beginning to seep through. Tears were useless enough, she thought, but at least when they were private no one saw your control fail.

"This is a great spot," he said conversationally. He kept her hand in his even when her fingers flexed for release. "Privacy, a kick-ass view, the smell of the sea just outside the door. Grounds could use some work."

The Joneses, he concluded, didn't spend enough time outside. Across the tumbling lawn there were a pair of grand old trees that begged to have a hammock stretched between them. He doubted Miranda had ever explored the miracles of a hammock in the shade on a summer afternoon.

There were shrubs, ragged from winter, that he imagined bloomed beautifully—and without any care—in the spring. There were bare patches in the lawn, crying out to be reseeded and fed.

But the fact that there was grass, shrubs, old trees, and an impressive windbreak of pines on the north side indicated that someone had cared enough once to plant—or at least to hire a staff to plant.

He might have been an urbanite through and through, but he appreciated rural atmosphere.

"You're not taking care of what you have here. You surprise me, Miranda. I'd think a woman with your practical nature would insist on maintaining her property and guarding a legacy like this."

"It's a house."

"Yeah, it is. It should be a home. Did you grow up here?"

"No." Her head felt stuffy and thick from the weeping. She wanted to go back inside, take some aspirin, lie down in a dark room. But she didn't have quite enough strength worked up to resist when he pulled her along the cliff path. "It was my grandmother's."

"Makes more sense. I couldn't see your father choosing to live here as an adult. Wouldn't suit him at all."

"You don't know my father."

"Sure I do." The wind whipped, circling them as they climbed. Centuries of its constant stroking had worn the rocks here, made them smooth, rounded. They glowed like pewter in the sunlight. "He's pompous, he's arrogant. He has the kind of narrow focus that likely makes him brilliant in his field, and an inconsiderate human being. He didn't hear you," he added when they'd reached the flattened ledge that speared out over the sea. "Because he doesn't know how to listen."

"Obviously you do." Now she jerked her hand from his and defensively wrapped her arms around her body. "I don't know why it should surprise me that someone who steals other people's property for a living should stoop to eavesdropping on private conversations."

"I don't know either. But the real point is you've been left to twist in the wind. Now what are you going to do about it?"

"What can I do? Whatever authority I might have at the Institute, it still comes down to the fact that I work for them. I've been temporarily relieved of my duties, and that's that."

"That, if you have any spine, is never that until it's the way you want it."

"You don't know anything about it." She whirled on him, and the self-pity that had been in her eyes flashed away into fury. "They run the show, and they always have. Whatever gloss you put on it, I do what I'm told. I manage the Institute with Andrew because neither of them wanted to bother with the day-to-day business of it. And we've always known that they could pull that particular rug out from under us whenever they chose. Now they have."

"And you're going to tolerate being dumped on your ass this way? Kick back, Miranda." He grabbed a handful of her hair while the wind tossed the rest of the hot red curls madly. "Show them what you're made of. The Institute isn't the only place you can shine."

"Do you think there's any major museum or lab that would have me after this? The Fiesole bronze has ruined me. I wish to God I'd never seen it."

Defeated, she sat on the rocks, staring out at the point where the lighthouse stood like white marble against a hard blue sky.

"So, start your own lab."

"That's a pipe dream."

"A lot of people said the same thing to me when I wanted to open the gallery in New York." He sat beside her, cross-legged.

She let out a short laugh. "The difference here might just be that I don't intend to steal to outfit a business."

"We all do what we do best," he said lightly. He took out a cigar, cupped his hands around the tip as he lighted it. "You have contacts, don't you? You've got a brain. You've got money."

"I've got a brain and money. The contacts . . ." She moved her shoulders. "I can't count on them now. I love my work," she heard herself say. "I love the structure of it, the discovery. Most people think of science as a series of steps forged in concrete, but it's not. It's a puzzle, and not all of the pieces will ever be firmly in place. When you're able to fit some of them together, to see an answer, it's thrilling. I don't want to lose that."

"You won't, unless you give up."

"The minute I saw the Fiesole bronze, understood what the project was, I was totally entranced in the possibilities. I knew it was part ego, but who cared? I'd authenticate it, I'd prove how smart and clever I was, and my mother would applaud. The way mothers do watching their children on stage at a school play. With sentimental enthusiasm and pride." She dropped her head on her knees. "That's pathetic."

"No, it's not. Most of us go through adulthood performing for our parents, and hoping for that applause."

She turned her head to study him. "Do you?"

"I still remember the opening of my New York gallery. The moment my parents walked inside. My father in his good suit—the one he always wore to weddings and funerals—and my mother in a new blue dress, and her hair ruthlessly styled from a trip to Betty's Salon. I remember the look on their faces. Sentimental enthusiasm and pride." He laughed a little. "And not a little bit of shock. It mattered to me."

Turning her head, she rested her chin on her hands and looked out to sea again where the waves broke strong and white and cold. "I remember the look on my mother's face when she fired me from the Fiesole project." She sighed. "I would have handled disappointment or regret better than that ice-edged disdain."

"Forget the bronze."

"How can I? It's what started this whole downhill slide. If I could just go back and see where I went wrong . . ." She pressed her fingers to her eyes. "Test it again like I did the *David*."

Slowly, she lowered her hands. Her palms had gone damp. "Like the *David*," she murmured. "Oh my God." She sprang to her feet so quickly, for one wild moment Ryan feared she meant to jump.

"Hold on." He took a firm hold of her hand as he got to his feet. "You're a little too close to the edge to suit me."

"It's like the *David*." She shoved away from him, then grabbed his jacket. "I followed procedure, step by step. I know what I had in my hands. I know it." She pushed him again, spun away with a clatter of boots on rock. "I did everything right. I detailed everything. The measurements, the formulas, the corrosion levels. I had all the facts, all the answers. Someone switched it."

"Switched it?"

"Like the *David*." She rapped a fist on his chest as if to knock the truth into him. "Just like the *David*. What Ponti's lab had was a forgery, but it wasn't the same bronze. It was a copy. It had to be a copy."

"That's a pretty big leap, Dr. Jones." And the possibilities swam like fine wine in his head. "Interesting."

"It fits. It makes sense. It's the only thing that makes sense."

"Why?" He lifted his eyebrows. "Why isn't it more logical that you made a mistake?"

"Because I didn't. Oh, I can't believe I let this cloud what I know." She pulled her hands through her hair, pressing her fists to the side of her head. "I wasn't thinking clearly. When you're told you're wrong often enough, strongly enough, you believe it. Even when you aren't wrong."

She began to walk, in those long, purposeful strides, letting the wind clear her head, letting her blood bubble. "I'd have gone on believing it, if it hadn't been for the *David*."

"Good thing I stole it."

She slanted a look at him. He was matching his pace to hers, and appeared to be enjoying a casual walk on a breezy afternoon. "Apparently," she muttered. "Why that piece? Why did you steal that particular piece?"

"I told you, I had a client."

"Who?"

His lips curved. "Really, Miranda, some things are sacred."

"They could be connected."

"My *David* and your lady? That's reaching."

"My David and *my* lady—and it's not that long a reach. They're both bronzes, both Renaissance works, Standjo and the Institute are connected, and I worked on both. Those are facts. Both were genuine, both were replaced by copies."

"And those are speculations, not facts."

"It's an educated and logical theory," she corrected, "and the basis for a preliminary conclusion."

"I've known this client for several years. Believe me, he isn't interested in complicated plots and schemes. He simply sees something he wants, puts in an order. If I think it's doable, I do it. We keep it simple."

"Simple." It was an attitude she was grateful she would never understand.

"And," he added, "he would hardly have commissioned me to steal a forgery."

Her brow creased at that. "I still believe whoever replaced the *David* replaced *The Dark Lady*."

"I'll agree it's a definite, and intriguing, possibility."

"I'd be able to solidify that conclusion if I was able to examine both pieces and compare them."

"Okay."

"Okay, what?"

"Let's do it."

She stopped at the base of the lighthouse, where the shale crunched under her feet. "Do what?"

"Compare them. We have one. It's just a matter of getting the other."

"Stealing it? Don't be ridiculous."

He grabbed her arm as she turned away. "You want to know the truth, don't you?"

"Yes, I want the truth, but I'm not flying to Italy, breaking into a government facility, and stealing a worthless copy."

"No reason we can't take something worthwhile while we're there. Just a thought," he added when her mouth dropped open. "If you're right, and we prove it, you'll more than salvage your reputation. You'll make it."

It was impossible, insane. It couldn't be done. But she saw the gleam in his eye and wondered.

"Why would you bother? What would you get out of it?"

"If you're right, it brings me a step closer to the original *David*. I have my reputation to salvage too."

And if she was right, he thought, and *The Dark Lady* was real, he'd be a step closer to that as well. He'd find her. What a marvelous addition she would make to his private collection.

"I'm not breaking the law."

"You already are. You're standing here with me, aren't you? You're an accessory after the fact, Dr. Jones." He swung his arm companionably over her shoulder. "I didn't hold a gun to your head or a knife to your back. You took me in past your security," he continued, walking back toward the house. "You've spent the day with me, fully aware I'm holding stolen property. You're already in." He gave her a friendly kiss on top of the head. "Might as well see it through."

He checked his watch, calculated. "You go up and pack. We'll need to swing through New York first. I have some things to tidy up there, and I need to pick up some clothes and tools."

"Tools?" She pushed her hair away from her face. Better not to know, she decided. "I can't just fly off to Italy. I have to talk to Andrew. I have to explain."

"Leave him a note," Ryan suggested, and pulled open the back door. "Make it brief, and tell him you're going away for a couple of weeks. Leave it at that, and you leave him out of it if the cops get too nosey."

"The police. If I leave this way before the investigation is complete, they might think I was involved."

"Adds to the excitement, doesn't it? Better not use your phone," he murmured. "Always a possibility of the records being checked. I'll get mine out of my bag. I need to call my cousin Joey."

Her head was reeling. "Your cousin Joey?"

"He's a travel agent. Go pack," he repeated. "He'll get us on the first flight out. Don't forget your passport—and your laptop. We'll want to finish going through those personnel files."

She tried a deep breath. "Anything else I should bring along?"

"An appetite." He pulled his phone out of his bag. "We should be in New York in time for dinner. You're going to love my mother's linguine."

It was nearly six before Andrew managed to get home. He'd tried to call Miranda half a dozen times, but had only reached their answering machine. He wasn't certain what shape he'd find her in—manic with temper or desolate with hurt. He hoped he was prepared to deal with either, or both.

But all he found was a note on the refrigerator.

Andrew, I'm sure you're aware I've been ordered to take a leave of absence from the Institute. I'm sorry to leave you in the lurch at a time like this. I don't want to say I don't have a choice, so I'll say I'm making the only one that works for me. I'll be gone for a couple of weeks. Please, don't worry. I'll be in touch when I can.

Don't forget to take out the trash. There's enough roast left over from Sunday to keep you going for another meal or two. See that you eat.

Love,
Miranda

"Shit." He yanked the note free and read it through again. "Where are you?"

CHAPTER FOURTEEN

"I DON'T SEE WHY WE DIDN'T JUST FLY TO FLORENCE." Miranda was well past second thoughts and into third thoughts by the time Ryan took the wheel of a natty little BMW and navigated out of La Guardia. "If we're going to do something this insane, there's no point in taking a detour."

"It isn't a detour, it's a scheduled stop. I need my things."

"You could have bought clothes in Italy."

"I probably will. If the Italians dressed the world, it would be a much more attractive place. However, there are certain things I need that can't always be easily bought in the retail market."

"Your tools," she muttered. "Burglary tools."

"Among others."

"Fine, fine." She shifted in her seat, drummed her fingers on her knee. Somehow, she had to accept the fact that she was now working with a criminal. A thief, who by definition was without integrity.

Without his help, she saw no way she would ever see the bronze again—or the forgery. And there *was* a forgery, she assured herself. It was a logical theory, one that required more data and study in order to be proven.

If she swallowed her pride and took the theory to her mother? The idea nearly made Miranda laugh. Elizabeth would dismiss it, and her daughter, in a snap, putting it down to arrogance, stubbornness, and a bit of desperation.

And not entirely without cause, Miranda admitted.

The only one who was willing to listen, to explore the possibility, was a professional thief who was certainly working toward his own ends—and expected her to hand over the Donatello *Venus* as a consultant fee.

Well, they would see about that.

He was a factor in the equation, she reminded herself, nothing more. Finding and authenticating *The Dark Lady* was more important than the formula she used to gain that end.

"There's no reason to go into Brooklyn."

"Sure there is." Ryan thought he had a pretty good idea what was running around in that admirable brain of hers. She had a very expressive face—when she didn't know anyone was paying attention to her. "I miss my mother's cooking."

He beamed at her and zipped around a poky sedan. It was so easy to read her. She was hating every minute of this, juggling the pros and cons in her mind to try to find full justification for the choice she'd made. "And I have a couple of things to straighten out, familywise, before I go to Italy. My sister's going to want shoes," he muttered. "She always wants shoes. She's addicted to Ferragamo."

"You steal shoes for your sister?"

"Please." Genuinely insulted, he scowled at traffic. "I'm not a shoplifter."

"Excuse me, but stealing is stealing."

His scarred eyebrow arched wickedly. "Not by a long shot."

"And there's no reason for me to go to Brooklyn. Why don't you just drop me off at whatever hotel I'm staying in."

"First, you're not staying in a hotel. You're staying with me."

Her head whipped around, her eyes narrowed. "I certainly am not."

"And second, you're going to Brooklyn because, as you appear to have forgotten, we're joined at the hip until this is finished. Where I go you go . . . Dr. Jones."

"That's ridiculous." And inconvenient. She needed time alone, time completely to herself in order to put everything down on paper in an orderly fashion. To weigh and consider. He hadn't given her time to think. "You said yourself I'm too deeply involved to do anything but cooperate. If you don't trust me, it's only going to complicate matters."

"Trusting you would complicate matters," he corrected. "Your problem is you've got a conscience. It's going to kick in from time to time and tempt you to call some cop and confess all." He reached over to pat her hand. "Just consider me the bad angel on your shoulder, kicking the good angel in the face whenever he starts spouting about honesty and truth."

"I'm not staying with you. I have no intention of sleeping with you."

"Now you've done it. What's the point of living?"

The laughter in his voice put her teeth on edge so that she had no choice but to speak through them. "You know very well you want me to sleep with you."

"It's been my lifelong dream, and now it's crushed. I don't know how I'm going to go on."

"I despise you." She hissed it out, and when he laughed again, she did her ego and her temper the favor of staring out the side window and ignoring him for the rest of the drive.

She didn't know what she'd expected, but it wasn't the pretty two-level house with yellow trim in a quiet neighborhood.

"You grew up here?"

"Here? No."

He smiled at the shock in her voice. He imagined she'd expected him to take her to some nasty little slum where the sound of raised voices was as pervasive as the smell of garlic and garbage.

"The family moved here about ten years ago.

Come on, they're expecting us, and Mama's likely got some antipasto ready."

"What do you mean expecting?"

"I called to let her know we were coming."

"You called? Who am I supposed to be?"

"That's a question everyone has to decide for themselves."

"What did you tell her?" Miranda demanded, and clung to the handle as he leaned across to open her door.

"That I was bringing a woman home to dinner." He stayed where he was a moment, his body angled and pressed to hers, his face close. "Don't be shy. They're very easy people."

"I'm not shy." But there was the faintly sick sensation in her stomach she experienced whenever she had to meet new people on a social level. In this case, she told herself, such things were absurd. "I just want to know how you've explained . . . Stop that," she demanded when his gaze lowered and lingered on her mouth.

"Hmm." He really wanted to take a slow, tasty bite of that stubborn bottom lip. "Sorry, I was distracted. You smell . . . interesting, Dr. Jones."

The moment called for action and movement—and not the ridiculous fantasy that leaped into her brain of grabbing two handfuls of his hair and yanking his mouth to hers. Instead she slapped one hand on his chest, yanked the door open with the other, and scooted out.

He chuckled a little—which helped relieve the

ball of tension that had gathered low in his gut, and climbed out the opposite side. "Hey, Remo."

The big brown dog who'd been sleeping in the yard uncurled himself, let out one bark that echoed like a cannon blast, then jumped lovingly on Ryan. "I thought you were going to learn some manners." Grinning, he scratched the delighted dog's ears. "What happened to obedience school? You flunked out again, didn't you?" Ryan asked as they headed toward the door.

As if avoiding the question, the dog slid his eyes to the side and gazed at Miranda. His tongue lolled out in a canine grin.

"Not afraid of dogs, are you?"

"No, I like them," she replied as Ryan pushed open the front door. Through it emerged the sound of the evening news, voices, male and female, raised in what appeared to be a bitter and violent argument, delicious aroma of roasted garlic and spices, and a large spotted cat who dashed for freedom and began an immediate war with the dog.

"Home sweet home," Ryan murmured, and pulled her into the melee.

"If you can't behave like a decent human being, I don't want you to speak to any of my friends, ever again."

"All I did was mention that if she had some really basic plastic surgery, she would improve her looks, her self-esteem, and her sex life."

"You're a pig, Patrick."

"Yeah, well, your friend has a nose like a tail fin on a fifty-seven Chevy."

"Not only a pig, but a shallow, superficial asshole on top of it."

"I'm trying to hear the news, here. Take it outside until the sports are over, for sweet Christ's sake."

"This," Miranda said in prim and precise tones, "is obviously a bad time."

"No, this is normal," Ryan assured her, and dragged her into the spacious, cluttered, and noisy living room.

"Hey, Ry!"

The man—boy really, Miranda noted as he turned with a grin nearly as lethal as Ryan's—took a few gangly strides and punched Ryan in the shoulder. A sign, Miranda assumed, of affection.

His dark hair was curly, his eyes a glinting golden brown in a face that Miranda supposed had caused the girls in his high school to sigh into their pillows at night.

"Pat." With equal affection, Ryan caught him in a headlock for the introduction. "My baby brother Patrick, Miranda Jones. Behave," he warned Patrick.

"Sure. Hey, Miranda, how's it going?"

Before she could answer, the young woman Patrick had been arguing with stepped up. She gave Miranda a long measuring look as she slipped her arms around Ryan and rubbed cheeks. "Missed you. Hello, Miranda, I'm Colleen." She didn't offer a hand, but kept her arms proprietarily around her brother.

She had the onyx and gold good looks of the

Boldaris, and a sharp, assessing gleam in her eyes.

"It's nice to meet you, both." Miranda offered Colleen a cool smile, and let it warm a little for Patrick.

"You gonna leave the girl at the door all day, or you bringing her in so I can get a look at her?" This boomed out of the living room and had all three Boldaris grinning.

"I'm bringing her in, Papa. Let's have your coat."

She gave it up with some reluctance, heard the door close at her back with the enthusiasm of a woman hearing a cell snap shut.

Giorgio Boldari rose out of his easy chair and politely muted the television. Ryan hadn't gotten his build from his father, Miranda decided. The man who studied her was short, stocky, and sported a graying moustache over his unsmiling lips. He wore khakis, a neatly pressed shirt, scuffed Nikes, and a medallion of the Madonna on a chain around his neck.

No one spoke. Miranda's ears began to buzz with nerves.

"You're not Italian, are you?" he asked at length.

"No, I'm not."

Giorgio pursed his lips, let his gaze skim over her face. "Hair like that, you probably got some Irish in you."

"My father's mother was a Riley." Miranda fought back the urge to shift her feet and lifted a brow instead.

He smiled then, fast and bright as lightning. "This

one's got a classy look to her, Ry. Get the girl some wine, for God's sake, Colleen. You gonna leave her standing here thirsty? Yankees blew it today. You follow baseball?"

"No, I—"

"Ought to. It's good for you." Then he turned to his son and enveloped Ryan in a fierce bear hug. "You should stay home more."

"I'm working on it. Mama in the kitchen?"

"Yeah, yeah. Maureen!" The shout could have cracked concrete. "Ryan's here with his girl. She's a looker too." He sent Miranda a wink. "How come you don't like baseball?"

"I don't dislike it, in particular. I just—"

"Ryan played third base—hot corner. He tell you that?"

"No, I—"

"Carried a four twenty-five batting average his senior year. Nobody stole more bases than my Ryan."

Miranda shifted her eyes to Ryan. "I bet."

"We got trophies. Ry, you show your girl your trophies."

"Later, Papa."

Colleen and Patrick went back to arguing, in hissy undertones, as she brought in a tray of glasses. The dog was barking incessantly at the front door, and Giorgio shouted again for his wife to come the hell out and meet Ryan's girl.

At least, Miranda thought, she wasn't going to be required to make a great deal of conversation.

These people simply took over, carrying on as if there was no stranger in the house.

The house itself was cluttered, full of light and art. She saw Ryan had been right about his mother's watercolors. The three dreamy New York street scenes on the wall were lovely.

There was an odd and intriguing tall tangle of black metal—most likely his father's work—behind a couch with thick blue cushions peppered with dog hair.

There were trinkets and framed snapshots everywhere, a ratty knotted rope on the floor that showed evidence of Remo's teeth, and a scatter of newspapers and magazines on the coffee table.

No one scurried to pick them up, to make excuses for the clutter.

"Welcome to the Boldaris'." With a twinkle in his eye, Ryan took two glasses off the tray, handed her one, and toasted. "Your life may never be the same."

She was beginning to believe him.

Even as she took the first sip, a woman hurried into the room wiping her hands on an apron splattered with sauce. Maureen Boldari was a good three inches taller than her husband, slim as a willow, and possessed of striking black-Irish looks. Her glossy hair waved attractively around her strong face, and vivid blue eyes sparkled with pleasure as she opened her arms.

"There's my boy. Come kiss your mama."

Ryan obeyed, lifting her off her feet as he did so and making her let loose a rich, hearty laugh. "Patrick, Colleen, stop that bickering before I give the pair of you the back of my hand. We've got company. Giorgio, where are your manners? Turn that television off. Remo, stop that barking."

And as it was all done, quickly and without comment, Miranda got a solid clue as to who ran the household.

"Ryan, introduce me to your young lady."

"Yes, ma'am. Maureen Boldari, the love of my life, meet Dr. Miranda Jones. Pretty, isn't she, Mama?"

"Yes, she is. Welcome to our home, Miranda."

"It's very kind of you to have me, Mrs. Boldari."

"Good manners," Maureen said with a brisk nod. "Patrick, bring out the antipasto, and we'll get acquainted. Ryan, show Miranda where she can freshen up."

Ryan led her out of the living room, down a short hall, and into a small pink and white powder room. She grabbed his shirt in her fist.

"You told them we were involved."

"We are involved."

"You know what I mean," she said in the same furious whisper. "Your girl? That's ridiculous."

"I didn't tell them you were my girl." Because it amused him, he lowered his voice to a whisper as well. "I'm thirty-two, they want me married and making babies. They assume."

"Why didn't you make it clear we were business associates?"

"You're beautiful, you're single, you're female.

They wouldn't have believed we were just business associates. What's the big deal?"

"For one, your sister looked at me as if she'd pop me in the nose if I didn't adore you enough—for another, it's just deceitful. Not that such niceties as honesty matter to you."

"I'm always honest with my family."

"Sure you are. Undoubtedly your mother is very proud of her son the thief."

"Of course she is."

She stuttered, losing whatever it was she'd planned to say. "Are you trying to convince me that she knows you steal?"

"Sure she does. Does she look stupid?" He shook his head. "I don't lie to my mother. Now, hurry up in there, will you?" He gave her a nudge into the powder room when she only gaped at him. "I'm hungry."

He wasn't hungry for long. No one could have been. There was, in short order, enough food being offered to feed a small and starving Third World army.

Because there was company, they had the meal in the dining room, with its attractive striped walls and handsome mahogany table. There was good china, the glint of crystal, and enough wine to float a battleship.

Conversation never lagged. In fact, if you didn't heave your words out fast and furiously, there was no room for them. When she noted that the level of her wineglass rose back up to the rim whenever she sipped, Miranda left it alone and concentrated on the food.

Ryan had been right about one thing. She loved his mother's linguine.

She was brought up-to-date on the family. Michael, the second son, ran Boldari Gallery, San Francisco. He was married to his college sweetheart and had two children. The last tidbit of info was delivered by the proud grandpa with a meaningful look at Ryan and an eyebrow-wiggling grin for Miranda.

"You like children?" Maureen asked her.

"Um, yes." In a vague and cautious manner, Miranda thought.

"Center your life, children do. Give you real purpose, and celebrate the love that brings a man and woman together." Maureen passed a basket of irresistible bread to Miranda.

"I'm sure you're right."

"Take my Mary Jo."

And Miranda was treated to the virtues of her eldest daughter, who owned a boutique in Manhattan, *and* had three children.

Then there was Bridgit, who'd taken a sabbatical from a career in publishing in order to stay at home with her baby daughter.

"You must be very proud of them."

"They're good kids. Educated." She beamed at Ryan as she said it. "All my children went to college. Patrick's a freshman. He knows all about computers."

"Really." It seemed a much safer topic, so Miranda smiled at him. "It's a fascinating field."

"It's like playing games for a living. Oh, Ry, I've got some of the data you asked me to access."

"Great."

"What data?" Colleen stopped eyeing Miranda and narrowed her eyes suspiciously at Ryan.

"Just cleaning up a little business, baby." He gave her hand a casual squeeze. "Mama, you outdid yourself tonight."

"Don't change the subject, Ryan."

"Colleen." Maureen's voice was mild, with honed steel beneath. "We have company. Help me clear the table. I made tiramisu, your favorite, Ry."

"We're going to discuss this," Colleen said between her teeth, but rose obediently to clear plates.

"Let me help." Miranda started to rise and was waved back by her hostess.

"Guests don't clear. You sit."

"Don't worry about Colleen," Patrick said the moment she was out of earshot. "We'll handle her."

"Shut up, Patrick." Though Ryan smiled over at Miranda, she caught a glint of discomfort in his eyes. "I don't think we mentioned what Colleen does."

"No, you didn't."

"She's a cop." With a sigh, he rose. "I'll give them a hand with the coffee."

"Oh, wonderful." Blindly, Miranda reached for her wine.

* * *

She kept out of the way, obeying the house rules by retiring to the living room after coffee and dessert. Since Giorgio was busy grilling her on what she did, why she wasn't married, her mind was well engaged. No one seemed bothered by the angry words coming out of the kitchen.

When Colleen stormed out, Patrick only rolled his eyes. "Here she goes again."

"You promised, Ry. You gave your word."

"I'm keeping it." Obviously frustrated, he dragged a hand through his hair. "I'm just finishing what I started, baby. Then it's done."

"And what does she have to do with it?" She jabbed a finger at Miranda.

"Colleen, it's not polite to point," Giorgio told her.

"Oh hell." And tossing something uncomplimentary in Italian over her shoulder, Colleen strode out of the house.

"Damn it." Ryan blew out a breath, offered Miranda an apologetic smile. "Be right back."

"Um . . ." She sat another moment, nearly squirming as Giorgio and Patrick stared at her. "I'll go see if Mrs. Boldari needs any help after all."

She escaped into what she hoped was some area of sanity. The kitchen was big and airy and carried the warm, friendly smells of the meal. With its bright counters and sparkling white floor, it was a picture out of a grocery store checkout magazine.

Dozens of incomprehensible pictures executed with crayon crowded the front of the refrigerator. There was a bowl of fresh fruit on the table, and cafe curtains at the windows.

Normality, Miranda decided.

"I hoped you'd bend your rule and let me give you a hand."

"Sit." Maureen gestured to the table. "Have coffee. They'll finish arguing soon. I should wallop them both for making a scene in front of company. My kids." She turned to an efficient home cappuccino maker and began to fix a cup. "They got passion, good brains, and wide stubborn streaks. Take after their father."

"Do you think so? I see a lot of you in Ryan."

It was exactly the right thing to say. Maureen's eyes turned warm and loving. "The firstborn. No matter how many you have, there's only one first. You love them all—so much it's a wonder your heart doesn't break from it. But there's only one first. You'll know, one day."

"Hmmm." Miranda declined to comment as Maureen frothed the milk. "It must be a little worrying, having a child go into law enforcement."

"Colleen, she knows what she wants. Never goes any way but forward, that girl. One day, she'll be a captain. You'll see. She's mad at Ryan," she continued conversationally, as she set the cup in front of Miranda. "He'll charm her out of it."

"I'm sure he will. He's very charming."

"Girls always chased after him. But my Ryan's very particular. He's got his eye on you."

It was time, Miranda decided, to put the record straight. "Mrs. Boldari, I don't think Ryan was completely clear about this. We're just business associates."

"You think so?" Maureen said placidly, and turned back to load the dishwasher. "He doesn't look good enough to you?"

"He looks very good, but—"

"Maybe because he comes from Brooklyn and not Park Avenue he isn't classy enough for a Ph.D.?"

"No, not at all. It's simply . . . It's simply that we're business associates."

"He doesn't kiss you?"

"He—I . . ." For God's sake, was all she could think, and filled her mouth with hot foamy coffee to shut it up.

"I thought so. I'd worry about that boy if he didn't kiss a woman who looks like you. He likes brains too. He's not shallow. But maybe you don't like the way he kisses. It matters," she added while Miranda stared into her coffee. "A man doesn't get your blood up with his kisses, you aren't going to have a happy relationship. Sex is important. Anybody who says different never had good sex."

"Oh my," was all she could think of.

"What? You don't think I know my boy has sex? You think I have brain damage?"

"I haven't had sex with Ryan."

"Why not?"

"Why not?" Miranda could only blink as Maureen tidily closed the dishwasher and began to fill the sink to wash the pots. "I barely know him." She couldn't believe she was having this conversation. "I don't just have sex with every attractive man I meet."

"Good. I don't want my boy going around with easy women."

"Mrs. Boldari." She wondered if it would help to bang her head on the table. "We're not going around. Our relationship is strictly a business one."

"Ryan doesn't bring business associates home to eat my linguine."

Since she had no comment for that, Miranda shut her mouth again. She glanced up with relief as Ryan and his sister came through the archway.

As expected, he'd charmed Colleen out of her snit. The two of them, Miranda noted, were smiling, their arms around each other's waists. For the first time, Colleen sent Miranda a friendly look.

"Sorry about that. Just a few things we needed to straighten out."

"No problem."

"So . . ." Colleen sat at the table, rested her feet on the opposite chair. "Do you have any solid feeling for who might have stolen the original bronze?"

Miranda just blinked at her. "Excuse me?"

"Ryan filled me in. Maybe I can help you sort it out."

"Six months out of the academy and she's Sherlock Holmes." Ryan bent over, kissed her hair. "Want me to dry the pots, Mama?"

"No, it's Patrick's turn." She glanced around. "Somebody steal something from your lady?"

"I did," he said easily, and joined the women at the table. "It turned out to be a forgery. We're straightening it out."

"Good."

"Wait. Wait just a minute." Miranda lifted both hands. "Good? Is that what you said? Good? You're telling me you know your son's a thief?"

"What, am I a moron?" Maureen neatly wiped her hands before fisting them on her hips. "Of course I know."

"I told you she knew," Ryan pointed out.

"Yes, but—" She simply hadn't believed it. Baffled, she shifted, studied Maureen's pretty face. "And that's just dandy with you? That's just fine? And you—" She pointed at Colleen. "You're a police officer. Your brother steals. How do you resolve the two?"

"He's retiring." Colleen lifted her shoulders. "A little behind schedule."

"I don't understand." She pressed her lifted hands to her head. "You're his mother. How can you encourage him to break the law?"

"Encourage?" Maureen gave that rich laugh again. "Who had to encourage him?" Deciding to give her guest the courtesy of an explanation, she set down her dishcloth. "Do you believe in God?"

"What? What does that have to do with this?"

"Don't argue, just answer. Do you believe in God?"

Beside Miranda, Ryan grinned. She couldn't know it, but when his mother used that tone it meant she'd decided she liked you.

"All right, yes."

"When God gives you a gift, it's a sin not to use it."

Miranda closed her eyes a moment. "You're saying that God gave Ryan a talent, and that it would be a sin for him not to break into buildings and steal?"

"God could've given him a gift for music, like He did my Mary Jo, who plays the piano like an angel. God gave him this gift instead."

"Mrs. Boldari—"

"Don't argue," Ryan murmured. "You'll just give yourself a headache."

She scowled at him. "Mrs. Boldari," she tried again, "I appreciate your loyalty to your son, but—"

"Do you know what he does with this gift?"

"Yes, as a matter of fact."

"He buys this house for his family because the old neighborhood isn't safe anymore." She opened her arms to encompass the lovely kitchen, then wagged a finger. "He sees that his brothers and sisters get a college education. None of this would be. However hard Giorgio and I worked, you can't send six kids to college on teachers' salaries. God gave him a gift," she said again, and rested her hand on Ryan's shoulder. "You going to argue with God?"

Ryan was right again. She did have a headache. She nursed it with silence during the drive to Manhattan. She wasn't sure which baffled her more just then, the stand Maureen had taken to defend her son's choice of career, or the warm hugs she'd been given by each family member before they left.

Ryan let her have her quiet. When he pulled up in front of his building, he gave the keys to the doorman. "Hi, Jack. Arrange to have this rental returned to the airport, would you, and send Dr. Jones's bags—they're in the trunk—up to my apartment."

"Sure thing, Mr. Boldari. Welcome home." The twenty that slipped discreetly from palm to palm had Jack's smile widening. "Have a nice evening."

"I don't understand your life," Miranda began as he escorted her through an elegant lobby decked out with glossy antiques and attractive art.

"That's all right. I don't understand yours either." He stepped into an elevator and used a key to access the top floor. "You must be worn out. Jack'll have your things up in a minute. You can get comfortable."

"Your mother wanted to know why I wasn't having sex with you."

"I wonder the same thing all the time." The elevator opened into a spacious living area done in bold blues and greens. Wide terrace windows offered a pricey view of New York.

He'd obviously indulged himself in his affection for the finer things, she decided with a quick scan. Art Deco lamps, Chippendale tables, Baccarat crystal.

She wondered how much of it he'd stolen.

"All purchased legitimately," he said, reading her perfectly. "Well, that Erté lamp was hot, but I couldn't resist it. Want a nightcap?"

"No, no I don't."

The floor was glossy honey-toned wood accented with one of the most beautiful Orientals she'd ever seen. Art on the walls ranged from a misty Corot to a soft, lovely watercolor of what she recognized as the Irish countryside.

"Your mother's work."

"Yes, she's good, isn't she?"

"Very. Confusing, but very good."

"She likes you."

With a sigh, Miranda wandered to the window. "I like her too, for some reason."

Her own mother had never hugged her that way, with a good, solid squeeze that communicated approval and affection. Her own father had never grinned at her with that lively twinkle in his eyes, as Ryan's father had.

She wondered how, despite it all, his family had seemed so much more blissfully normal than her own.

"That'll be your bags." When the buzzer sounded, Ryan moved over to check the intercom, then released the elevator. The delivery was made quickly, with another exchange of bills. When the elevator whispered closed again, Ryan left her bags where they were and crossed to her.

"You're tense," he murmured after he began kneading her shoulders. "I'd hoped an evening with my family would relax you."

"How does anyone relax with all that energy around them?" She arched back against his hands before she could stop herself. "You must have had an interesting childhood."

"I had a terrific childhood." Far from the privileged one she'd known, and from all appearances, a great deal more loving. "Long day," he murmured, and because he knew she was beginning to relax, bent down to nibble at her neck.

"Yes, very. Don't."

"I was about to work my way around . . . here." He turned her, covered her mouth with his and stole her breath.

His mother had said kisses should get the blood up. Hers was up, bubbling close under her skin, swimming in her head, pumping much too hard and fast through her veins.

"Don't," she said again, but it was a weak protest, easily ignored by both of them.

He could feel the need simmering inside her. It didn't matter that it wasn't for him in particular. He wouldn't let it matter. He wanted her, wanted to be the one to crack through the shield and discover the volcano he was sure was inside of her.

Something about her pulled at him with a slow and steady strength that refused to be ignored.

"Let me touch you." Even as he asked, he took, his hands running up her sides to skim her breasts. "Let me have you."

Oh, yes. The sigh of it circled around in her cloudy brain as if searching for a place to land. *Touch me. Have me. God, please don't let me think.*

"No." It was a shock to hear herself say it. To realize she was pulling away even as she yearned to strain closer. "This won't work."

"It was working just fine for me." He hooked his hand in the waistband of her trousers and gave her a yank. "And I'd say it was working just fine for you too."

"I won't be seduced, Ryan." She concentrated on the annoyed flash in his eyes and ignored the screams of her own system for the release his mouth had promised. "I won't be had. If we're going to finish this arrangement successfully, it has to be on a business level. And only that level."

"I don't like that level."

"That's the deal, and it's nonnegotiable."

"Your tongue ever get frostbite when you use that tone?" He jammed his hands in his pocket as she studied him balefully. "Okay, Dr. Jones, it's all business. I'll show you your room."

He walked back to pick up her suitcases and carried them up a fluid curve of metal stairs with a soft green patina. Then, setting her bags down just inside the door, he nodded. "You should find this comfortable enough, and private. We're booked out tomorrow evening. That'll give me time to tie up a few loose ends here. Sleep well," he added, and shut the door in her face before she had the chance to shut it in his.

She started to shrug, then her eyes widened when she heard the click of a lock. In one leap she was at the door rattling the knob.

"You son of a bitch. You can't lock me in here."

"An ounce of prevention, Dr. Jones." His voice was soft as silk through the door. "Just to make sure you stay where I put you until tomorrow."

He walked away whistling while she pounded and promised vengeance.

CHAPTER FIFTEEN

THOUGH SHE KNEW IT WAS A USELESS GESTURE, Miranda locked the door to the bathroom in the morning. She showered quickly, struggling to keep one eye on the door in case Ryan decided he wanted to play games.

She wouldn't have put it past him.

Once she was safely bundled into her robe, she took her time. She wanted to be completely dressed, with a confident shield of makeup and tidily groomed hair, before she saw him. There would be, she determined, no cozy little breakfast chat in pajamas.

Of course, he had to let her out first. The bastard.

"Let me out of here, Boldari," she called as she rapped smartly on the door.

Her answer was silence. Incensed, she knocked harder, shouted louder, and began to add inventive threats.

Kidnapping, she decided; she'd add kidnapping to the list of charges against him. She hoped the other inmates at whatever federal facility he spent the rest of his life in rejoiced in torturing him.

Frustrated, she started to rattle the knob. It turned smoothly under her hand and caused her angry flush to deepen into embarrassment.

She stepped out, glanced cautiously down the hallway. Doors were open, so she walked to the first one, determined to confront him.

She found herself in a library with floor-to-ceiling shelves stocked with books, cozy leather chairs, a small marble fireplace with an ornate pendulum clock gracing the mantel. A hexagon-shaped glass cabinet held an impressive collection of Oriental snuff bottles. She sniffed once. He might be slick on taste and culture, but he was still a thief.

She tried the next doorway and found his bedroom. The big half-tester with rococo head and foot boards was impressive enough, but the fact that it was tidily made, with the pearl-gray duvet cover nicely fluffed, had her brow lifting. Either he hadn't slept in it, or his mother had trained him very well.

After meeting Maureen, she voted for the latter.

A very masculine room, she decided, yet subtly sensual with jade-green walls and creamy trim. Sinuous women in the Art Deco style he seemed fond of held frosted-glass shades that would soften the light. An oversized chair in that same moonlight gray was tilted invitingly toward a full-sized fireplace fashioned of rose-veined marble. Ornamental lemon trees in huge urns flanked the wide window where the curtain had been drawn open to let in the sunlight and the view.

The chest of drawers was Duncan Phyfe, and along with the bronze of the Persian god Mithras was a scatter of loose change, a ticket stub, a book of matches, and other ordinary contents of a man's pocket.

She was tempted to poke into his closet, open drawers, but resisted. It wouldn't do for him to pop in while she was at it and get the impression she was at all interested.

There was a third room, obviously an office of a man who could afford the best for his at-home work. Two computers, both with laser printers, the expected fax and desktop copier, a two-line phone, oak filing cabinets. Sturdy oak shelves held books and trinkets and dozens of framed photographs of his family.

The young children would be his nieces and nephews, she thought. Pretty faces mugging for the camera. The serene Madonna-like woman holding an infant was likely his sister Bridgit, the sleekly handsome man with the Boldari eyes would be Michael, and the woman his arm was draped around his wife. They lived in California, she remembered.

There was a shot of Ryan with Colleen, grinning identical grins, and a group picture of the entire family obviously taken near Christmas. The lights from the tree were prettily blurred behind the crowd of faces.

They looked happy, she thought. Unified, and

not at all stiff the way people often appeared in posed photos. She found herself lingering over them, studying another of Ryan kissing the hand of his sister, who wore a princess-in-a-fairy-tale wedding gown, and the glow that matched it.

Envy moved through her before she could stop it. There were no sentimental photographs arranged in her home to capture family moments.

She wished, foolishly, that she could slide into one of those photographs, snuggle under one of those casually welcoming arms and feel what they felt.

Feel love.

She shook the thought off, turned determinedly away from the shelves. It wasn't the time to speculate on why the Boldari family was so warm, and her own so cold. She needed to find Ryan and give him a piece of her mind while her annoyance was still fresh.

She headed downstairs, biting her tongue to keep from calling his name. She didn't want to give him the satisfaction. He wasn't in the living room, nor in the somewhat hedonistic den with its big screen TV, complicated stereo, and full-sized pinball machine—appropriately titled "Cops and Robbers."

She imagined he thought that ironic.

Nor was he in the kitchen. But there was a halfpot of coffee left on warm.

He wasn't in the apartment at all.

She snatched up the phone with some wild idea of calling Andrew and telling him everything. There was no dial tone. Cursing viciously, she dashed back out into the living room and jabbed the button on the elevator. It didn't make a sound. Snarling, she turned to the door, found it locked.

Eyes narrowed, she flicked on the intercom and heard nothing but static.

The son of a bitch had unlocked the bedroom, but he'd simply expanded the perimeters of her cage.

It was after one before she heard the quiet hum of the elevator. She hadn't whiled away the morning. She'd taken the opportunity to go over every inch of his living quarters. She'd pawed through his closet without guilt. He definitely leaned toward Italian designers. She'd riffled through his drawers. He preferred sexy silk boxers, and shirts and sweaters of natural fibers.

The desks—bedroom, library, and office—had all been annoyingly locked. She'd wasted quite a bit of time attacking the locks with hairpins. The passwords on his computers had blocked her, the stone terrace off the living room had charmed her, and the caffeine she'd continued to drink as she pried had her system jumping.

She was more than ready for him when he walked through the elevator door.

"How dare you lock me in this way. I'm not a prisoner."

"Just a precaution." He set aside the briefcase and shopping bags he carried.

"What's next? Handcuffs?"

"Not until we know each other better. How was your day?"

"I—"

"Hate, loathe, and despise me," he finished as he took off his coat. "Yes, we've covered that." He hung it up neatly. She'd been right, his mother had trained him well. "I had a few errands I had to run. I hope you made yourself at home while I was out."

"I'm leaving. I must have been temporarily insane when I thought we could work together."

He waited until she was at the base of the stairs. "*The Dark Lady* is being held in a storeroom at the Bargello until it can be decided where she came from, and who cast her."

She stopped, as he'd known she would, and turned slowly back. "How do you know?"

"It's my business to know. Now, with or without you, I'm going to Italy and liberating her. I can, with little trouble, find another archeometrist, and will eventually figure out just what happened and why. You walk out, you're all the way out."

"You'll never get it out of the Bargello."

"Oh yes." His smile was quick and wolfish. "I will. You can have a pass at her once I do, or you can run along back to Maine and wait for your parents to decide you're not grounded anymore."

She let the last comment pass. She supposed it was close enough to the truth. "How will you get it out?"

"That's my problem."

"If I'm going to agree with this moronic plan, I have to have details."

"I'll fill you in on what you need to know as we go along. That's the deal. In or out, Dr. Jones. Time's wasting."

It was here, she realized, where she crossed the line, passed the point of no return. He was watching her, waiting, with just enough arrogance in his eyes to scrape at her pride.

"If you manage to perform a miracle and actually get inside the Bargello, you take nothing but the bronze. It isn't a shopping spree."

"Agreed."

"If we do end up in possession of the bronze, I'm in full charge of it."

"You're the scientist," he added with a smile. She was welcome to the copy, he thought. He wanted the original. "That's the deal," he repeated. "In or out?"

"In." Her breath exploded out. "God help me."

"Good. Now." He opened the briefcase, tossed items onto the table. "These are for you."

She picked up the dark blue book. "This isn't my passport."

"It is now."

"This isn't my name—how did you get this picture?" She stared down at the image of herself. "This is the photo in my passport."

"Exactly."

"No, *my* passport. And my driver's license," she continued, snatching it up. "You stole my wallet."

"Borrowed certain items in your wallet," he corrected.

She vibrated. There was no other word for it.

"You came in my room while I was sleeping and took my things."

"You were restless," he remembered. "Lots of tossing and turning. Maybe you should try meditation to release some of that tension."

"That's despicable."

"No, it was necessary. It would have been despicable if I'd climbed into bed with you. Fun, but despicable."

She drew air in through her nose, looked down it. "What have you done with my proper identification?"

"It's safe. You won't need it until we get back. Just playing it on the side of caution, darling. If the cops are snooping around, better that they don't know you've left the country."

She tossed the passport down again. "I'm not Abigail O'Connell."

"Mrs. Abigail O'Connell—we're on our second honeymoon. And I think I'll call you Abby. It's friendly."

"I'm not pretending I'm married to you. I'd rather be married to a sociopath."

She was green, after all, he reminded himself. A little patience was in order. "Miranda, we're traveling together. We'll share a hotel suite. A married couple isn't going to raise eyebrows or cause questions to be asked. All this does is keep things simple. For the next several days, I'm Kevin O'Connell, your devoted spouse. I'm a stockbroker, you're in advertising. We've been married for five years, live on the Upper West Side, and we're considering starting a family."

"So now we're Yuppies."

"No one uses that term anymore, but basically yes. I got you a couple of credit cards there."

She glanced down at the table. "How did you get this identification?"

"Contacts," he said easily.

She imagined him in a dark, smelly room with an enormous man with a snake tattoo and bad breath who sold forged IDs and assault weapons.

It was nowhere close to the split-level townhouse in New Rochelle where Ryan's accountant cousin—second, once removed—created documents in his basement.

"It's illegal to enter a foreign country with false identification."

He stared at her for ten full seconds, then roared with laughter. "You're wonderful. Seriously. Now, I need a detailed description of the bronze. I need to be able to recognize her quickly."

She studied him, wondering how anyone could keep up with a man who flipped from hilarity to brisk business in the blink of an eye. "Ninety point four centimeters in height, twenty-four point sixty-eight kilograms in weight, a nude female with the blue-green patina typical of a bronze more than five hundred years old."

As she spoke, the image of it flashed brilliantly in her head. "She's standing on the balls of her feet, her arms lifted—it would be easier if I just sketched it for you."

"Great." He walked over to a cabinet, took a pad and pencil from a drawer. "As precise as you can. I hate to make mistakes."

She sat, and with a speed and skill that had his brows lifted, put the image in her mind on paper. The face, that sly and sensuous smile, the seeking, spread fingers lifted high, the fluid arch of the body.

"Gorgeous. Absolutely gorgeous," he murmured, struck by the power of the image as he leaned over Miranda's shoulder. "You're good. Do you paint?"

"No."

"Why not?"

"Because I don't." She had to struggle not to jerk her shoulder. His cheek nearly rested against her as she sketched in the last details.

"You have real talent. Why waste it?"

"I don't. A skilled sketch can be very helpful in my work."

"A gift for art should give you pleasure in your life." He took the sketch, studied it another moment. "You've got a gift."

She set her pencil down and rose. "The drawing's accurate. If you're lucky enough to stumble across it, you'll recognize the bronze."

"Luck has very little to do with it." Idly, he flicked a fingertip down her cheek. "You look a bit like her—the shape of the face, the strong bone structure. It would be interesting to see you with that cagey, self-aware smile on your face. You don't smile very often, Miranda."

"I haven't had much to smile about lately."

"I think we can change that. The car will be here

in about an hour—Abby. Take some time and get used to your new name. And if you don't think you can remember to call me Kevin . . ." He winked at her. "Just call me sweetheart."

"I will not."

"Oh, one last thing." He pulled a small jeweler's box out of his pocket. When he flipped the lid the flash of diamonds made her blink. "By the power invested in me, and so forth," he said, plucking it out of the box and taking her hand.

"No."

"Don't be such an idiot. It's window dressing."

It wasn't possible not to look down and be dazzled when he shoved it on her finger. The wedding band was studded with brilliant square-cut diamonds, four in all, that sparkled like ice. "Some window. I suppose it's stolen."

"You wound me. I've got a friend who runs a place in the diamond district. I got it wholesale. I need to pack."

She worried the ring on her finger while he started up the stairs. It was absurd, but she wished the ring hadn't fit quite so perfectly. "Ryan? Can you really do this?"

He sent her a wink over his shoulder. "Watch me."

He knew immediately she'd been into his things. She'd been neat, but not quite neat enough. In any case, she wouldn't have seen the small telltales he left scattered through his room—the single strand of hair placed over the knobs of his double closet doors, the slim bit of invisible tape over the top of his dresser drawer. It was an old habit, and one he'd never broken even with the high security in his building.

He only shook his head. She wouldn't have found anything he hadn't wanted her to find.

He opened his closet, pressed a mechanism hidden under a portion of the chair rail, and stepped into his private room. Selecting what he needed didn't take much time. He'd already thought it through. He would need his picks, the pocket electronics of his trade. The coil of thin, flexible rope, surgical gloves.

Spirit gum, hair color, a couple of scars, two pairs of glasses. He doubted the job would call for disguises, and if it went correctly, it wouldn't call for anything but the most basic of tools. Still, he preferred to be prepared for anything.

These he packed carefully in the false bottom of his suitcase. He added the expected choices a man on a romantic vacation to Italy would take, filling the case and a garment bag.

In his office he outfitted his own laptop, chose the disks he wanted. He clicked off his mental list as he packed, adding a few items he'd picked up at Spy 2000 downtown and had beefed up himself.

Satisfied, he locked his current identification in the safe behind the complete volumes of Edgar Allan Poe—the father of the locked-door mystery—and on impulse took out the plain gold band he kept there.

It had been his grandfather's wedding ring. His mother had given it to him at the wake two years ago. Though he'd had occasion to wear a wedding ring as cover before, he'd never used this one.

Without questioning why he wanted to this time, he slipped it on, locked up, and went back for his suitcases.

The intercom buzzed, announcing the car, as he carried them downstairs. Miranda had already brought her things down. Her suitcases, laptop, and briefcase were stacked neatly. Ryan lifted his brows.

"I like a woman who knows how to be ready on time. All set?"

She drew a deep breath. This, she thought, was it. "Let's get going. I hate to rush at the airport."

He smiled at her. "That's my girl," he said, and bent down to pick up one of her cases.

"I can carry my own things." She pushed his hand away and picked it up herself. "And I'm not your girl."

With a shrug he stepped back, waiting until she'd managed to sling straps over her shoulders, heft the cases. "After you, Dr. Jones."

It shouldn't have surprised her that he'd managed to book two first-class seats on ridiculously short notice. Because she jolted every time the flight attendant addressed her as Mrs. O'Connell, Miranda buried herself in the pages of Kafka immediately after takeoff.

Ryan passed some time with the latest Lawrence Block burglar novel. Then sipped champagne and watched Arnold Schwarzenegger kick big-time ass on his video screen. Miranda drank mineral water and tried to concentrate on a nature documentary.

Midway over the Atlantic, the restless night caught up with her. Doing her best to ignore her seat companion, she took her seat back down, stretched out, and ordered her brain to sleep.

She dreamed of Maine, of the cliffs with the sea thrashing below, and a thick gray fog that smothered shapes. The light flicked in a blurry swath, and she used it to guide her toward the lighthouse.

She was alone, so completely alone.

And she was afraid, terribly afraid.

Stumbling, groping, fighting not to let her breath sob out no matter how it burned her lungs. A woman's laughter, soft and menacing, taunted her so that she ran.

And running, found herself on the edge of the cliff over a boiling sea.

When a hand gripped hers, she held on tight. *Don't leave me alone*.

Beside her, Ryan looked down at their joined hands. Hers were white knuckled even in sleep. What chased her there, he wondered, and what kept her from reaching out?

He soothed her fingers with his thumb until they relaxed. But he kept her hand in his, finding it curiously comforting as he closed his own eyes and slept.

CHAPTER SIXTEEN

"THERE'S ONLY ONE BEDROOM." MIRANDA SAW nothing of the lovely suite but the single bedroom with its gracious king-sized bed and elegant white coverlet.

In the parlor, Ryan opened the double doors and stepped out on an enormous terrace where the air was ripe with spring and the Italian sun shone cheerfully on the soft red rooftops.

"Check this view. This terrace is one of the reasons I wanted to book this room again. You could live out here."

"Good." She pushed open the doors from the bedroom and stepped out. "Why don't you plan to do just that?" She would not be charmed by the throat-aching view of the city, nor the cheerful geraniums that lined the boxes just under the stone parapet. Nor the man who leaned over them, looking as though he'd been born to stand in precisely that spot.

"There's only one bedroom," she repeated.

"We're married. Which reminds me, how about getting me a beer?"

"I'm sure there's a certain kind of woman who finds you irresistibly amusing, Boldari. I don't happen to be that certain kind." She stepped up to the rail. "There is only one bed in the only one bedroom."

"If you're shy, we can take turns on the parlor sofa. You first." He draped an arm over her shoulders and added a friendly squeeze. "Relax, Miranda. Getting you in the sack would be fun, but it's not my first priority. A view like this makes up for a long plane flight, doesn't it?"

"The view isn't my first priority."

"It's here, might as well appreciate it. There's a young couple who lives in that flat, there." He steered her over a bit and pointed to a top-floor window on a soft yellow building just to the left. "They'd work on the rooftop garden on Saturday mornings together. And one night they came out and made love there."

"You watched them?"

"Only until the intent was unmistakable. I'm not a pervert."

"The jury's still out on that one. You've been here before, then."

"Kevin O'Connell stayed here for a few days last year. Which is why we're using him again. In a well-run hotel like this, the staff tends to remember guests—more so if they tip well, and Kevin's a generous soul."

"Why were you here as Kevin O'Connell?"

"A little matter of a reliquary with a bone fragment of Giovanni Battista."

"You stole a relic? A *relic*? John the Baptist's bone?"

"A fragment thereof. Hell, pieces of him are scattered all over Italy—especially here, where he's patron saint." He couldn't help himself, he got a huge kick out of her staggered shock. "Very popular guy, old Johnny. Nobody's going to miss a splinter or two of bone."

"I don't have words," Miranda murmured.

"My client had cancer—convinced himself that the relic would cure him. Of course, he's dead, but he lived nine months longer than the doctors gave him. So who's to say? Let's get unpacked." He patted her arm. "I want a shower, then we'll get to work."

"Work?"

"I've got some shopping to do."

"I'm not spending the day looking for Ferragamos for your sister."

"That won't take long, and I'll need trinkets for the rest of the family."

"Look, Boldari, I think we have a higher priority than gathering souvenirs for your family."

He infuriated her by leaning over and kissing the tip of her nose. "Don't worry, darling. I'll buy you something too. Wear comfortable shoes," he advised her, and strolled back inside to shower.

* * *

He bought a fluid gold bracelet set with emerald cabochons in a shop on the Ponte Vecchio—his mother's birthday was coming up—and had it sent back to the hotel. Obviously enjoying the press of tourists and bargain hunters who swarmed the bridge over the placid Arno, he added gold chains in shimmering Italian gold, marcasite earrings, and Florentine-style brooches. For his sisters, he told Miranda as she waited impatiently and refused to be charmed by the tumbling glitter in display windows.

"Stand here long enough," he commented, "you can hear every language in the world."

"Have we stood here long enough?"

He slipped an arm around her shoulders, shaking his head as she stiffened. "Don't you ever let yourself fall into the moment, Dr. Jones? It's Florence, we're standing on the oldest of the city's bridges. The sun's shining. Take a breath," he suggested, "and drink it in."

She nearly did, nearly leaned into him and did just that. "We didn't come here for the atmosphere," she said, in what she hoped was a tone cool enough to dampen his enthusiasm and her own uncharacteristic urges.

"The atmosphere's still here. And so are we." Undaunted, he took her hand and pulled her along the bridge.

The little shops and stands appeared to delight him, Miranda noted, watching him bargain for leather bags and trinket boxes near the Piazza della Repubblica.

She ignored his suggestion that she treat herself to something, and giving her attention to the architecture, waited for him in simmering silence.

"Now, this is Robbie." He took a tot-sized black leather jacket with silver trim from a rack.

"Robbie?"

"My nephew. He's three. He'd get a big kick out of this."

It was beautifully made, undoubtedly expensive, and adorable enough to have her pressing her lips together to keep them from curving. "It's completely impractical for a three-year-old."

"It was made for a three-year-old," he corrected. "That's why it's little. *"Quanto?"* he asked the hovering merchant, and the game was on.

When he'd finished the round, he headed west. But if hc'd hoped to tempt her with the flawless fashions of the Via dei Tornabuoni, he underestimated her willpower.

He bought three pairs of shoes in Ferragamo's cathedral to footwear. She bought nothing—including a gorgeous pair of pearl-gray leather pumps that had caught her eye and stirred her desire.

The credit cards in her wallet, she reminded herself, weren't stamped with her name. She'd go barefoot before she used one.

"Most women," he observed as he walked toward the river, "would have a dozen bags and boxes by now."

"I'm not most women."

"So I've noticed. You'd look damn good in leather, though."

"In your pathetic fantasies, Boldari."

"There's nothing pathetic about my fantasies." He stepped to a storefront and opened a glass door.

"What now?"

"Can't come to Florence without buying some art."

"We didn't come here to buy anything. This is supposed to be business."

"Relax." He took her hand, bringing it up in a sweep to his lips. "Trust me."

"Those are two phrases that will never go together when applied to you."

The shop was crowded with marble and bronze reproductions. Gods and goddesses danced to lure tourists into plunking down their gold cards and purchasing a copy of a master's work or an offering by a new artist.

Patience straining, Miranda prepared to waste another precious hour while Ryan fulfilled his family obligations. But he surprised her by nodding toward a slender statue of Venus within five minutes.

"What do you think of her?"

Soberly, she stepped up, circled the polished bronze figure. "It's adequate, not particularly good, but if one of your legion of relatives is looking for some lawn art, it would do well enough."

"Yeah, I think she'll do well enough." He aimed a delighted smile toward the clerk, then made Miranda's brows draw together as he fumbled with guidebook Italian.

Throughout the shopping spree, he'd spoken the language fluidly, often peppering his speech with casual colloquialisms. Now he slaughtered the most basic of phrases with a miserable accent that had the clerk beaming at him.

"You're American. We can speak English."

"Yeah? Thank God." He laughed and tugged Miranda by the hand to bring her closer. "My wife and I want something special to take home. We really like this piece. It'll look great in the sunroom, won't it, Abby?"

Her answer was a "hmmm."

He didn't bargain well this time, either, just winced over the price, then pulled her away as if to hold a private consult.

"What's this all about?" She found herself whispering because his head was bent close to hers.

"I wouldn't want to buy it without being sure my wife approved."

"You're a jackass."

"That's what I get for being a considerate husband." He lowered his head, kissed her firmly on the mouth—and only by instinct avoided her teeth. "Promise me you'll try that again later."

Before she could retaliate, he turned back to the clerk. "We'll take her."

When the deal was made, the statue wrapped and boxed, he refused the offer to send it to their hotel.

"That's okay. We're about to head back anyway." He hefted the bag, then put an arm around Miranda, bumping her with one of the two cameras slung over his shoulders. "Let's get some of that ice cream on the way, Abby."

"I don't need any ice cream," she muttered when they stepped outside again.

"Sure you do. Gotta keep your energy up. We've got one more stop to make."

"Look, I'm tired, my feet hurt, and I don't care for shopping. I'll just meet you back at the hotel."

"And miss all the fun? We're going to the Bargello."

"Now?" What chased up her spine was a combination of dread and excitement. "We're going to do it now?"

"Now we're going to play tourist some more." He stepped off the curb, giving her room on the narrow sidewalk. "We'll check the place out, get a feel for things, take some pictures." He winked. "Case the joint, as they say in the movies."

"Case the joint," she murmured.

"Where are the security cameras? How far from the main entrance is Michelangelo's *Bacchus*?" Though he knew, precisely. It wouldn't be his first trip, under any guise. "How far is it across the courtyard? How many steps to the first-floor loggia? When do the guards change shift? How many—"

"All right, all right, I get the point." She threw up her hands. "I don't know why we didn't go there in the first place."

"Everything in its time, honey. Abby and Kevin

would want to see some of the city on their first day, wouldn't they?"

She imagined they looked exactly like American tourists—cameras, shopping bags, and guidebooks. He bought her an ice cream cone as they walked. Because she decided it might help cool the hot ball of tension in her stomach, she licked at the tart, frothy lemon ice as he strolled along, pointing out buildings, statues, loitering at shop windows or over menus posted outside trattorias.

Perhaps there was a point to it all, she decided. No one would look twice at them, and if she concentrated, she could almost believe she was meandering through the city for the first time. It was a bit like being in a play, she thought. *Abby and Kevin's Italian Vacation*.

If only she weren't such a lousy actress.

"Fabulous, isn't it?" He paused, his fingers twining with hers as he studied the magnificent cathedral that dominated the city.

"Yes. Brunelleschi's dome was a revolutionary achievement. He didn't use scaffolding. Giotto designed the campanile, but didn't live to see it completed." She adjusted her sunglasses. "The neo-Gothic marble facade echoes his style, but was added in the nineteenth century."

She brushed at her hair and saw him smiling at her. "What?"

"You have a nice way with a history lesson, Dr. Jones." When her face went carefully blank, he framed it with his hands. "No, don't. That wasn't a dig, it was a compliment." His fingers brushed her cheekbones lightly. So many sensitive spots, he mused. "Tell me something else."

If he was laughing at her, he was doing a good job of disguising it. So she took a chance. "Michelangelo carved his *David* in the courtyard of the Museo dell'Opera del Duomo."

"Really?"

He said it so seriously her lips twitched. "Yes. He also copied Donatello's *Saint John* for his own *Moses*. It would have been a compliment. But the pride of the museum, I think, is his *Pietà*. The figure of Nicodemus is believed to be a self-portrait and is brilliantly done. But the figure of Mary Magdalene in the same sculpture is inferior, and obviously the work of one of his students. Don't kiss me, Ryan," she said it quickly, closing her eyes as his mouth hovered a breath from hers. "It complicates things."

"Do they have to be simple?"

"Yes." She opened her eyes again, looked into his. "In this case, yes."

"Normally I'd agree with you." Thoughtfully, he skimmed the pad of his thumb over her lips. "We're attracted to each other, and that should be simple. But it doesn't seem to be." He dropped his hands from her face to her shoulders, skimmed them down her arms to her wrists. Her pulse was rapid and thick, and should have pleased him.

But he stepped back. "Okay, let's keep it as simple as possible. Go stand over there."

"Why?"

"So I can take your picture, honey." He tipped

his sunglasses down and winked at her. "We want to show all our friends back home, don't we, Abby?"

Though she considered it overkill, she posed in front of the grand Duomo with hundreds of other visitors and let him snap pictures of her with the magnificent white, green, and rose marble at her back.

"Now you take one of me." He walked over holding out his snazzy Nikon. "It's basically point and shoot. You just—"

"I know how to work a camera." She snatched it from him. "Kevin."

She moved back, blocked and focused. Maybe her heart tripped a little. He was such a staggering sight, tall and dark and grinning cockily at the camera.

"There. Satisfied now?"

"Almost." He snagged a couple of tourists who happily agreed to take a picture of the young Americans.

"This is ridiculous," Miranda muttered as she found herself posing once again, this time with Ryan's arm around her waist.

"It's for my mother," he said, then followed impulse and kissed her.

A flock of pigeons swarmed up with a rush of wings and a flutter of air. She had no time to resist, less to defend. His mouth was warm, firm, sliding over hers as the arm around her waist angled her closer. The quiet sound she made had nothing to do with protest. The hand she lifted to his face had everything to do with holding him there.

The sun was white, the air full of sound. And her heart trembled on the edge of something extraordinary.

It was either pull away or sink, Ryan thought. He turned his lips into the palm of her hand. "Sorry," he said, and didn't smile—couldn't quite pull it off. "I guess I fell into the moment."

And leaving her there with her knees trembling, he retrieved his camera.

He strapped it back on, picked up the shopping bag, then with his eyes on hers, held out a hand. "Let's go."

She'd almost forgotten the purpose, almost forgotten the plan. With a nod, she fell into step with him.

When they reached the gates of the old palace, he tugged the guidebook out of his back pocket, like a good tourist.

"It was built in 1255," he told her. "From the sixteenth to the mid-nineteenth century it was a prison. Executions were carried out in the courtyard."

"Apt under the circumstances," she muttered. "And I know the history."

"Dr. Jones knows the history." He gave her butt an affectionate pat. "Abby, honey."

The minute they were inside the principal ground-floor room, he dug out his video camera. "Great place, isn't it, Abby? Look at this guy—he's knocked back a few, huh?"

He aimed the camera at the glorious bronze of the drunken *Bacchus,* then began to slowly pan the room. "Wait until Jack and Sally see these. They'll be green."

He swung the camera toward a doorway where a guard sat keeping an eye on the visitors. "Wander around," he told her under his breath. "Look awed and middle-class."

Her palms were sweating. It was ridiculous, of course. They had a perfect right to be here. No one could possibly know what was going on inside her head. But her heart pounded painfully in her throat as she circled the room.

"Wonderfully awful, isn't it?"

She jolted a little when he came up beside her as she pretended to study Bandinelli's *Adam and Eve*. "It's an important piece of the era."

"Only because it's old. It looks like a couple of suburbanites who hang out at a nudist colony every other weekend. Let's go see Giambologna's birds in the loggia."

After an hour, Miranda began to suspect that a great deal of criminal activity involved the tedious. They went into every public room, capturing every inch and angle on camera. Still, she'd forgotten that the Sala dei Bronzetti held Italy's finest collection of small Renaissance bronzes. Because it made her think of the *David,* her nerves began to twitch again.

"Haven't you got enough yet?"

"Nearly. Go flirt with the guard over there."

"I beg your pardon."

"Get his attention." Ryan lowered the camera and briskly undid the top two buttons on Miranda's crisp cotton blouse.

"What do you think you're doing?"

"Making sure his attention's focused on you, *cara.* Ask him some questions, use bad guidebook Italian, bat your eyes and make him feel important."

"What are you going to do?"

"Nothing if you can't hold his eye for five minutes. Give me that long, ask him where the bathroom is, then head there. Meet me back in the courtyard in ten."

"But—"

"Do it." He snapped it out, with a flick of steel. "There's just enough people in here that I should be able to pull this off."

"Oh God. All right." Her stomach tilted down toward her shaky knees as she turned away to approach the guard.

"Ah . . . *scusi,*" she began, giving the word a hard American accent. "*Per favore* . . ." She watched the guard's eyes dip to the opening of her blouse, then skim back up to her face with a smile. She swallowed hard, then spread her hands helplessly. "English?"

"*Sì, signora,* a little."

"Oh, wonderful." She experimented with fluttering her lashes and saw by the warming of the guard's smile that such pitiful ploys actually worked. "I studied up on Italian before I left, but it just gets all jumbled up in my mind. Such a scatterbrain. It's terrible, isn't it, that Americans don't speak a second language the way most Europeans do?"

The way his eyes were glazing, she deduced she was speaking much too quickly for him to follow. All the better. "Everything's so beautiful here. I wonder if you could tell me anything about . . ." She chose a sculpture at random.

Ryan waited until he saw the guard's focus fix on Miranda's cleavage, then slipping back, he took a thin pick out of his pocket and went to work on a side door.

It was easy enough, even dealing with it behind his back. The museum hardly expected its visitors to come armed with lockpicks or to want entrance to locked rooms in broad daylight.

The floor plan of the museum was on a disk in his files. As were dozens of others. If his source was to be trusted, Ryan would find what he wanted beyond the door, in one of the jumbled storerooms on this level.

He kept one eye on the security camera, biding his time until a group of art lovers shuffled in front of him.

Before they'd gone by, he was through the door and closing it softly behind him.

He took one long breath of appreciation, tugged on the gloves he'd tucked in his pocket, then flexed his fingers. He couldn't take much time.

It was a rabbit warren of little rooms crowded with statues and paintings, most of which were in desperate need of restoration. Generally, he knew, those who made their living through or around art weren't the most organized of souls.

Several pieces caught his eye, including a sad-eyed Madonna with a broken shoulder. But he was looking for another type of lady altogether—

The sound of tuneless whistling and clicking foot-steps sent him searching quickly for cover.

She waited the ten minutes, then fifteen. By twenty she was wringing her hands on the bench where she sat in the courtyard and imagining what it would be like to spend some time in an Italian prison.

Maybe the food would be good.

At least they didn't kill thieves these days, and hang their corpses from the Bargello's windows as a testament to rough justice.

Once again she checked her watch, rubbed her fingers over her mouth. He'd been caught, she was sure of it. Right now he was being interrogated in-side some hot little room, and he'd give up her name without a qualm. The coward.

Then she saw him, strolling across the courtyard like a man without a care in the world and no shadow of larceny in his heart. Her relief was so great that she sprang up, threw her arms around him.

"Where have you been? I thought you'd been—"

He kissed her as much to stop her babbling as to take advantage of the situation. "Let's go get a drink. We'll talk about it," he said against her mouth.

"How could you just leave me out here like this? You said ten minutes—it's been nearly half an hour."

"It took me a little longer." They were still mouth to mouth, and he grinned at her. "Miss me?"

"No. I was wondering what was on the menu in jail tonight."

"Have a little faith." He clasped hands, swinging arms with her as they walked. "Some wine and cheese would be nice right now. The Piazza della Signoria isn't as picturesque as others, but it's close."

"Where did you go?" she demanded. "I fiddled around with the guard as long as I could, and when I looked around, you were gone."

"I wanted to see what was behind door number three. That place might have been a palace once, and a cop shop later, but the interior doors are child's play."

"How could you take a chance like that, breaking into an off-limits area with a guard not three yards away?"

"Usually that's the best time." He glanced in a shop window as they passed and reminded himself to carve out some more time for shopping. "I found our lady," he said casually.

"It's irresponsible, foolish, and nothing more than an egocentric . . . What?"

"I found her." His grin flashed like the Tuscan sun. "And I don't think she's too happy being tucked away in the dark to gather dust. Patience," he told her before she could question him. "I'm thirsty."

"You're thirsty? How can you think about wine and cheese, for God's sake? We should be doing something. Planning out our next step. We can't just sit under an awning and drink Chianti."

"That's just what we're going to do—and stop looking over your shoulder as if the *polizia* were on our tail."

He pulled her toward one of those wide awnings in front of a bustling trattoria, maneuvered her through the tables to an empty one.

"You're out of your mind. Shopping, buying souvenirs, scouting out leather jackets for toddlers, wandering around the Bargello as if you've never been there before. And now—"

She broke off, shocked, when he pushed her into a chair. His hand closed hard over hers as he leaned across the table. The smile he sent her was as tough and chilly as his voice.

"Now, we're just going to sit here awhile, and you're not going to give me any trouble."

"I—"

"No trouble at all." The smile turned easy as he glanced up at the waiter. Since the cover seemed absurd at the moment, he rattled off a request for a bottle of local wine and a selection of cheeses in perfect Italian.

"I'm not tolerating your feeble attempts at bullying me."

"Sweetheart, you're going to tolerate what I tell you to tolerate. I've got the lady."

"You're laboring under— *What?*" The color that had rushed into her face faded again. "What do you mean you've got the lady?"

"She's sitting under the table."

"Under the—" When she would have scraped her chair back and dived under, he simply tightened his grip on her hand until she had to muffle a yelp.

"Look at me, *cara,* and pretend you're in love." He brought her bruised fingers to his lips.

"Are you telling me that you walked into a museum in broad daylight and walked out with the bronze?"

"I'm good. I told you."

"But just now? Now? You were only gone for thirty minutes."

"If a guard hadn't wandered into the storage area to sneak a wine break, I'd have cut that in half."

"But you said we had to check the place out, to tape it, to take measurements, get the feel."

He kissed her fingers again. "I lied." He kept her hand in his, kept his eyes dreamily on hers while the waiter set their wine and cheese on the table. Recognizing lovers, the waiter smiled indulgently and left them alone.

"You lied."

"If I'd told you I was going in to get it, you'd have been nervous, jumpy, and very likely have screwed things up." He poured wine for both of them, sampled and approved. "The wine from this region is exceptional. Aren't you going to try it?"

Still staring at him, she lifted her glass and

downed the contents in several long swallows. She was now an accessory to theft.

"If you're going to drink like that, you better soak some of it up." He sliced off some cheese, offered it. "Here."

She pushed his hand away and reached for the bottle. "You knew going in that you were going to do this."

"I knew going in that if the opportunity presented itself, I'd make the switch."

"What switch?"

"The bronze we bought earlier. I put that in her place. I told you, most people see what they expect to see. There's a bronze statue of a woman sitting in the storeroom. Odds are no one's going to notice it's the wrong bronze for a bit."

He sampled some cheese, approved, and built some onto a cracker. "When they do, they'll look for the right one, likely figure it was moved. And when they don't find her, they won't be able to pinpoint when she was taken. If our luck holds, we'll be back in the States by that time anyway."

"I need to see it."

"There's time for that. I gotta tell you, knowingly stealing a forgery . . . it just doesn't give you that rush."

"Doesn't it?" she murmured.

"Nope. And I'm going to miss that rush when I'm fully retired. You did a good job, by the way."

"Oh." She didn't feel a rush at all, just a sinking sensation in her stomach.

"Distracting the guard. Better fortify yourself." He offered cheese again. "We've still got work to do."

It was surreal, sitting in the hotel room and holding *The Dark Lady* in her hands. She examined it carefully, noting where samples and scrapings had been taken, judging the weight, critiquing the style.

It was a beautiful and graceful piece of work, with the blue-green patina giving it the dignity of age.

She set it on the table beside the *David*.

"She's gorgeous," Ryan commented as he puffed on his cigar. "Your sketch of her was very accurate. You didn't capture the spirit, but you certainly got the details. You'd be a better artist if you put some heart into your work."

"I'm not an artist." Her throat was dry as dust. "I'm a scientist, and this isn't the bronze I tested."

He lifted a brow. "How do you know?"

She couldn't tell him it felt wrong. She couldn't even acknowledge to herself that it simply didn't give her the same tingle in her fingertips when she held it. So she gave him facts.

"It's very possible for someone with training to recognize the work of the twentieth century just by a visual exam. In this case I certainly wouldn't depend on that alone. But I took scrapings. Here, and here." She used a fingertip to point to the back of the calf, the curve of the shoulder. "There's no sign of them on this piece. Ponti's lab took scrapings from the back, and the base. Those aren't my marks. I need equipment and my notes to verify, but this isn't the bronze I worked on."

Considering, Ryan tapped his cigar in an ashtray. "Let's verify it first."

"No one will believe me. Even when I verify it, no one will believe this isn't the bronze." She looked over at him. "Why should they?"

"They'll believe you when we have the original."

"How—"

"One step at a time, Dr. Jones. You're going to want to change. Basic black works best for an entertaining evening of breaking and entering. I'll arrange for transportation."

She moistened her lips. "We're going into Standjo."

"That's the plan." He sensed her waffling and leaned back in his chair. "Unless you want to call your mother, explain all this to her and ask her to give you a little lab time."

Miranda's eyes cooled as she rose. "I'll change."

The bedroom door didn't have a lock, so she dragged over the desk chair and lodged the back under the knob. It made her feel better. He was using her, was all she could think, as if she were just another tool. The idea of them being partners was an illusion. And now she'd helped him steal.

She was about to break into her family's business. And how would she stop him if he decided to do more than run a few basic tests?

She could hear him talking on the phone in the parlor, and took her time changing into a black shirt and slacks. She needed a plan of her own, needed to enlist someone she could trust.

"I've got to run down to the desk," he called out.

"Snap it up in there. I'll only be a minute, and I need to change too."

"I'll be ready." And the minute she heard the door shut, she was dragging the chair away from the door. "Be there, be there, be there," she murmured frantically, as she yanked her address book out of her briefcase. Flipping through, she found the number and made the call.

"Pronto."

"Giovanni, it's Miranda."

"Miranda?" It wasn't pleasure in his voice, but caution. "Where are you? Your brother's been—"

"I'm in Florence," she interrupted. "I need to see you right away. Please, Giovanni, meet me inside Santa Maria Novella. Ten minutes."

"But—"

"Please, it's vital." She hung up quickly, then moving fast, covered the bronzes sloppily in bubble wrap and stuffed them back in their bag. She grabbed the bag and her purse, and ran.

She took the stairs, hurrying down the carpeted treads with her heart banging in her chest, her arms straining against the weight of the bag. She pulled up short at the base, eased out.

She could see Ryan at the desk, chatting cheerfully with the clerk. She couldn't risk crossing the lobby, and tried to slide invisibly around the corner and jog through the lounge. She kept going, through the glass doors that led to the pretty courtyard, with its sparkling swimming pool and shady trees. Pigeons scattered as she raced through.

Though the bag weighed heavily, she didn't stop

for breath until she'd circled the building and made it out to the street. Even then, she took only time enough to shift hands, readjust the weight, cast one nervous glance behind her. Then she headed straight for the church.

Santa Maria Novella, with its beguiling patterns of green and white marble, was just a short walk from the hotel.

Miranda controlled her need to run and walked into its cool, dim interior. Her legs wobbled as she headed down and found a seat near the left of the chancel. Once there, she tried to understand what the hell she was doing.

Ryan was going to be furious, and she couldn't be sure just how much violence simmered under that elegant surface. But she was doing the right thing, the only logical thing.

Even the copy had to be protected until there was resolution. You couldn't trust a man who stole for a living.

Giovanni would come, she told herself. She'd known him for years. However flirtatious, however eccentric he might be, he was at heart a scientist. And he'd always been her friend.

He would listen, he would assess. He would help.

Trying to calm herself, she shut her eyes.

There was something in the air of such places, temples of age and faith and power. Religion had always been, on some levels, about power. Here, that power had manifested itself in great art, so much of it paid for from the coffers of the Medicis.

Buying their souls? she wondered. Balancing out their misdeeds and sins by creating grandeur for a church? Lorenzo had betrayed his wife with the Dark Lady—however acceptable such affairs had been. And his greatest protégé had immortalized her in bronze.

Had he known?

No, no, she remembered, he'd been dead when the bronze was cast. She would have been making the transition to Piero, or one of the younger cousins.

She wouldn't have given up the power her beauty granted her by turning away a new protector. She was too smart for that, too practical. To prosper, or even to survive during that period, a woman needed the shield of a man, or her own wealth, a certain acceptable lineage.

Or great beauty with a cool mind and heart that knew how to wield it.

Giulietta had known.

Shivering, Miranda opened her eyes again. It was the bronze, she reminded herself, not the woman that mattered now. It was science, not speculation that would solve the puzzle.

She heard the rapid footsteps and tensed. He'd found her. Oh God. She jumped up, whirled, and nearly wept with relief.

"Giovanni." Her limbs went weak as she stepped forward and wrapped her arms around him.

"*Bella,* what are you doing here?" He returned the embrace with a combination of exasperation and affection. "Why do you call me with fear in your voice and ask me to meet you like a spy?" He glanced over at the high altar. "And in church."

"It's quiet, it's safe. Sanctuary," she said with a weak smile as she drew back. "I want to explain, but I don't know how much time I have. He knows I'm gone by now, and he'll be looking for me."

"Who knows?"

"Too complicated. Sit down a minute." Her voice was a whisper, as suited churches and conspiracies. "Giovanni, the bronze. *The Dark Lady*—it was a forgery."

"Miranda, my English comes and goes, but to be a forgery makes it necessary to have something to forge. The bronze was a fake, a bad joke, a . . ." He groped for a word. "Bad luck," he decided. "The authorities have questioned the plumber, but it appears he was no more than a dupe. Is this the word? Someone hoped to pass the statue off as genuine, and nearly succeeded."

"It *was* genuine."

He took her hands. "I know this is difficult for you."

"You saw the test results."

"*Sì,* but . . ."

It hurt, seeing both doubt and suspicion in the eyes of a friend. "Do you think I doctored them?"

"I think there were mistakes. We moved too fast, all of us. Miranda—"

"The pace doesn't alter the results. That bronze was real. This one is a forgery." She reached down and brought the wrapped bronze to the top of the bag.

"What is this?"

"It's the copy. The one Ponti tested."

"*Dio mio!* How did you get it?" His voice rose on the question, causing a few heads to turn. Wincing, he leaned closer and whispered. "It was being held in the Bargello."

"That's not important. What is important is that this is not the bronze we worked on. You'll be able to see that for yourself. Once you have it in the lab."

"In the lab? Miranda, what madness is this?"

"This is sanity." She had to cling to that. "I'm barred from Standjo. The records are all there, Giovanni, the equipment is there. I need your help. There's a bronze *David* in this bag as well. It's a forgery. I've already tested it. But I want you to take them both in, examine them, run what tests you can. You'll compare the results of the Fiesole Bronze with the ones that were run on the original. You'll prove it's not the same bronze."

"Miranda, be sensible. Even if I do as you ask, I'll only prove you were wrong."

"No. You get my notes, your own. Richard's. You run the tests, you compare. We couldn't all have been wrong, Giovanni. I'd do it myself, but there are complications."

She thought of Ryan, furious, tearing the city apart to find her and the bronzes. "And running them myself won't convince anyone. It needs to be objective. I can't trust anyone but you."

She squeezed his hands, knowing she played on his weakness for friendship. She could have stopped the tears that swam into her eyes, but they were genuine. "It's my reputation, Giovanni. It's my work. It's my life."

He cursed softly, then winced when he remembered where he was, quickly added a prayer and the sign of the cross.

"This will only make you unhappy."

"I can't be any more unhappy. For friendship, Giovanni. For me."

"I'll do what you ask."

She squeezed her eyes shut as her heart swelled with gratitude. "Tonight, right away."

"The sooner it's done, the better. The lab, it's closed for a few days, so no one will know."

"Closed, why?"

He smiled for the first time. "Tomorrow, my lovely pagan, is Good Friday." And this was not the way he'd intended to spend his holiday weekend. He sighed, nudged the bag with his foot. "Where will I reach you when it's done?"

"I'll reach you." She leaned forward to touch her lips to his. "*Grazie, Giovanni. Mille grazie*. I'll never be able to repay you for this."

"An explanation when it's done would be a fine start."

"A full one, I promise. Oh, I'm so glad to see you. I wish I could stay, but I have to get back, and . . . well, I suppose we'd say face the music. I'll find a way to call you in the morning. Take good care of them," she added, and nudged the bag toward him with her foot. "Wait a minute or two before you leave, will you. Just in case."

She kissed him again, warmly, then left him.

Because she looked neither right nor left, she didn't see the figure standing in the dimness, turned as if to contemplate the faded frescoes of Dante's Inferno.

She didn't feel the fury, or the threat.

It was as if a burden had been lifted, the weight that had pressed down on her head, her heart, her conscience. She stepped outside, into the gilded light from the sun that was melting into the west. On the off chance that Ryan was out on foot searching for her, she walked in the opposite direction of the hotel, toward the river.

It wouldn't do, she thought, to have him find her before she and Giovanni had plenty of distance between them.

It was a long walk, and gave her time to calm herself, time to think, and time, for once, to wonder about the couples who strolled along, hand in hand, who shared long looks or long embraces. Giovanni had once told her romance lived in Florentine air, and she had only to sniff at it.

It made her smile, then it made her sigh.

She simply wasn't fashioned for romance. And hadn't she proven it? The only man who'd ever stirred her to the point of aching was a thief with no more integrity than a mushroom.

She was better, much better off alone. As she'd always been.

She reached the river, watched the dying sun sprinkle its last lights on the water. When the roar of an engine sounded behind her, when that engine revved violently, impatiently, she knew he'd found her. She'd known he would.

"Get on."

She glanced back, saw his furious face, the way that anger could turn those warm golden eyes to deadly ice. He was all in black now, as she was, and astride a blue motorbike. The wind had blown his hair into disorder. He looked dangerous, and absurdly sexy.

"I can walk, thanks."

"Get on, Miranda. Because if I have to get off and put you on, it's going to hurt."

Since the alternative was to run like a coward, and likely be run over for her trouble, she shrugged carelessly. She walked to the curb, swung a leg over to sit behind him. She gripped the back of the seat for balance.

But when he took off like a bullet, survival instinct took over and had her wrapping her arms tightly around him.

CHAPTER SEVENTEEN

"I GUESS I SHOULD HAVE USED THE HANDCUFFS after all." After taking the narrow, winding streets with a reckless and risky speed that suited his mood, Ryan jerked the bike to a halt in the Piazzale Michelangelo.

It seemed apt, and it gave them a heart-shattering view of Florence, with the Tuscan hills rising beyond. As well as the privacy he wanted should he decide to commit violence.

It was nearly empty, with the vendors that crowded the area gone for the day and a broody storm gathering in the western sky, where the sun clung tenuously to the horizon.

"Off," he ordered, and waited for her to pry her hands from their death grip around his waist. He'd given her a couple of good scares on the ride. He'd meant to.

"You drive like a lunatic."

"Half Italian, half Irish. What do you expect?" He swung off himself, then dragged her to the wall, where Florence spread like an old jewel below. There were still a few tourists taking pictures of the grand fountain, but since they were Japanese he thought he could risk ripping into her in either English or Italian. He chose the latter because he considered it more passionate.

"Where are they?"

"Safe."

"I didn't ask how they were, but where. What have you done with the bronzes?"

"The sensible thing. It's going to storm," she said as lightning licked the sky with the same edgy sizzle as the nerves riding in her stomach. "We should get inside somewhere."

He simply pushed her back against the wall, and held her there, body against body. "I want the bronzes, Miranda."

She kept her eyes on his. She wouldn't appeal to the handful of lingering tourists for help. This, she promised herself, she would deal with on her own. "They're worthless to you."

"That's for me to decide. Damn it, I trusted you."

Now her eyes fired back. "You mean you couldn't lock me into the suite the way you did in your apartment." She kept her voice low, its already husky tone rough with temper. "You couldn't make me wait the way you did at the Bargello while you went ahead and acted without telling me what you planned to do. This time *I* went ahead."

He put his arms around her so that they looked

like desperate lovers too involved with each other to notice storm or city. His grip shortened her breath considerably. "Went ahead and what?"

"Made arrangements. You're hurting me."

"Not yet I'm not. You had to give them to someone. Your mother. No," he decided when she continued to stare at him. "Not your mother. You're still hoping to make her grovel for doubting you. Got a boyfriend here in Florence, Dr. Jones, someone you could sweet-talk into tucking the bronzes away until you figure I'd give up? Now I want the bronzes—both of them."

Thunder grumbled, rolled closer.

"I told you, they're safe. I made arrangements. I did what I thought best."

"Do I look like I give a rat's ass what you think?"

"I want to prove they're copies. So do you. If I run the tests and the comparisons, it could be claimed I slanted them. We'd be no better off than we are now. It was your job to get the bronze from the Bargello, it's mine to determine how to prove it's a forgery."

"You gave them to someone from Standjo." He drew back only far enough to take her face in his hands. "What kind of idiot are you?"

"I gave them to someone I trust, to someone I've known for years." She took a deep breath, hoping to trade temper for reason. "He'll do the work because I asked him. And tomorrow, I'll contact him and get the results."

He had a vicious urge to bounce her head off the wall, just to see if it was really as hard as he suspected. "Follow this logic, Dr. Jones. *The Dark Lady* is a forgery. Therefore someone at Standjo made the copy. Someone who knows what the tests would show, how to make it look real enough to pass prelims, someone who likely has a source who'd pay some excellent lire for the real thing."

"He wouldn't do that. His work's important to him."

"Mine's important to me. Let's go."

"Where?"

He was already dragging her across the plaza to the bike when the first fat drops of rain fell. "To the lab, sweetheart. We'll check up on your friend's progress."

"Don't you understand? If we break into the lab, the tests will be moot. No one will believe me."

"You forget. I already believe you. That's part of the problem. Now get on, or I leave you here and take care of business myself."

She considered it, then decided the last thing Giovanni needed was a furious Ryan breaking into the lab. "Let him do the tests." She pushed at her wet hair. "It's the only way they'll have validity."

He simply gunned the engine. "Get on."

She got on, and as he tore out of the plaza she tried to convince herself she'd make him see reason once they got to Standjo.

Half a block from Standjo he pulled the bike into a small forest of others along the curbing. "Be quiet," he said, jumping off to remove pouches from the saddlebags. "Do what you're told, and carry this." He shoved one of the bags into her hands, then took her arm in a firm grip and led her down the street.

"We'll go in the back, just in case anyone's curious enough to be looking out into the rain. We'll cross directly over the photo lab to the stairs."

"How do you know the setup?"

"I do my research. I've got blueprints of the whole facility on disk." He drew her around the back of the building, then pulled out a pair of surgical gloves. "Put these on."

"This isn't going to—"

"I said be quiet and do what you're told. You've already caused me more trouble than necessary. I'm going to disable the alarm in this sector, which means you don't go more than one foot away from me while we're inside."

He pulled on his own gloves as he spoke, and thought nothing of the rain now pounding over them. "If we need to access another area of the building, I'll deal with the security from inside. It'll be easier. There're no guards, it's all electronic, so it's unlikely we'd run into anyone but your good pal over a holiday weekend."

She started to protest again, then backed off. It occurred to her that once she was inside, she'd have Giovanni behind her. Surely the two of them could handle one irritating thief.

"If he's not inside, with the bronzes, I'm going to make you very sorry."

"He's there. He gave me his word."

"Yeah, like you gave me yours." He approached the door, setting down his bag to prepare to work.

Then his eyes narrowed as he studied the fixture beside the door. “Alarm’s off,” he murmured. “Your friend’s careless, Dr. Jones. He didn’t reset the system from inside.”

She ignored the rippling chill over her skin. “I suppose he didn’t think it necessary.”

“Um-hmm. Door’s locked, though. That would be automatic once it was shut. We’ll fix that.”

He unrolled a soft leather strip, using his body to shield his tools as best he could. He’d have to wipe them down well later, he mused. Couldn’t risk rust.

“This shouldn’t take long, but keep your eye out anyway.”

He hummed lightly, a tune she recognized as a passage from *Aida*. She crossed her arms over her chest, turned her back to him, and stared into the driving rain.

Whoever had installed security hadn’t wanted to deface the beautiful old door with dead bolts. The brass knobs were sad-faced cherubs that suited the medieval architecture and guarded a series of efficient but aesthetically discreet locks.

Ryan blinked rain out of his eyes and wished vaguely for an umbrella.

He had to work by feel alone. The pounding of the rain prevented him from hearing that faint and satisfying click of tumblers. But the sturdy British locks surrendered, degree by degree.

“Bring the bag,” he told her when he pulled the heavy door open.

He used his penlight to guide them to the stairs.

"You explain to your friend that I'm helping you out, and I'll take it from there. That is, if he's here."

"I said he'd be here. He promised me."

"Then he must like to work in the dark." He shined his light straight ahead. "That's your lab, right?"

"Yes." Her brows drew together. It was black as pitch. "He just hasn't gotten here yet."

"Who turned off the alarm?"

"I . . . He's probably in the chem lab. That's his field."

"We'll check that out in a minute. Meanwhile we'll just see if your notes are still in your office. Through here?"

"Yes, through the doors and to the left. It was only my temporary office."

"You put the data on your computer's hard drive?"

"Yes."

"Then we'll get it."

The doors were unlocked, which gave him an unhappy feeling. Deciding to err on the side of caution, he shut off his flashlight. "Stay behind me."

"Why?"

"Just do it." He eased through the door, blocking her body with his. For several humming seconds he listened, and hearing nothing but the whoosh of air through the vents, reached over to turn on the lights.

"Oh God." Instinctively, she gripped his shoulder. "Oh my God."

"I thought scientists were tidy," he murmured.

It looked as if someone had indulged in a vicious tantrum, or a hell of a party. Computers were smashed, and the glass from monitors and test tubes littered the floor. Worktables had been overturned, papers scattered. Stations that had been surgically ordered were now a jumble of wreckage. The stench of chemicals unwisely mixed smeared the air.

"I don't understand this. What's the point of this?"

"It wasn't burglary," he said easily. "Not with all these computers busted instead of lifted. Looks to me, Dr. Jones, like your friend's come and gone."

"Giovanni would never do this." She pushed past Ryan to kick her way through the rubble. "It had to be vandals, kids on a rampage. All this equipment, all this data." She mourned it even as she stormed through the room. "Destroyed, ruined."

Vandals? He didn't think so. Where was the graffiti, where was the glee? This had been done in rage, and with purpose. And he had a hunch it was going to circle right around on them.

"Let's get out of here."

"I have to check the other sections, see how extensive the damage is. If they got to the chem lab—"

She broke off, shoving her way through the mess with the terrible idea of a gang of young hoods with a volatile supply of stolen chemicals.

"You can't fix it," he muttered under his breath,

and started after her. When he caught up, she was standing in an open doorway, staring, swaying.

Giovanni had kept his promise, and he wasn't going anywhere. He lay on his back, his head twisted at an odd angle and resting in a dark, glossy pool. His eyes, open and dull, were fixed on *The Dark Lady,* who lay with him, her graceful hands and smiling face covered with blood.

"Sweet Jesus." It was as much prayer as oath as Ryan jerked her back, forced her around so that she stared into his eyes instead of at what lay in the room beyond. "Is that your friend?"

"I . . . Giovanni." Her pupils had dilated with shock and her eyes were as black and lifeless as a doll's.

"Hold it together. You have to hold it together, Miranda, because we might not have much time. Our fingerprints are all over that bronze, do you understand?" And the bronze had recently graduated from forgery to murder weapon. "Those are the only ones the cops will find on it. We've been set up here."

There was a roaring in her ears—the ocean rising up to strike rock. "Giovanni's dead."

"Yeah, he is—now stand right here." For expedience sake, he propped her against the wall. He stepped into the room, breathing through his teeth so as not to absorb the smell of death. The room reeked with it, and the smell was obscenely fresh. Though it made him grimace, he picked up the bronze, stuffed it into his bag. Doing his best to stop his gaze from locking on the face staring up at him, he did a quick search of the wrecked room.

The *David* had been heaved into a corner. The dent in the wall showed where it had struck.

Very smart, he thought as he pushed it into the bag. Very tidy. Leave both pieces and tie it together. Tie it right around Miranda's neck like a noose.

She was exactly as he'd left her, but now she was shaking and her skin was the color of paste.

"You can walk," he said roughly. "You can run if you have to, because we've got to get out of here."

"We can't—can't leave him. In there. Like this. Giovanni. He's dead."

"And there's nothing you can do for him. We're going."

"I can't leave him."

Rather than wasting time arguing, he caught her up in a fireman's carry. She didn't struggle, only hung limply and repeated the same words over and over like a chant. "I can't leave him. I can't leave him."

He was out of breath by the time he hit the outside door. Still, he shifted her weight, opened the door only far enough to give him a view of the street. He saw nothing out of place, but the back of his neck continued to prickle as though it felt the business end of a blade.

When they were out in the rain, he dumped her on her feet and shook her hard. "You don't fall apart until we're out of here. Put it on ice, Miranda, and do what needs to be done next."

Without waiting for her assent, he pulled her around the building and down the street. She slid on the bike behind him, held on so that he could feel the jumping skip of her heart against his back as he drove through the rain.

He wanted to get her inside quickly, but forced himself to drive through the city, taking narrow side streets at random to be certain they weren't being followed. Whoever had killed Giovanni might have been watching the building, waiting for them. He was reserving judgment on that until he managed to get the full story out of Miranda.

Satisfied there was no tail, he parked in front of the hotel. He gathered his bags, then turned to push the wet hair out of her face. "You listen to me. Pay attention." He held on to her face until her glazed eyes focused. "We have to cross the lobby. I want you to walk straight to the elevator. I'll handle the clerk. You just go and stand by the elevator. Understand?"

"Yes." It felt as if the words came from somewhere over the top of her head rather than out of her mouth. Words floating there, meaningless and confusing.

When she walked it was like swimming through syrup, but she walked, intensely focused on the gleaming doors of the elevators. That was her goal, she thought. She just had to walk to the elevator.

Dimly she heard Ryan talking with the desk clerk,

a rumble of male laughter. She stared at the door, reached out and ran her fingertip down the surface as if to gauge the texture. So smooth and cool. Odd, she'd never noticed that before. She laid her palm on it as Ryan came up beside her and pushed the up button.

It rumbled, like the thunder, she realized. Gears shifting, engaging. And the door made a soft hissing sound when it opened.

She didn't have any more color in her cheeks than the corpse they'd left behind, Ryan noted. And her teeth were starting to chatter. He imagined she was chilled to the bone. God knew he was, and not just from an open ride in drenching rain.

"Just walk down the hall," he ordered, shifting his bags so that he could wrap an arm around her waist. She didn't lean on him, didn't seem to have enough substance in her body to give weight, but he kept his arm around her until they were inside the suite.

He locked the door, added the safety latch before taking her into the bedroom. "Get out of the wet clothes, into a robe." He'd have preferred to dump her in a hot bath, but was afraid she'd just slip under and drown.

He checked the terrace doors, made certain they too were locked before he searched out a bottle of brandy from the minibar. He didn't bother with glasses.

She was sitting on the bed, exactly as he'd left her. "You've got to get out of those clothes," he told her. "You're soaked through."

"I—My fingers don't work."

"Okay, okay. Here, swallow."

He broke the seal on the bottle, then held it to her lips. She obeyed mindlessly, until the fire spurted down her throat and into her belly. "I don't like brandy."

"I don't like spinach, but my mother made me eat it. One more time. Come on, be a good soldier." He managed to pour another swallow down her throat before she sputtered and pushed his hand away.

"I'm all right. I'm all right."

"Sure you are." Hoping to ease the queasiness in his own stomach, he tipped back the bottle and took a healthy gulp himself. "Now the clothes." He set the bottle aside and went to work on the buttons of her shirt.

"Don't—"

"Miranda." Realizing his legs weren't completely steady, he sat beside her. "Does it look like I'm going to cop a feel here? You're in shock. You need to get warm and dry. So do I."

"I can do it. I can." She got shakily to her feet and stumbled into the bath.

When the door clicked shut, he resisted the urge to open it again to be certain she wasn't in a heap on the floor.

For a moment he lowered his head into his hands, ordered himself to breathe, just breathe. It was his first up-close and personal experience with violent death. Fresh, violent, and real, he thought, and took one more shot of brandy from the bottle.

It wasn't an experience he wanted to repeat.

"I'm going to order up some food. Something hot." He peeled out of his wet jacket as he spoke. Keeping an eye on the door, he stripped, tossed his wet clothes aside, and pulled on slacks and a shirt.

"Miranda?" With his hands in his pockets, he frowned at the door. Modesty be damned, he decided, and pushed it open.

She'd put on a robe, but her hair was still streaming with wet as she stood in the center of the room, her arms wrapped tight around her body as she rocked herself. She sent Ryan one look of unspeakable misery. "Giovanni."

"Okay, all right." He put his arms around her, cradled her head on his shoulder. "You did good, you did fine. It's okay to fall apart now."

She only clenched and unclenched her hands against his back. "Who could have done that to him? He's never hurt anyone. Who could have done that?"

"We'll figure it out. We will. We're going to talk about it, step by step." He cuddled her closer, stroking a hand down her wet hair as much to soothe himself as her. "But your mind has to be clear. I need your brain. I need your logic."

"I can't think. I keep seeing him, lying there. All the blood. He was my friend. He came when I asked him to. He . . ."

And the full horror of it struck her, a brutal slice to the heart that cleared her head to shocking, vicious clarity. "Oh God, Ryan. I killed him."

"No." He pulled her back so that their eyes were level again. "Whoever bashed in the back of his head killed him. You get over that, Miranda, because it's not going to help."

"He was only in there tonight because of me. If I hadn't asked him, he'd have been at home, or out on a date, or sitting in some trattoria drinking wine with friends."

She pressed her fisted hands to her mouth, the eyes over them swimming with horror. "He's dead because I asked him to help me, because I didn't trust you and because my reputation is so important, so vital, I had to have it done my way." She shook her head. "I'm never going to get over that."

However miserable her eyes, her color was back and her voice was stronger. Guilt could energize as well as paralyze. "Okay, then use it. Dry your hair while I order some food. We've got a lot to talk about."

She dried her hair, and slipped into white cotton pajamas, then wrapped the robe over them. She would eat, she told herself, because she would be ill if she didn't. She needed to be well, strong, and clearheaded if she was going to avenge Giovanni.

Avenge? she thought with a shudder. She'd never believed in vengeance. Now it seemed perfectly sane, perfectly logical. The term "an eye for an eye" circled grimly in her head. Whoever killed Giovanni had used her as a weapon as cold-bloodedly as they'd used the bronze.

Whatever it took, however long it took, she would see that they paid for it.

When she came out of the bedroom, she saw that Ryan had ordered the waiter to set up the meal on the terrace. The rain had stopped and the air was fresh. The table sat cheerfully under the bright green-and-white-striped awning and candles flickered over the linen cloth.

She supposed it was designed to make her feel better. Because she was grateful to him, she did her best to pretend it did.

"This looks very nice." She managed what passed for a smile. "What are we eating?"

"Minestrone to start, then a couple of Florentine steaks. It'll help. Sit and eat."

She took a chair, even picked up her spoon and sampled the soup. It stuck like paste in her throat, but she forced herself to swallow. And he was right, the heat of it thawed some of the ice in her belly.

"I need to apologize to you."

"Okay. I never turn down an apology from a woman."

"I broke my word to you." She lifted her gaze, locked on his. "I never meant to keep it. I told myself a promise to a man like you didn't have to be kept. That was wrong of me, and I'm sorry."

The simplicity, the quiet tone, touched his heart. He'd have preferred it otherwise. "We're going at this at cross-purposes. That's the way it is. Still, we've got a mutual goal. We want to find the original bronzes. And now someone's upped the stakes. It may be smarter for you to back off, let this go. Proving you were right isn't worth your life."

"It cost me a friend." She pressed her lips together, then made herself spoon up more soup. "I won't back off, Ryan. I couldn't live with myself if I did. I don't have many friends. I'm sure that's my fault. I don't relate well to people."

"You're being too hard on yourself. You relate fine when you let your guard down. Like you did with my family."

"I didn't let my guard down. They just didn't pay any attention to it. I envy you what you have with them." Her voice trembled a little, so she shook her head and forced down more soup. "The unconditional love, the sheer delight all of you have with each other. You can't buy that kind of gift." She smiled a little. "And you can't steal it."

"You can make it. It just takes the wanting to."

"Someone has to want the gift you're making." She sighed and decided to risk a sip of wine. "If my parents and I had a better relationship, you and I wouldn't be sitting here right now. It really goes back to that. Dysfunction doesn't always show itself in raised voices and fists. Sometimes it can be insidiously polite."

"Have you ever told them how you feel?"

"Not the way I imagine you mean." She looked past him, over the city where the lights gleamed and the moon was beginning to ride the clearing sky. "I'm not sure I knew how I felt until recently. And it doesn't matter now. Finding who did this to Giovanni matters."

He let it rest, and since he'd decided it was his turn to deal with practicalities, he removed the covers from the steaks. "Nobody understands the way a slice of red meat should be treated better than the Florentines. Tell me about Giovanni."

It was a fist to the heart and the shock of it had her staring at him. "I don't know what you want me to say."

"First tell me what you knew about him and how you came to know it." It would ease her in, he thought, to the details he wanted most.

"He's—He was brilliant. A chemist. He was born here in Florence, and joined Standjo about ten years ago. He worked here primarily, but did some time in the lab at the Institute. That's where I worked with him initially, about six years ago the first time."

She lifted a hand and rubbed at her temple. "He was a lovely man, sweet and funny. He was single. He enjoyed women, and was very charming and attentive. He noticed details about you. If you wore a new blouse or did your hair a different way."

"Were you lovers?"

She winced, but shook her head. "No. We were friends. I respected his abilities, very much. I trusted his judgment, and I depended on his loyalty. I used his loyalty," she said quietly, then pushed away from the table to walk to the parapet.

She needed a moment to adjust, yet again. He was dead. She couldn't change it. How many times, she thought, for how many years, would she find herself adjusting to those two single facts?

"It was Giovanni who called me to tell me the bronze had been discredited," she continued. "He didn't want me unprepared when my mother contacted me."

"So, he was in her confidence?"

"He was part of my team here, on the project. And he'd been called on the carpet when my findings were questioned." Steadier, she walked back to the table, sat again. "I used his loyalty, and our friendship. I knew I could."

"Today was the first time you talked to him about the bronze being a copy?"

"Yes. I called him when you went downstairs. I asked him to meet me inside Santa Maria Novella. I told him it was urgent."

"Where did you call him?"

"At the lab. I knew I could catch him before the end of the workday. I took the bronzes, and I went down the stairs, out the back courtyard while you were at the desk. He came right away. It couldn't have been more than fifteen minutes."

Enough time, Ryan mused, for him to have told someone of the call. The wrong someone. "What did you tell him?"

"Almost everything. I explained that I had the bronze that Ponti had tested, that it wasn't the same one we'd worked on. I told him as much as I could about the *David*. I don't think he believed me. But he listened."

She stopped pushing her steak around on her plate. Pretending to eat was too much effort. "I asked him to take the bronzes into the lab, to run tests, to do a comparison. I said I'd contact him tomorrow. I didn't give him the hotel because I didn't want him to call or come over. I didn't want you to know what I'd done with the bronzes."

Ryan sat back, deciding neither of them was going to do the meal justice. Instead he took out a cigar. "That may very well be why we're sitting here, enjoying the moonlight."

"What do you mean?"

"Put your brain to work, Dr. Jones. Your friend had the bronzes, and now he's dead. The murder weapon and the *David* were left on the scene. What connects the two? You do."

He lighted the cigar to give her time to absorb the thought. "If the cops had found those statues on the crime scene, they'd have gone hunting for you. Whoever did it knows you've put enough together to look for answers, and that you're skirting the law enough to prevent you from bringing in the police."

"Killing Giovanni to implicate me." It was too cold, too hideous to be contemplated. And too logical to ignore.

"An added benefit. If he was straight, he'd have begun to wonder himself after the tests. He'd take another look at your notes, your results."

"That's why the lab was trashed," she murmured. "We'll never find my documentation now."

"Taken or destroyed," Ryan agreed. "Your friend was in the way. And Miranda, so are you."

"Yes, I see." Somehow it was better that way, easier. "It's more important than ever to find the original. Whoever replaced it killed Giovanni."

"You know what they say about killing? The first one's tough. After that, it's just business."

She ignored the chill that danced over her skin. "If that means you want to end our deal here and now, I won't blame you."

"Wouldn't you?" He leaned back again, drawing idly on the cigar. He wondered how much the fact that she would think him a coward played into it. And how much the need to protect her weighed on the decision he'd already made. "I finish what I start."

Relief spread like a river, but she picked up her wineglass, raised it in a half-salute. "So do I."

CHAPTER EIGHTEEN

IT WAS STILL SHY OF MIDNIGHT WHEN CARLO LEFT THE trattoria and began to walk home. He'd promised his wife he wouldn't be out late. The boundaries of their marriage included one evening a week for him to sit and drink and tell lies with his friends. Sofia had her evening as well, a gossipfest at her sister's, which he supposed amounted to the same thing.

Habitually he stayed till twelve, or a bit after, drawing the male oasis out, but just lately he'd been cutting it short. He'd been the butt of jokes since the papers had announced his *Dark Lady* was a hoax.

He didn't believe it, not for a minute. He'd held the statue in his hands, he'd felt the whisper of breath on his cheeks. An artist recognized art. But whenever he said so, his friends laughed.

The authorities had grilled him like a criminal. *Dio*

mio, he'd done nothing but what was right. Perhaps he'd made a small error of judgment by taking the statue out of the villa.

But he had found her, after all. He had held her in his hands, looked at her face, felt her beauty and her power like wine in his blood. She had transfixed him, he thought now. Bewitched him. And still, in the end he'd done the right thing and given her up.

Now they tried to say she was nothing. A clever scheme to dupe the art world. He knew, in his heart, in his bones, that was a lie.

Sofia said she believed him, but he knew she didn't. She said it because she was loyal and loving, and because it caused less arguing in front of the children. The reporters he'd talked to had taken down all his statements, and had made him sound like a fool.

He'd tried to talk to the American woman, the one who ran the big laboratory where his lady had been taken. But she wouldn't listen. He'd lost his temper with her, demanded to speak to the Dr. Miranda Jones who had proven his lady was real.

The *direttrice* had called security and had him tossed out. It had been humiliating.

He should never have listened to Sofia, he thought now as he made his way down the quiet road outside the city toward home, stumbling a bit as the wine brooded in his head. He should have kept the lady for himself as he'd wanted to. He had found her, he had taken her out of the damp, dark cellar and brought her into the light. She belonged to him.

Now, even though they claimed she was worthless, they wouldn't give her back to him.

He wanted her back.

He'd called the lab in Rome and demanded the return of his property. He had shouted and raved and called them all liars and cheats. He'd even called America and left a desperate and rambling message on Miranda's office machine. He believed she was his link to his lady. She would help him, somehow.

He couldn't rest until he saw the lady again, held her in his hands.

He would hire a lawyer, he decided, inspired by wine and the humiliation of sly laughter. He would call the American woman again, the one in the place called Maine, and convince her it was all a plot, a conspiracy to steal the lady from him.

He remembered her picture from the papers. A strong face, an honest one. Yes, she would help.

Miranda Jones. She would listen to him.

He didn't glance behind him when he heard the oncoming car. The road was clear, and he was well onto the shoulder. He was concentrating on the face from the papers, on what he would say to this woman scientist.

It was Miranda and *The Dark Lady* who occupied his mind when the car struck him at full speed.

Standing on the terrace in the strong morning light, Miranda gazed out at the city. Perhaps for the first time she fully appreciated the beauty of it. The end of Giovanni's life had irrevocably changed hers.

Somewhere inside her a dark place would remain, formed of guilt and sorrow. And yet, she sensed more light than she had ever known before. There was an urgency to grab hold, to take time, to savor details.

The quiet kiss of the breeze that fluttered over her cheeks, the flash of sun that shimmered over city and hill, the warm stone under her bare feet.

She wanted to go down, she realized. To get dressed and go out and walk the streets without destination, without some purpose driving every step. Just to look in store windows, to wander along the river. To feel alive.

"Miranda."

She drew in a breath, glanced over her shoulder and saw Ryan standing in the terrace doorway. "It's a beautiful morning. Spring, rebirth. I don't think I really appreciated that before."

He crossed the terrace, laid a hand over hers on the parapet. She might have smiled if she hadn't seen the look in his eye. "Oh God. What now? What happened?"

"The plumber. Carlo Rinaldi. He's dead. Hit and run, last night. I just heard it on the news." Her hand turned in his, gripped. "He was walking home near midnight. There weren't many more details." A cold fury worked through him. "He had three children, and another on the way."

"It could have been an accident." She wanted to cling to that, thought she might have been able to if she hadn't looked into Ryan's eyes. "But it wasn't. Why would anyone kill him? He isn't connected to the lab. He can't know anything."

"He's been making a lot of noise. For all we know, he might have been in on the whole thing from the beginning. Either way, he found it, he had it for several days. He would have studied it. He was a loose end, Miranda, and loose ends get snipped."

"Like Giovanni." She moved away from him. She could live with it, she told herself. She had to. "Was there anything in the news about Giovanni?"

"No, but there will be. Get dressed. We're going out."

Out, she thought, but not to wander the streets, to stroll along the river, to just be. "All right."

"No arguments?" He raised an eyebrow. "No where, what, why?"

"Not this time." She stepped into the bedroom and closed the doors.

Thirty minutes later, they were at a phone booth and Ryan was doing something he'd avoided all of his life. He was calling the cops.

He pitched his voice toward the upper scale, used a nervous whisper and colloquial Italian to report a body in the second-floor lab at Standjo. He hung up on the rapid questions. "That should do it. Let's get moving in case the Italian police have caller-ID."

"Are we going back to the hotel?"

"No." He swung onto the bike. "We're going to your mother's. You navigate."

"My mother's?" Her vow not to question was

swallowed up in shock. "Why? Are you crazy? I can't take you to my mother's."

"I figure there won't be a nice linguine and red sauce for lunch, but we'll catch a pizza on the way. That should give it enough time."

"For what?"

"For the cops to find the body, for her to hear about it. What do you figure she'll do when she does?"

"She'll go straight to the lab."

"That's what I'm counting on. That should give us a nice window to search her place."

"We're going to break into my mother's home?"

"Unless she leaves a spare key under the mat. Put this on." He pulled a ball cap out of the saddlebags. "The neighbors will spot that hair of yours a mile away."

"I don't see the point in this," Miranda said an hour later, sitting on the bike behind him half a block down from her mother's home. "I can't justify breaking into my mother's home, rummaging through her things."

"Any paperwork dealing with your tests that was kept at the lab is a loss. There's a chance she might have copies here."

"Why would she?"

"Because you're her daughter."

"It wouldn't matter to her."

But it matters to you, Ryan thought. "Maybe, maybe not. Is that her?"

Miranda looked back at the house, caught herself ducking behind Ryan like a schoolgirl playing hooky. "Yes, I guess you called this part of it."

"Attractive woman. You don't look much like her."

"Thank you so much."

He only chuckled and watched Elizabeth, ruthlessly groomed in a dark suit, unlock her car. "Keeps her cool," he noted. "You wouldn't know to look at her that she's just been told her business has been broken into, and one of her employees is dead."

"My mother isn't given to outward displays of emotion."

"Like I said, you're not much like her. Okay, we'll walk down from here. She won't be back for a couple of hours, but we'll do this in one to keep it simple."

"There's nothing simple here." She watched him sling his bag over his shoulder. Oh yes, she decided, her life would never be the same. She was a criminal now.

He walked right up to the front door and rang the bell. "She have a staff? A dog? A lover?"

"She has a housekeeper, I believe, but not a live-in. She doesn't care for pets." She tugged the ball cap more securely over her hair. "I don't know anything about her sex life."

He rang the bell again. There wasn't much more embarrassing to his mind than stepping into what you believed was an empty home to do your job, and discovering the owner was home sick with the flu.

He slipped out his picks and defeated the locks in little more time than if he'd used a key. "Alarm system?"

"I don't know. Probably."

"Okay, we'll deal with it." He stepped in, saw the panel on the wall, and the light indicating the system required a code. He had a minute, he concluded, and pulling out a screwdriver, removed the facing, snipped a couple of wires, and put it to rest.

Because the scientist in her couldn't help but admire his quick, economic efficiency, she made her voice bland. "You make me wonder why anyone bothers with this sort of thing. Why not just leave the doors and windows open?"

"My sentiments exactly." He winked at her, then scanned the foyer. "Nice place. Very appealing art—a bit on the static side but attractive. Where's her office?"

She only stared at him a moment, wondering why she found his casual critique of her mother's taste amusing. She should have been appalled. "Second floor, to the left I think. I haven't spent a great deal of time here."

"Let's try it." He climbed up a graceful set of stairs. Place could have done with a bit more color, he thought, a few surprises. Everything was as perfect as a model home and had the same unoccupied feel. It was certainly classy, but he much preferred his own apartment in New York or Miranda's elegantly shabby house in Maine.

He found the office feminine but not fussy, polished but efficient, cool but not quite brittle. He wondered if it reflected the occupant, and thought it likely.

"Safe?"

"I wouldn't know."

"So, look around," he suggested, and began to do so by tipping forward the backs of paintings. "Here it is, behind this very nice Renoir print. I'll deal with this, you go through the desk."

She hesitated. Even as a child she'd known better than to enter any room of her mother's without permission. She would never have strolled in and borrowed earrings or copped a spritz of perfume. And she certainly would never have touched the contents of her mother's desk.

It appeared she was about to make up for lost time.

She shoved aside the conditioning of a lifetime and dived in, with a great deal more enthusiasm than she'd ever admit.

"There are a lot of files here," she told Ryan while she flipped through. "Most seem to be personal. Insurance, receipts, correspondence."

"Keep looking."

She sat in the desk chair—another first—and pawed through another drawer. Excitement was bubbling in her belly now, guilty, shameful excitement.

"Copies of contracts," she murmured, "and reports. I guess she does some work here. Oh." Her fingers froze. "The Fiesole Bronze. She has a file."

"Take it. We'll look through it later." He listened to the last tumbler click into place. "Now I have you, my little beauty. Very nice, very nice," he whispered, opening a velvet case and examining a double rope of pearls. "Heirlooms—they'd suit you."

"Put those back."

"I'm not stealing them. I don't do jewelry." But he opened another box and hmmed at the glitter of diamonds. "Very classy earrings, about three carats each, square-cut, looks like Russian whites, probably first water."

"I thought you didn't do jewelry."

"Doesn't mean I don't have an interest. These would be killers with your ring."

"It's not my ring," she said primly, but her gaze shifted to the diamond winking on her finger. "It's window dressing."

"Right. Look at this." He pulled out a thin plastic holder. "Look familiar?"

"The X rays." She was away from the desk and grabbing for them in two thumping heartbeats. "The computer printouts. Look, look at them. It's there. You can see it. The corrosion level. Just look. It's there. It's real."

Suddenly swamped with emotion, she pressed the heel of her hand to her brow and squeezed her eyes shut. "It's there. I wasn't wrong. I didn't make a mistake."

"I never thought you did."

She opened her eyes again, smiled. "Liar. You broke into my bedroom and threatened to strangle me."

"I said I could strangle you." He circled her throat

with his hands again. "And that was before I knew you. Tidy up, honey. We've got enough to keep us busy for a while."

They spent the next several hours in the hotel suite, with Miranda going over the copies of her reports line by line and Ryan huddled at his computer.

"It's all here. Everything I did, stage by stage. Every test, every result. Admittedly, it's light on documentation, but it stands. Why didn't she see that?"

"Take a look at this and see if I've got it right."

"What?"

"I've done a cross-check." He motioned her over. "These are the names I come up with. People who had access to both bronzes. There's probably more, but these are the key players."

She rose and read over his shoulder. She only set her teeth when she noted her name topped the list. Her mother was there, as was her father, Andrew, Giovanni, Elise, Carter, Hawthorne, Vincente.

"Andrew didn't have access to *The Dark Lady.*"

A tendril of the hair she'd pinned up fell and tickled his cheek. The immediate tightening of his loins had him letting out a long quiet breath. If nothing else, he thought, her hair was going to drive him to drink before they were done.

"He's connected to you, your mother, and Elise. Close enough."

She sniffed and shoved her glasses more securely on her nose. "That's insulting."

"I want to know how accurate it is. Save the comments."

"It's fairly complete, and insulting."

Oh yeah, there was that prissy tone of voice too. It just destroyed him with wanting to turn it into moans. "Was Hawthorne's wife with him in Florence?"

"No."

"Richard's divorced." What the hell, he thought, and tortured himself by turning his head just enough to get a good solid sniff of her hair. "Was he a couple when he did his stint in Maine?"

"I don't know. I barely met him. In fact, I didn't remember him until he reminded me we'd met." Annoyed, she turned her head, found her eyes locked on his—and something in his wasn't focused on work. Her heart did a quick cartwheel and shot little springs of lust into her belly. "Why does it matter?"

"Why does what matter?" He wanted that mouth. Goddamn it, he was entitled to that mouth.

"The, uh . . . Richard being divorced."

"Because people tell their lovers and spouses all kinds of confidential things. Sex," he murmured, and wrapped that loose tendril around his finger, "is a great communicator."

One tug, he thought, one little tug and her mouth would be on his. He'd have all that hair in his hands, all the wild, curling mass of it. He'd have her naked in five minutes. Except for the glasses.

He was starting to have incredible fantasies about Miranda wearing only her glasses.

It was with real regret that he didn't tug, but unwound her hair, turned, and scowled at the screen.

"We need to go through the worker bees too, but we need a break."

"A break?" There wasn't a single organized thought in her mind. Her nerves were sizzling along the surface of her skin like little licks of lightning.

If he touched her now, if he kissed her now, she knew she'd go off like a rocket. She straightened, closed her eyes. And yearned.

"What did you have in mind?"

"Let's put this away, and go have a meal."

Her eyes popped open again. "A what?"

"Food, Dr. Jones." He tapped keys, concentrating, and didn't see her scrub her hands over her face behind his back.

"Yes, food." Her voice shook slightly—laughter or despair, she couldn't be sure. "Good idea."

"What would you like for your last night in Florence?"

"The last night?"

"Things might get sticky here. We're better off working on home ground."

"But if *The Dark Lady* is here—"

"We'll come back for her." He shut off his machine, pushed away from the little desk. "Florence isn't a big city, Dr. Jones. Sooner or later, someone you know is going to spot you." He flicked a finger over her hair. "You just don't blend. Now, fast, fancy, or rowdy?"

Home. She discovered she very much wanted to go home, to see it with these new eyes. "I think I'd like rowdy for a change."

"Excellent choice. I know just the place."

It was loud, it was crowded, and the harsh lights bounced off the unapologetically garish paintings that crowded the wall. They suited the hanks of hanging sausages and whole smoked hams that were the restaurant's primary decor. Tables were pushed together so that diners—friends and strangers alike—ate the hearty portions of meat and pasta elbow to elbow.

They were wedged in a corner by a round man with a stained apron who took Ryan's order for a bottle of local red with a nod. At Miranda's left was one half of a gay American couple who were touring Europe. They shared a basket of bread while Ryan engaged them in conversation with an ease and openness Miranda admired.

She would never have talked to strangers in a restaurant except in the most limited fashion. But by the time the wine was set on the table and poured, she knew they were from New York, ran a restaurant in the Village, and had been together for ten years. It was, they said, their anniversary trip.

"It's our second honeymoon." Enjoying himself, Ryan picked up Miranda's hand and kissed it. "Right, Abby darling?"

At sea, she stared at him, then responded to his light kick under the table. "Oh, yes. Um . . . we couldn't afford a honeymoon when we were first married. Kevin was just getting started and I was . . . only a junior exec at the agency. Now we're treating ourselves before kids come along."

Stunned at herself, she gulped down wine while Ryan beamed at her. "It was worth the wait. You breathe romance with every inhale in Florence."

Defying every law of physics, the waiter pushed his way through the excuse for space between the tables and demanded what they wanted.

Less than an hour later, Miranda wanted more wine. "It's wonderful. It's a wonderful place." She shifted in her chair to smile affectionately at a table of Brits who chatted in polite voices while a table of Germans beside them downed local beer and sang. "I never go to places like this." It all spun in her head, scents, voices, wine. "I wonder why."

"Want some dessert?"

"Sure I do. Eat, drink, and be merry." She poured another glass of wine and grinned tipsily at him. "I love it here."

"Yes, I can see that." He nudged the bottle farther out of her reach and signaled the waiter.

"Weren't they a nice couple?" She smiled sentimentally at the space their table companions had recently vacated. "They were really in love. We're going to look 'em up, right, when we get home? No, when *they* get home. *We're* going home tomorrow."

"We'll try the zabaglione," Ryan told the waiter, eyeing Miranda under lifted brows as she began to hum along with the drunk Germans. "And cappuccino."

"I'd rather have more wine."

"Not a good idea."

"Why not?" Filled with love for her fellowman, she picked up her glass and drained it. "I like it."

"It's your head," he said with a shrug when she snagged the bottle again. "Keep it up, and you're not going to have a pleasant flight home."

"I'm a very good flier." Eyes narrowed, she poured until the wine was precisely a half-inch from the rim of the glass. "See that, steady as a rock. Dr. Jones is always steady." She giggled and leaned forward conspiratorially. "But Abby's a lush."

"Kevin is more than a little concerned that she's going to pass out at the table so that he has to carry her home."

"Nah." She rubbed the back of her hand over her nose. "Dr. Jones wouldn't permit that. Too embarrassing. Let's walk down by the river. I want to walk by the river in the moonlight. Abby'll let you kiss her."

"That's an interesting offer, but I think we'd better get you home."

"I love Maine." She leaned back, swinging the glass in her hand. "I love the cliffs and the fog and the waves crashing and the lobster boats. I'm going to plant a garden. This year I'm really going to do it. Mmmm." This was her opinion of the creamy dessert set in front of her. "I like indulging." She set the glass down long enough to dive a spoon in. "I never knew that about me," she said with her mouth full.

"Try the coffee," he suggested.

"I want the wine." But when she grabbed for it, he snatched it up.

"Can I interest you in something else?"

She studied him thoughtfully, then grinned. "Bring me the head of the Baptist," she ordered, then collapsed into giggles. "Did you really steal his bones? I just can't understand a man who'd steal the bones of a saint. But it's fascinating."

Time to go, Ryan decided, and quickly dug out more than enough lire to cover the tab. "Let's take that walk, honey."

"Okay." She popped up, then had to brace a hand against the wall. "Oh my, there's quite a bit of gravity in here."

"Maybe there's not as much outside." He scooped an arm around her waist and pulled her through the restaurant, laughing himself as she called cheerful goodbyes.

"You're a handful, Dr. Jones."

"What was the name of that wine? It was lovely wine. I want to buy a case of it."

"You were doing a good job of working your way through a case." He guided her along the uneven sidewalk, across the quiet street, grateful they'd opted to walk rather than take the scooter. He'd have had to tie her on.

"I'm going to paint my shutters."

"Good idea."

"Your mother has yellow shutters. So cheerful. Everyone in your family is so cheerful." Wrapping an arm around his waist in turn, she led him in a wide, drunken circle. "But I think a nice bright blue would suit my house. A nice bright blue, and I'll put a rocker on the front porch."

"Nothing like a porch rocker. Watch your step, up the curb. Atta girl."

"I broke into my mother's house today."

"I heard that somewhere."

"I'm sharing a hotel suite with a thief and I broke into my mother's house. Coulda robbed her blind."

"You only had to ask. Left turn, that's the way. Almost there."

"It was great."

"What was?"

"The breaking in. I didn't want to say so at the time, but it was great." She threw up her arms and caught him neatly on the chin. "Maybe you could teach me how to pick locks. Wouldya do that, Ryan?"

"Oh yeah, that's going to happen." He wiggled his jaw and steered her toward the front entrance of the hotel.

"I could seduce it out of you." She turned, plowing into him at the edge of the elegant lobby carpet, and crushed her mouth against his before he could gain his balance. This time his head spun as she sucked the blood right out of it.

"Miranda—"

"That's Abby to you, pal," she murmured as the desk clerk discreetly averted his eyes. "So how about it?"

"Let's talk upstairs." He dragged her toward the elevator and out of sight.

"Don't want to talk." She plastered herself against him and attacked his earlobe with her teeth. "I want wild, crazy sex. Right now."

"Who doesn't?" said the male half of a formally dressed couple who stepped off the elevator.

"See?" Miranda pointed out as Ryan yanked her into the car. "He agrees with me. I wanted to jump you ever since I saw you and heard the ping."

"Ping." He was becoming breathless trying to unwind her from around him.

"I hear pings with you. My head's just full of pings right now. Kiss me again, Ryan. You know you want to."

"Cut it out." A little desperately, he shoved at her hands before they could unbutton his shirt. "You're hammered."

"What do you care?" She threw back her head and laughed. "You've been trying to get me into bed all along. Now's your chance."

"There are rules," he muttered, lurching like a drunk as she draped herself over him. One of them, he thought, needed a cold shower.

"Oh, now there're rules." Laughing, she tugged his shirt free of his slacks. As her hands streaked over his back, around to his belly, he fought to shoot the key into the lock.

"God help me. Miranda—Jesus Christ." Those busy hands had worked their way down. Look, I said no." His eyes were crossed when they stumbled inside together. "Get ahold of yourself."

"Can't. Got ahold of you." She released him only long enough to bounce up, wrap her legs around his waist, fist her hands in his hair, and fuse her mouth to his. "I want you. Oh I want you." Her breath came fast as her lips raced over his face. "Make love with me. Touch me. I want your hands on me."

They already were. He couldn't stop them from molding that tight lovely bottom. His blood was screaming for her, his tongue tangling with hers. The little beam of sanity that remained in his mind was growing dimmer.

"You're going to hate both of us in the morning."

"So what?" She laughed again, and her eyes were wildly blue as they looked into his. She shook back her hair, turning his system into one pulsing gland. "This is now. Fall into the moment with me, Ryan. I don't want to go there alone."

Their gazes remained locked as he carried her through the doorway into the bedroom. "Then let's see how long now can last. And remember, Dr. Jones." He caught her bottom lip in his teeth, bit, tugged, released. "You asked for it."

They fell on the bed together, with the moonlight streaming through the doors and shadows dancing in the corners. The weight of him thrilled her, the hard lines of his body pressing hers onto the mattress. Their mouths met again in a kiss that was near violent with greed, then went on and on with tongues hotly tangled, teeth nipping.

She wanted all, then more. Everything, then the impossible. And knew with him she'd find it.

She molded herself to him, unwilling to take the passive role now. The rough movements made her head spin, her breath come out on moaning laughter. Oh God, she was free. And alive, so alive. In her rush to feel flesh, she tugged at his shirt, popping buttons off the elegant silk.

"Oh yes," she whispered when he ripped the sleeve of her blouse. "Hurry."

He couldn't have slowed the pace any more than he could stop time. His quick and clever hands were rough as they yanked off her bra, then filled themselves with her breasts.

White as marble, soft as water.

When touch wasn't enough, he twisted her under him again and devoured.

She cried out, arching as his lips and teeth and tongue laid siege to her. Her nails dug into his back, scraped along the tensed ridge of muscle as shock waves of pleasure swarmed through her body. Sensations slammed into her in a riotous confusion of glorious aches and dark delights and raw nerves.

"Now. Now. Right now."

But his mouth streaked down her torso. Not yet. Not nearly yet.

He yanked the neat cotton slacks down her hips and plunged his tongue into the center of that driving heat. She came instantly, violently, all but paralyzing them both with the glory of it. She sobbed out his name, her fingers tangling in his hair as release built back to need, and need ground desperately toward demand.

Her body was a miracle, a work of art, with long legs and torso, milk pale skin, quivering muscles.

He wanted to savor it, to lick his way up, then down again. He wanted to bury his face in that free fall of hair until he was deaf and blind.

But the animal inside him clawed frantically for freedom.

They rolled again, wrestling over the bed and tormenting each other with nips and gropes.

Vision blurred, lungs burned as another orgasm erupted, raging through her system, spiking it with outrageous energy. Her breath was a series of short screams burning in her chest, her body unbearably awake to every touch, every taste.

His face seemed to swim over hers, then came into focus, every feature distinct as if etched with a diamond on glass. Their breath mingled, her hips arched up. And he drove into her.

All movement stopped for one humming and timeless instant. Joined, with him buried deep inside her, they watched each other. Slowly, in one long stroke, she took her hands down his back, then gripped his hips.

Together, they began to move, the speed building and rising, bodies slick with sweat sliding, pleasure tumbling over pleasure until it battered the system and overpowered the mind.

All, and then more, she thought dizzily as she climbed toward the peak. Everything, then the impossible. She found it as she clamped herself around him and shattered.

CHAPTER NINETEEN

IT WAS THE BRILLIANT WASH OF SUNLIGHT THAT WOKE her. For one horrible moment, she thought her eyes were on fire, and beat on them with her open palms before she was fully coherent.

She discovered she was not spontaneously combusting. And that she was not alone in bed. The best she could manage was a muffled moan as she squeezed her aching eyes shut again.

What had she done?

Well, it was pretty obvious what she'd done—in fact, if memory served, she'd done it twice. In between which, Ryan had made her swallow three aspirin and a small ocean of water. She supposed it was that small consideration that was currently keeping her head in place on her shoulders.

Cautiously, she slid her glance over. He was flat on his stomach, his face buried in the pillow. She imagined he wasn't too wild about the brilliance of the sun either, but neither of them had had their mind on pulling the drapes the night before.

Oh, good God.

She'd jumped him, groped at him, torn at his clothes like a madwoman.

And even now, in the full light of day, her mouth watered at the thought of doing it all again.

Slowly, hoping to preserve her dignity at least long enough to get into the shower, she eased from the bed. He didn't move a muscle or make a sound, and thankful for this small blessing, she made the dash into the bathroom.

Fortunately for her state of mind, she didn't see him pop one eye open and grin at her naked butt.

She talked to herself through the shower, pitifully grateful for the hot steam of the water. It eased some of the aches away. But the deeper ones, the sweeter ones that she accepted came from good, healthy sex remained.

She took another three aspirin anyway, hoping.

He was on the terrace when she came out, chatting casually with the room service waiter. Since it was too late to duck back inside, she managed a small smile for both of them.

"*Buon giorno*. The day is beautiful, *sì*? You enjoy." The waiter took the signed bill with a small bow. *"Grazie. Buon appetito."*

He left them alone with a table full of food and a pigeon who walked along the ledge of the terrace wall, eyeing the offerings avariciously.

"Well . . . I . . ." She stuffed her hands in her robe pockets because they wanted to flutter.

"Have some coffee," he suggested. He wore soft gray slacks and a black shirt that made him look very at ease and cosmopolitan. And made her remember her hair was damp and tangled.

She nearly leaped at the diversion, but shook her head. She was a woman who faced the music squarely. "Ryan, last night . . . I think I should apologize."

"Really?" He poured two cups of coffee and made himself comfortable at the table.

"I had too much to drink. That's not an excuse, just a fact."

"Darling, you were plowed. Cute too," he added, studying her as he added jam to a croissant. "And amazingly agile."

She closed her eyes, gave in, and sat down. "My behavior was inexcusable and regrettable, and I'm sorry. I put you in a very awkward position."

"I recall several positions." He sipped his coffee, charmed at the faint blush that worked its way up her throat. "None of which were the least awkward."

She picked up her coffee, sipped fast, and scalded her tongue.

"Why does it need to be excused?" he wondered, choosing a little cake from the basket and putting it on her plate. "What's the point in regrets? Did we hurt anyone?"

"The issue is—"

"The issue—if there has to be one—is we're both single, unattached, healthy grown-ups who have a strong attraction for each other. Last night we acted on it." He took the cover from a glistening golden omelet. "I for one enjoyed myself, very much." He cut the omelet in two and added a portion to her plate. "How about you?"

She'd been conscientiously set to humiliate herself, to apologize, to take full responsibility. Why wasn't he letting her? "You're missing the point."

"No, I'm not. I don't agree with the point you're fumbling to make. Ah, there, a little flash of that chilly temper in your eyes. Much better. Now, while I appreciate the fact that you're sensible enough not to put the blame on me for taking advantage of the situation—as you were tearing off my clothes—it's just as foolish to blame yourself."

"I'm blaming the wine," she said stiffly.

"No, you already said that wasn't an excuse." He laughed, took her hand and put a fork in it. "I wanted to make love with you the minute I saw you—wanted it more the longer I knew you. You fascinate me, Miranda. Now eat your eggs before they get cold."

She stared down at her plate. It wasn't possible to be annoyed with him. "I don't have casual sex."

"You call that casual?" He blew out a long breath. "God help me when we get serious."

She felt her lips twitch and gave up. "It was fabulous."

"I'm glad you remember. I wasn't sure how clear your mind would be. I wish we had more time here." He toyed with her damp hair. "Florence is good to lovers."

She took a long breath, looked directly into his

eyes, and made what for her was an unprecedented commitment. "Maine's beautiful in the spring."

He smiled and stroked a finger down her cheek. "I'm going to enjoy experiencing it."

The Dark Lady stood under a single beam of light. The one who studied her sat in the dark. The mind was cold, calm, and clear, as it had been when murder was done.

Murder had not been planned. The driving forces had been power and what was right. If all had gone correctly, if all had gone well, violence would not have been necessary.

But it had not gone correctly, or well, so adjustments had been made. The blame for the loss of two lives lay with the theft of the *David.* Who could have anticipated, who could have controlled such an event?

It would be termed a wild card. Yes, a wild card.

But murder was not as abhorrent as one would think. That too brought power. Nothing and no one could substantiate the existence of *The Dark Lady* and be permitted to exist. That was simple fact.

It would be taken care of, it would be dealt with, cleanly, completely, and finally.

When the time was right it would end. With Miranda.

It was a pity such a bright and clever mind had to be destroyed. Reputation alone would have sufficed once. Now, everything had to be taken. There was no room for sentiment in science, or in power.

An accident perhaps, though suicide would be best.

Yes, suicide. It would be so . . . satisfying. How odd not to have anticipated how satisfying her death would be.

It would take some thought, some planning. It would take . . . A smile spread as slyly as that on the glorious face of the bronze. It would take patience.

When *The Dark Lady* was left alone under that single beam of light, there was no one to hear the quiet laughter of the damned. Or the mad.

Spring was drifting over Maine. There was a softness in the air that hadn't been there even a week before. Or at least Miranda hadn't felt it.

On its hill, the old house stood with its back to the sea, its windows going gold in the setting sun. It was good to be home.

She stepped inside and found Andrew in the den, keeping company with a bottle of Jack Daniel's. Her quietly optimistic mood plummeted.

He got to his feet quickly, swaying a little. She noted that it took his eyes several seconds to focus, that he hadn't shaved in the last day or two, that his clothes were wrinkled.

He was, she realized, well drunk, and likely had been for a couple of days.

"Where've you been?" He took a couple of lurching steps, then caught her up in a sloppy hug. "I've been worried about you. I called everybody I could think of. Nobody knew where you'd gone."

Despite the heavy fumes of whiskey that hung around him, she knew his concern was sincere. Though she hugged him back, wanting that connection, her intention of telling him everything wavered. How much could a drunk be trusted?

"I'm on leave," she reminded him. "I left you a note."

"Yeah, and it didn't tell me dick." He drew back, studied her face, then patted her head with one of his big hands. "When the old man came to the Institute, I knew we were hip-deep. I got back here as soon as I could, but you were already gone."

"They didn't leave me any choice. Did he come down hard on you?"

"No more than expected." He shrugged that off. Even with the whiskey hampering his instincts he could see something was different. "What's going on, Miranda? What'd you do?"

"I went away for a few days." She made the decision to keep what she knew to herself, with regret. "I ran into Ryan Boldari in New York."

She turned away because she was a poor liar under the best of circumstances. And had never lied to Andrew. "He's back in Maine now. He's going to stay here for a few days."

"Here?"

"Yes, I . . . We're involved."

"You're—Oh." He ran his tongue around his teeth and tried to think. "Okay. That was . . . quick."

"Not really. We have a lot in common." She

didn't want to dwell on that. "Has there been any progress in the investigation?"

"We hit a snag. We can't find the documentation on the *David*."

Though she'd been expecting this, her stomach jumped. She ran a nervous hand over her hair and prepared to continue the deception. "Can't find it? It should be in the files."

"I know where it should be, Miranda." Irritated, he picked up the bottle and poured another drink. "It's not there. It's not anywhere in the Institute. I've looked everywhere." He pressed his fingers to his eyes. "Insurance company's balking. If we don't come up with it, we're going to take the loss. You did the testing."

"Yes," she said carefully. "I did the testing. I authenticated the piece, and the documentation was properly filed. You know that, Andrew. You worked on it too."

"Yeah, well, it's gone now. The insurance company's rejecting the claim until they have documents, our mother is threatening to come in and see why we're so inept that we lose not only a fine piece of art but its paperwork, and Cook's giving me the fucking fish eye."

"I'm sorry I left you alone with this." Sorrier now that she could see how he was handling it. "Andrew, please." She walked over and took the glass out of his hand. "I can't talk to you when you're drunk."

He only smiled, dimples popping into his cheeks. "I'm not drunk yet."

"Yes, you are." She'd been there herself recently enough to know the signs. "You need to get into a program."

The dimples faded. Jesus Christ, was all he could think. Just what he needed. "What I need is a little cooperation and support." Irked, he snatched the glass back and took a long gulp. "Maybe you're sorry you left me alone with this, but that's just what you did. And if I want a few drinks after a miserable day of dealing with the police, running the Institute, and tap dancing for our parents, it's nobody's fucking business."

As she stared at him her chest tightened, squeezing her heart with the pressure. "I love you." The words hurt, just a little, because she knew neither of them said them often enough. "I love you, Andrew, and you're killing yourself in front of my eyes. That makes it my business."

There were tears in her eyes and in her voice that played on his guilt and infuriated. "Fine, I'll kill myself in private. Then it won't be any of your goddamn business." He grabbed the bottle and strode out.

He hated himself for it, for putting that disappointment and hurt in the eyes of the only person he'd ever been able to fully depend on. But goddamn it to hell and back, it was his life.

He slammed the door of his bedroom, didn't notice the stench of stale whiskey from his binge the night before. He sat in a chair and drank straight from the bottle.

He was entitled to relax, wasn't he? He got his

work done, he did his job—for all the good it did him—so why did he have to get grief for having a couple of drinks?

Or a couple dozen, he thought with a snicker. Who was counting?

Maybe the blackouts worried him a little, those weird and empty pockets of time he couldn't seem to account for. That was probably stress, and a good stiff drink was the best solution to stress.

You bet it was.

He told himself he missed his wife, though it was becoming more and more difficult to bring up a clear picture of her face, or to remember the exact pitch of her voice. Occasionally, when he was sober, he had a flash of truth. He didn't love Elise any longer—and maybe had never loved her as much as he liked to think. So he drank to blot out that truth, and allowed himself to enjoy the sense of betrayal and misery.

He was beginning to see the value of drinking alone now that Annie had barred him from her place. Alone, you could drink until you couldn't stand, and when you couldn't stand you lay down and passed out. It got a man through the night.

A man had to get through the night, he thought, brooding at the bottle before tipping it back again.

It wasn't that he had to drink. He was in control of it and could quit whenever he wanted. He didn't want, that was all. Still, he'd stop, cold turkey, just to prove to Miranda, to Annie, to every damn body they were wrong about him.

People had always been wrong about him, he

decided, stewing in resentment. Beginning with his parents. They'd never known who the hell he was, what he wanted, much less what the hell he needed.

So fuck them. Fuck all of them.

He'd quit drinking, all right. Tomorrow, he thought with another chuckle as he lifted the bottle.

He saw the lights cut across the room. Headlights, he decided after a long, wavering study where his mind blinked out and his mouth hung open. Company's coming. Probably Boldari.

He took another long gulp and grinned to himself. Miranda had a boyfriend. He'd get some mileage out of that. It had been a long time since he'd been able to tease his sister over something as interesting as a man.

Might as well get started on it now, he decided. He got to his feet, snorting with laughter as the room revolved. Join the circus, see the world, he thought, and stumbled toward the door.

He'd just find out what old Ryan Boldari's intentions were. Yes indeed. He had to show that slick New Yorker that little Miranda had herself a big brother looking out for her. He took another long chug from the bottle as he lurched down the hall, and grabbing the banister at the top of the steps, looked down.

There was his baby sister, right at the foot of the steps, in a hot liplock with New York. "Hey!" He called out, gesturing wildly with the bottle, then laughing when Miranda whirled around. "Whatcha doing with my sister, Mr. New York?"

"Hello, Andrew."

"Hello, Andrew my ass. You sleeping with my sister, you bastard?"

"Not at the moment." He kept his arm around Miranda's rigid shoulders.

"Well, I wanna talk to you, buddy." Andrew started down, made it halfway on his feet, and tumbled the rest. It was like watching a boulder fall down a cliff.

Miranda leaped forward, kneeling beside his sprawled body. There was blood on his face, which terrified her. "Oh God. Andrew."

"I'm all right. I'm all right," he muttered, shoving at her hands as they poked and probed for broken bones. "Just took a little spill's all."

"You could have broken your neck."

"Steps are a tricky thing," Ryan said mildly. He crouched beside Miranda, noting that the cut on Andrew's forehead was shallow, and Miranda's hands were shaking. "Why don't we get you back up them, clean you up?"

"Shit." Andrew brushed his fingers over his forehead, studied the smear of blood. "Look at that."

"I'll get the first-aid kit."

Ryan glanced over at Miranda. She'd gone pale again, but her eyes were shuttered. "We'll take care of it. Come on, Andrew. My brother tripped over a curb the night of his bachelor party and did more damage than this." He was hauling Andrew to his feet as Miranda got to hers. But when she started to go up with them, Ryan shook his head at her.

"No women. This is a guy thing. Right, Andrew?"

"Damn right." Boozily he made Ryan his best friend. "Women are the root of all evil."

"God love them."

"I had one for a while. She dumped me."

"Who needs her?" Ryan steered Andrew to the left.

"That's the spirit! I can't see a fucking thing."

"There's blood dripping into your eye."

"Thank Christ, thought I'd been struck blind. Know what, Ryan Boldari, pal?"

"What's that?"

"I'm going to be really sick now."

"Oh yeah." Ryan dragged him into the bathroom. "You are."

What a family, Ryan thought as he held Andrew's head and wondered vaguely if it was possible to throw up internal organs. If not, Andrew was giving it the old college try.

By the time it was over, Andrew was wrecked, white as death and trembling. It took three tries for Ryan to prop him on the toilet seat so he could deal with the cut on his face.

"Must've been the fall," Andrew said weakly.

"You threw up the best part of a fifth," Ryan said as he wiped blood and sweat away. "You embarrassed yourself and your sister, took a header that would have snapped several bones if they hadn't been permeated with whiskey, you smell like a four o'clock bar and look worse. Sure, it was the fall."

Andrew closed his eyes. He wanted to curl up somewhere and sleep until he died. "Maybe I had a couple too many. Wouldn't have if Miranda hadn't started on me."

"Save the lame excuses. You're a drunk." Ruthlessly, Ryan swabbed antiseptic over the wound and felt no sympathy when Andrew sucked in his breath. "At least be man enough to take the responsibility for it."

"Fuck you."

"That's a clever and original comeback. You shouldn't need stitches, but you're going to have a hell of a black eye to go with the war wound." Satisfied, he pulled Andrew's ruined shirt over his head.

"Hey."

"You need a shower, pal. Trust me."

"I just want to go to bed. For God's sake, I just want to lie down. I think I'm dying."

"Not yet, but you're on your way." Grimly, Ryan pulled him to his feet, bracing himself to hold the weight while he reached out and turned on the shower. He decided it was more trouble than it was worth to remove Andrew's pants, so dragged him half dressed into the tub.

"Jesus. I'm going to be sick again."

"Then aim for the drain," Ryan suggested, and held him in place even when Andrew began to sob like a baby.

It took the best part of an hour to pour Andrew into bed. When he came downstairs Ryan noted that the shattered glass from the bottle had been swept up, and the splash of whiskey that had hit walls and floors on the fall had been scrubbed.

When he couldn't find Miranda in the house, he grabbed a jacket and headed outside.

She was on the cliffs. He studied the silhouette she made there, alone, tall, slender, against the night sky, with her hair blowing free and her face turned to the sea.

Not just alone, he thought. Lonely. He didn't think he'd ever seen anyone lonelier.

He climbed up to her, draped the jacket over her shoulders.

She'd managed to steady herself. Somehow the restless tossing of the sea could always calm her. "I'm terribly sorry you were dragged into that."

Her voice was cool, he noted. Automatic defense. Her body was stiff, and still turned away from him. "I wasn't dragged in. I was here." He laid his hands on her shoulders, but she stepped away.

"That's the second time you've had to deal with an embarrassingly drunk Jones."

"One night's foolishness is a long distance from what your brother's doing to himself, Miranda."

"However true that is, it doesn't change the facts. We behaved badly, and you cleaned up the mess. I don't know if I could have handled Andrew tonight by myself. But I would have preferred it."

"That's too bad." Annoyed, he spun her around to face him. "Because I was here, and I'm going to be here for a while."

"Until we find the bronzes."

"That's right. And if I'm not done with you by then . . ." He cupped her face, lowered his head and took her mouth in an angry and possessive kiss. "You'll have to deal with it."

"I don't *know* how to deal with it." Her voice rose over the crash of waves. "I'm not equipped for this, for you. Every relationship I've ever had has ended badly. I don't know how to handle that kind of emotional tangle, no one in my family does, so they just untangle at the first possible opportunity."

"You've never tangled with me before." It was said with such blatant arrogance she might have laughed. Instead she turned away, stared at the steady circling beam from the lighthouse.

He would be the one to run when it was done, she thought. And this time, with him, she was desperately afraid she would suffer. It didn't matter that she understood why he was there, what his primary purpose was. She would suffer when he left her.

"Everything that's happened since I met you is foreign to me. I don't function well without guidelines."

"You've been winging it pretty well so far."

"Two men are dead, Ryan. My reputation's in ruins, my family is more divided than ever. I've broken the law, I've ignored ethics, and I'm having an affair with a criminal."

"But you haven't been bored, have you?"

She let out a weak laugh. "No. I don't know what to do next."

"I can help you with that." He took her hand and began to walk. "Tomorrow's soon enough to take the next steps. Soon enough to talk about what they should be."

"I need to put everything in order." She glanced back toward the house. "I should check on Andrew first, then organize."

"Andrew's asleep, and he's not going to surface until tomorrow. Organizing takes a clear, focused mind. You've got too much on yours to be clear or focused."

"Excuse me, but organization is my life. I can organize three different projects, outline a lecture, and teach a class at the same time."

"You're a frightening woman, Dr. Jones. Then let's say *I'm* not clear or focused. And I've never been inside a lighthouse." He studied it as they approached, enjoying the way its beam cut through the dark and lay shimmering on the surface of the sea. "How old is it?"

She let out a breath. If it was avoidance, so be it. "It was built in 1853. The structure is original, though my grandfather had the interior revamped in the forties with the idea of using it as his art studio. The fact is, according to my grandmother, he used it for illicit sexual affairs because it amused him to have them within sight of the house and in such an obviously phallic symbol."

"Good old Grandpa."

"He was only one of the insufferable emotionally stunted Joneses. His father—again according to my grandmother, who was the only one who would discuss such matters—flaunted his mistresses in public and conceived several illegitimate children he refused to acknowledge. My grandfather carried on that lofty tradition."

"The Joneses of Jones Point are many."

She waited for the insult to sink in, then shook her head. It was amusement she felt instead. "Yes, I suppose so. In any case, my great-grandmother chose to ignore his habits and spent most of the year in Europe, avenging herself by squandering as much of his money as was possible. Unfortunately, she chose to travel back to the States on a luxurious new ship. They called it the *Titanic*."

"Really?" Ryan was close enough to see the rusted lock on the thick wooden door. "Cool."

"Well, she and her children boarded a lifeboat and were rescued. But she caught pneumonia from the exposure in the North Atlantic, and died of it a few weeks later. Her husband mourned by taking up with an opera singer shortly thereafter. He was killed when the opera singer's husband, being somewhat displeased with the arrangement, set the house where they were living in sin on fire."

"I imagine he died happy." Ryan took a Leatherman knife kit out of his pocket, chose his tool, and went to work on the lock.

"Don't. I have a key in the house if you want to see the inside."

"This is more fun, and quicker. See?" He replaced the knife, opened the door. "Damp," he said, and took out his penlight to shine it around the large lower room. "Yet cozy."

The walls were paneled with old-fashioned knotty pine that reminded him of a suburban rec room from the fifties. Various shapes were tucked efficiently under holland covers, and a small fireplace, layered with cold gray ash, was built into the far side.

He thought it was a shame that whoever had designed this area had chosen to build in the walls to square them off rather than going with the round.

"So, is this where Grandpa entertained his ladies?"

"I imagine." She pulled the jacket more securely around her shoulders. The air inside was chilly and stale. "My grandmother detested him, but she stayed in the marriage, raised my father, then nursed her husband through the last two years of his life. She was a wonderful woman. Strong, stubborn. She loved me."

He turned back, skimmed the back of his hand over her face. "Of course she did."

"There's no of course when it comes to love in my family." Because she saw the flicker of sympathy in his eyes, she turned away. "You'd see more in here if you wait for daylight."

He said nothing for a moment. He remembered he'd once thought she had a cold streak. It was rare for him to be so completely wrong when analyzing a mark. She'd been a mark then, and now . . . That was something to think about later.

It wasn't coldness inside her, but a well-built defense against hurts of a lifetime. From neglect, indifference, from the very coldness he'd believed lived in her.

He walked around, pleased when he spotted both an oil lamp and candles. He lighted both, appreciating the eerie glow they gave the room.

"Spooky." He put his penlight away and grinned at her. "You ever come in here as a kid and look for ghosts?"

"Don't be ridiculous."

"Honey, you had a deprived childhood. We'll have to make up for that. Come on."

"What are you doing?"

"Going up." He was already climbing the metal tight-winder stairs.

"Don't touch anything." She scurried after him as the lights he carried sent bobbing glows and shadows against the walls. "It's all automated now."

He found a small bedroom, with little more than a stripped mattress that looked inhabitable and a scruffy chest of drawers. The grandmother, he decided, had likely pirated the place of any valuables. Good for her.

He walked over and admired the view from the porthole-style window. The sea raged, sliced by the light, churning under it, through it. Small islands, like humped backs, brooded off the ragged coastline. He caught the sway of buoys, heard the hollow bong of them punch through the sweeping crash and suck of sea.

"Great spot. Drama, danger, and challenge."

"It's rarely calm," she said from behind him. "There's a view of the bay from the other window. "Some days, or nights, the water there is as smooth as glass. It looks as though you could walk on it, all the way to shore."

He glanced over his shoulder. "Which do you like best?"

"I'm fond of both, but I suppose I'm usually drawn to the sea."

"Restless spirits are drawn to restless spirits."

She frowned at that, brooding after him as he moved out of the room. No one, she thought, would term her a restless spirit. Least of all herself.

Dr. Miranda Jones was stable as granite, she thought. And often, too often, just as boring.

With a vague shrug she followed him into the pilot room.

"Amazing place." He was already ignoring her order and touching what he chose.

The equipment was efficiently modern and hummed along as the great lights circled overhead. The room was round, as it should have been, with a narrow ledge circling outside. The iron rails were rusted, but he found them charming. When he stepped out, the wind slapped at him like an insulted woman and made him laugh.

"Fabulous. Damned if I wouldn't have brought my women here too. Romantic, sexy, and just a little scary. You ought to fix it up," he said, glancing back at her. "It'd make a terrific studio."

"I don't need a studio."

"You would if you worked on your art, the way you should be."

"I'm not an artist."

He smiled, stepped back inside and closed out the wind. "I happen to be a very important art broker, and I say you are. Cold?"

"A little." She was hugging herself inside the jacket. "It's very damp in here."

"You're going to have rot if you don't deal with that. That would be a crime. I'm also an expert on crime." He put his hands on her arms, rubbing to warm her with friction. "The sea sounds different from in here. Mysterious, almost threatening."

"During a good nor'easter, it would sound a lot more threatening. The light still functions to guide ships and keep them from coming too close to the shallows and the rocks. Even with it, there were a number of wrecks off the coast last century."

"The ghosts of shipwrecked sailors, rattling bones, haunting the shore."

"Hardly."

"I can hear them." He slipped his arms around her. "Moaning for mercy."

"You hear the wind," she corrected, but he'd managed to draw a shudder out of her. "Seen enough?"

"Not nearly." He lowered his mouth to nibble on hers. "But I intend to."

She tried to wiggle free. "Boldari, if you think you can seduce me inside a damp and dusty lighthouse, you're delusional."

"Is that a dare?" He nipped around to the side of her neck.

"No, it's a fact." But the muscles in her thighs were already going lax. He had the most inventive tongue. "There's a perfectly good bedroom in the house, several in fact. They're warm, convenient, and have excellent mattresses."

"We'll have to try them out, later. Have I mentioned what a delightful body you have, Dr.

Jones?" His hands were already busy exploring it. Those quick and clever fingers flipped open the hook of her slacks, drew the zipper down before she could do more than gasp out a protest.

"Ryan, this isn't the place for—"

"It was good enough for Grandpa," he reminded her, then slowly slipped his fingers inside her. She was already hot, already wet, and he kept his eyes on hers, watching them go blind and dark and desperate. "Just let go. I want to feel you come, right here. I want to watch what I do to you take you over."

Her body gave her no choice. It hummed like a well-oiled machine toward one purpose, one goal. The long, deep thrill slid through her, a sudden tangling of circuits, a sparking of nerve ends, then a long liquid wave of pleasure that swamped the system.

Her head fell back on a moan, and he moved in to ravage the exposed column of her throat. "Still cold?" he murmured.

"No, God, no." Her skin was on fire, her blood pumping like a hot river beneath it. Gripping his shoulders for balance, she rocked against his busy hand.

Now, when his mouth came back to hers, she answered the demand with one of her own. Time and place were nothing against the hard and driving need.

Her slacks pooled at her feet, the jacket slipped from her shoulders. Pliant as softened wax, she molded against him as he braced her on the counter where equipment whirred efficiently to send the light circling the sea.

"Lift your arms, Miranda."

She obeyed, her breath snagging on every inhale as he slowly slipped her sweater up. He watched nervy pleasure flicker over her face as he used his thumbs to trace her nipples through the thin fabric of her bra.

"No wine tonight to blur the edges." His fingers skimmed lightly over the swell above the simple white silk. "I want you to feel everything, to wonder what you'll feel next." He nudged one strap down with a fingertip, then the other, lowered his head to nibble at her bare shoulders.

It was like being . . . sampled, she thought as her heavy eyes shut. Savored, lavishly savored. His tongue licked lightly over her flesh, his teeth grazed, and his fingertips slid up and down, up and down the sides of her body, gradually, thrillingly lowering the thin swatch of cotton at her hips.

He stood intimately between her spread legs while she gripped the edge of the counter and understood what it was to be completely under someone else's control. To want to be. To crave it.

Everything he did to her was a shock, a jolt to the ruthlessly ordered pattern of her mind, that only seconds later was desired again and welcomed.

A part of her brain knew the image she made, almost naked, skin flushed, body arched in surrender while the man who handled her was fully dressed.

But when he slipped the bra aside, lowered that skilled mouth to her breast, she didn't care.

He hadn't known she could be like this, or how powerful an arousal it was to have a strong and cautious woman yield to him completely. She was his, utterly, to take pleasure from, to give pleasure to. But the thrill of that, rather than dark and edgy, was almost unbearably tender.

The backwash from the great light slid over her, turning her skin to brilliant white; then it was gone, leaving her glowing gold in the flicker of candlelight. Her hair, so recently chased by the wind, tumbled like silken fire over her shoulders. Her mouth, soft and swollen, parted under his.

The kiss deepened, warmed, and delved beyond the heady desire neither had anticipated. For a moment they clung together, staggered. And trembled.

It was like a dream now where the air was thick and sweet. Hot candy, melted over slow heat.

Neither noticed the damp or the chill. They lowered to a floor that was layered with dust, that was hard and cold, and drew together as gently as a couple on a feather bed.

Without words, she removed his shirt, her hands steady. And she pressed her lips to his heart, lingering there because she knew that somehow he'd stolen hers.

He wanted to give her tenderness here, the compassion in mating as well as the thrill. So he was gentle with his mouth, with his hands, loving her in a way that gleamed with emotion as well as need.

A murmur, a sigh, a long slow arch toward warm waves that cradled rather than battered.

So when she wrapped around him, pressing her face into his throat, he stroked, he soothed, he gave himself the gift of that same tenderness.

When he shifted her over him, cupping her hips until she took him in, took him deep, she knew what it was to love her lover.

CHAPTER TWENTY

MIRANDA AWOKE BESIDE RYAN FOR THE SECOND morning in a row, and on another continent. It was an oddly thrilling experience that seemed both carelessly wicked and decidedly sophisticated.

Sinning in style.

She had an urge to comb her fingers through his hair, play them over his face, explore that dashing little scar over his eye. Foolish, sentimental little strokes and pats that might lead to slow and lazy morning sex.

It was so odd, all these feelings crowding inside of her, taking up room she hadn't known she had in store, warming up places she'd assumed would always stay cool and uninhabited. So much more inside her now, she thought, than that first hot gush of lust. Too much more, and it left her completely vulnerable.

And that was terrifying.

So instead of touching what she wanted to touch, she eased out of bed and tiptoed into the shower as she had done the morning before. This time, however, she'd barely dunked her head under the spray, when arms slid around her waist.

"Why do you do that?"

She waited until her heart had dropped back in place. "Do what?"

"Sneak out of bed in the morning. I've seen you naked already."

"I didn't sneak." She tried to wiggle free, but his teeth clamped lightly on her shoulder. "I just didn't want to wake you."

"I know a sneak when I see one." He lifted a brow at her mutter. "And saying 'pot' and 'kettle' doesn't apply. I have never sneaked out of a woman's bed. In yes, out no."

"Very funny. Now if you'll excuse me, I'm trying to shower."

"I'll help you." More than willing to assist, he picked up the soap, sniffed it, then began to rub it over her back. It was, he thought, a very excellent back.

"I mastered the art of the shower years ago. I can do it solo."

"Why?" Because her voice had been delightfully prim, he turned her around, snuggling her wet, slippery body against his.

"Because it's . . ." She could feel her color rise and hated it. "It's personal."

"Oh, I see," he said, tongue planted in cheek. "And the sex wasn't personal?"

"It's different."

"Okay." With his eyes laughing into hers, he skimmed his soap-slicked hands over her breasts. "We'll compromise and combine the two."

It was far from the brisk and basic hygiene she'd had in mind.

When she was gulping in steam and quaking from the aftershocks, he nuzzled at her throat. "That," he said, "was personal." Then he sighed. "I have to go to Mass."

"What?" She shook her head, sure there was water in her ears. "Did you say you had to go to Mass?"

"Easter Sunday."

"Yes, yes, it is." Struggling to keep up with him, she shoved dripping hair out of her eyes. "It seems like an odd line of thought, under the circumstances."

"They might not have had the benefit of indoor plumbing in biblical times, but they had plenty of sex."

She supposed he had a point, but it still made her vaguely uncomfortable to think of religion when his wet hands were sliding over her wet butt.

"You're Catholic." At his lifted brow she shook her head. "Yes, I know, Irish and Italian, what else could you do? I didn't realize you practiced."

"Mostly I'm lapsed." He stepped out of the shower, handed her a towel and got one for himself. "And if you tell my mother I said that, I'll swear you're a dirty, rotten liar. But it's Easter Sunday." He gave his hair a quick rub, then draped the towel around his hips. "If I don't go to Mass, my mother will kill me."

"I see. I feel obliged to point out that your mother isn't here."

"She'll know." He said it mournfully. "She always knows, and I'll go straight to hell because she'll see to it." He watched her align the ends of the towel, wrap, then neatly tuck them between her breasts. The efficiency of the gesture did nothing to detract from the sexiness of it. The room smelled of her—clean soap with woodsy overtones. Abruptly, he didn't want to leave her, not even for an hour.

The realization had him rolling his shoulders as if he needed to displace a sudden and uncomfortable weight.

"Why don't you come with me? You can wear your Easter bonnet."

"Not only don't I own a bonnet, of any kind, but I have to get my thoughts in order." She took a portable hair dryer from the cabinet beside the sink. "And I need to talk to Andrew."

He'd been toying with the idea of afternoon Mass so he could slip the knot on her towel. But he put that aside now. "What do you intend to tell him?"

"Not very much." And it shamed her. "Under the circumstances, as long as he's . . . I hate that he's drinking like this. I hate it." It shamed her too that when she drew in a breath it was shaky. "And for a minute last night, I hated him. He's all I've ever had, and I hated him."

"No you didn't. You hated what he's doing."

"Yes, you're right." But she knew what had

bloomed inside her when she looked up and saw him weaving at the top of the steps. "In any case, I have to talk to him. I'll have to tell him something. I've never lied to him before, not about anything."

There was nothing Ryan understood more than family ties, or the knots they could tie themselves into. "Until he deals with his drinking, he's not the man you know, or one you can trust."

"I know." It was eating at her heart.

In the bathroom in the next wing, where the smell of stale vomit still hung in the air, Andrew leaned on the sink and forced himself to study the face in his mirror.

It was gray, the eyes bloodshot, the skin pasty. His left eye was a sunburst of bruising and above that was a shallow cut perhaps an inch in length. It ached like a fever.

He couldn't remember more than pieces from the evening before, but what did swim back into his mind made his raw stomach clench again.

He saw the image of himself, standing at the top of the stairs, waving a nearly empty bottle and shouting down, slopping the words out while Miranda stared up at him.

And there had been something like loathing in her eyes.

He closed his own. It was all right, he could control it. Maybe he'd stepped over a line the night before, but he wouldn't do it again. He'd take a couple of days off from drinking, prove to everyone he could. It was the stress, that was all. He had reason to be stressed.

He downed some aspirin, pretended his hands weren't shaking. When he dropped the bottle and pills spilled out on the tile, he left them there. He walked out, carrying his sickness with him.

He found Miranda in her office, dressed casually in a sweater and leggings, her hair bundled on top of her head and her posture perfect as she worked at her computer.

It took him more time than he cared to admit to gather the courage to step inside. But when he did, she glanced over, then quickly clicked her data to save and blanked the screen.

"Good morning." She knew her voice was frigid, but couldn't find the will to warm it. "There's coffee in the kitchen."

"I'm sorry."

"I'm sure you are. You may want to put ice on that eye."

"What do you want from me? I said I'm sorry. I had too much to drink. I embarrassed you, I acted like an idiot. It won't happen again."

"Won't it?"

"No." The fact that she didn't give an inch infuriated him. "I went past my limit, that's all."

"One drink is past your limit, Andrew. Until you accept that, you're going to continue to embarrass yourself, to hurt yourself and the people who care about you."

"Look, while you've been off having your little fling with Boldari, I've been here, up to my ears, dealing with business. And part of that business is your screwup in Florence."

Very slowly, she got to her feet. "I beg your pardon?"

"You heard me, Miranda. I'm the one who's had to listen to our mother and our father complain and bitch about the mess with that bronze of yours. And I'm the one who spent days looking for the goddamn documents on the *David*—that you were in charge of. I'm taking the heat for that too because you're out of it. You can waltz off and spend your time fucking some—"

The crack of her hand across his face shocked them both, left them staring and breathless. She curled her fingers into her stinging palm, pressed it to her heart, and turned away from him.

He stood where he was, wondering why the new apology that ached in his heart couldn't be forced out of his mouth. So, saying nothing at all, he turned and walked out.

She heard the slam of the front door moments later, then looking out the window, saw his car drive off.

All of her life, he'd been her rock. And now, she thought, because she simply wasn't capable of enough compassion, she'd struck out when he needed her. And she'd pushed him away.

She didn't know if she had it in her to pull him back.

Her fax phone rang, then picked up the transmission with its high-pitched squeal. Rubbing the tension out of the back of her neck, Miranda walked over as the message slid into the tray.

Did you think I wouldn't know? Did you enjoy Florence, Miranda? The spring flowers and the warm sunshine? I know where you go. I know what you do. I know what you think. I'm right there, inside your mind, all the time.

You killed Giovanni. His blood's on your hands.

Can you see it?

I can.

With a sound of fury, Miranda crushed the paper into a ball, heaved it across the room. She pressed her fingers to her eyes, waiting for the red haze that was fury and fear to fade. When it had, she walked over calmly, picked up the paper, smoothed it out with great care.

And put it neatly into the drawer with the other two.

Ryan came back with an armload of daffodils so bright and sunny she couldn't do anything but smile. But because it didn't reach her eyes, he tipped up her chin.

"What?"

"It's nothing, they're wonderful."

"What?" he repeated, and watched her struggle to overcome her habitual reluctance to share trouble.

"Andrew and I had a scene. He left. I don't know

where he's gone, and I know there's nothing I can do about it."

"You have to let him find his own level, Miranda."

"I know that too. I need to put these in water." On impulse she picked up her grandmother's favored rose medallion vase, and taking it to the kitchen, busied herself arranging the flowers on the kitchen table. "I've made some progress, I think," she told him. "I've put together some lists."

She thought about the fax, wondered if she should tell him. Later, she decided. Later when she'd thought it all through.

"Lists?"

"Organizing thoughts and facts and tasks on paper. I'll go get the hard copies so we can go over them."

"Fine." He opened the refrigerator, perused the contents. "Want a sandwich?" Since she was already gone, he shrugged and began to decide what an inventive man could put together.

"Both your lunch meat and your bread are on the edge," he told her when she came back in. "But we risk it or starve."

"Andrew was supposed to go to the market." She watched him slice undoubtedly soft tomatoes and frowned. He looked very much at home, she decided. Not just helping himself to the contents of the kitchen, but preparing them.

"I suppose you can cook."

"No one got out of our house unless they could cook." He glanced her way. "I suppose you don't."

"I'm a very good cook," she said with some annoyance.

"Really? How do you look in an apron?"

"Efficient."

"I bet you don't. Why don't you put one on and let me see?"

"*You're* fixing lunch. I don't need an apron. And just as a passing observation, you're a bit locked into regular meals."

"Food's a passion." He licked tomato juice, slowly, from his thumb. "I'm very locked into regular passions."

"So it would seem." She sat and tapped the edges of her papers together to align them. "Now—"

"Mustard or mayo?"

"It doesn't matter. Now, what I've done—"

"Coffee, or something cold?"

"Whatever." She heaved out a breath, telling herself he couldn't possibly be interrupting her train of thought just to annoy her. "In order to—"

"Milk's off," he said, sniffing the carton he pulled out of the fridge.

"Dump the damn stuff down the sink then, and sit down." Her eyes flashed as she looked up, and caught him grinning at her. "Why do you purposely aggravate me?"

"Because it puts such pretty color in your face." He held up a can of Pepsi. "Diet?"

She had to laugh, and when she did, he sat down at the table across from her. "There, that's better," he decided, pushed her plate closer, then picked up his own sandwich. "I can't concentrate on anything but you when you're sad."

"Oh, Ryan." How could she possibly defend her heart against these kinds of assaults? "I'm not sad."

"You're the saddest woman I've ever known." He kissed her fingers. "But we're going to fix that. Now what have you got?"

She gave herself a moment to regain her balance, then picked up the first sheet. "The first is an amended draft of the list you had of personnel with access to or contact with both of the bronzes."

"Amended."

"I've added a tech who I remembered flew in from Florence to work with Giovanni on another project during the given time period. He was only here for a few days, as I recall, but for accuracy's sake should be included. His name wasn't on the records we accessed because he was, technically, employed by the Florence branch and only here on temporary loan. I also added length of employment, which may factor into loyalty, and base salaries, as it could be assumed that money is a motivation."

She'd also alphabetized the names, he noted. God love her. "Your family pays well." He'd noted that before.

"Quality staff demands appropriate financial reward. On the next list I worked up a probability ratio. You'll note my name remains, but the probability is low. I know I didn't steal the originals. I've taken Giovanni off as he couldn't have been involved."

"Why?"

She blinked up at him. *His blood's on your hands.* "Because he was murdered. He's dead."

"I'm sorry, Miranda, that only makes him dead. It's still possible he was involved, and killed for any number of reasons."

"But he was testing the bronzes when he was killed."

"He'd have needed to, to be sure. Maybe he was panicking, demanding a bigger cut, or just pissed off one of his associates. His name stays on."

"It wasn't Giovanni."

"That's emotion, not logic, Dr. Jones."

"Very well." Jaw stiff, she added Giovanni's name. "You may disagree, but I've rated my family low. In my opinion they don't apply here. They've no reason to steal from themselves." He only looked at her, and after a long moment, she pushed the sheet aside.

"We'll table the probability list for now. Here I've made a time line, from the date the *David* came into our hands, the length of time it remained in the lab. Without my notes and records, I can only guess at the times and dates of the individual tests, but I believe this is fairly close."

"You made graphs and everything." He leaned closer, admiring the work. "What a woman."

"I don't see the need for sarcasm."

"I'm not being sarcastic. This is great. Nice color," he added. "You put it at two weeks. But you wouldn't have worked on it seven days at a stretch or twenty-four hours a day."

"Here." She referred him to another chart and felt only a little foolish. "These are approximated times the *David* was locked in the lab vault. Getting to it would have required a key card, security clearance, a combination, and a second key. Or," she added, tilting her head, "a very good burglar."

His gaze slid over to hers, dark gold and mocking. "I was in Paris during this time."

"Were you really?"

"I have no idea, but in your probability ratio I don't compute because there would have been no reason for me to steal a copy and get sucked into this mess if I'd already taken the original."

Head angled, she smiled sweetly. "Maybe you did it just to get me in bed."

He glanced up, grinned. "Now, there's a thought."

"That," she said primly, "was sarcasm. This is a time line of the work period on *The Dark Lady.* We have the records on this, and it's very fresh in my mind, so this is completely accurate. In this case, the search for documentation was still ongoing, and the authentication not yet official."

"Project terminated," Ryan read, and glanced at her. "That was the day you got the ax."

"If you prefer to simplify, yes." It still stung both pride and heart. "The following day, the bronze was transferred to Rome. The switch had to be made in that small window of time, as I'd run tests on it just that afternoon."

"Unless it was switched in Rome," he murmured.

"How could it have been switched in Rome?"

"Did anyone from Standjo go along for the transfer?"

"I don't know. Someone from security, perhaps my mother. There would have been papers to sign on both ends."

"Well, it's a possibility, but only gives them a few extra hours in any case. They had to be ready, the copy fully prepared. The plumber had it for a week—or so he said. Then the government took it over, another week for them to fiddle with the paperwork and contract Standjo. Your mother contacts you and offers you the job."

"She didn't offer me the job, she ordered me to come to Florence."

"Mmm." He studied her chart. "Why did it take you six days between the phone call and the flight? Your description doesn't lead me to believe she's a patient woman."

"I was told—and had planned—to leave the following day, two at the most. I was delayed."

"How?"

"I was mugged."

"What?"

"This very large man in a mask came out of nowhere, put a knife to my throat." Her hand fluttered there as if to see if the thin trickle of blood was indeed only a bad memory.

Ryan took her fingers to draw them away and look for himself, though he knew there was no mark. Still, he could imagine it. And his eyes went flat.

"What happened?"

"I was just coming back from a trip. Got out of the car in front of the house, and there he was. He took my briefcase, my purse. I thought he was going to rape me, and I wondered if I had a chance to fight him off, against that knife. I have a bit of a phobia about knives."

When her fingers trembled lightly, he tightened his grip. "Did he cut you?"

"A little, just . . . just enough to scare me. Then he knocked me down, slashed my tires, and took off."

"He knocked you down?"

She blinked at the cold steel in his voice, at the unbearable tenderness of his fingers as they stroked over her cheek. "Yes."

He was blind with fury at the thought of someone holding a knife to her throat, terrorizing her. "How bad were you hurt?"

"Nothing, just bruises and scrapes." Because her eyes began to sting, she lowered her gaze. She was afraid that the emotions flooding through her were showing—the wonder and bafflement of her feelings for him. No one but Andrew had ever looked at her with that kind of concern, that kind of care.

"It was nothing," she said again, then stared helplessly as he tipped up her chin and touched his lips to each of her cheeks.

"Don't be kind to me." A tear spilled over before she could blink it away. "I don't handle it well."

"Learn." He kissed her again, lightly, then

brushed the tear away with his thumb. "Have you ever had trouble like that before around here?"

"No, never." She managed one hitching breath, then a steadier one. "That's why I was so shocked, I guess, so unprepared. It's a very low-crime area. The fact is this was such an aberration it played on the local news for days."

"They never caught him?"

"No. I couldn't give them a very detailed description. He wore a mask, so I could only give them his build."

"Give it to me."

She didn't want to recall the incident, but knew he would push her until she relented. "White male, six four or five, two-fifty, two-sixty, brown eyes. Muddy brown. Long arms, big hands, left-handed, wide shoulders, short neck. No distinguishing scars or marks—that I could see."

"Seems like you gave them quite a bit, considering."

"Not enough. He never spoke, not a word. That was another thing that frightened me. He went about everything so quickly, so silently. And he took my passport, driver's license. All my ID. It took me several days, even pulling strings, to arrange for new ones."

A pro, Ryan concluded. With an agenda.

"Andrew was furious," she remembered with a ghost of a smile. "He walked around the house every night for a week with a golf club—a nine iron, I think—hoping the man would come back so he could beat him to a pulp."

"I appreciate the sentiment."

"That's a man's reaction. I'd have preferred to handle it myself. It was humiliating to know that I hadn't fought back, I just froze."

"Someone holds a knife to your throat, freezing is the intelligent choice."

"I was more frightened than hurt," she murmured, and stared hard at the surface of the table.

"I'm sorry you were either. He didn't go for the house?"

"No, just grabbed my purse, my briefcase, slugged me and ran."

"Jewelry?"

"No."

"Were you wearing any?"

"Yes, I was wearing a gold chain and watch—the police wondered about that too. But I had my coat on. I don't suppose he saw them."

"This watch?" He held up her wrist, examining the slim eighteen-karat Cartier. An idiot could fence it for a grand, minimum, he mused. "A hit and grab like that doesn't sound like an amateur who'd miss this sort of easily liquidated asset. And he doesn't force you into the house, steal any number of excellent and portable items."

"The police figured he was someone passing through, short of cash."

"He might figure you had a couple hundred on you if he was lucky. Not worth armed robbery."

"People kill for designer tennis shoes."

"Not this kind of deal. He was after your ID, darling, because someone didn't want you to get to

Florence too soon. They needed time to get to work on the copy, and couldn't afford you underfoot until they had it under way. So they hired a pro. Someone who wouldn't be messy or make stupid mistakes. And they paid him enough so he wouldn't be greedy."

The explanation was so simple, so perfect, she only stared, wondering why she hadn't made the connection herself. "But the police never suggested that."

"The cops didn't have all the data. We do."

Slowly, she nodded, and slowly the anger began to inch up into her chest, into her throat. "He held a knife to my throat for my passport. It was all to delay me. To give them more time."

"I'd say the probability ratio is very high. Run through it again for me, step by step. It's a long shot, but maybe some of my connections can tag your man."

"If they can," she said soberly, "I don't want to meet your connections."

"Don't worry, Dr. Jones." He turned her hand over and kissed her palm. "You won't."

There was no place to buy a bottle on Easter Sunday. When he caught himself driving around and around, looking for one, Andrew began to shake. It wasn't that he needed one, he told himself. He wanted one, and that was different. He just wanted a couple of drinks to smooth out the edges.

Damn it, everybody was on his back. Everything rested on him. He was sick to death of it. So fuck them, he decided, tapping his fist on the wheel. Fuck them all.

He'd just keep driving. He'd head south and he wouldn't stop until he was damn good and ready. He had plenty of money, what he didn't have was any fucking peace.

He wouldn't stop until he could breathe again, until he found a goddamn liquor store that was open on a goddamn Sunday.

He glanced down, stared at the fist that was ramming over and over into the steering wheel. The fist that was bloody and torn and seemed to belong to someone else. Someone that scared the hell out of him.

Oh God, oh God. He was in trouble. With his hands trembling, he jerked the car to the curb, and leaving the engine running, rested his head on the wheel and prayed for help.

The quick knuckle rap on the window had him jolting up and staring through the glass at Annie's face. Head cocked, she made a circling motion with her finger, telling him to roll down the window. It wasn't until he saw her that he realized he'd headed for her house.

"What are you doing, Andrew?"

"Just sitting here."

She shifted the small bag she carried and studied his face. It was a mess, she noted, bruised, sick in color, worn out. "You piss somebody off?"

"My sister."

Her eyebrows rose high. "Miranda punched you in the eye?"

"What? No. No." Embarrassed, he probed around the ache with his fingertips. "I slipped on the stairs."

"Really?" Her eyes were narrowed now, focused on the fresh cuts and seeping blood on his knuckles. "Did you punch the stairs?"

"I . . ." He held up his hand, his mouth going dry as he stared at it. He hadn't even felt the pain. What was a man capable of when he stopped feeling pain? "Can I come in? I haven't been drinking," he said quickly, when he saw the rejection in her eyes. "I want to, but I haven't been."

"You won't get a drink in my place."

"I know." He kept his gaze steady. "That's why I want to come up."

She studied him another moment, then nodded. "Okay."

She unlocked her door and walked in to set her bag on a table covered with papers and forms and files, some of which were anchored with an adding machine.

"I'm doing my taxes," she explained. "That's why I went out to get this." She took an economy-sized bottle of extra-strength Excedrin out of the bag. "You got a Schedule C, you got a headache."

"I've already got the headache."

"Figured. Let's do some drugs." With a half-smile, she turned to pour two glasses of water. She opened the bottle and shook out two tablets for each of them. Solemnly, they swallowed.

She moved back, took a bag of frozen peas out

of the freezer. "Put that on your hand for now. We'll clean it up in a bit."

"Thanks." He might not have felt the pain when he'd pounded the steering wheel, but he was feeling it now. From wrist to fingertip his hand was one obscene scream. But he bit back the wince as he laid the cold bag over it. He'd done enough to damage both ego and manhood in front of Annie McLean.

"Now, what did you do to piss off your sister?"

He very nearly lied, made up some idiotic sibling spat. Ego and manhood aside, he couldn't manage to lie to those quiet, assessing eyes. "It might have been getting stinking drunk and humiliating her in front of her new boyfriend."

"Miranda's got a guy?"

"Yeah, sort of sudden. Nice enough. I entertained him by falling down the stairs, then throwing up part of my stomach lining."

Sympathy fluttered in her stomach, but she only cocked her head. "You've been a busy boy, Andrew."

"Oh yeah." He tossed the bag of peas into the sink so he could pace. He had jitters tangled around his jitters. Couldn't keep still. His fingers patted at his thighs, at his face, at each other as he prowled. "Then this morning, I decided to round things out by jumping all over her about work, family problems, her sex life." He traced his fingers over his cheek, remembering the jolt of shock when she'd slapped him.

Because she caught herself taking a step toward

him, Annie turned and rooted out antiseptic from a cabinet behind her. "It was probably the sex life crack that did it. Women don't like their brothers poking into that area."

"Yeah, maybe you're right. But we've got a lot of trouble at the Institute. I'm under a lot of stress right now."

She pursed her lips, glanced down at the piles of papers and forms, the envelopes of receipts, the worn-down stubs of pencils, and the reams of adding machine tape. "If you're breathing, you have stress. You drink yourself blind, the stress is right there when your vision clears up."

"Look, maybe I've got a little problem. I'm going to deal with it. I just need to take a little time, give my system a rest. I—" He pressed his fingers to his eyes, swayed.

"You've got a big problem, and you can deal with it." She crossed to him, took his wrists and tugged his hands down so he would look at her. "You need a day, because it's only today that has to count."

"So far today sucks."

She smiled, rose on her toes to kiss his cheek. "It's probably going to get worse. Sit down. I'll doctor those knuckles, tough guy."

"Thanks." Then he sighed, said it again. "Thanks, Annie."

He kissed her cheek in turn, then rested his head against hers just for the comfort of it. She still held his wrists, lightly, and her fingers felt so competent, so strong, her hair smelled so fresh and simple. He pressed his lips to it, then to her temple.

Then somehow his mouth was on hers, and the taste of her was flooding his ragged system like sunlight. When her fingers flexed in his, he released them, but only to frame her face with his hands, to draw her into him, hold her there while the sheer warmth of her soothed like balm on a wound.

So many contrasts, was all he could think. The tough little body, the soft sweep of hair, the clipped voice and generous mouth.

The strength and the softness of her, so endearing, so familiar. And so necessary to him.

She'd always been there. He'd always known she'd be there.

It wasn't easy to break free. Not from his hold—she could have easily stepped away. His hands were gentle as bird wings on her face. The mouth both needy and tender.

She'd wondered, had let herself wonder once, if it would be the same. The feel of him, the taste. But that was long ago, before she'd convinced herself that friendship was enough. Now it wasn't easy to break free of what that one long quiet kiss stirred, what it asked, what it took out of her.

She needed all of her strength of will to step back from the slowly kindling need he'd brought back to life. A need, she told herself, that wouldn't help either of them.

He nearly pulled her back, was already reaching out blindly when she held up her hands, palms out, in warning. He jerked back as if he'd been slapped a second time.

"Oh Christ. I'm sorry. Annie, I'm sorry." What had he done? How could he have ruined the single friendship he didn't think he could live without? "I didn't mean to do that. I wasn't thinking. I'm sorry."

She let him wind down, let the miserable guilt settle on his face. "I bounced a two-hundred-pound man out of my bar last night because he thought he could buy me along with a beer and a bump." She clamped her hand around Andrew's left thumb and gave it a quick twist. His eyes widened, his breath hissed as she held it. "I could have you on your knees, pal, whimpering if I gave this one little digit a good yank back. We're not seventeen anymore, not quite so stupid and a hell of a lot less innocent. If I hadn't wanted your hands on me, you'd have been flat on your back, checking out the cracks in my ceiling plaster."

Sweat began to pearl on his forehead. "Ah, could you let go?"

"Sure." Obligingly, she released his thumb, and kept her eyebrows arrogantly cocked. "Want a Coke? You look a little sweaty." She turned and stepped to the refrigerator.

"I don't want to ruin things," he began.

"Ruin what?"

"Us. You matter, Annie. You've always mattered."

She stared blindly into the refrigerator. "You've always mattered too. I'll let you know when you ruin things."

"I want to talk about . . . before."

He waited while she popped the tops on two bottles. Grace in economy of motion, he thought, a steel spine in a well-toned body. Had he noticed those things before? Noticed the little flecks of gold in her eyes? Or had he just stored them up so they'd all come to him in a flood in a moment just like this?

"Why?"

"Maybe to face things—something I didn't realize until lately was stuck inside me." He flexed his fingers, felt the ache. "I'm not in the best shape right now, but I have to start somewhere. Sometime."

She set the bottles on the counter, forced herself to turn, to meet his eyes. And hers were swimming with emotions she'd struggled to keep locked in for years. "It's painful for me, Andrew."

"You wanted the baby." The breath he released hurt his chest. He'd never spoken of the baby before, not out loud. "I could see it in your face when you told me you were pregnant. It scared the hell out of me."

"I was too young to know what I wanted." Then she closed her eyes because it was a lie. "Yes, yes, I wanted the baby. I had this idiotic fantasy that I'd tell you, and you'd be happy and just sweep me up. Then we'd . . . Well, that's as far as it went. But you didn't want me."

His mouth was dry as dust, his gut raw. He knew one drink would smooth it all away. Cursing himself for thinking of that at such a time, he snagged one of the bottles off the counter and gulped down soda that seemed sickly and sweet. "I cared about you."

"You didn't love me, Andrew. I was just a girl you got lucky with on the beach one night."

He slammed the bottle down again. "It wasn't like that. Goddamn it, you know it wasn't like that."

"It was exactly like that," she said evenly. "I was in love with you, Andrew, and I knew when I lay down on the blanket with you that you weren't in love with me. I didn't care. I didn't expect anything. Andrew Jones of Jones Point and Annie McLean from the waterfront? I was young, but I wasn't stupid."

"I would have married you."

"Would you?" Her voice went chilly. "Your offer didn't even hit lukewarm."

"I know it." And that was something that had eaten away at him slowly, a nibble at a time, for fifteen years. "I didn't give you what you needed that day. I didn't know how. If I had, you might have made a different choice."

"If I'd taken you up on it, you would have hated me. When you offered, part of you already did." She moved her shoulders, picked up her own Coke. "And looking back, I can't blame you. I'd have ruined your life." The bottle froze halfway to her lips as he stepped toward her. The hot glint of fury in his eyes had her bracing against the counter. He snatched the bottle out of her hand, set it down, then took a hard grip on her shoulders.

"I don't know how it would have been—and that's something I've asked myself more than once over the years. But I know how it was. Maybe I wasn't in love with you, I don't know. But making love with you mattered to me." And that, he realized, was something else he'd never said aloud, something neither one of them had faced. "However badly I handled things afterward, that night mattered. And damn it, Annie, damn it," he added, giving her a brisk shake, "you might have made my life."

"I was never right for you," she said in a furious whisper.

"How the hell do you know? We never had a chance to find out. You tell me you're pregnant, and before I can absorb it, you had an abortion."

"I never had an abortion."

"You made a mistake," he said, tossing the words she'd once heaved at him back in her face. "And you fixed it. I would have taken care of you, both of you." Pain, long and shallowly buried, cracked through the surface in pummeling fists. "I would have done my best for you." His fingers tightened on her arms. "But it wasn't good enough. Okay, it was your decision, your body, your choice. But goddamn it, it was a part of me too."

She'd lifted her hands to push him away and now curled them into his shirt. His face was sheet-pale under the bruises, his eyes burning dark. The ache around her heart was for both of them now. "Andrew, I didn't have an abortion. I lost the baby. I told you, I had a miscarriage."

Something flickered deep in his eyes. His grip relaxed on her shoulders, and he stepped back. "You lost it?"

"I told you, when it happened."

"I always thought—I assumed you'd . . ." He turned away, walked to the window. Without thinking he yanked it open, and resting his palms on the sill, dragged in air. "I thought you told me that to make it easier on both of us. I figured that you hadn't trusted me enough to stand by you, to take care of you and the baby."

"I wouldn't have done that without telling you."

"You avoided me for a long time afterward. We never talked about it, never seemed to be able to talk about it. I knew you wanted the baby, and I thought—all this time—I thought that you'd terminated the pregnancy because I hadn't stood by you the way you needed."

"You—" She had to swallow the hot ball in her throat. "You wanted the baby?"

"I didn't know." Even now he didn't know. "But I've never regretted anything more in my life than not holding on to you that day on the beach. Then everything drifted, almost like it never happened."

"It hurt me. I had to get over it. Over you."

Slowly, he pulled the window down again. "Did you?"

"I made a life for myself. A lousy marriage, an ugly divorce."

"That's not an answer."

When he turned back, his eyes very blue and level on hers, she shook her head. "It's not a fair question just now. I'm not going to start something with you that's based on what was."

"Then maybe we'd better take a look at where we are, and start from there."

CHAPTER TWENTY-ONE

MIRANDA WENT BACK TO WORK ON THE COMPUTER, revising charts, making new ones. It kept her mind occupied, except for the times she caught herself looking out the window, willing Andrew's car to come up the hill.

Ryan had settled in the bedroom with his cell phone. She imagined he didn't want several of the calls he was making to pop up on her records. That was something she wasn't going to worry about.

He'd given her a whole new line of worry. If he was right, the quick and rough daylight robbery hadn't simply been a matter of chance, hadn't been some itinerant thief looking for fast cash. It had been a well-planned, carefully orchestrated part of the whole. She'd been a specific target, the motive behind it nothing more than delaying her trip to Italy and her work on the bronze.

Whoever had stolen it, copied it, had already decided to discredit her. Had that been personal, or the luck of the draw? she wondered. She believed, as she had few genuine friends, she had few genuine enemies. She'd simply avoided becoming close enough to anyone to create them.

But the messages coming over her fax were very personal.

The attack had been personal, she thought, designed to terrify. The silence, the little nick at the throat with the knife. Had that all been routine for the attacker, or had he been given instructions to leave his victim frozen in shock and fear?

It had cost her a large slice of her confidence, her sense of safety, certainly her dignity. And it had delayed her trip by almost a week. The delay had put her at odds with her mother before the project even began.

Layers, she mused, very cleverly applied layers that coated the core. Yet it hadn't begun with the attack, but with the forgery and theft of the *David.*

What had been going on in her life then? What was she missing that tied the one to the other?

She'd been working on her doctorate, she remembered. Splitting her time between the Institute, her studies, her thesis. Her social life, never a glitter ball of events, had been nil.

What had been going on around her? That, she realized, was harder to pin down. Paying attention to the people around her wasn't her strong suit. That was something she intended to change.

For now, she closed her eyes and tried to bring the time span, and the people in it, into focus.

Elise and Andrew had been married, and still by all appearances deeply in love. She could remember no fights or squabbles. Andrew's drinking had been routine, but nothing she'd worried about.

Then again, she'd done her best to give him and Elise as much privacy as possible.

Giovanni and Lori had entertained each other with a brisk, friendly affair. She'd known they were sleeping together, but since it hadn't interfered with the quality or quantity of their work, Miranda had kept out of that as well.

Her mother had come into the Institute briefly. A day or two, Miranda thought now. No longer. They'd had a handful of meetings, one stiff family dinner, and had parted ways.

Her father had stayed only long enough to see the bronze through initial testing. He'd only sat in on a portion of the meetings and had made some excuse to avoid attending the family meal.

Vincente and his wife had come in her father's place, but even their vivid personalities hadn't brightened the event. If memory served, Gina had come into the lab only once.

Richard Hawthorne she remembered only as a vague presence buried in books or hunched over a computer.

John Carter had been a constant presence, overseeing projects, worrying over reports. Miranda rubbed her temples as she struggled to pull in details. Had he been a little off his stride, sluggish, out of sorts? A touch of the flu, she remembered. He'd had a touch of the flu, but had worked through it.

How was she supposed to remember? In disgust, she dropped her hands. It had been routine, simply routine with her work as the driving force. Everything else was blips once she had that small, lovely statue in her hands.

She'd seen the acquisition of the *David* as another step in her career, and had used the authentication as the basis for one of her papers. She'd gotten quite a bit of attention for that, she recalled, in the academic and scientific worlds. She'd been invited to lecture on it and had won a considerable amount of acclaim.

It had, she supposed, been the true beginning of her rise in her career. That little bronze had lifted her out of the pack and put her solidly in the lead.

She stared blindly at the words on her screen, heard a dim buzzing in her ears.

The Fiesole Bronze would have sent her reputation rocketing. It would have cemented her as one of the top archeometrists in the world. Not just academic acclaim this time, but the lay press as well. We were talking Michelangelo here, romance, mystery, money. She shut her eyes and struggled to think it through.

Both pieces were hers. Both pieces had offered her a solid boost up the reputational ladder. And both pieces had been forged. What if they hadn't been the target at all?

What if she was?

She folded her hands, waited for her insides to

settle. It had logic, it had reason. It was more than plausible.

But where was the motive?

What other pieces had she authenticated that could be retested without too much speculation or comment within the Institute? The Cellini. Her stomach twisted painfully at the thought of it. The statue of Nike, she thought, forcing herself to be calm and thorough. There was the paperweight-sized bronze of Romulus and Remus nursing at the she-wolf.

She would have to get back into the lab. She would have to be sure none of those had been replaced with forgeries.

She jerked as the phone rang, stared at it for several long seconds before she picked up the receiver. "Hello?"

"Miranda. I have some difficult news."

"Mother." She rubbed a hand over her heart. *I think someone's trying to hurt me. I think they're trying to destroy me. It was real, the bronze was real. You have to listen.* But the words only raced in her head. "What is it?"

"Sometime on Thursday night the lab was broken into. Equipment, records, data were destroyed."

"Destroyed?" she said dully. *Yes, I'm being destroyed.*

"Giovanni . . ." The pause was long, and for the first time in too long to remember, Miranda heard raw emotion in her mother's voice. "Giovanni was killed."

"Giovanni." *You cared. Oh God, you cared.* She shut her eyes as tears began to swim. "Giovanni," she said again.

"From all appearances, he must have decided to come in and take advantage of the holiday quiet in the lab to work. We've been unable to tell what project he was dealing with. The police—"

Again that hitch in rhythm, and though the voice was stronger, it remained uneven. "The police are investigating, but they have no leads to date. I've been attempting to assist them for the last two days. The funeral is tomorrow."

"Tomorrow?"

"I thought it best that you hear it from me. I trust you'll inform Andrew. I realize you were fond of Giovanni. I believe we all were. There's no need for you to fly in for the services. They're to be simple and private."

"His family."

"I've spoken with his family. Though we've made arrangements to have donations to charity made in his name, I believe they would appreciate flowers. This is a very difficult time for all of us. I hope that you and I can put our professional differences aside and agree to send an arrangement as a family."

"Yes, of course. I could fly out tonight."

"That's neither necessary nor wise." Elizabeth's voice was brisk again. "The press is well aware that you worked together on the Fiesole Bronze. This has already been rehashed in the media. Your presence here would only stir it all up again. For

Giovanni's family's sake, the services should be kept quiet and dignified."

She remembered the words of the last fax again: *His blood's on your hands. Can you see it?* "You're right. There's nothing I can do there but make matters worse." She closed her eyes, the better to concentrate on keeping her tone even. "Do the police know why the lab was broken into? Was anything stolen?"

"It's difficult to tell, but it doesn't appear that anything was taken. A great deal was destroyed. The alarm was shut off, from inside. The authorities believe it's possible he knew his assailant."

"I'd like you to keep me informed of the progress. He mattered very much to me."

"I know you had a personal relationship."

"We weren't lovers, Mother." Miranda nearly sighed it. "We were friends."

"I didn't intend to—" Elizabeth stopped, remained silent for several seconds. "I'll see that you're kept up-to-date. If you go out of town, you might see that Andrew has your location this time."

"I plan to stay home," Miranda said. "And garden." She smiled a little as there was no response. "An enforced leave of absence gives me time to develop a hobby. They're supposed to be good for the soul."

"So I'm told. I'm glad you're making productive use of your time rather than brooding. Tell Andrew I want an update on the investigation there as soon as possible. I may be coming in for a short time, and would appreciate having everything dealing with the matter of the *David* recorded in a cohesive fashion."

I'll warn him. "I'll be sure he understands."

"Good. Goodbye, Miranda."

"Goodbye, Mother."

She replaced the receiver neatly, then sat staring at it until she realized Ryan had come in and stood behind her. "She had me fooled for a minute. I started to believe she was human. She sounded genuinely grieved when she told me about Giovanni. But before it was over, she reverted to her usual self. I'm to stay away because my presence at Giovanni's funeral would be disruptive."

Her instinct was to stiffen when his hands came to her shoulders. That alone infuriated her. She shut her eyes and willed herself to relax under his hands. "I'm instructed to inform Andrew of my location, should I choose to leave town again, and to tell him to give her an update, at the soonest opportunity, of the burglary investigation."

"She's got a lot on her mind, Miranda. Everyone in your family does just now."

"And when your family has a crisis, what do they do?"

He crouched, turned her swivel chair around until she faced him. "Your family and mine aren't the same, and can't be expected to react in the same way."

"No. My mother remains, at all times, the director. My father maintains his distance and general apathy, and Andrew drowns himself in a bottle. And what do I do? I ignore all of it as long as it's humanly possible so it won't interfere with my routine."

"That's not what I've seen."

"You've seen a blip on the screen, not the usual sweep." She nudged him aside so she could stand. "I'm going for a run."

"Miranda." He caught her arm before she could hurry out of the room. "If you didn't care, if they didn't matter to you, you wouldn't be so sad."

"I'm not sad, Ryan. I'm resigned." She shook free and walked out to change her clothes.

She didn't often run. She considered walking a more efficient and certainly more dignified method of exercise. But when events and emotions built up to a high inside her, she ran.

She chose the beach below the cliffs because the water was close and the air fresh. She headed north, digging into the shale while the waves gleefully attacked the rocky shore and spewed droplets of water into the sunlight. Gulls swooped, letting out their eerily feminine screams.

As her muscles warmed, she tugged off the light jacket and tossed it aside. No one would steal it. Crime, she thought with a giddy lurch in her stomach, was low in Jones Point.

Orange buoys bobbed on the surface of the dark blue water. Others, tall, gray, and weathered, swayed and spoke in hollow, mournful bongs. A short pier lay drunkenly askew in the water, ignored because neither she nor Andrew sailed. Farther out, boats skimmed and sailed as people took advantage of the hint of spring and a Sunday holiday.

She followed the curve of the beach, ignoring the burning in her calves and chest, the trickle of sweat between her breasts.

A lobster boat swayed on the current while the waterman in his bright red cap checked his pots. He lifted a hand and waved, and the simple gesture from a stranger made her eyes burn. While her vision blurred, she waved in return, then stopped, bending over, hands on knees, while her breath screamed out of her laboring lungs.

She hadn't run far, she thought, but she'd run too fast. She hadn't paced herself. Everything was happening too fast. She couldn't quite keep up, yet she didn't dare slow down.

And sweet God, she didn't even know where she was going.

There was a man in her house, a man she'd known for only a matter of weeks. A man who was a thief, likely a liar, and undoubtedly dangerous. Yet she'd put a part of her life in his hands. She'd become intimate with him, more intimate than she'd ever allowed herself to become with anyone.

She looked back and up and studied the moon-white spear of the lighthouse. She'd fallen in love with him inside that tower. It didn't matter if she'd been sliding toward it all along, it was there she'd fallen. And she had yet to be certain she would land on her feet.

He'd walk away when he finished what he had come to do. He'd be charming about it, and clever. Not cruel. But he would go back to his life. Hers, she realized, would still be in shambles.

They could find the bronzes, shore up their reputations, solve the puzzle, and even catch a killer. But her life would remain in shambles.

And with no precedent, no formula, no data, she couldn't make an educated guess on how long it would take her to rebuild it.

At the tips of her feet was the edge of a tidepool, the water calm and clear. Life scurried under it, in otherworldly colors and shapes.

When she was a child her grandmother had walked this beach with her—or with both her and Andrew. They'd studied the tidepools together, but it hadn't been like a lesson, some sneaky education ploy of adult to child.

No, she remembered, they had crouched down and looked for the pleasure of it. Had laughed when what appeared to be a rock squirted at them in annoyance.

Little worlds, her grandmother had called them. Ripe with passion, sex, violence, and politics—and often more sensible than the life that's led on the dry part of the planet.

"I wish you were here," Miranda murmured. "I wish I still had you to talk to."

She looked away from the busy world at her feet, out to sea again, let the wind rage through her hair, over her face. What was she to do now? she wondered. Now that she knew what it was to love someone until it hurt, to prefer the pain to the emptiness that had been so familiar it was rarely noticed?

She sat on the smooth dome of a rock, brought

her knees up to rest her head on them. This, she supposed, was what happened when the heart was allowed to control the mind, the actions, the decisions. With everything else in tatters around her, she was sitting on a rock, looking out to sea and brooding over a love affair that was destined to end.

An oystercatcher landed near the shoreline, then stalked up and down the verge looking important. It made her smile a little. Apparently even birds worry about appearances. Look at me, he seemed to say, I'm very cool.

"We'd see how cool you are if I'd brought some bread crumbs," she told him. "You'd be scrambling to gulp them all down before your buddies got wind of it and swooped down to fight you for them."

"I've heard that people who drink too much start believing in talking birds." Andrew saw her shoulders stiffen, but kept walking toward her. "You dropped this." He laid her jacket in her lap.

"I got too warm."

"You sit here without it after a run, you'll get chilled."

"I'm fine."

"Suit yourself." It took a great deal of courage for him to sit on the rock beside her. "Miranda, I'm sorry."

"I believe we've covered that ground."

"Miranda." He knew just how far he'd pushed her away when she wouldn't let him take her hand.

"I came down here to be alone for a while."

And he knew just how stubborn she could be

when she'd been crossed. "I've got a few things to say. When I'm done, you can hit me again if you want. I was way over the line this morning. There's no excuse for what I said to you. I didn't want to hear what you were saying to me, so I hit hard and low."

"Understood. We'll agree that we're better off staying out of each other's personal choices."

"No." This time he ignored her jerk away and clamped her hand. "No, we're not. We've always been able to depend on each other."

"Well, I can't depend on you anymore, Andrew, can I?" She looked at him now, saw how haggard his face was against the dark glasses he'd put on. He should have looked rakish, she thought. Instead he looked pitiful.

"I know I've let you down."

"I can take care of myself. You've let yourself down."

"Miranda, please." He'd known it wouldn't be easy, but he hadn't realized how completely her rejection would rip at him. "I know I've got a problem. I'm trying to come to terms with that. I'm . . . I'm going to a meeting tonight. AA."

He saw the flicker in her eyes, of hope, of sympathy, of love, and shook his head. "I don't know if it's going to be for me. I'm just going to go, listen, see how I feel about it."

"It's a good start, it's a good step."

He rose, stared out over the restless water. "When I left this morning, I went looking for a bottle. I didn't realize it, didn't consciously think about it. Not until I got the shakes, until I found myself driving around looking for a liquor store or a bar, anything that was open on a Sunday morning."

He looked down at his hand, flexed the fingers, felt the small aches. "It scared the hell out of me."

"I'll help you, Andrew. I've read all the literature. I've been to a couple of Alanon meetings."

He turned back to stare at her. She was watching him, twisting the jacket in her hands. And the hope was deeper in her eyes. "I was afraid you'd started to hate me," he said.

"I wanted to. Just can't." She wiped at tears. "I've been so angry with you, for taking you away from me. When you left today I kept thinking you'd come back drunk, or you'd finally be stupid enough to drive when you'd been drinking and kill yourself. I would have hated you for that."

"I went to Annie's. Didn't know I was going there either, until I was parked in front of her building. She's—I'm—Hell. I'm going to stay at her place for a few days. Give you some privacy with Ryan, give you and me a little space."

"Annie's? You're going to stay with Annie?"

"I'm not sleeping with her."

"Annie?" she said again, gaping at him. "Annie McLean?"

"Is that a problem for you?"

It was the defensive way he said it that had her lips curving up. "No, not at all. That's something I think I'd like very much to see. She's a strong-willed, ambitious woman. And she won't take any crap from you."

"Annie and I . . ." He wasn't sure how to explain it. "We've got a history. Maybe now we're going to see about having a present."

"I didn't know you were anything but friends."

He stared down the beach, thought he could almost pick out the spot where two reckless teenagers had lost their innocence. "We were, then we weren't. I don't know what we are now." But finding out, he thought, was giving him a direction and purpose he hadn't had in too long. "I'm sleeping on her couch for a couple of nights. I'm going to get my feet under me again, whatever it takes. But the odds are I'm going to disappoint you again before I do."

She'd read everything she could get her hands on about alcoholism, treatment, recovery. She knew about backsliding, starting over, failure. "You're not disappointing me today." She held out a hand, linking fingers tight when he took it. "I've missed you so much."

He picked her up off the rock to hold her. He knew she was crying, could feel it in the little quivers her body made against his. But she made no sound. "Don't give up on me, okay?"

"Tried. Can't."

He laughed a little and pressed his cheek to hers. "This thing you've got going with New York—"

"How come he was Ryan before, and now he's New York?"

"Because now he's messing around with my sister, and I'm reserving judgment. This thing you've got," he repeated. "It's working for you?"

She drew back. "It's working today."

"Okay. Since we've made up, why don't we go up and have a drink to celebrate." His dimples winked. "Drunk humor. How about a pot roast?"

"It's too late in the day to start one. I'll make you a very manly meatloaf."

"Good enough."

As they started back, she braced herself, knowing she would have to tell him and shatter the moment. "Andrew, Mother called a bit ago."

"Can't she take Easter off like everybody else?"

"Andrew." She stopped, kept a hand on his arm. "Someone broke into the lab in Florence. Giovanni was there, alone. He was murdered."

"What? Giovanni? Oh my God." He turned, walked to the edge of the water, stood there with the surf soaking his shoes. "Giovanni's dead? Murdered? What the hell is going on?"

She couldn't risk telling him. His strength of will, his emotions, his illness . . . it was too unstable a mix. "I wish I knew. She said the lab had been vandalized, equipment and records destroyed. And Giovanni . . . they think he was working late, and someone came in."

"A burglary?"

"I don't know. It doesn't seem . . . She said she didn't think anything of value had been taken."

"It makes no sense." He whirled around, his face grim and battered. "Someone breaks into the gallery here, takes a valuable bronze and doesn't squash a fly on his way in or out. Now someone breaks into the lab at Standjo, kills Giovanni, wrecks the place and takes nothing?"

"I don't understand it either." That, at least, was partially true.

"What's the connection?" he muttered, and had her gaping at him.

"Connection?"

"There are no coincidences." Jingling the change in his pocket, he began to walk up and down the beach. "Two break-ins, within a couple of weeks, at different divisions of the same organization. One lucrative and quiet, the other violent and without apparent reason. There's always a reason. Giovanni worked at both locations at some time." Behind the dark lenses, his eyes narrowed. "He did some of the work on the *David,* didn't he?"

"Ah . . . yes, yes, he did."

"The *David*'s stolen, the documents are missing, and now Giovanni's dead. What's the connection?" He didn't expect an answer, and she was spared from fumbling for a lie.

"I'm going to pass this on to Cook, for whatever good it does. Maybe I should go to Florence."

"Andrew." Her voice wanted to quake. She wouldn't risk him, wouldn't let him go anywhere near Florence. Or the person who had killed Giovanni. "That's not a good idea right now. You need to stay close to home, rebuild your routine and stability. Let the police do their jobs."

"It's probably better to try to figure it out from here, anyway," he decided. "I'm going up to call

Cook, give him something to chew on besides his Easter ham."

"I'll be there in a minute." She worked up a smile. "To start your Easter meatloaf."

He was distracted enough not to notice how quickly her smile slipped away into worry. But he spotted Ryan on the cliff path. Pride, ego, shame, and brotherly resistance built very quickly.

"Boldari."

"Andrew." Ryan decided to avoid an unproductive pissing match and stepped aside.

But Andrew was already primed. "Maybe you think since she's a grown woman and her family's screwed up that there's nobody to look out for her, but you're wrong. You hurt her, you son of a bitch, and I'll break you in two." His eyes went to slits when Ryan grinned at him. "You hear a joke?"

"No. It's just that the last part of that statement is very similar to what I said to my sister Mary Jo's husband when I caught them necking in his Chevy. I'd already dragged him out and punched him first, much to MJ's annoyance and distress."

Andrew rocked on his heels. "You're not my sister's husband."

"Neither was he, at the time." The words were out, glibly delivered before the potential meaning struck Ryan. The humor blinked out of his eyes and discomfort blinked on. "What I mean to say is—"

"Yeah?" Enjoying himself now, Andrew nodded. "What do you mean to say?"

A man could do a lot of thinking in the time it took to clear the throat. "I mean to say that I have a great deal of affection and respect for your sister. She's a beautiful, interesting, and appealing woman."

"You're light on your feet, Ryan." It seemed they were back to Ryan, for the moment. "Good balance." They both looked down to where Miranda stood on the narrow beach watching the waves rise.

"And she's not as sturdy as she thinks she is," Andrew added. "She doesn't let herself get too close to too many, because when she does, the soft center's exposed."

"She matters to me. Is that what you want to hear?"

"Yeah." Particularly, Andrew thought, since it had been said with a great deal of heat and some reluctance. "That'll do. By the way, I appreciate what you did for me last night, and for not rubbing my nose in it today."

"How's the eye?"

"Hurts like a bastard."

"Well then, that's punishment enough, I'd say."

"Maybe." He turned and started up the path. "We're having meatloaf," he called back. "Go make her put her jacket on, will you?"

"Yeah," Ryan murmured. "I think I'll do that." He started down, picking his way over rocks, skidding a bit on pebbles. She started up, steady as a mountain goat.

"Those aren't the right kind of shoes for this."

"You're telling me." Then he caught her against

him. "Your arms are cold. Why don't you have your jacket on?"

"The sun's warm enough. Andrew's going to an AA meeting tonight."

"That's great." He pressed his lips to her brow. "It's a good start."

"He can do it." The breeze tugged hair out of the elastic band she'd pulled on, and forced her to shake it out of her face. "I know he can. He's going to be staying with a friend for a couple of days, just to give himself time to steady a bit. And I think he's not quite comfortable with sleeping under the same room while we're . . . sleeping."

"Yankee conservatism."

"Don't knock a cornerstone." She drew in a breath. "There's something else. I told him about Giovanni. He's made the connection."

"What do you mean he's made the connection?"

"I mean for the past year or so he's been killing his brain cells, and I'd nearly forgotten how smart he is. He put it together in minutes. A connection between the break-in here, and the one there. He's going to talk to Detective Cook about it."

"Great, bring in the cops."

"It's the reasonable thing to do. It's too coincidental for Andrew." Speaking quickly, she ran back over what her brother had said. "He'll explore this. I didn't tell him what I know or suspect. I can't risk his state of mind right now when he should be concentrating on recovery, but I can't go on lying to him either. Not for much longer."

"Then we'll have to work faster." He had no intention of playing team ball, or sharing the bronzes. Once he had them, he was keeping them. "The wind's picking up," he commented, and draped an arm around her as they walked up the path. "I heard a rumor about meatloaf."

"You'll get fed, Boldari. And I can promise my meatloaf is very passionate."

"In some cultures meatloaf is considered an aphrodisiac."

"Really? Odd that was never covered in any of my anthropology courses."

"It only works if you serve it with mashed potatoes."

"Well then, I guess we'll have to test that theory."

"They can't be instant."

"Please. Don't insult me."

"I think I'm crazy about you, Dr. Jones."

She laughed, but the soft center her brother had spoken of was laid bare.

PART THREE

THE PRICE

Wrath is cruel, and anger is outrageous;
but who is able to stand before envy?
—Proverbs

CHAPTER TWENTY-TWO

THE COUNTRY QUIET KEPT RYAN AWAKE, AND MADE him think of New York. Of the comforting and continual buzz of traffic, of the pace that got into your blood so that you lengthened your stride to get to the next corner, beat the light, keep the clip steady.

Places this close to the ocean made you slow down. Once you slowed down, you could get settled in and rooted before you realized it was happening.

He needed to get back to New York, to his gallery, which he'd already left too long in other hands. Of course, he often did, but that was when he was traveling, moving from place to place. Not when he was . . . planted this way.

He needed to pull up stakes, and soon.

She was sleeping beside him, her breathing echoing the slow, steady ebb and flow of the sea outside. She didn't curl up against him, but maintained her own space and gave him his. He told himself he appreciated that. But he didn't. It irked him that she didn't cuddle and cling and at least pretend that she was trying to hold him down.

It would have been so much easier to resist staying if she did.

He couldn't concentrate this way. She was a constant distraction from the work at hand, just by being close enough to touch. She was an infinitely touchable woman if only because she was always vaguely surprised by little strokes and pats.

And because he wanted to do so, to nudge her awake and into arousal with little strokes and pats, with quiet sips and nibbles until she was hot and slippery and eager for him, he got out of bed.

Sex was supposed to be a simple form of entertainment, not an obsession, for God's sake.

He tugged on a pair of loose black pants, found a cigar and his lighter, and quietly opened her terrace doors and stepped out.

Breathing the air was like drinking a lightly chilled and mellow white, he decided. It could become a casual habit, one easily taken for granted. The height gave him a full view of the sea, of the ragged spit of land with the glowing spear of the lighthouse, and that spear's straight beaming lance.

It held a sense of age and tradition, of security again easily taken for granted by those who saw it day after day. Things changed slowly here, if they flexed their muscles and decided to change at all.

You would see the same view morning after morning, he decided. A similar scatter of boats over the same moody sea, and all with the beat and pulse of that sea as a backdrop. He could see the stars, brilliantly clear like bright studs pinned to velvet. The moon was waning, losing its edge.

He was afraid he was losing his.

Annoyed with himself, he lighted the cigar, blew a fume of smoke into the wind that never seemed to rest.

They were getting nowhere, he thought. Miranda could create her charts and graphs, calculate her time lines, and input her data until she generated reams of paperwork. None of it delved into the hearts and minds of the people involved. It couldn't touch on greed or anger, jealousy or hate. A chart couldn't illustrate why one human took the life of another over a piece of metal.

He needed to know the players, to understand them, and he'd barely begun.

He thought he'd come to know her. She was an efficient woman with a practical shell, an aloof nature that could, with the proper key, be unlocked to expose the warmth and needs under the surface. Her upbringing had been privileged and cold. She'd reacted to that by distancing herself from people, honing her mind, fixing her goals and setting along a straight, linear path to achieving them.

Her weakness was her brother.

They'd stuck together, bonding initially out of defense or rebellion or genuine affection. It didn't matter what had forged that bond; it existed, it was real and strong and unified them. What came out of it was loyalty and love. He'd seen for himself what

Andrew's drinking, his unpredictability had done to her. It left her shaken and angry and baffled.

And he'd seen the hope and the happiness in her eyes during the dinner they'd shared that evening. She believed he was climbing back toward the brother she'd known. She needed that belief, that faith. He couldn't stand the idea of shattering it.

So he would keep his suspicions to himself. He knew just what addictions, any kind of addictions, could do to warp a man. To make him consider and to make him commit acts he would never have considered or committed otherwise.

Andrew headed the Institute, he had power, the ease of motion within the organization to have managed the switch of the first bronze. The motive could have been money, or a simple lust to own, or the surrendering to blackmail. No one was in a better position to have orchestrated the thefts and the forgeries than one of the Joneses.

He considered Charles Jones. He'd been the one to discover the *David*. It wasn't unreasonable to theorize that he'd wanted it for himself. He would have needed help. Andrew? Possibly. Giovanni, just as possibly. Or any of the most trusted staff.

Elizabeth Jones. Proud, cold, driven. She'd based her life on art, the science of it rather than the beauty. She, like her husband, had put their family in the shadows in order to concentrate energy and time and effort on gaining prestige. Their own. Wouldn't a priceless statue make the perfect trophy for a lifetime of work?

Giovanni. A trusted employee. A brilliant scientist or he would never have been a part of Miranda's team. Charming, by her account. A single man who enjoyed flirting with women. Maybe he'd flirted with the wrong one, or had craved more than his position at Standjo offered.

Elise. Ex-wife. Ex-wives were often vengeful. She'd transferred from the Institute to Standjo, Florence. She was in a position of trust and power. She might have used Andrew, then discarded him. As lab manager, she'd be privy to all data. She would have held both bronzes in her hands. Had she coveted them?

Richard Hawthorne. Bookworm. Still waters often ran deep and often ran violent. He knew his history, knew how to research. His type was largely overlooked in favor of the more flamboyant, the more demanding. It could eat at a man.

Vincente Morelli, longtime friend and associate. With a very young, very demanding wife. He'd given the Institute and Standjo years of his life, of his work, of his skills. Why not cash in on more than a paycheck and a pat on the back for services rendered?

John Carter, with his worn shoes and ridiculous ties. Stable as granite. Why not just as hard? He'd been with the Institute for more than fifteen years, plodding his way along. Following orders, clinging to routines. Maybe he was still following orders.

Any one of them could have planned it, he decided. But he didn't believe any one of them could have executed two such flawless switches alone.

There was teamwork here, gears meshing. And a cool and clever mind behind it all.

He was going to need more than personnel records and time lines to uncover that mind.

He watched a star fall, streaking toward the sea with an arc of light. And he began to plan.

"What do you mean you're going to call my mother?"

"I'd call your father," Ryan said, peeking over her shoulder to see what she was up to on the computer, "but I get the impression your mother's more involved in the business. What are you doing there?"

"Nothing. Why are you going to call my mother?"

"What is that? A gardening web page?"

"I need some data, that's all."

"On flowers?"

"Yes." She'd already printed out several informative documents on soil treatments, perennials, and planting seasons, so she closed the page. "My mother?"

"In a minute. Why do you need data on flowers?"

"Because I'm going to start a garden, and I know nothing about it."

"So you're taking the scientific approach." He bent down to kiss the top of her head. "You really are cute, Miranda."

She removed her glasses and put them on the desk. "I'm delighted I've amused you. Now will you answer my question?"

"Your mother?" He sat on the desk, facing her.

"I'm going to call her to tell her my conditions for the loan of the Vasaris, and a Raphael and Botticelli."

"Raphael and Botticelli? You never agreed to loan us anything but the Vasaris."

"New deal. Five paintings—and I may let her talk me into tossing in a Donatello sculpture—a three-month loan, with the Boldari Gallery suitably acknowledged in all advertising, with the proceeds from the fund-raiser going to the National Endowment for the Arts."

"Fund-raiser?"

"I'll get to that. The reason I'm choosing the New England Institute of Art History is because of its reputation, its dedication to not only displaying art but teaching, restoring, studying, and preserving it. I was very impressed when I was here a few weeks ago and was taken through the facility by Dr. Miranda Jones."

He tugged on her hair, sent it tumbling to her shoulders as he liked it best. And ignored her curse of annoyance. "I was particularly intrigued by her idea of creating a display of the history and progress," he went on, "with its social, religious, and political underlayment, of the Italian Renaissance."

"Were you?" she murmured. "Were you really?"

"I was riveted." He picked up her hand to toy with her fingers and noted she'd taken off the ring he'd put there. The fact that the lack of it caused his brows to draw together in annoyance was something to ponder later. "I was struck by her vision of this showing, and by the idea of arranging a similar display, after the three-month period, in my own gallery in New York."

"I see. A partnership."

"Exactly. We were of one mind, and during the preliminary stages of discussion, you brought up the idea of holding a fund-raiser at the Institute, benefiting the NEA. As Boldari Galleries are staunch supporters of the organization, I was caught. It was very clever of you to dangle that lure."

"Yes," she murmured, "wasn't it?"

"I'm ready to move forward on this mutual project at the earliest possible date, but having been told that Dr. Jones is on a leave of absence, I'm quite concerned. I can't possibly work with anyone else. The delay has led me to consider working with the Art Institute in Chicago instead."

"She won't care for that."

"I didn't think she would." He nipped the pins out of her hand before she could bundle her hair back up, and carelessly tossed them over his shoulder.

"Damn it, Ryan—"

"Don't interrupt. We need you back inside the Institute. We need whoever's behind the forgeries to know you're back on the job. Then once we've got everything in place, we need everyone who was connected to the two bronzes here, together, in one spot."

"You may very well be able to manage the first. A display such as the one you're describing would be very prestigious."

She would have gotten up to retrieve the pins,

but he was playing with her hair again, watching her face as he gathered it, twined it. "Um. My mother appreciates the power of prestige. Obviously the second part would be a given after that. But I don't know how you expect to manage the last of it."

"I'll tell you." He grinned and leaned over to flick a finger down her cheek. "We're going to throw a hell of a party."

"A party? The fund-raiser?"

"That's right." He rose and began poking around on her shelves, in her drawers. "And we're going to have it in Giovanni's name, a kind of memorial."

"Giovanni." It turned her blood cold. "You'd use him for this? He's dead."

"You can't change that, Miranda. But we'll arrange it so that whoever killed him comes. And we'll be one step closer to the bronzes."

"I don't understand you."

"I'm working out the details. Don't you have a sketch pad?"

"Yes, of course." Wavering between irritation and confusion, she rose and took one from a filing cabinet.

"I should have known. Well, bring it along, get yourself a couple of pencils."

"Bring it along where?"

"To the back porch. You can sit and sketch your garden while I make some phone calls."

"You expect me to sketch a garden while all this is going on?"

"It'll relax you." He chose some pencils from her

desk, tucked them in his shirt pocket, picked up her glasses, tucked them in hers. "And you'll plant a better one if you know what you want to look at." He grabbed her hand and pulled her out of the room.

"When did you come up with all this?"

"Last night. Couldn't sleep. We're spinning wheels, when we need action. We've been letting someone else run the show, and we've got to start pushing the buttons."

"That's all very interesting and metaphorical, Ryan, but holding a fund-raiser in Giovanni's name won't guarantee his killer will show. And it certainly doesn't put the bronzes in our hands."

"One step at a time, baby. You going to be warm enough?"

"Don't fuss. Sitting outside and sketching isn't going to relax me. If we're going to pull off this display, I should be working on that."

"You'll be putting your nose to the grindstone soon enough."

Resigned, she stepped out on the porch. April had decided to make its entrance gently, bowing in balmy breezes and sunny skies. It could change, she knew, in a surprising instant to wet spring snow and high winds. It was part of the appeal, she supposed, the caprices of coastal weather.

"Just sit." He gave her a brotherly kiss on the brow. "I'll handle this part."

"Well then, I just won't worry my pretty little head."

He laughed and took out his cell phone. "The

only thing little about you, Dr. Jones, is your tolerance level. But somehow I find that alluring. What's your mother's number?"

She adjusted her thoughts, accepted that he was innately skilled at arousing and annoying—often simultaneously. "That's her home number," she told him after she'd recited it. "With the time difference, that's most likely where you'll find her."

As he punched it in, she looked out over the lawn. He would charm Elizabeth, Miranda decided. His talent with women was inarguable, and something it didn't suit her to consider too deeply. He would know just how to appeal to Elizabeth, as he'd known just how to appeal to her daughter. With enough time, she doubted there was a woman on the planet he couldn't convince to eat the menu selection of his choice right out of his talented hands.

She sighed, hearing the way his voice flowed over her mother's name as the connection was made. Then she blocked it out.

The shattering blue of the sky, the glimpses of sea and rock that sparkled under the sun only made her lawn look shabbier. She could see the paint peeling on the porch rail, and winter-browned weeds poking up through the chipped surface of the flagstones that formed a walkway to the cliffs.

Her grandmother had tended the house and the grounds as a mother tends beloved children, she remembered. Now she and Andrew had let it go, ignoring the small details, shrugging off what they considered the more tedious responsibilities.

Major repairs and maintenance were simple. You just hired someone to deal with it. She didn't think either she or Andrew had ever mowed their own lawn, raked leaves, pruned a bush, or yanked a weed.

It would be a good change, she thought. Something they could share. The manual labor, the satisfaction of seeing the improvements would be good therapy for him. And, she decided, for her. One way or another, the cycle her life was in just now would end. When it did, she would need something to fill the hole.

Casting her mind back, she tried to remember how the side garden had looked when she was a child and her grandmother had still been fit and well enough to tend it.

Tall spiky flowers, she recalled, with deep purple and deep red blooms. Something butter yellow and daisylike in a flower with stems that bent gracefully under the weight. Her pencil began to move as she brought it back into her mind. Clumps of green with a slender stem shooting up and ending with an upturned white cup. There was a scent too, from flowers that looked something like carnations with red and white blooms and a strong spicy fragrance.

Others with rich blue trumpets. Yes, and snapdragons. She was ridiculously thrilled she finally put a name to a variety.

While Ryan made his pitch on the phone to the mother, he watched the daughter. She was relaxing, he noted, smiling a little as she drew. Fast sketching, the kind that took innate talent and a good eye.

Her hair was tousled, her fingers long, the nails neat, short, and unpainted. She'd taken her glasses out of her pocket and put them on. Her sweater bagged at the shoulders, her trousers were the color of putty.

He thought she was the most stunning woman he'd ever seen.

And because thinking that, he lost his thread, he turned away and wandered to the far end of the porch.

"Please, call me Ryan. I hope I may call you Elizabeth. I'm sure you know just how brilliant and how delightful your daughter is, but I must tell you what a tremendous impression she made on me. When I learned she'd taken a leave of absence, well, disappointed is a mild term."

He listened for a moment, smiling to himself. He wondered if Miranda was aware her voice had that same upper-crust pitch when she was trying to disguise annoyance.

"Oh yes, I have no doubt there are members of the staff at the Institute who could take the basic idea and implement it. But I'm not interested in working with the second line. Although Lois Berenski at the Chicago Art Institute—you know Lois, I assume. . . . Yes. She's very competent and quite interested in this proposal. I've promised to get back to her within forty-eight hours, which is why I'm taking the liberty of bothering you at home. My preference is the Institute and Miranda, but if this can't be accomplished before my deadline, I'll have to . . ."

He trailed off, grinning openly now as Elizabeth began a hard sell. Getting comfortable, he swung a leg over the rail, straddling it while he let his gaze sweep the coast, watch the gulls swoop, and allowed Elizabeth to wheel and deal until she gave him exactly what he wanted.

It took forty minutes, during which time he wandered into the kitchen, made himself a small snack plate of crackers, cheese, and olives, and carried it back outside. When it was done, he and Elizabeth had agreed to have drinks the evening before the gala—he was calling it a gala now—and raise a toast to their mutual project.

He hung up, popped an olive in his mouth. "Miranda?"

She was still sketching, well into her third angle on her proposed garden. "Hmmm."

"Answer the phone."

"What?" She glanced up, vaguely annoyed with the interruption. "The phone's not ringing."

He winked. "Wait for it," he told her, then grinned when the kitchen phone pealed. "That'll be your mother. If I were you, I'd act surprised—and just a little reluctant."

"She agreed?"

"Answer the phone, and find out."

She was already leaping up, dashing into the house to snatch the phone off the hook. "Hello? . . . Hello, Mother." She pressed a hand to her speeding heart and listened.

It came as a demand, but that was to be expected. More, it was outlined as a fait accompli. Her leave was to be terminated, immediately, and she was to contact the Boldari Gallery and make arrangements to proceed. Her schedule was to be adjusted, this was to be priority, and the display would be conceived, planned, erected, and completed the second weekend in May.

"That's barely a month. How—"

"I realize it's a short amount of time for something of this scope, but Mr. Boldari has other commitments and conflicts. He'll work with Andrew on the publicity for the gala, with Vincente pitching in. Your only concern for the next four weeks is the display. He expects a great deal from you, Miranda, and so do I. Is that understood?"

"Of course." Absently she slipped off her glasses, hung them by the earpiece in her pocket. "I'll start right away. Giovanni—"

"The service was very lovely. His family appreciated the flowers. I'll be in close touch with you on this matter, Miranda, and expect to arrange my schedule to come in the first week of May, if possible, to supervise the final touches. Be sure to send me the proper reports."

"You'll get everything. Goodbye. . . . It's done," Miranda murmured as she replaced the receiver. "Just like that."

"I didn't mention Giovanni," Ryan told her. "That can't come from me. You'll have the idea for this tomorrow, and after running it by me and securing my agreement, you'll send her a memo."

He set his plate on the counter, chose a cracker for her and topped it with cheese. "Out of that will come the notion that all key staff members from all Jones organizations will attend the event in a show of unity, support, and respect."

"They'll come," she murmured. "My mother will see to it. But I don't see what good this does."

"Logistics. Everyone connected in one place, at one time." He smiled and ate another cube of cheese. "I'm looking forward to it."

"I have to get to work." She pushed both hands through her hair. "I have an exhibit to design."

"I'll be flying in from New York tomorrow."

She paused at the doorway and glanced back. "Oh, will you?"

"Yes. Morning flight. It's going to be a pleasure to see you again, Dr. Jones."

CHAPTER TWENTY-THREE

"IT'S GOOD TO HAVE YOU BACK." LORI SET A STEAMing cup of coffee on Miranda's desk.

"I hope you feel that way by the end of the week. I'm about to run you ragged."

"I can handle it." Lori touched a hand to Miranda's arm. "I'm so sorry about Giovanni. I know you were friends. We all liked him so much."

"I know." *His blood's on your hands.* "He'll be missed. I need to work, Lori, to dive in."

"All right." She walked to a chair, poised her pencil over her notebook. "Where do we start?"

Deal with what needs to be done, Miranda told herself. One step at a time. "Set up meetings with carpentry—get Drubeck. He did good work on the Flemish display a couple of years ago. I need to talk to legal, to contracts, and we'll need to pull someone out of research. I want someone who can check data quickly. I'll need ninety minutes with Andrew, and I want to be notified the moment Mr. Boldari arrives. Arrange for lunch to be set up in the VIP lounge—make it for one o'clock and see if Andrew can join us. Check with restoration. I want to know when works in progress of our era will be completed. And invite Mrs. Collingsforth to be my guest any day this week for tea—again we'll use the VIP lounge."

"Going after her collection?"

The avaricious look sharpened Miranda's eyes. "I think I can convince her she'd enjoy seeing her paintings in this showing, with a nice, tasteful brass plaque saying 'on loan from the collection of.' "

And if she couldn't convince Mrs. Collingsforth, Miranda thought, she'd sic Ryan on her.

"I'll need measurements of the South Gallery. If they aren't on record here, get me a tape measure. I want them today. Oh, and I want to see a decorator."

Lori's busy pencil paused. "A decorator?"

"I have an idea for . . . atmosphere. I need someone inventive, efficient, and who knows how to take orders instead of giving them." Miranda drummed her fingers. Oh yes, she knew what she wanted, right down to the last inch of fringe. "I'll need a drawing board in here, and one delivered to my home. Send a memo to Andrew, requesting that I be copied on all steps on the publicity and all conceptions for the fund-raiser. Mr. Boldari is to be put through at any time and is to be accommodated in his wishes whenever possible."

"Of course."

"I'll need to talk to security."

"Check."

"In four weeks, ask me for a raise."

Lori's lips curved. "Double check."

"Let's get started."

"One thing." Lori flipped her book closed. "You had a message on your machine. I left it on. It was in Italian, so most of it was lost on me."

She rose, moved over to click back the counter on Miranda's machine, punched it in. Immediately there was a flood of excited, emotional Italian. Mildly irritated, Miranda stopped the recording and began again with her mind adjusted to translate.

Dr. Jones, I must speak with you. I try to reach you here. There is no one else who will believe me. I am Rinaldi, Carlo Rinaldi. I found the lady. I held her. I know she is real. You know this is true. The papers, they said you believed in her. No one will listen to me. No one pays attention to a man like me. But you, you are important. You are a scientist. They will listen to you. Please, you will call me. We will talk. We know what we know. It must be proven. No one listens. Your mother, she tosses me out of her office. Tosses me out like a beggar or a thief. The government, they think I help make a fraud. This is a lie. A terrible lie. You know this is a lie. Please, we will tell everyone the truth.

He recited a phone number, twice, and repeated his plea.

And now he was dead, Miranda thought as the message ended. He'd asked her for help, but she hadn't been there. Now he was dead.

"What was it?" Concerned by the devastated look on Miranda's face, Lori reached out to touch her arm. "My Italian's limited to pasta orders. Is it bad news?"

"No," Miranda murmured. "It's old news, and I was too late."

She clicked the delete button but she knew the message from the dead would play in her mind for a long time.

It was good to be back in the saddle, to have specific tasks and goals. Ryan had been right about that, she decided. She'd needed action.

She was in restoration, checking out the progress of the Bronzino personally, when John Carter came in.

"Miranda. I've been trying to track you down. Welcome back."

"Thanks, John, it's good to be back."

He removed his glasses, polished them on his lab coat. "It's terrible about Giovanni. I can't take it in."

She had a flash, the sprawled body, the staring eyes, blood. "I know. He had a lot of friends here."

"I had to make the announcement yesterday. The lab's like a morgue." He puffed out his cheeks, blew out a breath. "I'm going to miss the way he'd perk things up whenever he came in for a few days. Anyway, we all wanted to do something. We came up with a few ideas, but the one everyone liked best was having a tree planted in the park. A lot of us take our lunch break there in good weather, and we thought it would make a nice memorial."

"I think that's lovely, John. Something he would have liked very much."

"I wanted to clear it with you first. You're still lab director."

"Consider it cleared. I hope the fact that I'm management doesn't mean I can't contribute to the fund."

"Everybody knows you were friends—that comes first."

"You, ah, spent time with him when he came here, and whenever you went over to Standjo."

"Yeah, he used to say I was a branch in the mud." Carter smiled wistfully. "He meant stick, but I got such a kick out of it, I never corrected him. He'd talk me into going out and sharing a bottle of wine or a meal. He'd say how he was getting me out of my rut, how he'd teach me to flirt with the pretty girls. Then he'd ask to see the latest pictures of my kids."

His voice thickened, his eyes glistened with moisture before he turned away and cleared his throat. "So I'll, ah, arrange for the tree."

"Yes, thank you, John." She turned away herself, ashamed that she'd let Ryan's suspicions lure her into probing into the man's grief.

"Meanwhile, um, I hope you'll get back to the lab soon. You're missed."

"I'll be swinging through, but I've got a priority project for the next few weeks."

"New Renaissance display." He managed a

smile again when she looked back at him. "If you could tap the grapevine around here, you'd have a hell of a potent wine. A major exhibit like that's just what we need after the bad taste we've got in our mouths over the break-in. Nice thinking."

"Yes, we'll . . ." She trailed off, spotting Detective Cook as he wandered in. "Sorry, John, I'd better deal with this."

"Yeah. . . . I don't know why." He lowered his voice to a whisper. "He makes me nervous. Looks like he suspects everybody of doing something."

With barely a nod for Cook, he scurried out, his dusty shoes scarcely making a sound.

"Detective? What can I do for you?"

"This is some setup you've got here, Dr. Jones." Rather than take out what he thought of as his close-up glasses, he squinted at the painting. "That's the real thing, isn't it?"

"Yes, it's a Bronzino. Sixteenth-century Italian Renaissance artist. The Institute is very pleased to have it. The owners have agreed to lend it to us for display."

"Mind if I ask what she's doing there?"

The restorer barely glanced at him, giving him one flick of a look from behind her magnifying goggles. "The painting was part of a collection, long neglected, of a recluse in Georgia," Miranda said. "This piece, as well as several others, suffered some damage—dirt, damp, direct sunlight for an unfortunate period of time. It's been cleaned. In itself that's a slow, careful process. We can't risk damaging the work, so it takes a great deal of time and skill. Now we're attempting to repair some damage to the paint. We use only ingredients which would have been available when the painting was created, so as to preserve its integrity. This takes research, talent, and patience. If we've done our job, the painting will be as it was when the artist finished it."

"A lot like police work," he commented.

"Is it?"

"It's a slow, careful process—you can't risk damaging the case. You only use information that comes through it. It takes research, a kind of talent," he said with a ghost of a smile. "And a hell of a lot of patience. You do it right, you got the whole picture when you're done."

"A very interesting analogy, Detective." And one that made her incredibly nervous. "And are you getting the whole picture?"

"Just bits and pieces, Dr. Jones. Just bits and pieces." He dug around in his pocket and came up with an open pack of Juicy Fruit. "Gum?"

"No, thank you."

"Quit smoking." He took out a piece, carefully unwrapped it and put the paper and the foil into his pocket again. "Still driving me nuts. Got this patch on, but it's not all it's cracked up to be, let me tell you. You smoke?"

"No, I don't."

"Smart girl. Me, I used to suck down two packs a day. Then it got to be you can't smoke here, you can't smoke there. You're catching a couple drags in some closet or going outside in the rain. Makes you feel like a criminal." He smiled again.

Miranda barely resisted shifting her feet, and instead imagined herself tapping her foot, snapping her fingers. "I'm sure it's a difficult habit to break."

"An addiction's what it is. It's a hard thing to face up to, an addiction. It can take over your life, make you do things you wouldn't do otherwise."

He knew about Andrew's drinking. She could see it in his eyes, and thought he wanted her to see it. "I never smoked," she said flatly. "Would you like to go to my office?"

"No, no, I won't keep you long." He drew a breath of air that smelled of paint and turpentine and commercial cleaner. "Didn't think I'd run into you at all, since I'd been told you were out on leave. Took a little vacation?"

She started to agree. She wasn't sure if it was instinct or simple fear that stopped her. "I'm sure you're aware that I was told to take leave, Detective, due to the break-in here, and some difficulties that came out of my trip to Florence last month."

She was quick, he thought, and not easily tripped. "I heard something about it. Another bronze piece, right? You had some trouble authenticating it."

"I don't think so. Others do." She moved away from the painting, well aware ears were pricked.

"It caused you some trouble anyway. Two bronzes. Funny, don't you think?"

"There's nothing funny to me about having my reputation on the line."

"I can understand that. Still, you only had to stay out a few days."

This time she didn't even hesitate. "It would have been longer, but we're beginning an important project that falls into my specific field of knowledge."

"Somebody mentioned that to me. And I heard about your man in Italy. The murder. That's a rough one."

Distress came into her eyes, made her look away. "He was a friend. A good one."

"Got any idea who'd take him out that way?"

She looked back now, coldly. "Detective Cook, if I knew who had crushed my friend's skull, I'd be in Florence, talking to the police."

Cook moved the gum to the other side of his mouth with his tongue. "I didn't know they'd released the fractured skull."

"My mother was informed," she said in the same chilly voice, "as was Giovanni's family." She could only pray that was true. "Are you investigating his murder, or our burglary?"

"Just curious. Cops are curious." He spread his hands. "I came in because your brother's got a theory on how maybe the two incidents are connected."

"Yes, he told me. Do you see a connection?"

"Sometimes you don't see it until you're on top of it. You also authenticated the, ah . . ." He took out his notebook, flipped through as if to refresh his memory. "Bronze *David,* sixteenth century, in the style of Leonardo."

Though she felt her palms go damp, she resisted rubbing them on her trousers. "That's correct."

"Nobody can seem to lay their hands on the paperwork for that, the reports, documents, pictures."

"Andrew told me that as well. I can only assume the thief took the authenticating documents as well as the bronze."

"That makes sense, but he'd have to know just where to look, wouldn't he? Camera blips only put him inside for . . ." He flipped pages again. "About ten minutes. He'd have to be fast as greased lightning to have added a trip to the lab for records. I did the route at a fast walk myself. Takes a full minute. That doesn't seem like much, but when you put it into an eight-to-ten-minute time span, it's a chunk."

She couldn't afford to allow her gaze to waver, her voice to weaken. "All I can tell you is the records were filed, and now they're missing, as is the bronze."

"You have many people work alone here at night, after hours? Like your friend in Florence."

"Occasionally, though it would only be senior staff. Security wouldn't allow anyone else entrance once the building was closed."

"Like you and your brother coming in the week after the burglary."

"Excuse me?"

"I got a statement here from your night security. He says that on March twenty-three, about two-thirty A.M., you called in and informed him you and

Dr. Andrew Jones were coming in to do some lab work. Would that be accurate?"

"I wouldn't argue with it."

"That's late hours you keep."

"Not habitually." Her heart was stampeding in her chest, but her hands were steady enough as she realigned a loosened pin in her hair. "We decided to come in and get some work done while it was quiet. Is that a problem, Detective?"

"Not for me. Just keeping it tidy." He tucked his notebook away, scanned the room again. "You know, it's hard to find a paper clip out of place here. You and your brother run a tidy, organized place."

"At home he leaves his socks on the living room floor and never puts his keys in the same place twice." Was she getting too good at this? she wondered. Was she, in some nasty little way, actually starting to enjoy dancing with a cop?

"I bet you do—keep everything in its place, I mean. I bet you put everything in the same place every time. A routine, a habit."

"You could call it an addiction." Yes, she realized, in some small way she was enjoying it. Enjoying the fact that she was holding her own. "Detective, I have an appointment very soon, and I'm pressed for time."

"Didn't mean to keep you so long. Appreciate the time, and the explanation," he added, gesturing toward the painting. "Looks like an awful lot of work. Almost be easier to paint the whole thing over again."

"Then it wouldn't be a Bronzino."

"A lot of people wouldn't know the difference. You would." He nodded at her. "I bet you could spot a forgery just by eyeballing it."

She wondered if the blood had drained from her face or if it merely seemed that way. He'd gotten so close, and so quickly, while she'd been smugly congratulating herself on playing her part to perfection.

"Not always. A visual study isn't, can't be conclusive if the fake is well executed. It takes laboratory tests."

"Like the ones you run here, the ones you were doing in Florence last month."

"Yes, exactly like those." The sweat that ran in a thin trail down her back was ice cold. "If you have an interest, I can arrange a demonstration. But not at the moment," she said with a glance at her watch. "I really—" She broke off, swamped by a war of relief and nerves when Ryan came through the door.

"Miranda. How nice to see you again. Your assistant said I might find you here." Butter smooth, he took her hand, brought it to his lips. "I'm sorry, I'm a bit late. Traffic."

"That's all right." She heard the words but couldn't feel her own mouth move. "I've been tied up for a while. Detective Cook—"

"Oh yes, we met, didn't we?" Ryan offered a hand. "The morning after the burglary here. Has there been any progress?"

"We're working on it."

"I'm sure you are. I don't mean to interrupt. Shall I wait for you in your office, Miranda?"

"Yes. No. Are we finished for now, Detective?"

"Yes, ma'am. I'm glad to hear you're not put off by the theft here, Mr. Boldari. Not everyone would loan a gallery all that art after its security was breached."

"I have every confidence in Dr. Jones, and the Institute. I'm sure my property will be well protected."

"Still, it wouldn't hurt to add on a few men."

"It's being done," Miranda told Cook.

"I could give you the names of a couple of good cops who moonlight in private security."

"That's very kind of you. You could give the names to my assistant."

"No problem, Dr. Jones. Mr. Boldari." There was something between those two, Cook thought as he headed out the door. Maybe it was just sex. And maybe it was something else.

And there was something, a definite something, about Boldari. Maybe everything about him checked out neat as pins in a cushion, but there was something.

"Ryan—"

He cut Miranda off with an almost undetectable shake of the head. "I'm sorry you haven't recovered your property."

"We, ah, haven't given up on it. I've arranged for lunch in our VIP lounge. I thought that would give us time to go over some of the plans for the exhibit."

"Perfect." He offered her his arm. "I'm anxious to hear your plans in more detail." He walked her down the hall, up the stairs, keeping up inane chatter until they were safely alone in the small, elegant lounge. "Had he been grilling you for long?"

"It seemed like all my life. He talked about forgeries, wanted to know if I could detect one by just looking."

"Really." The table was already set for three, with appetizers of crackers and black olive pâté on hand. He spread one. "He's a sharp cop, though the Columbo routine wears a little thin."

"Columbo?"

"Lieutenant Columbo." Ryan bit into the cracker. "Peter Falk, cheap cigar, rumpled trench coat." When she only looked blank, he shook his head. "Your education in popular culture is sadly lacking. Doesn't matter." He waved it away. "He may actually be some help in all this before it's over."

"Ryan, if he makes the connection, if he pursues that angle, it could lead him to you. You've got the forgeries."

"It won't lead him to me, or to you. And in a month, give or take a few days, I won't have the forgeries. I'll have the originals. And we'll both polish the smear off our reputations."

She pressed her fingers to her eyes and tried to bring back that momentary sense of satisfaction she'd experienced. It just wasn't there. "I don't see how this is going to work."

"You have to trust me, Dr. Jones. This is my particular field of expertise." He gestured toward the place settings. "Who's joining us?"

"Andrew."

"You can't tell him, Miranda."

"I know." She linked her hands together and came perilously close to wringing them. "He's trying to get his life back. I'm not going to add to his stress by telling him I'm involved in planning a robbery."

"If things go according to plan, it'll be a burglary, and," he added, taking her hands to soothe her nerves, "all we're doing is taking back what was stolen. So why don't we say you're involved in planning a recovery?"

"That doesn't make it less of a crime. That doesn't make me feel less guilty when Cook gives me that hound-on-the-scent look and asks me about forgeries."

"You handled him."

"And I was starting to enjoy it," she muttered. "I don't know what's happening to me. Every step I'm taking or planning to take is outside the law."

"Inside, outside." He gave a slight shrug. "The line shifts more often than you might think."

"Not my line, Ryan. My line's always been firmly dug in one place." She turned away. "There was a message on my phone machine here. From Carlo Rinaldi."

"Rinaldi?" He set down the cracker he'd just spread. "What did he want?"

"Help." She squeezed her eyes shut. She wasn't helping anyone, except possibly herself. What did that make her? "He asked me for help. No one believed him about the bronze. He must have gone to see my mother, because he said she tossed him out of her office. He said I was the only one who could help him prove the bronze was authentic."

"And that's what you're going to do."

"He's dead, Ryan. He and Giovanni are dead. There's nothing I can do to help them."

"You're not responsible for what happened to them. You're not," he insisted, turning her to face him. "Now ask yourself this . . ." He held her shoulders firmly, kept their gazes locked and on level. "Do you think either of them would want you to stop until you've finished? Until you're able to prove the bronze is genuine? Until by proving that, you're able to point the finger at whoever killed them?"

"I don't know. I can't know." She drew in a breath, let it out slowly. "But I do know I can't live with myself unless I do finish. One asked me for help, the other did me a favor. I can't stop until I've finished."

"The line's shifted, Miranda. Whoever killed them drew it this time."

"I want revenge." She shut her eyes. "I keep waiting to feel ashamed of that, but I don't. I can't."

"Darling, do you always question every human emotion you feel?"

"I suppose I've been feeling a lot more of them lately. It makes it difficult to think in a logical pattern."

"You want to think in a logical pattern? I'll help you. I want to hear your plans for the exhibition."

"No you don't."

"Of course I do. The Boldari Gallery is lending you some very important pieces." He lifted her hand to his lips. "I want to know what you intend to do with them. This is business."

"Ryan—" She wasn't sure what she wanted to say, and never had the chance to say it as Andrew opened the door and came in.

"Things are moving fast," he commented, eyeing the way Ryan nibbled on his sister's fingers.

"Hello, Andrew." Ryan lowered Miranda's hand, but kept it in his.

"Why don't the two of you tell me what's going on here?"

"Happy to. We decided to go ahead with our earlier plan for a cooperative loan between my gallery and your organization. Expanded on it. It has the benefit of raising a great deal of money for the NEA, and putting Miranda back where she belongs."

Ryan turned to the table, lifted a glass pitcher and poured three glasses of water. "Your mother was very enthusiastic about the project."

"Yeah, I've spoken with her." Which partially explained his sour mood, he supposed. "She told me you called her from New York."

"Did she?" With a smile, Ryan passed the glasses out. "I imagine she assumed that's where I was. Why don't we let her, and everyone else, go on assuming that? So much less complicated. Miranda and I prefer to keep our personal relationship private."

"Then you shouldn't stroll through the building holding hands. The gossip mill's already chewing up the grist."

"That's not a problem for me—is that a problem for you?" he asked Miranda, then continued smoothly before she could speak. "Miranda was about to tell me her plans for the exhibit. I have some ideas of my own for that, and the gala. Why don't we sit down and see what we can come up with?"

Deciding it was best, Miranda stepped between them. "This will be an important event for us, for me personally. I'm grateful that Ryan wants to go ahead with it. It got me back here, Andrew, and I need to be here. All that aside, an exhibit of this scope is something I've hoped to do for years. Which is one of the reasons I can move quickly on implementing it. It's been in my head a long time."

She laid a hand on his arm. "After what happened in Florence, Mother would never have given me this chance unless Ryan had demanded to work with me."

"I know. Okay, I know. Maybe it just takes me longer to switch gears these days."

"But you're all right?"

"I haven't had a drink. Day three," he said with a thin smile. And two nights of sweats and shakes and desperation. "I don't want to go there with you, Miranda."

"Okay." She let her hand drop. It seemed they both had their secrets now. "I'll tell catering we're ready for lunch."

* * *

It isn't fair, it isn't right. She *has no business being back, being in charge again. I won't have her ruining my plans. I won't allow it. Years I've waited, sacrificed.* The Dark Lady *is mine. She came to me, and in that sly smile I saw a kindred spirit, a mind that could wait and watch and plan and accumulate power like coins in a jar. And in that smile I saw, finally, the means to destroy all of my enemies. To take what was mine, what was always mine.*

I had ruined her. I had done it.

The hand that wrote began to shake, used the pen like a blade to stab at the page in the diary, viciously, until the room was full of ragged breathing. Gradually all movement stopped, and the breathing became slow and deep and even, almost trancelike.

Control was slipping, sliding out of those competent fingers, leaking out of that strong and calculating mind. But it could still be wrenched back. The effort was painful, but it could still be done.

This is only a reprieve, a few weeks in the eye of the storm. I'll find a way to make her pay, to make them all pay for what was denied me. The Dark Lady *is still mine. We've killed together.*

Miranda has the forgery. It's the only explanation. The police don't have the weapon. How unlike her, how bold of her to go to Florence, to find a way to steal the bronze. I hadn't thought such actions were in her nature. So I didn't anticipate, didn't add the possibility into the equation.

I won't make that mistake again.

Did she stand and stare down at Giovanni? Was there horror and fear in her eyes? Oh, I hope so. Is fear dogging her still, like a baying hound snapping at her heels?

It is, I know it is. She ran back to Maine. Does she look nervously over her shoulder even as she strides down the hallowed halls of the Institute? Does she know, somewhere inside, that her time is short?

Let her have her reprieve, let her bask in the power she's done nothing to earn. It will be all the sweeter when she's stripped of it once and for all.

I'd never planned to take her life as well. But plans change.

When she's dead, her reputation devoured by scandal, I'll weep at her grave. They will be tears of triumph.

CHAPTER TWENTY-FOUR

THE FALSE MOUSTACHE ITCHED AND WAS PROBABLY unnecessary. As were the contacts that changed his eyes from brown to an indistinct hazel and the long blond wig he'd fashioned into a streaming ponytail. His face and any exposed skin had been carefully lightened, toning down the gold hue to the pale and pasty complexion of a man much happier out of the sun.

Three earrings glittered on his right earlobe, wire-framed glasses with tiny round rosy lenses were perched on his nose. He rather liked the bloom they gave everything.

He'd chosen his wardrobe with care. Tight, pegged red pants, a saffron silk shirt with flowing sleeves, black patent leather boots with small heels.

After all, he didn't want to be subtle.

He looked like a desperately fashionable, fanatically artsy type just skirting the edge of reasonable taste. He'd seen enough of the breed in his career to know the right moves, the right speech patterns.

He checked his face in the rearview mirror of the midsized sedan he'd chosen from Rent-A-Wreck. The car hadn't been a pleasure to drive, but it had gotten him the sixty-odd miles to Pine State Foundry. He had hopes it would get him back to the coast when he was finished.

He took his cheap, scarred faux-leather portfolio case out of the car with him. Inside were dozens of sketches—most of which he'd borrowed, so to speak, from Miranda.

The forgery of the *David* had to have been cast somewhere, he thought. Somewhere, due to time constraints, locally. And this was the closest foundry to the Institute. The one, his quick search of records indicated, the staff and students used habitually.

He took out a roll of peppermints and began chewing one as he studied the foundry. The place was a scar on the hillside, he decided. Ugly brick and metal jagging up, spreading out, with towers puffing smoke. He wondered how closely they skirted EPA regulations, then reminded himself that wasn't his problem, or his mission.

Tossing his ponytail behind his back, he slung the strap of the portfolio over his shoulder and headed in the direction of a low metal building with dusty windows.

In the heeled boots, adding a little swish was a matter of course.

Inside was a long counter with metal shelves behind, stuffed with fat ring binders, plastic tubs filled with hooks and screws, and large metal objects that defied description. At the counter on a high stool, a woman sat paging through a copy of *Good Housekeeping.*

She glanced up at Ryan. Her eyebrows shot up instantly, her gaze skimmed up and down. The slight smirk wasn't quite disguised. "What can I do for you?"

"I'm Francis Kowowski, a student at the New England Institute of Art History."

Her tongue was in her cheek now. She caught the scent of him and thought of poppies. For God's sake, what kind of man wanted to smell like poppies? "Is that so?"

"Yes." He moved forward, letting eagerness come into his eyes. "Several of my classmates have had bronzes cast here. That's my art. I'm a sculptor. I've just transferred to the Institute."

"Aren't you a little old to be a student?"

He worked up a flush. "I've only recently been able to afford to pursue . . . Financially, you see." He looked miserable, embarrassed, and touched the clerk's heart.

"Yeah, it's rough. You got something you want cast?"

"I didn't bring the model, just sketches. I want to be sure it's forged just exactly to my specifications." As if gaining confidence, he briskly opened the portfolio. "One of the other students told me about a small bronze that was done here—but he couldn't remember who'd done the casting. This is a sketch of the piece. It's David."

"Like in Goliath, right?" She tilted her head, turning the sketch around. "This is really good. Did you draw it?"

"Yes." He beamed at her. "I was hoping to find out who did the casting on this so I could make arrangements for him to do my work. It was about three years ago, though, according to my friend."

"Three years?" She pursed her lips. "That's going back a ways."

"I know." He tried the puppy look again. "It's vitally important to me to find out. My friend said that the piece was beautifully done. The bronze was perfect—and whoever did the foundry work used a Renaissance formula, really knew his craft. The sculpture was like museum quality."

He took out another sketch, showed her *The Dark Lady.* "I've worked desperately hard on this piece. It's taken all my energies. Almost my life, if you can understand." His eyes began to shine as she studied it.

"She's great. Really great. You oughta be selling these drawings, kid. Seriously."

"I make a little money doing portraits," he mumbled. "It's not what I want to do. It's just to eat."

"I bet you're going to be a big success."

"Thanks." Delighted with her, he let tears swim into his eyes. "It's been such a long haul already, so many disappointments. There are times you could just give up, just surrender, but somehow . . ."

He held up a hand as if overcome. Sympathetically, she popped a tissue out of a box and handed it to him.

"Thank you. I'm so sorry." He dabbed delicately under his tinted lenses. "But I know I can do this. I have to do this. And for this bronze, I need the best you've got. I've saved enough money to pay whatever you charge, extra if I have to."

"Don't worry about extra." She patted his hand, then turned to her computer terminal. "Three years back. Let's see what we can find out. Odds are it was Whitesmith. He gets a lot of the work from students."

She began to click and clack with inch-long red nails, and shot him a wink. "Let's see if we can get you an A."

"I appreciate this so much. When I was driving up here, I just knew this was going to be a special day for me. By the way, I just love your nails. That color is fabulous against your skin."

It took less than ten minutes.

"I bet this is the one. Pete Whitesmith, just like I figured. He's top of the line around here, and most anywhere else if you ask me. Did a job for this kid—I remember this kid. Harrison Mathers. He was pretty good too. Not as good as you," she added, sending Ryan a maternal smile.

"Did he get a lot of work done here? Harrison, I mean."

"Yeah, several pieces. Always hung around over Pete's shoulder. Nervous kid. Here it shows a small bronze nude of David with sling. That's the one."

"That's great. Amazing. Whitesmith. He still works here?"

"Sure, he's a cornerstone. You go on over to the foundry. Tell Pete Babs said to treat you right."

"I don't know how to thank you."

"How much would you charge to do a drawing of my kids?"

"For you, absolutely free." He shined a smile at her.

"Sure I remember it." Whitesmith mopped at his face under the bill of a stained blue cap. He had a face that should have been carved in granite, all blocky square and deep grooves. He was built like a bullet, broad at the base, narrow at the shoulders. His voice rose over the roar of furnaces, the hard clangs of metal.

"This was the piece?"

Whitesmith stared at the sketch Ryan showed him. "Yep. Harry was mighty particular about this one. Had the formula for the bronze written out—wanted me to add some lead so it'd cure faster, but otherwise it was an old formula. I'm coming up on break, let's take this outside."

Grateful, Ryan followed him out of the heat and noise.

"I've been casting for twenty-five years," Whitesmith said, lighting his break Camel and blowing the smoke into the lightly chilled air. "I gotta say, that piece was a little gem. Ayah. One of my favorites."

"You did others for him too?"

"Harry, sure. Four, maybe five in a couple-year

period. This was the best of the lot, though. Knew we had something special when he brought in the mold and wax copy. Now that I think on it . . ." And he did, taking a long deep drag, blowing it out. "That was the last piece I did for him."

"Was it?"

"Ayah. I don't recollect seeing young Harry after that. Students at the Institute . . ." He shrugged his thin shoulders. "They come and they go."

"Did he work with anybody else?"

"No, far as I know, I did all Harry's casting. He was interested in the process. Not all the students give a hot damn about this end of it. Just what they think of as art." He sneered a little. "Lemme tell you, pal, what I do is goddamn art. A good foundryman is an artist."

"I couldn't agree more. That's why I was so desperate to find you—the artist who worked on this wonderful little *David*."

"Yeah, well." Obviously pleased, Whitesmith sucked in smoke. "Some of those artist types are snots, pure and simple sons of bitches. Figure a guy like me's just a tool. I gotta be an artist and a scientist. You get a prize-winning sculpture outta here, you got me to thank for it. Most don't bother, though."

"I knew a foundryman in Toledo." Ryan sighed lustily. "I considered him a god. I hope Harrison was properly appreciative of your work."

"He was okay."

"I guess he used a flexible mold for the *David*."

"Yeah, silicon. You gotta be careful there." Whitesmith jabbed with his cigarette for emphasis, then nipped it between his thumb and forefingers and flicked it away in a long, high arch. "You can get distortions, shrinkage. But the kid knew his stuff. He went with the lost-wax method for the model. Me, I can work with all of them, wax, sand, plaster investment. Do the finishing and tool work if the client wants. And I stick with my work, all the way. Don't like being rushed, either."

"Oh, did Harry rush you?"

"On that last piece he was a pain in the ass sideways." Whitesmith snorted through his nose. "You'da thought he was Leonardo da fucking Vinci on deadline." Then he shrugged. "Kid was okay. Had talent."

Though it was a long shot, Ryan took out the sketch of *The Dark Lady.* "What do you think of her?"

Whitesmith pursed his lips. "Well now, that's a sexy broad. Wouldn't mind casting her. What are you using for her?"

A little knowledge, Ryan thought, could be a dangerous thing. Or it could be just enough. "Wax with a plaster investment."

"Good. We can work fine with that. Fire the plaster right here too. You don't want air bubbles in that wax, ace."

"No indeed." Ryan slipped the sketch away again. The man was too solid, he thought, too cooperative to be involved. "So did Harry ever come around with anyone?"

"Not that I recollect." Whitesmith's eyes narrowed. "Why?"

"Oh, I just wondered if the friend who told me about the piece, and you, ever came by with him. He spoke so highly of your work."

"Ayah, and who'd that be?"

"James Crispin," Ryan improvised. "He's a painter, so he wouldn't have come around unless he was hanging with Harry. I've researched the formula," he added. "If I bring it in along with the wax cast and mold, you'll do the work?"

"That's what we're here for."

"I appreciate it." Ryan held out a hand. "And I'll be in touch."

"I like the look of your lady there," Whitesmith added, with a nod toward Ryan's portfolio as he turned back to the foundry door. "Don't get the chance to work on anything that classy often. I'll treat her right."

"Thanks." Whistling lightly, Ryan walked back toward the car. He was congratulating himself on an easy and successful morning's work when another car pulled into the lot.

Cook got out, stretched his back, gave Ryan a mild stare.

"Morning."

Ryan nodded, adjusted his pretty rose-colored glasses and slid behind the wheel of his rented car while Cook walked to the offices.

Close, very close, Ryan thought. But there'd been no flicker of recognition in those cop eyes. For now, he was still one short step ahead.

* * *

Once he was back in the house by the cliffs, he removed the moustache, took off the wig, gratefully blinked out the contacts. The precaution had been necessary after all, he thought as he happily removed the ridiculous shirt.

Apparently Cook had forgery on the brain.

That was fine. When the job was over, having Cook's investigation slanted toward most of the truth would be an advantage.

Now it was only mildly unnerving.

He removed the makeup from his face, throat, and hands, brewed a pot of coffee, and settled down to work.

There were eight students who'd used the foundry in those critical two weeks. He'd already eliminated three off the top, as their projects had been too large.

Now thanks to good old Babs and Pete, he had the one he wanted. It didn't take much time to go back into the records he'd already accessed from the Institute. And there he found Harry's class during that final semester. Renaissance Bronzes, The Human Form.

And Miranda had taught the course.

He hadn't figured that, he realized. He'd wanted to see another name. Carter's, Andrew's, anyone he could concentrate on uncovering. Then he realized he should have expected it. The *David* had been hers, *The Dark Lady* had been hers. She was the key, the core, and he was beginning to believe she was the reason.

One of her students had cast a bronze *David.* *The* bronze *David,* Ryan had no doubt.

He skimmed further, calling up final grades. She was tough, he thought with a smile. Miranda didn't hand out A's like candy. Only four out of her twenty students had rated one, with the edge slanted heavily toward B's, a scatter of C's.

And one Incomplete.

Harrison K. Mathers. Incomplete, no final project. Class dropped.

Now why would you do that, Harrison K., Ryan wondered, when you went to the trouble to have a bronze figure cast ten days before the due date, unless you'd never intended to worry about the grade?

He looked up Mathers's records, noted that he'd attended twelve classes at the Institute over a two-year period. His grades were admirable . . . until the last semester, when they took a sharp nose-dive.

Taking out his cell phone, he dialed the number listed under Harrison's personal information.

"Hello?"

"Yes, this is Dennis Seaworth in student records from the New England Institute. I'm trying to reach Harrison Mathers."

"This is Mrs. Mathers, his mother. Harry doesn't live here anymore."

"Oh, I see. We're doing an update on our students, trying to gather input for next year's classes. I wonder if you could put me in touch with him."

"He moved out to California." She sounded

weary. "He never finished his classes at the Institute."

"Yes, we have those records. We're hoping to discover if and why any of our former students were dissatisfied with the program here."

"If you find out, tell me. He was doing so well there. He loved it."

"That's good to know. If I could talk to him?"

"Sure." She recited a number with a San Francisco area code.

Ryan dialed the West Coast number and was told by a recording the number had been disconnected.

Well, he thought, a trip to California would give him a chance to see his brother Michael.

"Harrison Mathers."

With the most recent plans for the exhibit still crowded in her head, Miranda frowned at Ryan. "Yes?"

"Harrison Mathers," he repeated. "Tell me about him."

She slipped out of her jacket, hung it in the foyer closet. "Do I know a Harrison Mathers?"

"He was a student of yours a few years ago."

"You'll have to give me more than a name, Ryan. I've had hundreds of students."

"You taught him a course on Renaissance bronzes three years ago. He got an Incomplete."

"An Incomplete?" She struggled to reorder her thoughts. "Harry." It came back to her with both pleasure and regret. "Yes, he took that course.

He'd been studying at the Institute for several years, I think. He was talented, very bright. He started out with me very well, both in papers and in sketching."

She circled her neck as she walked into the parlor. "I remember he started to miss class, or come in looking as if he'd been up all night. He was distracted, his work suffered."

"Drugs?"

"I don't know. Drugs, family problems, a girl." She moved her shoulders dismissively. "He was only nineteen or twenty, it could have been a dozen things. I did talk to him, warn him that he needed to concentrate on his work. It improved, but not a great deal. Then he stopped coming in, just before the end of the course. He never turned in his final project."

"He had one cast. At the Pine State Foundry the second week in May. A bronze figure."

She stared, then lowered herself into a chair. "Are you trying to tell me he's involved in this?"

"I'm telling you he had a figure cast, a figure of David with sling. A project he never turned in. He was there while the *David* was being tested, and he dropped out shortly after. Was he ever in the lab?"

The sick and uneasy rolling was back in her stomach. She remembered Harry Mathers. Not well, not clearly, but well enough for it to hurt. "The entire class would have been taken through the lab. Any student is taken through the labs, restoration, research. It's part of the program."

"Who'd he hang with?"

"I don't know. I don't get involved in my students' personal lives. I only remember him as clearly as I do because he had genuine talent and he seemed to waste it at the end."

She felt the beginnings of a headache creep in behind her eyes. Oddly enough, for hours that day she'd forgotten everything but the exhibit—the thrill of the planning. "Ryan, he was a boy. He couldn't have been behind a forgery like this."

"When I was twenty I stole a thirteenth-century Madonna mosaic from a private collection in Westchester, then went out and had pizza with Alice Mary Grimaldi."

"How can you possibly brag about something like that?"

"I'm not bragging, Miranda. I'm stating a fact, and pointing out that age has nothing to do with certain types of behavior. Now if I wanted to brag, I'd tell you about the T'ang horse I stole from the Met a few years back. But I won't," he added. "Because it upsets you."

She only stared at him. "Is that your way of trying to lighten the mood?"

"Didn't work, did it?" And because she suddenly looked so tired, he walked over to take the bottle of white wine he'd already opened, and poured her a glass. "Try this instead."

Instead of drinking, she passed the glass from hand to hand. "How did you find out about Harry?"

"Just basic research, a short field trip." The unhappy look that came into her eyes distracted him.

He sat on the arm of the chair and began to rub her neck and shoulders. "I've got to go out of town for a few days."

"What? Where?"

"New York. There are some details I have to deal with, several of which involve the transport of the pieces for this exhibit. I also need to go out to San Francisco and find your young Harry."

"He's in San Francisco?"

"According to his mama, but his phone's been disconnected."

"You found all this out today?"

"You've got your work, I've got mine. How's yours coming?"

She ran her hands nervously through her hair. Those thief's fingers were magic and were loosening muscles she hadn't realized were knotted. "I—I chose some fabric for drapings, and worked with the carpenter on some platforms. The invitations came in today. I approved them."

"Good, we're on schedule."

"When are you leaving?"

"First thing in the morning. I'll be back in a week or so. And I'll keep in touch." Because he could feel her begin to relax, he played with her hair. "You might want to see if Andrew will move back in so you're not alone."

"I don't mind being alone."

"I mind." He picked her up, slid into the chair, and settled her on his lap. Since she wasn't going to drink it, he took the glass of wine out of her hand and set it aside. "But since he's not here at the moment . . ." He cupped the back of her neck and brought her mouth to his.

He'd meant to leave it at that, a kiss, a nuzzle, a quiet moment. But the taste of her was warmer than he'd expected. The morning-in-the-woods scent of her skin more provocative than it should have been. He found himself nipping his teeth into that soft lower lip, licking at the little ache as she shivered once.

And when her arms tightened around him and her mouth moved urgently under his, he lost himself, slipped into her, surrounded himself with her.

Curves, lines, scent, flavors.

His busy hands unfastened the buttons of her blouse, skimmed under to bare those shoulders, to trace hypnotically over the swell of her breasts.

Sighs, moans, shudders.

"I can't get enough of you." His words were more irritated than pleased. "I always think I have, then I only have to see you to want you."

And no one had ever wanted her like this. She felt herself falling, deep, deeper, into the rippling warm waters of a wide well of sensation. Just feelings, no thoughts, no reason. Just needs, basic as breath.

His fingers played over her breasts, silky bird wings of motion. His tongue followed them as he shifted her, nudging her up until his mouth could close hotly over her so that the echoing tug low in her belly mirrored the aches. He caught her nipple in his teeth, a light bite, a small exquisite pain.

Willing, eager, she arched back, giving herself to him, to the moment, delighting in his single focus.

To feed on her.

Just as intent, she took her hands over him, stroking, sliding, seeking, finding her way under his shirt to flesh. Sampling that flesh and feeding herself as they rolled from the chair to the rug.

Her legs parted, trapping him in that erotic V, her hips arched so that heat pressed against heat, each movement tormenting them both.

He needed to be in her, to fill her, to bury himself in her. The primal need to possess, to be possessed, had them both grappling with clothes, gasping for air as they tumbled over the floor.

Then she was astride him, her body bent forward, her palms pressed to his chest so their mouths could tangle again. Slowly, slowly, he lifted her hips. Their eyes locked, both dark and glazed. Finally, finally, she lowered herself to him, took him in, held him there with muscles clamped and trembling.

Then she rode, body arched back, hair flowing like wild red rain over her shoulders, her eyes narrowed to slits as pleasure overwhelmed. Speed ruled now. Here was energy, electric waves of power that swam into the blood, whipped at the heart, fueled the body to bursting.

Faster, harder, deeper, with his fingers digging desperately into her hips, her breath expelling in harsh sobs. The orgasm lanced through her, the desperate edge of it racking her, wrecking her.

Still he drove into her, his grip locking her to him

as he pushed her higher with strong, steady thrusts.

A roaring filled her head, like a sea warring with a gale, and the next wave was scorching, tossing her up on one long, hot sweep.

She thought she heard someone scream.

And he saw her, in that mindless moment, hair tumbled, body arched, arms lifted, her eyes half closed, her lips curved in a smile of sly female awareness.

She was as priceless, as alluring and magnificent as *The Dark Lady,* and just as powerful. As his own release burst through him, he had one clear thought.

Here was his destiny.

Then his mind was wiped clean as the same wave caught him and flipped him over the edge.

"Good God." It was the best he could do. Never before had he lost himself so utterly in a woman or felt so bound to one. Though she still shuddered, she seemed to melt onto him, her body sliding down until her gasps were muffled against his throat.

"Miranda." He said her name once, stroking a hand down her back, up again. "Christ, I'm going to miss you."

She kept her eyes closed, said nothing at all. But she let herself sink in, let herself go, because a part of her didn't believe he'd come back.

He was gone when she awoke in the morning, leaving only a note on the pillow beside her.

Good morning, Dr. Jones. I made coffee. It'll be fresh enough unless you oversleep. You're out of eggs. I'll be in touch.

Though it made her feel foolish as a lovesick teenager, she read it half a dozen times, then got up to tuck it like a declaration of undying devotion in her jewelry case.

The ring he'd pushed onto her finger, the ring she'd kept foolishly in a velvet-lined square box in the case, was gone.

His plane landed at nine-thirty and Ryan was uptown at his gallery by eleven. It was a fraction of the size of the Institute, more like a sumptuous private home than a gallery.

The ceilings soared, the archways were wide, and the stairs curved, giving the space an airy and fluid feel. The carpets he'd chosen to scatter over the marble and hardwood floors were as much works of art as the paintings and sculptures.

His office there was on the fourth level. He'd kept it small in order to devote every available space to public areas. But it was well and carefully appointed and lacked no comfort.

He spent three hours at his desk catching up on work with his assistant, in meetings with his gallery director approving sales and acquisitions, and arranging for the necessary security and transportation for the pieces to be shipped to Maine.

He took time to schedule interviews with the press regarding the upcoming exhibit and fund-raiser, decided to shuffle in a fitting for a new tux, and called his mother to tell her to buy a new dress.

He was sending the whole family to Maine for the gala.

Next on the schedule was a call to his travel agent cousin.

"Joey, it's Ry."

"Hey, my favorite traveling man. How's it going?"

"Well enough. I need a flight to San Francisco, day after tomorrow, open-end return."

"No problemo. What name you want to use?"

"Mine."

"There's a change. Okay, I'll get you booked and fax you the itinerary. Where you at?"

"Home. You can book flights for my family, going to Maine." He gave his cousin the dates.

"Got it. All first-class, right?"

"Naturally."

"Always a pleasure doing business with you, Ry."

"Well, that's nice to hear because I have a favor to ask."

"Shoot."

"I'm going to give you a list of names. I need to find out what kind of traveling these people have been doing. For the last three and a half years."

"Three and a half years! Jesus Christ, Ry."

"Concentrate on international flights, to and from Italy in particular. Ready for the names?"

"Look, Ry, I love you like a brother. This kind of thing'll take days, maybe weeks, and it's dicey. You don't just punch a few buttons and get that kind of info. Airlines aren't supposed to give it out."

It was a song and dance he'd heard before. "I've got season tickets to the Yankees. VIP lounge with locker room passes."

There was a short silence. "Give me the names."

"I knew I could count on you, Joey."

When he was done, he kicked back in his chair. He took the ring he'd given Miranda out of his pocket, watched it shine in the light coming through the filtered glass at his back.

He thought he would have his friend the jeweler pop the stones and make them into earrings for her. Earrings were safer than a ring. Women, even bright, practical women, could get the wrong idea about a ring.

She'd appreciate the gesture, he thought. And he was going to owe her something, after all. He'd have the earrings made, then have them shipped to her when he—and the bronzes—were a comfortable distance away.

He imagined, once she had a chance to think it through, she'd conclude that he'd acted in the only logical fashion. No one could expect him to come out of his last job empty-handed.

He put the ring back in his pocket so he'd stop imagining what it had looked like on her hand.

She was going to get what she needed, he reminded himself, and when he rose his fingers were still toying with the ring. They would prove her bronze had been genuine, they'd uncover a forger, a murderer, and she'd be haloed in the spotlight with her reputation glinting like gold.

He had several clients who would pay a delightful fee for a prize like *The Dark Lady.* He had only to choose the lucky winner. And that fee would cover his time, his expenses, his aggravation, with a nice little bonus like cream over the top.

Unless he decided to keep it for himself. She would be, without question, the prize of his private collection.

But . . . business was business. If he found the right client—and gained the right fee—he could start a new gallery in Chicago or Atlanta or . . . Maine.

No, he'd have to stay clear of Maine after this was done.

A pity, he thought. He'd come to love it there, near the sea, near the cliffs, catching scents of water and pine. He'd miss it.

He'd miss her.

It couldn't be helped, he told himself. He had to neatly close out one area of his life and start a new one. As a completely legitimate art broker. He'd keep his word to his family, and he'd have kept his word to Miranda. More or less.

Everyone would go back where they belonged.

It was his own fault if he'd let his feelings get a little too tangled up. Most of that, he was sure, was due to the fact they'd been virtually living together for weeks now.

He liked waking up beside her, a little too much. He enjoyed standing with her on the cliffs, listening to that husky voice, nudging one of those rare smiles out of her. The ones that reached her eyes and took that sad look out of them.

The fact was—the very worrying fact was—there was nothing about her that didn't appeal to him.

It was a good thing they had their own spaces back for a while. They would put it all back in perspective with a little distance.

But he wondered why, as he nearly convinced himself this was true, he felt a nasty little ache around his heart.

She tried not to think about him. To wonder if he thought of her. It was more productive, she told herself, to focus entirely, exclusively, on her work.

It would very likely be all she had left before much longer.

She nearly succeeded. Through most of the day she had dozens of details demanding her skill and attention. If her mind wandered once or twice, she was disciplined enough to steer it back to the task at hand.

If a new level of loneliness had been reached in only a single day, she would learn to adjust.

She would have to.

Miranda was about to shut down for the day and take the rest of her work home when her computer signaled an incoming e-mail. She finished her long, detailed post to the decorator she'd contracted regarding the lengths of fabrics required, copying both Andrew and the proper procurement clerk in requisitions.

She scanned the post, made a few minor adjustments, then clicked to both send and receive. Her incoming mail flashed on-screen under the header A DEATH IN THE FAMILY.

Uneasy, she clicked on read.

You have the False Lady. There's blood on her hands. She wants it to be yours. Admit your mistake, pay the price and live. Go on as you are, and nothing will stop her.

Killing becomes her.

Miranda stared at the message, reading each word over and over until she realized she was curled in the chair, rocking.

They wanted her to be afraid, to be terrified. And oh God, she was.

They knew she had the forgery. It could only mean someone had seen her with Giovanni, or that he had told someone. Someone who had killed him, and wished her dead.

Struggling for control, she studied the return address. Lost1. Who was Lost1? The url was the standard route all Standjo organizations used for electronic mail. She did a quick name search, but found nothing, then hit the reply button.

Who are you?

She left it at that and sent. In took only seconds for the message to flash across her screen denying her. Not a known user.

He'd been quick, she decided. But he had taken a chance sending her the post. What could be sent could surely be traced. She printed out a hard copy, saved the post to a file.

A glance at her watch told her it was nearly six. There was no one to help her now. No one was waiting for her.

She was alone.

CHAPTER TWENTY-FIVE

"SO, HAVE YOU HEARD FROM RYAN?"

Miranda checked off items on the list fixed to her clipboard as she supervised the maintenance crew in the removal of selected paintings from the wall in the South Gallery.

"Yes, his office faxed the details of the transportation schedule. All items will arrive next Wednesday. I'm having a team of our security meet their security at the airport."

Andrew studied her profile for another moment, then shrugged. They both knew that wasn't what he'd meant. Ryan had already been gone a week.

He dug into the bag of pretzels he'd taken to eating by the pound. They made him thirsty, and when he was thirsty he drank gallons of water. Then he had to piss like a racehorse.

He'd worked it out in his mind that all the liquid was flushing toxins out of his system.

"Ms. Purdue and Clara are dealing with the caterer," he told her. "We don't have a final count for attendees, but they'd like the menu approved. I'd like you to take a look at it before we sign the final contract. It's really your show."

"It's *our* show," Miranda corrected, still checking off her list. She wanted both the paintings and the frames cleaned before the opening, and had sent a memo to restoration giving them priority.

"It better be a good one. Closing off this gallery has a lot of the visitors grumbling."

"If they come back in a couple of weeks, they'll get more than their money's worth." She took off her glasses and rubbed her eyes.

"You've been putting in a lot of hours on this."

"There's a lot to do, and not much time to do it. Anyway, I like being busy."

"Yeah." He rattled his pretzels. "Neither one of us is looking for loose time right now."

"You're doing okay?"

"Is that the code for are you drinking?" It came out with an edge he hadn't intended. "Sorry." His fingers dived into the bag again. "No, I'm not drinking."

"I know you're not. It wasn't code."

"I'm dealing with it."

"I'm glad you came back home, but I don't want you to feel you have to be there with me if you'd rather be with Annie."

"The fact that I've figured out I want to be with Annie makes it a little rough to stay there sleeping on her couch. If you get the picture."

"Yeah, I get the picture." She crossed over to dip into the pretzels herself.

"Any idea when Ryan's getting back?"

"Not exactly."

They stood for a moment, each crunching pretzels and contemplating the annoyance of sexual frustration. "Wanna go out and get drunk later?" Andrew grinned at her. "Just a little recovery humor."

"Ha ha." She dug into the bag, came up with a few grains of salt, sighed. "Got any more of these?"

Ryan's first stop in San Francisco was the gallery. He'd chosen the old warehouse in the waterfront district because he'd wanted a lot of space, and had decided to separate his business from the dozens of galleries downtown.

It had worked, making Boldari's more exclusive, unique, and allowing him to provide fledgling artists with a chance to show their work in a top-flight gallery.

He'd decided on a casual ambiance rather than the elegance he'd created in New York. Here, paintings might be spotlighted against raw brick or wood, and sculpture often stood on rough metal columns. Wide, unframed windows provided a view of the bay and the busy tourist traffic.

A second-floor cafe provided artists and art lovers with foamy cappuccino and lattes at tiny tables reminiscent of a sidewalk trattoria while they looked down on the main gallery, or gazed up at the third-floor studios.

Ryan settled himself at one of the tables and grinned across at his brother Michael. "So, how's business?"

"Remember that metal sculpture you told me looked like a train wreck?"

"I think my opinion was it looked like the wreck of a circus train."

"Yeah, that was it. We sold it yesterday for twenty thousand and change."

"A lot of people have more money than taste. How's the family?"

"See for yourself. You're expected for dinner."

"I'll be there." He leaned back, studying his brother as Michael ordered coffee for both of them.

"It suits you," Ryan commented. "Marriage, family, the house in the burbs."

"It better, I'm in for the duration. And a good thing for you. It helps keep Mama off *your* ass."

"It doesn't help much. I saw her yesterday. I'm supposed to tell you she needs new pictures of the kids. How is she supposed to remember what they look like if you don't send pictures?"

"We sent her ten pounds of pictures last month."

"You can deliver the next batch in person. I want you and the family to come in for the exhibit and fund-raiser at the Institute. You got the memo on that, right?"

"Yeah, I got it."

"Any problem with the scheduling?"

Michael considered as their coffee was served.

"None that I can think of. We should be able to make it. The kids always love a chance to go into New York and see the family, fight with their cousins, have Papa sneak them candy. And it'll give me a chance to see this Ph.D. Mama told us about. What's she like?"

"Miranda? Smart, very smart. Capable."

"Smart and capable?" Michael sipped his coffee, noting the way his brother's fingers lightly tapped the table. Ryan wasn't often given to restless or wasted motion, he thought. The smart, capable woman was on his mind—and his nerves. "Mama said she's a looker, lots of red hair."

"Yeah, she's a redhead."

"You usually go for blondes." When Ryan only arched an eyebrow, Michael laughed. "Come on, Ry, spill it. What's the story?"

"She's beautiful. She's complicated. It's complicated," he decided, and finally realized he was tapping his fingers. "We're doing business together on a couple of levels."

This time Michael's brow lifted. "Oh really?"

"I don't want to get into that right now." Missing her was like a fire in his gut. "Let's just say we're working together on a couple of projects, this exhibit for one. And we have a personal relationship. We're enjoying each other. That's all."

"If that were all, you wouldn't look so worried."

"I'm not worried." Or he hadn't been until she'd sneaked into his head again. "It's just complicated."

Michael made a "hmm" of agreement and decided he was going to enjoy telling his wife that Ryan was well and truly hooked on a redheaded Ph.D. from Maine. "You've always been able to work your way out of complications."

"Yeah." Since it made him feel better to think so, Ryan nodded. "In any case, that's only part of the reason I'm here. I'm looking for a young artist. I've got an address, but I thought I'd see if you knew him. Harrison Mathers? Sculptor."

"Mathers." Michael's forehead creased. "Doesn't ring a bell right off. I can check, look through the files to see if we've taken any of his work."

"We'll do that. I don't know if he's still at this address."

"If he's in San Francisco and looking to sell art, we'll find him. Have you seen his work?"

"I believe I have," Ryan murmured, thinking of the bronze *David.*

Mathers's last known address was a third-floor walk-up apartment on the wrong side of downtown. Light rain was falling as Ryan approached Mathers's building. A small group of young men huddled in a doorway, their eyes scanning the street, looking for trouble.

On the line of pitifully narrow mailboxes built into the wall of the dank foyer, Ryan saw "H. Mathers" in 3B.

He headed up the stairs into the faint smell of urine and stale vomit.

On the door of 3B someone had painted an excellent study of a medieval castle, complete with turrets and drawbridge. It resembled a fairy tale, a dark one, Ryan thought, when you noticed the single face in the top window gazing out in screaming horror.

Harry, he mused, had talent and an excellent sense of his current circumstances. His home might be his castle, but he was a terrified prisoner in it.

He knocked and waited. Almost immediately the door behind him opened. Ryan shifted to the balls of his feet, and turned.

The woman was young, and might have been attractive if she hadn't already dressed her face for the night's work. It was a whore's makeup, heavy on the lips and eyes. The eyes, under the weight of shadow and lashes, were hard as Arctic ice. Her hair was plain brown and cut short as a boy's. He imagined she used a wig during working hours.

Though he took all this in, as well as the lush body carelessly displayed in a short, flowered robe, his attention centered on the big, black .45 in her hand. Its muzzle was as wide as the Pacific and pointed dead-center at his chest.

He decided it was best to keep his eyes on hers, his hands in plain view, and his explanation simple.

"I'm not a cop. I'm not selling anything. I'm just looking for Harry."

"I thought you were the other guy." Her voice was straight out of the Bronx, but didn't make him feel any more secure.

"Let me just say, under the circumstances, I'm

glad I'm not. Could you point that cannon somewhere else?"

She studied him another moment, then shrugged. "Yeah, sure." She lowered it, and leaned against the doorjamb. "I didn't like the look of the other guy. Didn't like his attitude neither."

"As long as you're holding that gun, I'll adjust my attitude any way you like."

She grinned at that, a quick flash that nearly overcame the sex doll makeup. "You're okay, Slick. What do you want with Rembrandt?"

"A conversation."

"Well, he ain't there, and ain't been around for a few days. That's what I told the other guy."

"I see. Do you know where Harry is?"

"I mind my own business."

"I'm sure you do." Ryan held one hand palm out, moved the other slowly to his wallet. He saw her lips purse in consideration as he took out a fifty. "Got a few minutes?"

"I might. Another fifty'd buy you an hour." But she shook her head. "Slick, you don't look like the type who pays to party."

"Conversation," he said again, and held out the fifty.

It only took her three seconds to reach out, nip the bill with the lethal tips of blood-red fingernails. "Okay, come on in."

The room held a bed, a single chair, two flea market tables, and a metal clothes rack crowded with bright, eye-catching colors and cheap fabrics. He'd been right about the wig, he noted. Two of them, a long, curly blond and a sleek raven-black, sat on Styrofoam heads.

A little desk held a dressing room mirror and a department store array of cosmetics.

While distressingly bare, the room was tidy as an accountant's spread sheet.

"For fifty," she told him, "you can have a beer."

"Appreciate it." While she moved toward the two-burner stove and midget refrigerator that constituted her kitchen, Ryan stepped up to a bronze dragon that guarded one of her flimsy tables.

"This is a very nice piece."

"Yeah, it's real art. Rembrandt did it."

"He has talent."

"I guess." She moved her shoulders, didn't bother to tug her robe back together. He was entitled to look at the merchandise, she thought, in case he wanted to invest another fifty. "I said how I liked it, and we worked out a trade." She smiled as she handed him a bottle of Budweiser.

"You're friendly with Mathers?"

"He's okay. Doesn't try to scam me for freebies. Once I had a john up here who wanted to use me for a punching bag instead of a mattress. Kid comes banging on the door when he heard I was in trouble. Yelled out how he was the cops." She snickered into her beer. "Asshole went out my window with his pants around his ankles. Rembrandt's okay. Gets a little down, smokes a lot of grass. That's an artist's thing, I guess."

"He have many friends?"

"Slick, nobody in this building has many friends.

He's been here a couple years now, and this is the first time I've seen two people come around to his door in one day."

"Tell me about the other guy."

She fingered the fifty in the pocket of her robe. "Big. Ugly face. Looked like meat to me, somebody's arm, you know. And you could tell he liked breaking legs. Said how he wanted to buy one of Rembrandt's statues, but that creep wasn't no art lover. Gave me grief when I said he wasn't around, and I didn't know where he was."

She hesitated a moment, then moved her shoulders again. "He was carrying. Had a bulge under his jacket. I shut the door in his fat face, and got out my friend there." She jerked her head toward the pie-plate-sized kitchen counter where she'd laid the .45. "You only missed him by a few minutes, that's why I thought you was him."

"How big was he, the other guy?"

"About six-four, maybe five, two-sixty easy. Gorilla arms and meat cleaver hands. Spooky eyes, like dirty ice, you know. Guy like that comes up to me on the stroll, I give him a pass."

"Good thinking." The description clicked very close to the man who'd attacked Miranda. Harrison Mathers was very lucky he wasn't home.

"So, what do you want with Rembrandt?"

"I'm an art dealer." Ryan took a business card from the case in his pocket, handed it to her.

"Classy."

"If you hear from Harry, or he comes back, give

him that, will you? Tell him I like his work. I'd like to discuss it with him."

"Sure." She rubbed a finger over the embossing, then lifted the dragon and set the card under its serpentine tail. "You know, Slick . . ." She reached out and trailed one of those scalpel-sharp nails down his shirt. "It's cold and rainy out there. You want to . . . converse a little more, I'll give you a discount."

He'd once been mildly in lust with a girl from the Bronx. The sentiment of it had him taking another fifty out of his wallet. "That's for the help, and the beer." He turned for the door, giving the dragon a last glance. "You get tight for money, take that to Michael at Boldari here on the waterfront. He'll give you a good price for it."

"Yeah. I'll keep that in mind. Come back anytime, Slick." She toasted him with the beer. "I owe you a free ride."

Ryan walked directly across the hall, finessed the lock, and was inside Mathers's apartment before his second fifty had been hidden away.

The room mirrored the one he'd just been in as to size. Ryan doubted the tanks for welding metal were approved by the landlord. There were several pieces in varying stages of work. None of them showed the insight or talent of the dragon he'd given a whore for sex. His heart was in bronzes, Ryan decided when he studied the small fluid nude standing on the stained tank of the toilet.

A self-critic, he thought. Artists could be so pathetically insecure.

He managed to search the entire apartment in under fifteen minutes. There was a mattress on the floor with a tangle of sheets and blankets, a cigarette-scarred dresser with drawers that stuck.

Over a dozen sketch pads, most of them filled, were stacked on the floor. Miranda had been right, Ryan mused as he flipped through, he had a good hand.

The only things in the apartment that appeared well cared for were the art supplies, which were arranged on army-gray metal shelves and stacked in plastic milk cartons.

The kitchen held a box of Rice Krispies, a six-pack of beer, three eggs, moldy bacon, and six packages of frozen dinners. He also found four neatly rolled joints hidden in a jar of Lipton tea bags.

He found sixty-three cents in change and a long-forgotten Milky Way bar. There were no letters, no notes, no stash of cash. He located the final disconnect notice for the phone crumpled in the trash along with the empties for another six-pack.

Nowhere was there a clue where Harry had gone or why, or when he intended to return.

He'd be back, Ryan mused, giving the room one more scan. He wouldn't abandon his art supplies or his stash of dope.

And when he came back, he'd call the minute he had his hands on the business card. Starving artists could be temperamental, but they were also predictable. And every mother's son or daughter of them hungered for one thing more than food.

A patron.

"Come home soon, Harry," Ryan murmured, and let himself out.

CHAPTER TWENTY-SIX

MIRANDA STARED DOWN AT THE FAX THAT HAD JUST hummed out of her machine. This one was all in caps, as if the sender was screaming the words.

I HAVEN'T ALWAYS HATED YOU. BUT I WATCHED YOU. YEAR AFTER YEAR. DO YOU REMEMBER THE SPRING YOU GRADUATED FROM GRAD SCHOOL—WITH HONORS, OF COURSE—AND HAD AN AFFAIR WITH THE LAWYER. CREG ROWE WAS HIS NAME, AND HE BROKE IT OFF, DUMPED YOU BECAUSE YOU WERE TOO COLD AND DIDN'T PAY ENOUGH ATTENTION TO HIS NEEDS. REMEMBER THAT, MIRANDA?

HE TOLD HIS FRIENDS YOU WERE A MEDIOCRE FUCK. I BET YOU DIDN'T KNOW THAT. WELL, NOW YOU DO.

I WASN'T VERY FAR AWAY. NOT VERY FAR AWAY AT ALL.

DID YOU EVER FEEL ME WATCHING YOU?

DO YOU FEEL IT NOW?

THERE ISN'T MUCH TIME LEFT. YOU SHOULD HAVE DONE WHAT YOU WERE TOLD. YOU SHOULD HAVE ACCEPTED THE WAY THINGS WERE. THE WAY I WANTED THEM TO BE. MAYBE GIOVANNI WOULD BE ALIVE IF YOU HAD.

DO YOU EVER THINK OF THAT?

I DIDN'T ALWAYS HATE YOU, MIRANDA. BUT I DO NOW.

CAN YOU FEEL MY HATE?

YOU WILL.

The paper trembled in her hands as she read it. There was something horribly childlike about the big block letters, the schoolyard-bully taunts. It was meant to hurt, humiliate, and frighten, she told herself. She couldn't allow it to succeed.

But when the buzzer on her intercom sounded, her breath caught on a gasp and her fingers clenched and crumpled the edges of the fax. Foolishly she laid it on her desk, smoothing out the creases precisely as she answered Lori's page.

"Yes?"

"Mr. Boldari is here, Dr. Jones. He wonders if you have a moment to see him."

Ryan. She nearly said his name aloud, pressed her fingertips to her lips to keep the word in her mind only. "Would you ask him to wait, please."

"Of course."

So he was back. Miranda rubbed her hands over her cheeks to bring color back into them. She had her pride, she thought. She was entitled to her pride. She wasn't going to rush through the door and throw herself into his arms like some moonstruck lover.

He'd been gone nearly two weeks, and not once had he called her. Oh, there'd been contact, she thought as she hunted up her compact and used the stingy mirror to smooth her hair, to add lipstick. Memos and telexes and e-mail and faxes, all sent by some office drone and signed in his name.

He hadn't bothered to ease away kindly when he was done with her. He'd had his office staff do it for him.

She wouldn't make a scene. They still had business, on several levels. She would see it through.

He wouldn't have the satisfaction of knowing she'd needed him. Had needed him every day and night of those two weeks.

She steadied herself, unlocking a drawer to lay the latest fax on a pile of others. They'd been coming in daily now, some only a line or two, others rambling like the one today. The printout of the e-mail was with them, though Lost1 had never contacted her again.

She locked the drawer, pocketed the key, then went to the door.

"Ryan." She sent him a polite smile. "Sorry to keep you waiting. Please, come in."

At her desk, Lori shifted her eyes from face to face, cleared her throat. "Should I hold your calls?"

"No, that won't be necessary. Would you like some—"

She never finished. As she closed the door behind them, he pressed her back against it and crushed his mouth to hers in a fiercely hungry kiss that battered against the wall she'd so carefully built.

Fisting her hands, she kept her arms at her sides and gave him nothing back, not even the passion of resistance.

When he drew away—his eyes narrowed in speculation—she inclined her head and shifted aside. "How was your trip?"

"Long. Where did you go, Miranda?"

"I've been right here. I'm sure you want to see the final design. I have the drawings. I'll be happy to take you down and show you what we've finished so far. I think you'll be pleased."

She moved to the drawing board and began unrolling a large sheet of paper.

"That can wait."

She looked up, angled her head. "Did you have something else in mind?"

"Entirely. But obviously that can wait as well." His eyes remained narrowed as he crossed to her, as if he were seeing her for the first time and taking in all the details. When they were eye to eye, he cupped a hand under her chin, slowly spread his fingers over her cheek.

"I missed you." He said it with a hint of puzzlement in his voice, as if he'd just solved a complex riddle. "More than I intended to, expected to. More than I wanted to."

"Really?" She stepped away because his touch left her shaken. "Is that why you called so often?"

"That's why I didn't call." He dipped his hands in

his pockets. He felt like a fool. And there was a nervous flutter in his stomach that warned him a man could experience emotions more alarming than foolishness. "Why didn't you call me? I made certain you knew how to reach me."

She tilted her head. It was an odd and rare sight, she thought. Seeing Ryan Boldari uncomfortable. "Yes, your various assistants were very efficient in giving me your whereabouts. As the project here was proceeding on schedule, there wasn't any reason to bother you about it. And since you seem to have decided to handle the other area of business on your own, there was little I could do about it."

"You weren't supposed to matter quite so much." He rocked back on his heels as he spoke, as if trying to find his balance. "I don't want you to matter this much. It's in my way."

She turned aside, hoping she was quick enough to keep him from seeing the hurt she knew flashed into her eyes. Anything that potent, that keen, had to show. "If you'd wanted to end our personal relationship, Ryan, you could have done it less cold-bloodedly."

He laid his hands on her shoulders, then tightened his grip, spun her angrily around when she tried to wrench away. "Do I look like I want to end it?" He dragged her toward him, covering her mouth with his again, holding her there as she struggled for freedom. "Does that feel like I want to end it?"

"Don't play with me this way." She stopped fighting, and her voice was shaky and weak. She could despise herself for it, but she couldn't change it. "I'm not equipped for this kind of game."

"I didn't know I could hurt you." As his anger drained, he rested his brow against hers. The hands that had gripped her shoulders gentled and skimmed lightly down her arms. "Maybe I wanted to see if I could. That doesn't say much for me."

"I didn't think you were coming back." Desperate for distance and the control she hoped came with it, she eased out of his arms. "People have a remarkably easy time walking away from me."

He saw now that he'd damaged something very fragile, and something he hadn't recognized as precious. Not just her trust in him, but her belief in them. He didn't think or plan or calculate the odds, he just looked at her and spoke. "I'm halfway in love with you. Maybe more. And nothing about it is easy."

Her eyes went dark, her cheeks went pale. She laid a hand on the edge of her desk as she felt her balance shift. "I—Ryan . . ." No amount of effort could catch any of the words spinning around in her head and form them into coherent thought.

"No logical response for that, is there, Dr. Jones?" He stepped to her, took her hands. "What are we going to do about this situation?"

"I don't know."

"Whatever it is, I don't want to do it here. Can you leave?"

"I . . . Yes, I suppose."

He smiled, brushed his lips over her fingers. "Then come with me."

They went home.

She assumed he'd want to go somewhere quiet, where they could talk, sort through these emotions that were so obviously foreign to both of them. Perhaps a restaurant, or the park, since spring was dancing prettily into Maine.

But he'd driven up the coast road, and neither of them spoke. She watched the land narrow, the water, quietly blue in the midday sunlight, close in on either side.

On the long rocky beach to the east, a woman stood watching a young boy dance in the playful surf and toss bread crumbs to greedy gulls. The road curved just close enough for Miranda to see the wide, delighted grin on his face as the birds swooped down to snag the feast.

Beyond them, the soft red sails of a schooner held the wind and cruised snappily southward.

She wondered if she'd ever been as innocently happy as that young boy, or as confidently peaceful as the schooner.

On the sound side, the trees were dressed in that tender green of April, more haze than texture. She loved that look the best, she realized, that delicate beginning. Odd that she'd never known that about herself. As the road climbed, the trees stirred, swaying under a soft spring sky laced with white clouds as harmless as cotton.

And there, on the edges of the hill where the old house stood, was the sudden ocean of cheery yellow. A sea of daffodils, a forest of forsythia, both of which had been planted before she was born.

He surprised her by stopping the car and grinning. "That's fabulous."

"My grandmother planted it all. She said that yellow was a simple color, and it made people smile."

"I like your grandmother." On impulse he got out, walked to the verge, and picked her a handful of the yellow trumpets. "I don't think she'd mind," he said as he climbed back inside and held them out.

"No, she wouldn't." But she found herself wanting to weep.

"I brought you daffodils once before." He laid a hand on her cheek until she turned her head to look at him. "Why don't they make you smile?"

With her eyes closed she pressed her face to the flowers. Their scent was unbearably sweet. "I don't know what to do, about what I feel. I need steps, I need reasonable, comprehensive steps."

"Don't you ever just want to stumble, and see where you fall?"

"No." But she knew that's exactly what she'd done. "I'm a coward."

"You're anything but that."

She shook her head, fiercely. "When I step into emotional territory, I'm a coward, and I'm afraid of you."

He dropped his hand, shifted position so he gripped the steering wheel with both of them. Arousal and guilt churned in his belly. "That's a dangerous thing to tell me. I'm capable of using that, taking advantage of that."

"I know it. Just as you're capable of stopping by the side of the road and picking daffodils. If you were only capable of one of those moods, I wouldn't be afraid of you."

Saying nothing, he restarted the car, drove slowly up the curved lane and parked at the front of the house. "I'm not willing to shift back and make it only business between us. If you think that's an option here, you're mistaken."

She jolted when his hand whipped out, gripped her chin. "Badly mistaken," he added, and the silky threat in his voice had her pulse pounding with panicked excitement.

"However I feel, I won't be pressured." She put her hand to his wrist and shoved. "And I keep my options open."

With that said, she pushed the door open and got out of the car, missing his lightning grin. And the heat in his eyes.

"We'll see about that, Dr. Jones," he murmured, and followed her up the steps.

"Whatever our personal relationship, we have priorities. We need to go over the plans for the exhibit."

"We will." Ryan jingled the change in his pocket as Miranda unlocked the front door.

"I need you to give me more details on what you expect to happen when we have everyone together."

"You'll get them."

"We need to talk all of this through, step by step. I need to have it organized in my mind."

"I know."

She closed the door. They stood staring at each

other in the quiet foyer. Her throat went desert dry as he stripped off his leather jacket, watched her.

Like hunter to prey, she thought, and wondered why that sensation should be so damn delightful. "I have a copy of the design here. Up in my office. Here. All the paperwork. Copies are upstairs."

"Of course you do." He took a step forward. "I wouldn't expect anything less. Do you know what I want to do to you, Dr. Jones? Right here, right now." He stepped closer, stopped just short of touching her though he could feel the urgent need for her pulsing in every cell.

"We haven't resolved anything in that area. And we need to deal with business." Her heart was knocking against her ribs like a rude and impatient guest banging at a locked door. "I have the copies here," she said again. "So I could work on them when I wasn't . . . there. Oh God."

They leaped at each other. Hands tugging and fumbling with clothes, mouths bumping, then fusing. Heat spewed up like a geyser erupting and scorching them with steam.

She dragged desperately at his shirt. "Oh God, I hate this."

"I'll never wear it again."

"No, no." A shaky laugh trembled out of her throat. "I hate being so needy. Touch me. I can't stand it. Touch me."

"I'm trying to." He yanked at the trim paisley vest she wore under her tweed jacket. "You would pick today to wear all these damn clothes."

They made it to the base of the stairs, stumbled.

The vest went flying. "Wait. I have to—" His fingers dived into her hair, scattering pins as they curled in that rich mass of red.

"Miranda." His mouth was on hers again, oceans of need cresting in that one bruising meeting of lips.

He swallowed her moans, his own, fed on them as they tripped up another two steps. She was tugging his shirt out of his waistband, struggling to drag it down his arms, gasping for air, sobbing for more as finally, finally her hands found flesh.

His muscles quivered under her hands. She could feel his heart pounding, as wildly as hers. It was just sex. It solved nothing, proved nothing. But God help her, she didn't care.

Her starched cotton shirt caught on her wrists at the cuffs and for a moment she was bound by it, thrilling, helpless as he shoved her back against the wall and feasted on her breasts.

He wanted a war, vicious, primal, savage. And found it in himself, in her feral response and demand. His fingers rushed down, unhooking the mannish trousers, sliding over her, into her so that her hips pushed forward. She came brutally, choking out his name as her body quaked from the shock.

Her mouth streaked over his face, his throat, her hands dug into his hips, tore at his clothes and drove him mad. He plunged into her where they stood, driving her hard against the wall, driving himself deeper and deeper.

She clawed at him now, her nails raking down his back. The sounds she made, primitive groans, wanton cries, throaty whimpers, called to his blood. When she went limp, he lifted her by the hips, blind and deaf to everything but the mindless need to take, and take and take. Each violent stroke was a possession.

Mine.

"More." He panted it out. "Stay with me. Come back."

"I can't." Her hands slid off his damp shoulders. Her mind and body drained.

"Take more."

She opened her eyes, found herself trapped in his. So dark, so hot, the deep gold glittering like sunburst and focused only on her. Her skin began to quiver again, little jolts of need that shimmered at the nerve endings and spread. Then those jolts turned to aches, raw, pulsing aches that turned each breath to a senseless moan. Pleasure had claws, and they ripped at her, threatened to tear her to pieces.

When she screamed, he buried his face in her hair and let himself crash.

It was like surviving a train wreck, Ryan decided. Barely surviving. They were sprawled on the floor, bodies tangled and numb, minds destroyed. She was lying across him, simply because they'd gone down that way—her midriff over his belly, her head facedown against the Persian runner.

Every few minutes, her stomach would quiver, so he knew she was still alive.

"Miranda." He croaked it out, realizing suddenly

his throat was wild with thirst. Her response was something between a grunt and a moan. "Do you think you can get up?"

"When?"

He laughed a little and reached down to rub her bottom. "Now would be good." When she didn't move, he growled, "Water. I must have water."

"Can't you just push me?"

It wasn't quite as simple as that, but he managed to extract himself from beneath her limp body. He braced a hand on the wall to keep his balance as he walked down the stairs. In the kitchen, he stood naked, gulped down two glasses of tap water, then poured a third. Steadier, he started back, his smile spreading when he scanned the scatter of clothes and flowers.

She was still on the floor at the top of the steps, on her back now, eyes shut, one arm flung out over her head, hair a glorious tangle that clashed with the deep red of the runner.

"Dr. Jones. What would the *Art Revue* say about this?"

"Hmm."

Still grinning, he crouched, nudged the side of her breast with the glass to get her attention. "Here, you could probably use this."

"Mmm." She managed to sit up, took the glass in both hands and downed every drop. "We never made it to the bedroom."

"There's always next time. You look very relaxed."

"I feel like I've been drugged." She blinked, focused on the painting on the wall behind him, and stared at the white bra that hung celebrationally from the top corner of the frame. "Is that mine?"

He looked back, ran his tongue over his teeth. "I don't believe I was wearing one."

"My God."

He had to give her points for speedy recovery as she leaped up and snatched it loose. With her eyes wide now and little gasps of distress sounding in her throat, she began to rush around gathering clothes, trying to save the flowers they'd crushed.

Ryan leaned his back against the wall and watched the show.

"I can't find one of my socks."

He smiled as she stared down at him, rumpled clothes pressed to her breasts. "You're still wearing it."

She glanced down, saw the traditional argyle on her left foot. "Oh."

"It's a cute look for you. Got a camera?"

Since the moment seemed to call for it, she dumped the clothes on his head.

At Ryan's insistence, they took a bottle of wine out to the cliffs and sat in the warm spring sun. "You're right," he said. "It's beautiful in the spring."

The water went from a pale blue at the horizon to a deeper hue where boats plied its surface, then to a dark, rich green near the shore where it spewed and beat against rock.

The wind was kind today, a caress instead of a slap.

The pines that lined the side of the land and marched up the rise showed fresh and tender new growth. The hardwoods showed the faintest blush of leaves to come.

No one walked the ragged sweep of beach below or disturbed the scatter of broken shells tossed up during a recent storm. He was glad of it, glad the boats were distant and toylike, the buoys silent.

They were alone.

If he looked back toward the house, he could just see the shape of the old south garden. The worst of the deadwood and thorny brown weeds had been cleared away. The dirt looked freshly turned and raked. He could see small clusters of green. She said she would garden, he remembered, and she was a woman who followed through.

He'd like to watch her at work, he realized. He'd very much enjoy seeing her kneeling there, concentrating on bringing the old garden back to life, making those sketches she'd drawn a reality.

He'd like to see what she made bloom there.

"We should be in my office working," she said as guilt began to prick through the pleasure of the afternoon.

"Let's consider this a field trip."

"You need to see the final design for the exhibit."

"Miranda, if I didn't trust you there, completely, you wouldn't have my property." He sipped his wine and reluctantly shifted his thoughts to work. "In any case, you sent my office daily reports on it. I imagine I've got the picture."

"Working on it's giving me some time to put other

things in perspective. I don't know what we can accomplish by all this, other than the obvious benefit to your organization and mine, and a hefty contribution to NEA. The other—"

"The other's progressing."

"Ryan, we should give all the information we can to the police. I've thought about this. It's what should have been done right from the start. I let myself get caught up—my ego, certainly, and my feelings for you—"

"You haven't told me what those are. Are you going to?"

She looked away from him, watched the tall iron buoys wave gently and without sound. "I've never felt for anyone what I feel for you. I don't know what it is, or what to do about it. My family isn't good with personal relationships."

"What does your family have to do with it?"

"The Jones curse." She sighed a little because she didn't have to glance back to know he smiled. "We always screw it up. Neglect, apathy, self-absorption. I don't know what it is, but we're just no good at being with other people."

"So you're a product of your genes, and not your own woman."

Her head twisted sharply, making him grin at the quick insult in her eyes. Then she controlled it and inclined her head. "That was very good. But the fact remains that I'm nearly thirty years old and I've never had a serious, long-term relationship. I don't know if I'm capable of maintaining one."

"First you have to be willing to find out. Are you?"

"Yes." She started to rub her nervous hand on her slacks, but he took it, held it.

"Then we start from there. I'm as much out of my element as you are."

"You're never out of your element," she murmured. "You have too many elements."

He laughed and gave her hand a squeeze. "Why don't we behave like a comfortable couple and I'll tell you about my trip to San Francisco?"

"You saw your brother."

"Yes, he and his family will be coming out for the gala. The rest of the family will come in from New York."

"All of them? All of your family's coming?"

"Sure. It's a big deal. Anyway, I should warn you, you're going to be checked out thoroughly."

"Wonderful. One more thing to be nervous about."

"Your mother's coming. And your father—which is a small dilemma, as he thinks I'm someone else."

"Oh God, I forgot. What will we do?"

"We won't know what in the world he's talking about." Ryan merely grinned when she gaped. "Rodney's British, I'm not. And he's not nearly as good-looking as I am, either."

"Do you really think my father's going to fall for something like that?"

"Of course he will, because that's our story and we're sticking to it." He crossed his ankles, drew in the cool, moist air. And realized he hadn't been completely relaxed for days. "Why in the world would I have introduced myself to him as someone else—particularly since I was in New York when he came to see you. He'll be confused, but he's hardly going to stand there and call Ryan Boldari a liar."

She let it simmer a moment. "I don't see what choice we have, and my father certainly doesn't pay close attention to people, but—"

"Just follow my lead there, and smile a lot. Now, when I was in San Francisco I looked up Harrison Mathers."

"You found Harry?"

"I found his apartment. He wasn't there. But I spent an interesting half hour with the hooker across the hall. She told me he's been gone a few days, and that—"

"One moment." She tugged her hand free of his and held up a single finger. "Would you mind repeating that?"

"He'd been gone a few days?"

"No, there was something about you spending time with a prostitute."

"It was well worth the fifty—well, hundred actually. I gave her another fifty when we were done."

"Oh, would that have been like a tip?"

"Yeah." He beamed at her. "Jealous, darling?"

"Would jealousy be inappropriate?"

"A little jealousy is very healthy."

"All right, then." She bunched her recently freed hand into a fist and rammed it into his stomach.

He wheezed out a breath, sat up cautiously in case she decided to hit him again. "I stand corrected. Jealousy is definitely unhealthy. I paid her to talk to me."

"If I thought otherwise, you'd be well on your way to the rocks down below." This time she smiled while he eyed her warily. "What did she tell you?"

"You know, that Yankee cool can be just a little frightening, Dr. Jones. She told me that I was the second man who'd come by that day looking for him. She had a very large gun pointed at me at the time."

"A gun. She had a gun?"

"She didn't like the look of the first guy. Women in her line of work generally know how to size a man up quickly. From her description, I'd say she was right about him—you'd know that firsthand. I think he was the one who attacked you."

Her hand went quickly to her throat. "The man who was here, who stole my purse? He was in San Francisco?"

"Looking for young Harry—and my guess is, your former student was lucky not to be home. He's tied in, Miranda. Whoever he made the bronze for, whoever he gave or sold it to, doesn't want him around any longer."

"If they find him—"

"I arranged for someone to keep an eye out for him. We'll have to find him first."

"Maybe he ran away. Maybe he knew they were looking for him."

"No, I looked around his place. He left all his art

supplies, a small stash of grass." Ryan leaned back on his elbows again and watched the clouds puff lazily across the sky. "I didn't get the impression he'd left in a particular hurry. The advantage is we know someone's looking for him. At this point, no one knows we are. The way the kid's been living, either he didn't get much for the forgery, or he blew it fast and hasn't explored the wonderful world of blackmail."

"Would they have threatened him first?"

"What would be the point? They didn't want him to run. They'd want to eliminate him, quick and quiet." But there was something in her eyes. "Why?"

"I've been getting . . . communications." It was a clean, professional word and made her less jittery.

"Communications?"

"Faxes, for the most part. For some time now. They've been coming daily since you left. Faxes, one e-mail, here and at the office."

Again, he sat up. This time his eyes were narrow and cool. "Threats?"

"Not exactly, or not really threats until most recently."

"Why didn't you tell me?"

"I *am* telling you."

"Why the hell didn't you let me know this was going on all along?" The blank look she sent him had him getting to his feet so quickly he knocked the glass aside and sent it tumbling over the rocks. "It never occurred to you, did it? To tell me you were being stalked this way, frightened this way?

Don't tell me you weren't frightened," he tossed out before she could speak. "I can see it in your face."

He saw, she thought, entirely too much, too easily. "What could you have done about it?"

He stared at her, eyes smoldering, then jamming his hands in his pockets, turned away. "What do they say?"

"Various things. Some of them are very calm, short and subtly threatening. Others are more disjointed, rambles. They're more personal, they talk about things that happened or little events in my life."

Because a hunted feeling crept up her spine, she got to her feet. "One came after Giovanni . . . after Giovanni," she repeated. "It said his blood was on my hands."

He had no choice but to put his own resentment and hurt aside. It surprised him how much there was of both that she hadn't trusted him. Hadn't counted on him. But now he turned back, looked her straight in the eye.

"If you believe that, if you let some anonymous bastard push you into believing that, you're a fool, and you're giving them exactly what they want."

"I know that, Ryan. I understand that perfectly." She thought she could say it calmly, but her voice broke. "I know it's someone who knows me well enough to use what would hurt me most."

He moved to her, wrapped his arms tightly around her. "Hold on to me. Come on, hold on." When her arms finally encircled him, he rubbed his cheek over her hair. "You're not alone, Miranda."

But she had been, for so long. A man like him would never know what it was like to stand in a roomful of people and feel so alone. So alien. So unwanted.

"Giovanni—he was one of the few people who made me feel . . . normal. I know whoever killed him is sending me the message. I know that in my head, Ryan. But in my heart, I'll always be to blame. And they know it."

"Then don't let them use you, or him, this way."

She'd closed her eyes, so overwhelmed with the comfort he'd offered. Now she opened them, stared out toward the sea as his words struck home. "Using him," she murmured. "You're right. I've been letting them use him to hurt me. Whoever it is hates me, and made certain I knew it in the fax that came today."

"You have copies of them all?"

"Yes."

"I want them." When she started to pull away, he held her in place, stroked her hair. Didn't she feel herself trembling? he wondered. "The e-mail. Did you trace it?"

"I didn't have any luck. The user name doesn't show up on the server—it's the server we use here and at Standjo."

"Did you keep it on your machine?"

"Yes."

"Then we'll trace it." Or Patrick would, he thought. "I'm sorry I wasn't here." He drew back, framed her face. "I'm here now, Miranda, and no one's going to hurt you while I am." When she didn't answer, he tightened his grip, looked carefully at her face. "I don't make promises lightly, because I don't break them once I do. I'm going to see this through with you, all the way. And I won't let anything happen to you."

He paused, then took what he considered a dangerous step toward a nasty edge. "Do you still want to talk to Cook?"

She'd been so sure that was the right thing. So sure, until he'd looked at her and promised. Until by doing so, he'd made her believe, against all common sense, that she could trust him.

"We'll see it through, Ryan. I guess neither one of us could swallow anything less."

"Put the base directly over the mark." Miranda stood back, watching the two burly men from maintenance haul the three-foot marble stand to the exact center of the room. She knew it was the exact center, as she'd measured it three times personally. "Yes, perfect. Good."

"Is that the last one, Dr. Jones?"

"In this area, yes, thank you."

She narrowed her eyes, envisioning the Donatello bronze of Venus bathing in place on the column.

This gallery was devoted to works of the Early Renaissance. A prized Brunelleschi drawing was matted behind glass and two Masaccio paintings were ornately framed and already hung, along with a Botticelli that soared twelve feet and showed the majestic ascension of the Mother of God. There was a Bellini that had once graced the wall of a Venetian villa.

With the Donatello as the central point, the display showcased the first true burst of artistic innovation that was not simply the foundation for the brilliance of the sixteenth century, but a period of great art in itself.

True, she considered the style of the period less emotional, less passionate. The figural representation even in Masaccio's work was somewhat static, the human emotions more stylized than real.

But the miracle was that such things existed, and could be studied, analyzed centuries after their execution.

Tapping her finger to her lips, she studied the rest of the room. She'd had the tall windows draped in deep blue fabric that was shot with gold. Tables of varying heights were also spread with it, and on the glittering fabric were the tools of artists of that era. The chisels and palettes, the calipers and brushes. She'd chosen each one herself from the museum display.

It was a pity they had to be closed under glass, but even with such a rich and sophisticated crowd, fingers could become sticky.

On an enormous carved wooden stand a huge Bible sat open to pages painstakingly printed in glorious script by ancient monks. Still other tables were strewn with the jewelry favored by both men and women of the period. There were embroidered slippers, a comb, a woman's ivory trinket box, each piece carefully chosen for just that spot. Huge iron candle stands flanked the archway.

"Very impressive." Ryan stepped between them.

"Nearly perfect. Art, with its social, economic, political, and religious foundations. The mid–fourteen hundreds. The birth of Lorenzo the Magnificent, the Peace of Lodi, and the resulting balance, however precarious, of the chief Italian states."

She gestured to a large map, dated 1454, on the wall. "Florence, Milan, Naples, Venice, and of course, the papacy. The birth too of a new school of thought in art—humanism. Rational inquiry was the key."

"Art's never rational."

"Of course it is."

He only shook his head. "You're too busy looking into the work to look at it. Beauty," he said, gesturing to the serene face of the Madonna, "is a most irrational thing. You're nervous," he added when he took her hands and felt the chill on her skin.

"Anxious," she corrected. "Have you seen the other areas?"

"I thought you'd walk me through."

"All right, but I don't have much time. I'm expecting my mother within the hour. I want everything in place when she gets here."

She walked with him through the room. "I've left wide traffic patterns, putting the sculptures—with the Donatello bronze as the centerpiece—out into the room for a full circling view. People should be free to wander, then to move through this egress into the next gallery, the largest, which represents the High Renaissance."

She stepped through. "We'll continue the theme here of showing not only the art itself, but what surrounded it, underlay it, inspired it. I've used more gold in here, and red. For power, for the church, royalty."

Her heels clicked on the marble floor as she circled, studying details, looking for any slight adjustment that needed to be made. "This era was richer and had more drama. So much energy. It couldn't last, but during its brief crest, it produced the most important works of any era before or since."

"Saints and sinners?"

"I'm sorry?"

"The most popular models of art, saints and sinners. The raw yet elegant sexuality and selfishness of the gods and goddesses, juxtaposed with the brutality of war and cheek by jowl with the grand suffering of the martyr."

He studied the beatific if somewhat baffled face of Saint Sebastian, who was about lanced through with arrows. "I never got martyrs. I mean, what was the point?"

"Their faith would be the obvious answer."

"No one can steal your faith, but they can sure as hell take your life—and in nasty, inventive ways." He hooked his thumbs in his front pockets. "Arrows for the ever popular Sebastian, roasting alive for good old Saint Lorenzo. Crucifixions, body parts lopped off with glee and abandon. Lions, tigers, and bears. Oh my."

She chuckled in spite of herself. "That is why they're martyrs."

"Exactly." He turned away from Sebastian and beamed at her. "So you're faced with the pagan horde and their primitive yet hideously efficient implements of torture. Why not just say, 'Sure, no problem, boys and girls. What god would you prefer I worship today?' What you say doesn't change what you think or what you believe, but they can certainly change your status of living."

He jerked a thumb toward the canvas. "Just ask poor beleaguered Sebastian."

"I can see you'd have prospered during persecutions."

"Damn right."

"What about words like courage, conviction, integrity?"

"Why die for a cause? Better to live for it."

While she pondered his philosophy and searched for the flaws in it, he strolled over to study a table artfully crowded with religious artifacts. Silver crucifixes, chalices, relics.

"You've done an amazing job here, Dr. Jones."

"I think it works very well. The Titians will be the major focal point of this room, along with your Raphael. It's a magnificent piece, Ryan."

"Yes, I like it quite a lot. Want to buy it?" He turned to grin at her. "The beauty of my business, Dr. Jones, is that everything has a price. Meet it, and it's yours."

"If you're serious about selling the Raphael, I'll

work up a proposal. A great many of our pieces, however, are donated or on permanent loan."

"Not even for you, darling."

She only moved her shoulders. She hadn't expected anything else. "I'd put *The Dark Lady* there," she said suddenly. "Every time I imagined this room, worked on the angles, the flow, the theme, I'd see it standing on a white column with grapevines twining down. Right here." She stepped forward. "Under the light here. Where everyone could see it. Where I could see it."

"We'll get it back, Miranda."

She said nothing, annoyed with herself for daydreaming. "Do you want to see the next room? We have your Vasaris up."

"Later." He stepped to her. It had to be done. He'd intended to tell her immediately, but he hadn't been able to face putting that haunted look back into her eyes. "Miranda, I got a call from my brother in San Francisco. From Michael. A body was pulled out of the bay last night. It was Harry Mathers."

She only stared, her eyes locked on his for a long silent moment before she simply closed them and turned away. "It wasn't an accident. It wasn't random."

"The news reports my brother's heard don't give many details. Just that he was killed before he was dumped in the water."

His throat had been slit, Ryan thought, but there was no reason to add that detail. She already knew the who and why. What good would it do for her to know the how?

"Three people now. Three people dead. And for what?" With her back still to him she stared up at the glorious face of the Madonna. "For money, for art, for ego? Maybe all three."

"Or maybe none of those, not really. Maybe it's you."

The quick stabbing pain in her heart had her shuddering once before she turned back. He saw the fear in her eyes, and knew that fear wasn't for herself. "Because of me? Someone could hate me that much? Why? I can't think of anyone I've had that kind of impact on, anyone I've hurt so deeply they would murder to protect a lie that ruins my professional reputation. For God's sake, Ryan, Harry was only a boy."

Her voice was grim now, sharp with the fury that rolled in behind the fear. "Just a boy," she repeated, "and he was snipped off like a loose thread. Just as carelessly as that. Who could I matter to so much they would have a boy killed that way? I've never mattered to anyone."

That, he thought, was the saddest thing he'd ever heard anyone say. Sadder still was the fact that she believed it. "You make more of an impact than you realize, Miranda. You're strong, you're successful. You're focused on what you want and where you want to go. And you get there."

"I haven't stepped over anyone on the way."

"Maybe you didn't see them. Patrick's been working on tracing that e-mail you received."

"Yes." She pushed a hand through her hair. Didn't see them? she wondered. Could she be that self-absorbed, that remote, that cold? "Did he manage it? It's been more than a week now. I thought he must have given up."

"He never does when he has his teeth into a computer puzzle."

"What is it? What are you trying not to tell me?"

"The user name was attached very briefly to an account. Put on and taken off, and buried under a great deal of computer jargon."

She felt the cold ball form in her stomach. It would be bad, she knew. Very bad. "What was the account?"

He laid his hands on her shoulders. "It was your mother's."

"That's not possible."

"The message was routed out of Florence, on that area code, and under the account registered to Elizabeth Standford-Jones, and under her password. I'm sorry."

"It can't be." She pulled away from him. "No matter how much—how little—no matter what," she managed. "She couldn't do this. She couldn't hate me this much. I can't accept that."

"She had access to both bronzes. No one would question her. She sent for you, then she fired you and sent you home. She pulled you away from the Institute. I'm sorry." He put his hand to her cheek. "But you're going to have to consider the facts."

It was logical. It was hideous. She closed her eyes, and let his arms come around her.

"Excuse me."

She jerked in his arms as if they were bullets and

not words at her back. Very slowly, she turned, took a long bracing breath. "Hello, Mother."

Elizabeth didn't look as though she'd spent the last several hours flying across an ocean and dealing with the small annoyances that come with international travel. Her hair was perfectly coiffed, her steel-blue suit showed not a single crease or wrinkle.

Miranda felt as she always did when faced with her mother's unwavering perfection—tousled, awkward, ungainly. Now suspicion was added to the mix. Could this woman who'd preached integrity all of her life have betrayed her own daughter?

"I apologize for interrupting your . . . work."

Too accustomed to parental disapproval to react, Miranda merely nodded. "Elizabeth Standford-Jones, Ryan Boldari."

"Mr. Boldari." Elizabeth assessed the situation, decided that the gallery owner had demanded Miranda's participation in the project for more reasons than her qualifications. Because the results benefited the Institute, she put warmth in her smile. "How nice to finally meet you."

"A pleasure." He crossed the room to take her hand, noting that mother and daughter didn't even bother with the cool air kisses women often exchanged. "I hope your flight was uneventful."

"It was, thank you." A beautiful face, she thought, and a smooth manner. The photographs she'd seen of him in art magazines over the years hadn't quite been able to capture the power of the combination. "I apologize for not being able to get away sooner as I'd planned. I hope the project is progressing as you anticipated, Mr. Boldari."

"Ryan, please. And it's already exceeded my expectations. Your daughter is everything I could wish for."

"You've been busy," she said to Miranda.

"Very. We've closed off the wing on this level to the public for the last two days. The team's put in a lot of hours, but it's paying off."

"Yes, I can see it is." She scanned the room, impressed and pleased, but only said, "You have work to do yet, of course. You'll be able to tap the talents of Standjo now. Several staff members flew out today, and a few others will be here by tomorrow. They know they're at your disposal. Elise and Richard are here now, along with Vincente and his wife."

"Does Andrew know Elise is here?"

Elizabeth raised her eyebrows. "If he doesn't, he will shortly." And the warning in her tone was clear. No personal family business was to be discussed or allowed to interfere. "Your father is due in tonight. He'll be a tremendous help with the final selections of the artifacts."

"I've already made the final selections," Miranda said flatly.

"It's rare that any project of this size can't benefit from a fresh eye."

"Are you planning to take me off *this* project too?"

There was a moment when it appeared Elizabeth would respond. Her lips trembled open, but then firmed again as she turned to Ryan. "I'd very much like to see your Vasaris."

"Yes, Ryan, show her the Vasaris. They're in the next area. If you'll both excuse me, I have an appointment."

"I feel obliged to tell you, Elizabeth," Ryan began when Miranda walked out, "that this very impressive exhibit wouldn't have been possible without your daughter. She conceived it, designed it, and has implemented it."

"I'm well aware of Miranda's talents."

"Are you?" He said it mildly, with a slight and deliberately mocking lift of brow. "Obviously I'm mistaken then. I assumed since you didn't comment on the results of four weeks of intense work on her part, you found them lacking in some way."

Something flickered in her eyes that might have been embarrassment. He hoped it was. "Not at all. I have every confidence in Miranda's capabilities. If she has a flaw it's overenthusiasm and the tendency to become too personally involved."

"Most would consider those assets rather than flaws."

He was baiting her, but she couldn't see the reason for it. "In business, objectivity is essential. I'm sure you'd agree."

"I prefer passion in all things. Riskier, but the benefits are much more rewarding. Miranda has passion, but she tends to repress it. Hoping, I'd guess, for your approval. Do you ever give it?"

Temper showed coldly on her, a chill in the eyes, frost lining the voice. "My relationship with Miranda isn't your concern, Mr. Boldari, any more than your relationship with her is mine."

"Odd. I'd say the opposite was true, since your daughter and I are lovers."

Her fingers tightened briefly on the strap of the slim leather attaché case she carried. "Miranda is an adult. I don't interfere with her personal affairs."

"Just her professional ones, then. Tell me about *The Dark Lady.*"

"I beg your pardon?"

"The Dark Lady." He kept his eyes on hers. "Where is she?"

"The Fiesole Bronze," Elizabeth said evenly, "was stolen from a storeroom at the Bargello several weeks ago. Neither I nor the authorities have any idea of its current location."

"I wasn't speaking of the copy, but of the original."

"Original?" Her face remained blank. But he saw something behind it. Knowledge, shock, consideration—it was difficult to be sure with a woman with such rigid control.

"Elizabeth?" A group of people came in, with Elise in the forefront. Ryan saw a small, finely built woman with a pixie crop of hair and big, brilliant eyes. One step behind was a balding, pale-faced man he tagged as Richard Hawthorne, then a lushly built Sophia Loren look-alike with her arm through that of a robust man with olive skin and glossy white hair. The Morellis, he decided. Hovering over them, beaming loving avuncular smiles, was John Carter.

"Excuse me." Elise linked her pretty hands together. "I didn't know you were busy."

More grateful for the interruption than she would allow to show, Elizabeth made introductions.

"It's so nice to meet you," Elise told him. "I was in your gallery in New York only last year. It's a treasure. And this." Her eyes shone as she turned a circle. "This is glorious. Richard, get your nose away from that map and look at the paintings."

He turned, a sheepish smile on his face. "I can never resist a map. It's an excellent exhibit."

"You must have worked like dogs." Vincente gave Carter a hearty slap on the back.

"I expected to be called on to scrub floors at any moment. Miranda had us jumping through hoops." Carter smiled sheepishly again. "The restoration on the Bronzino was only finished yesterday. I heard everyone in the department shuddered when they saw her coming. Every department head's been chugging Maalox for the past two weeks. Doesn't seem to bother Miranda. Woman's got nerves of steel."

"She's done a brilliant job." Elise glanced around again. "Where is she?"

"She had an appointment," Elizabeth said.

"I'll catch up with her later. I hope she'll put us to work."

"She knows you're available."

"Good. I, um, I thought I'd see if Andrew's free for a few moments." She sent Elizabeth an apologetic and wistful smile. "I'd like to see how he's doing. If you don't need me just now."

"No, go ahead." She glanced over with mild amusement as Gina Morelli exclaimed and cooed over the display of jewelry. "Richard, I know you've been chafing to visit the library."

"I'm predictable."

"Enjoy yourself."

"We'll know where to find him," Vincente said. "He'll be buried in books. Me, I'll wait for Gina to study and covet every bauble—then she'll drag me shopping." He shook his head. "She too is predictable."

"Two hours," Elizabeth announced, in the tone of the director. "Then we'll meet back here and do what needs to be done."

Elise hesitated outside the door of Andrew's office. His assistant was away from her desk, and she was grateful. Ms. Purdue was devoted to Andrew and wouldn't approve of an ex-wife's unscheduled visit. She heard his voice through the open door. It was a strong voice and brought her an odd nostalgia.

She'd always liked his voice. The clear tone of it, the upper-crust accent, faintly Kennedyesque, she thought. She supposed, in her way, she'd seen him as a kind of scion of that type of high-powered, successful New England family.

There had been such potential in their marriage, she thought. She'd had such hopes. But in the end, there'd been nothing to do but divorce and move on. From what she knew, she had moved on with considerably more success than Andrew.

Though she was aware of the regret in her eyes, she fixed on a bright smile and rapped lightly on the jamb.

"We're expecting five hundred guests," he said into the phone, then glanced up and froze.

It all flooded back in individual drops of memory. The first time he'd seen her when she took over the job as assistant lab manager at his father's recommendation. In a lab coat and goggles. The way she'd pushed the goggles up to rest on her head when Miranda introduced them.

The way she'd laughed and told him it was about time, when he finally worked up the nerve to ask her out.

The first time they'd made love. And the last.

The way she'd looked on their wedding day, radiant, delicate. The way she'd looked when she told him it was over, so cold and distant. And all the moods in between that had slipped from hope and happiness to dissatisfaction, disappointment, then lack of interest.

The voice on the phone was a buzzing in his ears. His hand fisted under the desk. He wished to God there was a drink in it.

"I'll need to get back to you on the rest, but all the details are in the press release. I'm sure we can arrange for a short interview tomorrow night during the event. . . . You're welcome."

"I'm sorry, Drew," she began when he hung up. "Ms. Purdue isn't at her desk, so I thought I'd take the chance."

"It's all right." The foolish words scraped at his throat. "Just another reporter."

"The event is generating a lot of positive press."

"We need it."

"It's been a difficult couple of months." He didn't rise as she thought he would, so she stepped into the room and faced him with his desk between them. "I thought it would be best, easier for both of us, if we had a few minutes. I wouldn't have come, but Elizabeth insisted. And I have to admit, I would have hated to miss all of this."

He couldn't take his eyes off her, no matter how it burned his heart. "We wanted all the key staff members here."

"You're still so angry with me."

"I don't know what I am."

"You look tired."

"Putting this thing together hasn't left a lot of time for R and R."

"I know this is awkward." She reached out a hand, then drew it back again, as if realizing it wouldn't be welcomed. "The last time we saw each other was—"

"In a lawyer's office," he finished.

"Yes." Her gaze dropped. "I wish it could have been handled differently. We were both so hurt and angry, Drew. I was hoping by now we could at least be . . ."

"Friends?" He let out a bitter laugh that didn't hurt nearly as much as the innocuous word he'd forced through it.

"No, not friends." Those fabulous eyes of hers

went soft and damp with emotion. "Just something less than enemies."

It wasn't what she'd expected, this hard-eyed, cynical look. She'd expected regret, unhappiness, even a spurt of anger. She'd been prepared for any and all of that. But not for this tough shield that bounced all her efforts back at her.

He'd loved her. She knew he'd loved her, and had held on to that even as she signed her name on the divorce papers.

"We don't have to be enemies, Elise. We don't have to be anything anymore."

"All right, this was a mistake." She blinked, once, twice, and the tears were gone. "I didn't want any difficulties to spoil tomorrow's success. If you were upset and started drinking—"

"I've quit drinking."

"Really." Her voice was cool again, and the grim amusement in it sliced bloodlessly. It was a talent of hers he'd forgotten. "Where have I heard that before?"

"The difference is it has nothing to do with you now, and everything to do with me. I emptied plenty of bottles over you, Elise, and I'm done with it. Maybe that disappoints you. Maybe you're insulted that I'm not crawling, not devastated to see you standing there. You're not the center of my life anymore."

"I never was." Her control cracked enough to let the words snap through. "If I had been, you'd still have me."

She spun around and rushed out. By the time

she got to the elevator, tears were stinging her eyes. She punched the button with her fist.

He waited until the rapid click of her heels had echoed away before lowering his head to the desk. His stomach was in ragged knots and screaming for a drink, just one drink to smooth it all away.

She was so beautiful. How could he have forgotten how beautiful she was? She'd belonged to him once and he'd failed to hold her, to hold their marriage, to be the man she needed.

He'd lost her because he hadn't known how to give enough, to love enough, to be enough.

He had to get out. Get air. He needed to walk, to run, to get the scent of her perfume out of his system. He used the stairs, avoiding the wing with all the bustle of work, slipped through the thin, early-evening visitors in the public areas and walked straight out.

He left his car in the lot and walked, walked until the worst of the burning in his gut had eased. Walked until he no longer had to concentrate to draw and release each breath evenly. He told himself he was thinking clearly now, perfectly clearly.

And when he stopped in front of the liquor store, when he stared at the bottles promising relief, enjoyment, escape, he told himself he could handle a couple of drinks.

Not only could he handle them, he *deserved* them. He'd earned them for surviving that face-to-face contact with the woman he'd promised to love, honor, and cherish. Who'd promised him the same. Until death.

He stepped inside, stared at the walls with bottles dark and light lining the shelves. Fifths and pints and quarts just waiting, just *begging* to be selected.

Try me and you'll feel better. You'll feel fine again. You'll feel fan fucking-tastic.

Glossy bottles with colorful labels. Smooth bottles with manly names.

Wild Turkey, Jim Beam, Jameson.

He picked up a bottle of Jack Daniel's, running a finger over the familiar black label. And sweat began to pool at the base of his spine.

Good old Jack. Dependable Jack Black.

He could taste it on his tongue, feel the heat slide down his throat and fall welcome to warm his belly.

He took it to the counter and his fingers felt fat and clumsy as he reached for his wallet.

"This be all?" The clerk rang up the bottle.

"Yes," Andrew said dully. "That's it for me."

He carried it with him, tucked into its slim paper sack. He felt the weight of it, the shape of it as he walked.

A twist of the top, and your troubles were over. The nasty ball of pain in your gut forgotten.

As the sun set toward twilight and the air cooled, he went into the park.

The yellow trumpets of the daffodils were rioting, a small ocean of cheer backed by the more elegant red cups of tulips. The first leaves were unfurling on the oaks and maples that would offer shade when the summer heat pounded during its short stay in Maine. The fountain trickled, a musical dance at the center of the park.

Over to the left, swings and slides were deserted. Children were home being washed up for supper, he thought. He'd wanted children, hadn't he? Imagined making a family, a real family where those in it knew how to love, how to touch each other. Laughter, bedtime stories, noisy family meals.

He'd never pulled that off either.

He sat on a bench, staring at the empty swings, listening to the fountain play, and running his hand up and down the shape of the bottle in the thin paper bag.

One drink, he thought. Just one pull from the bottle. Then none of this would matter quite so much.

Two pulls, and you'd wonder why it ever had.

Annie drew two drafts while the blender beside her whirled with the fixings for a pitcher of margaritas. Happy hour on Friday nights was a popular sport. It was mostly the business crowd, but she had a couple of tables of college students taking advantage of the discount prices and free nibbles while they trashed their professors.

She arched her back, trying to work out the vague ache at the base of her spine as she scanned the room to be certain her waitresses were keeping the customers happy. She dressed the birdbath glasses with salt and lime.

One of her regulars was into a joke involving a

man and a dancing frog. She built him a fresh vodka collins and laughed at the punch line.

The TV above the bar was showcasing a night baseball game.

She saw Andrew come in, saw what he had in his hand. Her stomach took a slow nosedive, but she kept working. Replaced crowded ashtrays with fresh empties, mopped damp rings from the bar. Watched him walk to it, take a seat on a vacant stool, set the bottle on the bar.

Their eyes met over the brown paper sack. Hers were carefully blank.

"I didn't open it."

"Good. That's good."

"I wanted to. I still want to."

Annie signaled to her head waitress, then tugged off her bar apron. "Take over for me. Let's take a walk, Andrew."

He nodded, but he took the bag with him when he followed her out. "I went to a liquor store. It felt good to be in there."

The streetlights were shining now, little islands of light in the dark. End-of-the-week traffic clogged the streets. Opposing radio stations warred through open car windows.

"I walked to the park and sat on a bench by the fountain." Andrew shifted the bottle from hand to hand as if to keep it limber. "Nobody much around. I thought I could just take a couple of pulls from the bottle. Just enough to warm me up."

"But you didn't."

"No."

"It's hard. What you're doing is hard. And tonight, you made the right choice. Whatever it is, whatever's wrong, you can't add drinking to it."

"I saw Elise."

"Oh."

"She's here for the exhibit. I knew she was coming. But when I looked up and saw her, it just slammed into me. She was trying to make things better, but I wouldn't let her."

Annie hunched her shoulders, jammed her hands into her pockets, and told herself she was insane even pretending she and Andrew stood a chance. That she stood a chance. "You have to do what feels right to you there."

"I don't know what's right. I only know what's wrong."

He walked back to the same park, sat on the same bench and set the bottle beside him.

"I can't tell you what to do, Andrew, but I think if you don't resolve this and let it go, it's going to keep hurting you."

"I know it."

"She's only going to be here a few days. If you could make your peace with it, and with her, while she's here, you'd be better for it. I never made peace with Buster. The son of a bitch."

She smiled, hoping he would, but he only continued to watch her with those steady, serious eyes. "Oh, Andrew." She sighed, looked away. "What I mean is, I never made the effort so we could be civil, and it still eats at me some. He wasn't worth it, God knows, but it eats at me. He hurt me, in a lot of ways, so all I wanted to do in the end was hurt him right back. But worse. Of course, I never did because he never gave a shit."

"Why'd you stay with him, Annie?"

She pushed a hand through her hair. "Because I told him I would. Taking vows at the courthouse on your lunch hour's just the same as doing it in a big church in a fancy white dress."

"Yeah." He gave the hand that now held his a squeeze. "I know it. Believe it or not, I wanted to keep mine. I wanted to prove that I could. Failing at it was like proving I wasn't any different from my father, his father, any of them."

"You're yourself, Andrew."

"That's a scary thought."

Because he needed it, and so did she, she leaned forward, laid her lips on his, let them part when he reached for her. Took him in.

God help her.

She could feel the edge of desperation, but he was careful with her. She'd known too many men who weren't careful. The hand on his face stroked, felt the prickle of a day-old beard, then the smooth skin of his throat.

The needs that kindled inside her were outrageous, and she was afraid they wouldn't help either of them.

"You're not like them." She pressed her cheek to his before the kiss could weaken her too much.

"Well, not tonight anyway." He picked up the bottle, handed it to her. "There, that's a hundred percent profit for you."

There was a relief in it, he realized. The kind a man feels when he whips the wheel of his car just before plunging off a cliff. "I'm going to go to a meeting before I go home." He puffed out a breath. "Annie, about tomorrow night. It would mean a lot to me if you'd change your mind and come."

"Andrew, you know I don't fit in with all those fancy art people."

"You fit with me. Always have."

"Saturday nights are busy." Excuses, she thought. Coward. "I'll think about it. I've got to go."

"I'll walk you back." He rose, took her hand again. "Annie, come tomorrow."

"I'll think about it," she repeated without any intention of doing so. The last thing she wanted to do was go up against Elise on the woman's turf.

CHAPTER TWENTY-SEVEN

"YOU NEED TO GET OUT OF HERE."

Miranda glanced up from her desk, where she was buried in a sea of papers, saw Ryan watching her from the doorway. "At this moment, I basically live here."

"Why do you feel you have to do all of this yourself?"

She ran her pencil between her fingers. "Is there something wrong with the way it's being done?"

"That's not what I said." He walked over, laid his palms on the desk and leaned toward her. "You don't have to prove anything to her."

"This isn't about my mother. This is about making certain that tomorrow night is a success. Now I have several more details to see to."

He reached over, plucked the pencil out of her hand and snapped it in two.

She blinked, stunned by the ripe and ready temper in his eyes. “Well, that was mature.”

“It’s more mature than doing the same to that stiff neck of yours.”

If she’d held a silver shield and lowered it between them, it would have been no less tangible a block than the way her face closed up.

“Don’t you shut me out. Don’t you sit there and play with one of your ubiquitous lists as if there’s nothing more important to you than the next item to be crossed off. I’m not a fucking item, and I know just what’s going on inside you.”

“Don’t swear at me.”

He turned on his heel and started for the door. She expected him to go straight through, to keep going, as others had. Instead he slammed the door, locked it. She got shakily to her feet.

“I have no idea why you’re so angry.”

“Don’t you? You think I didn’t see your face when I told you where that e-mail had come from? Do you really believe you’re so in control, Dr. Jones, that the devastation doesn’t show?”

It was killing him. Her complexities and complications were killing him. He didn’t want them, he thought furiously. He didn’t want to find himself constantly compelled to fight his way through to her.

“I don’t believe I in any way attempted to kill the messenger,” she began.

“Don’t take that private-school tone with me either, it doesn’t work. I saw your face when your mother walked in. How everything inside you went on hold. Cold storage."

That got through, and stung. Brutally. "You asked me to accept the strong possibility that my mother used me, betrayed me, had me terrorized. That she's involved in a major art theft that's already resulted in three deaths. You asked me to do that, then you criticize the way I choose to deal with it."

"I'd rather have seen you shove her on her ass and demand an explanation."

"That might work in your family. We're not quite so volatile in mine."

"Yeah, yours prefers the carefully iced blade that slices bloodlessly. I can tell you, Miranda, heat's cleaner in the end and a hell of a lot more human."

"What did you expect me to do? Goddamn it, what? Scream at her, shout and rage and accuse?" She swept an arm over the desk, sending neatly arranged papers and carefully sharpened pencils flying. "Was I supposed to demand she tell me the truth? Confess or deny? If she hates me enough to have done this, she hates me enough to lie to my face."

She shoved her desk chair, sent it crashing into the wall. "She never loved me. Never gave me one free gesture of affection. Neither of them, not to me, to Andrew, or to each other. In my whole life neither of them ever said they loved me, never even bothered to lie so I could have the illusion. You don't know what it's like never to be held, never to be told, and to ache for it."

She pressed her hands to her stomach as if the pain centered there was unbearable. "To *ache* so hard and long that you have to stop wanting it or just die."

"No, I don't know what it's like," he said quietly. "Tell me."

"It was like growing up in a fucking laboratory, everything sterile and perfectly in place, documented, calculated, but without any of the joy of discovery. Rules, that's all. Rules of language, conduct, education. Do this and do it this way and no other, because no other is acceptable. No other is correct. How many of those rules has she broken if she's done this?"

Her breath was heaving, her eyes blazing, her fists clenched. He'd watched, he'd listened, and hadn't moved or raised his voice. The only sound in the room now was her own ragged breathing as she looked around her office at the destruction she'd caused.

Stunned, she shoved at her hair, rubbed her hand over her hard-pumping heart. For the first time she became aware there were tears streaming down her cheeks, so hot they should have burned her skin.

"Is that what you wanted me to do?"

"I wanted you to get it out."

"I guess I did." She pressed her fingers to her temples. "Tantrums give me a headache."

"That wasn't a tantrum."

She let out a weak laugh. "What would you call it?"

"Honesty." He smiled a little. "Even in my line of work I'm vaguely acquainted with the concept. You're not cold, Miranda," he said gently. "You're just scared. You're not unlovable, just unappreciated."

She felt the tears, stood helplessly as they overflowed. "I don't want it to be my mother who did this, Ryan."

He went to her, nudged her fingers away and replaced them with his own. "We have a good chance of having the answers within the next couple of days. This will be over."

"But I'll have to live with those answers."

He took her home and persuaded her to take a sleeping pill and go to bed early. The fact that he barely had to bully her into it only proved to him that she was running on fumes now.

When he was certain she was asleep, when Andrew was closed off in his own wing, Ryan changed into the dark sweater and jeans he preferred for nighttime breaking and entering.

He slipped his tools into his pocket, chose a soft-sided black briefcase with shoulder strap, in the event he found something he needed to transport back with him.

He found Miranda's keys efficiently zipped in the side pocket of her purse. He walked quietly outside, got behind the wheel of her car, and adjusted the seat to suit him before putting it in neutral and releasing the brake. The car coasted downhill with its headlights shut off.

He could have claimed to have been restless, to have borrowed the car to take a drive, had either she or Andrew heard the engine. But why lie when it wasn't necessary? He waited until he was a quarter of a mile down the drive, then turned on the ignition, switched on the lights.

Puccini was on the radio, and though he shared Miranda's fondness for opera, it didn't quite suit his mood. He noted the frequency, then hit scan. When he heard George Thorogood belting out "Bad to the Bone," he grinned to himself and let it rip.

Traffic thickened a little on the edge of town. People heading to parties, he thought, to weekend dates, or home from either because they weren't quite interesting enough. It was barely midnight.

A long way, he thought, from the city that never sleeps.

Early to bed, early to rise, these Yankees, he decided. Such an admirable people. He pulled into the hotel parking lot well away from the entrance. He was fairly certain the same admirable trait would hold true for the visitors from Florence. The seven-hour time difference could be a killer the first couple of days.

He'd stayed in the same hotel on his first trip, and knew the layout perfectly. He'd also taken the precaution of getting the room numbers for all the parties he intended to visit that night.

No one took notice of him as he crossed the lobby and walked directly to the elevators like a man in a hurry to get to his bed.

Elizabeth and Elise were sharing a two-bedroom suite on the top club level. The level required a key to release the elevator. And being a farsighted man—and because it was an old habit—he'd kept the access key when he checked out of the hotel himself.

He saw no lights under any of the three doors of the suite, heard no murmur of voices or television from inside.

He was inside the parlor himself in just under two minutes. He stood still, in the dark, listening, judging, letting his eyes adjust. As a precaution, he unlocked the terrace doors, giving himself an alternate route of escape should it become necessary.

Then he got to work. He searched the parlor first, though he doubted either woman would have left anything vital or incriminating in that area.

In the first bedroom he was forced to use the penlight, keeping it away from the bed, where he could hear the soft, steady sound of a woman breathing. He took a briefcase and a purse back into the parlor with him to search.

It was Elizabeth in the bed, he noted as he flipped through the wallet. He took everything out, going through every receipt, every scrap of paper, reading the notations in her datebook. He found a key just where her daughter kept hers—inside zipper pocket. A safe-deposit box key, he noted, and pocketed it.

He checked her passport, noting the stamps coincided with the dates his cousin had given him. It was Elizabeth's first trip back to the States in more than a year, but she'd taken two quick trips into France in the last six months.

He put everything but the key back where he'd found it, repeated the same process on her luggage; then while she slept he searched her closet, the dresser, the cosmetic case in the bathroom.

It took him an hour before he was satisfied and moved on to the second bedroom.

He knew Andrew's ex-wife very well by the time he was done. She liked silk underwear and Opium perfume. Though her clothes were on the conservative side, she favored the top designers. Expensive taste required money to indulge it. He made a note to check her income.

She'd brought work with her if the laptop on her desk was any indication. Which made her, in his mind, either dedicated or obsessive. The contents of her purse and briefcase were orderly, with no stray wrappers or scraps of papers. The small leather jewelry case he found contained a few good pieces of Italian gold, some well-chosen colored stones, and an antique silver locket containing a picture of a man facing a picture of a woman. They were faded black-and-white, and from the style he judged them to have been taken around World War II.

Her grandparents, he imagined, and decided Elise had a quietly sentimental streak.

He left the two women sleeping and moved down the hallway to Richard Hawthorne's room. He too was fast asleep.

It took Ryan ten minutes to find the receipt for a storage facility in Florence—which he pocketed.

It took him thirteen to find the .38. That, he left alone.

In twenty, he'd located the small notebook hidden inside a black dress sock. Scanning the cramped handwriting with his light, Ryan read quickly and at random. His lips tightened on a grim smile.

He tucked the notebook in his pocket and let Richard sleep. He was, Ryan thought as he slipped out, in for a rude awakening.

"Excuse me, did you just say you broke into my mother's bedroom last night?"

"Nothing was broken," Ryan assured her. He felt as though he'd been chasing after Miranda for hours, trying to steal a half hour alone with her.

"Her bedroom?"

"I went in through the parlor, if it makes you feel any better. There was hardly any point in getting them all here, in one spot, if I wasn't going to do something once they were. I got a safe-deposit key out of her purse. I found it odd she'd have one with her on a trip like this. But it's an American bank. A Maine bank—with a branch in Jones Point."

Miranda sat behind her desk, the first time she'd been off her feet since six that morning. It was now noon, and Ryan had finally buttonholed her during her meeting with the florist and given her the choice of walking to her office or being carried there.

"I don't understand, Ryan. Why would a key to a bank box be important?"

"People generally keep things there that are important or valuable to them—and that they don't want other people to get their hands on. In any case, I'll check it out."

He waited until Miranda opened her mouth, shut it again without saying a word. "I didn't find anything in Elise's room except for her laptop. Seemed strange to cart it all this way for a four-day trip when she'd be spending most of her time here. If I have time I'll go back in and see if I can open it up while she's out of the room."

"Oh, that would be best," she said with a breezy wave of her hand.

"Exactly. I found enough jewelry to break the back of an elephant in the Morelli suite. That woman has a serious glitter addiction—and if I can access Vincente's bank account, we'll see just how deep in debt he's gone to pay for it. Now your father—"

"My father? He didn't even get in until after midnight."

"You're telling me. I nearly bumped into him in the hall on my way out of your mother's suite. Handy of the hotel to put everyone on the same floor."

"We had the rooms blocked that way," she murmured.

"In any case, doing the other rooms first gave him time to settle in. He was out like a light. Did you know your father's been to the Cayman Islands three times in the last year?"

"The Caymans?" She wondered her head didn't simply tumble off onto the floor, by the way it was reeling.

"Popular spot the Caymans. Good for scuba, sunshine, and money laundering. Now all that is idle speculation. But I hit gold in Hawthorne's room."

"You had a very full night while I was asleep."

"You needed your rest. I found this." He took the storage receipt out of his pocket, unfolded it. "He rented this space the day after the bronze was brought to Standjo. The day before your mother called and sent for you. What did Andrew say about coincidences? There aren't any."

"People rent space for all sorts of reasons."

"They don't generally rent a small garage just outside of the city when they don't own a car. I checked, and he doesn't. Then there was the gun."

"Gun?"

"The handgun—don't ask me the make and model. I try to avoid guns, but it looked very efficient to me."

Idly, he took her coffeepot off the burner, sniffed, and was pleased to find what was left was still fresh. "I think there's a law about transporting weapons on airplanes," he added as he poured a cup. "I doubt he went through the proper channels to get it here. And why would a nice, quiet researcher need a gun to attend an exhibit?"

"I don't know. Richard and a gun. It doesn't make sense."

"I think it might, once you read this." He took the notebook out of his pocket. "You'll want to read it, but I'll give you the highlights. It describes a bronze, ninety point four centimeters, twenty-four point sixty-eight kilograms. A female nude. It gives test results on said bronze, dating it late fifteenth century in the style of Michelangelo."

He watched her cheeks drain of color and her eyes go glassy, then held out the coffee until she'd wrapped both hands around the cup. "The date of the first test is at nineteen hundred hours, on the date *The Dark Lady* was accepted and signed for at Standjo. I imagine the lab's closed at eight most nights."

"He ran tests on it, on his own."

"It lists them, step by step, giving times and results. Two solid nights' work, and it adds several points of research. The documentation. He found something you didn't, and he didn't tell you about. An old baptismal record from the Convent of Mercy, written out by the abbess on a male child, infant. The mother's name was recorded as Giulietta Buonadoni."

"She had a child. I'd read there was a child, possibly the illegitimate son of one of the Medicis. She sent him away, most likely for his own protection as there was political tension during that period."

"The child was baptized Michelangelo." He saw when the idea struck home. "One might speculate, after his papa."

"Michelangelo never fathered a child. He was, by all accounts, homosexual."

"That doesn't make him incapable of conceiving a child." But he shrugged. "Doesn't mean the kid was his either, but it does make the theory that they had a close personal relationship highly possible, and if they did . . ."

"It helps support the likelihood that he would have used her as a model."

"Exactly. Hawthorne thought it was important enough to record it in his little book—and to keep the information from you. If they were lovers, even once, or if they had a close enough platonic relationship that she would name her only child after him, it goes a long way toward concluding that he created the bronze of her."

"It wouldn't be proof, but yes, it would add weight. It makes it less and less likely that he'd never used her, and we have no documentation of any other sculpture or painting of Michelangelo's that uses Giulietta as a model. Oh, it's good," she murmured, shutting her eyes. "If nothing else, as a springboard to keep looking."

"He didn't want you to look."

"No, and I stepped in line in that area. I left nearly all of the research in his hands. What I did came primarily from sources he gave me. He recognized it, exactly as I did. Probably the minute he saw it."

"I'd say that's an accurate assumption, Dr. Jones."

She could see the sense of it now, the logic and

the steps. "Richard stole the bronze and copied it. And the *David,* he had to have taken that as well." Her fisted hand pressed against her midriff. "He killed Giovanni."

"It wouldn't be proof," Ryan said, laying the book on her desk. "But it would add weight."

"We need to take this to the police."

"Not yet." He laid his hand on the book before she could grab it. "I'd feel a lot more . . . confident of the outcome if we had the bronzes in hand before we talk to cops. I'll go to Florence tomorrow, check out his garage. If they're not there, they'll be in his apartment, or the record of where they are will be. Once we've got them, we'll work out what to tell the cops."

"He has to pay for Giovanni."

"He will. He'll pay for it all. Give me forty-eight hours, Miranda. We've come this far."

She pressed her lips together. "I haven't lost sight of what this can do for my career, or what it can mean to the art world. And I know we made a deal. But I'm asking you now to agree, to promise, that justice for Giovanni will come first."

"If Hawthorne's responsible for Giovanni, he'll pay. I'll promise you that."

"All right. We'll wait until you're back from Florence to go to the police. But tonight. How can we possibly go through with tonight? He'll be there. He's here now."

"Tonight goes as scheduled. You have hundreds of people coming," he went on before she could object. "It's all in place. You just ride the current.

The Institute, and my galleries, are too far into it to pull out. You're too far in. And we don't know if he acted alone."

She ran her hands up and down her arms. "It could still be my mother. It could be any of them."

There was nothing he could do about the haunted look in her eyes. "You have to handle it, Miranda."

"I intend to." She dropped her hands. "I will."

"Hawthorne's made a mistake. Now we'll see if he—or someone else—makes another one. When I have the bronzes, we'll give him to the cops. I have a feeling he won't want to hang alone."

She jumped to her feet. "Hang."

"It's an expression."

"But—prison or worse. That's what this means. Years, even a lifetime in prison or . . . If it's one of my family, if it's one of them, Ryan, I can't. No, I can't handle it. I was wrong."

"Miranda—" He reached for her hands, but she tossed them up in panic.

"No, no, I'm sorry. It's not right, I know it's not right. Giovanni, and that poor man with his wife, his children, but . . . if we find out it's one of them, I don't know if I can live with knowing I helped put them behind bars."

"Just a damn minute." He grabbed onto her before she could evade, surprising them both with the quick and hot spurt of temper. "Whoever's responsible for this put your life on the line. I'm going to see that they pay for that too."

"No, not my life. My reputation, the momentum of my career."

"Who hired that son of a bitch to terrorize you with a knife? Who's been sending you faxes to frighten you, to hurt you?"

"It must have been Richard." Misery swamped her eyes. "And if it wasn't, I can't be responsible for sending one of my family to prison."

"What's your alternative? To let them walk? To leave *The Dark Lady* wherever she is, destroy that book, forget what's been done?"

"I don't know. But *I* need time too. You asked for forty-eight hours. I'm asking you to give me the same. There has to be a middle ground. Somewhere."

"I don't think so." He picked up the book, balancing it on his palm as if weighing it. Then he held it out. "You take it, keep it."

She stared at it, taking it gingerly as if the leather would burn. "How am I going to get through the rest of the day? Through tonight?"

"With that Yankee spine of yours? You'll do just fine. I'll be with you. We're in this together."

She nodded, put the book in a drawer and locked it. Forty-eight hours, she thought. That was all the time she had to decide whether to make the book public, or to burn it.

It's going to be perfect. I know exactly how it will work now. It's all in place. Miranda put it all in place for me. All those people will be there, admiring the great art, sliding champagne down their throats, stuffing all the pretty canapés in their mouths. She'll move among them, gracious and cool. The brilliant Dr. Jones. The perfect Dr. Jones.

The doomed Dr. Jones.

She'll be her own centerpiece, basking in the compliments. A brilliant exhibition, Dr. Jones. A glorious display. Oh yes, they'll say it, and they'll think it, and the mistakes she made, the embarrassment she caused will fade into the background. As if all my work was nothing.

Her star's rising again.

Tonight, it falls.

I've planned my own exhibit for tonight, one that will overshadow hers. I've titled it Death of a Traitor.

I believe the reviews will be very strong.

CHAPTER TWENTY-EIGHT

NO ONE KNEW HER STOMACH WAS ALIVE WITH MANIC butterflies wielding tiny scythes. Her hands were cool and steady, her smile easy. Inside her mind she could see herself jittering with every step, stuttering through every conversation. But the shield was up, the unflappable Dr. Jones firmly in place.

She'd chosen to wear a long column of midnight blue with a high banded collar and sleeves that ended in narrow cuffs. She was grateful for the amount of flesh it covered, because she felt cold, so cold. She hadn't been warm since Ryan had given her the book.

She watched her mother, elegant as an empress in a gown of petal pink, working the crowd—a touch on the arm there, an offered hand or cheek. Always the right thing to say at the right time to the right person.

Her husband was beside her, of course, dashing

in his tuxedo, the well traveled adventurer with the interesting air of a scholar. How handsome they looked together, how perfect the Joneses of Jones Point appeared on the surface. Not a flaw to mar the polish. And no substance beneath the gloss.

How smoothly they worked as a team when they chose, she thought. They would choose for the Institute, for art, for the Jones reputation as they had never chosen for family.

She wanted to hate them for it, but she thought of the book and all she felt was fear.

She turned away from them and moved through the archway.

"You belong in one of those paintings behind you." Ryan took her hand, shifting her around moments before she approached another small group. "You look magnificent."

"I'm absolutely terrified." Then she laughed a little, realizing that only a few months ago she wouldn't have been able to tell anyone what was inside her. "I always seem to be in crowds."

"So we'll pretend it's just you, and just me. But one thing's missing. You need champagne."

"I'm sticking with water tonight."

"One glass, one toast." He handed her one of the flutes he'd taken from a roaming waiter. "To the very successful results of your work, Dr. Jones."

"It's difficult to enjoy it."

"Fall into the moment," he reminded her. "This is a good moment." He touched his lips lightly to hers. "I find your shyness endearing." He murmured it against her ear, causing more than one eyebrow to rise. "And your skill in masking it admirable."

The clouds in her eyes lifted. "Were you born with that talent or did you develop it?"

"Which? I have so many."

"The talent of knowing exactly the right thing to say at precisely the right time."

"Maybe I just know what you need to hear. There's dancing in the Center Hall. You've never danced with me."

"I'm a terrible dancer."

"Maybe you've never been properly led." It made her eyebrows lift in mild disdain, just as he'd hoped. "Let's find out."

He kept a hand at the small of her back as they maneuvered through the groups. He knew how to work a crowd as well, she noticed. How to charm with a few words, and keep moving. She could hear the faint strains of a waltz—piano and violin—the murmur of conversation, the occasional trill or rumble of laughter.

She'd had the Center Hall decorated with trailing vines and potted palms, all glittering with the tiny white Italian lights that reminded her of stars. Fragrant white lilies and blood-red roses speared out of crystal vases draped in gold ribbon. Every individual drop of the antique chandelier had been hand-washed in vinegar water for a brilliant waterfall sparkle.

Couples circled, pretty pictures in their formal dress, or stood sipping wine. Others gathered on the staircase, or sat in the chairs she'd had dressed in rose damask.

At least a dozen times she was stopped, congratulated. If there were occasional murmurs about the Fiesole Bronze, most people were discreet enough to wait until she was out of earshot.

"There's Mrs. Collingsforth." Miranda nodded to a woman with an amazing stack of white hair in a gown of maroon velvet.

"Of the Portland Collingsforths?"

"Yes. I want to make sure she has everything she needs—and to introduce you. She's very fond of attractive young men."

Miranda wound her way through to where the widow was sitting, keeping time to the music with her foot. "Mrs. Collingsforth, I hope you're enjoying yourself."

"Lovely music," she said in a voice like the caw of a crow. "Pretty lights. It's about time you put some punch into this place. Places that house art shouldn't be stuffy. Art's alive. Shouldn't be stored like corpses. And who might this be?"

"Ryan Boldari." He bent down to take her hand and kiss the gnarled knuckles. "I asked Miranda to introduce us, Mrs. Collingsforth. I wanted to thank you, personally, for your generosity in lending the Institute so many wonderful pieces from your collection. You've made the exhibit."

"If the girl threw more parties instead of burying herself in a laboratory, I'd have lent them to her sooner."

"I couldn't agree more." He beamed at Mrs. Collingsforth, making Miranda feel superfluous. "Art needs to be celebrated, not simply studied."

"Keeps herself glued to a microscope."

"Where one often misses the big picture."

Mrs. Collingsforth narrowed her eyes, pursed her lips. "I like you."

"Thank you. I wonder, madam, if I could impose on you for a dance."

"Well." Her eyes twinkled. "I'd enjoy that, Mr. Boldari."

"Please, call me Ryan," he requested as he helped her to her feet. He tossed Miranda one wolfish grin over his shoulder as he led Mrs. Collingsforth into the music.

"That was smooth," Andrew murmured at Miranda's shoulder.

"As grease on a tree limb. It's a wonder he doesn't slide off and break his neck." Because the champagne was still in her hand, she sipped. "Did you meet his family?"

"Are you kidding? I think every other person here is related to him. His mother collared me, wanting to know if we'd ever considered holding art classes for children here, and why not, didn't I like children? And before I knew it she was introducing me to this child psychologist—single, female," Andrew added. "She's great."

"The psychologist?"

"No—Well, she seemed very nice and nearly as confused as I was. Ryan's mother. She's great." His hands were in his pockets, then out, wrapped around the carved newel post, fiddling with his tie.

Miranda took one of them and squeezed. "I know this is hard for you. All these people—Elise."

"Sort of a minor trial by fire. Elise, the parents, me, and cases of free booze everywhere." He glanced toward the entrance again. Annie hadn't come.

"You need to keep busy. Do you want to dance?"

"You and me?" He shot her a stunned look, then dissolved in easy and genuine laughter. "We'd both end up in the ER with broken toes."

"I'll risk it if you will."

His smile went tender. "Miranda, you've always been a high point in my life. I'm okay. Let's just watch people who know what they're doing."

Then his smile stiffened. Miranda didn't have to shift her gaze to know he'd seen Elise.

She came up to them, a sleek fairy in filmy white. Even as Miranda wanted to resent, she saw the nervousness in Elise's eyes.

"I just wanted to congratulate you, both of you, on a wonderful and successful exhibit. Everyone's raving about it. You've done a fabulous job for the Institute, and the organization."

"We had a lot of help," Miranda said. "The staff put in long hard hours to make this happen."

"It couldn't be more perfect. Andrew." She seemed to take a deep gulp of air. "I want to apologize for making things difficult. I know my being here is awkward for you. I won't be staying much longer tonight, and I've decided to go back to Florence tomorrow."

"You don't have to change your plans for my benefit."

"It's for mine too." She looked at Miranda then, struggled with a smile. "I didn't want to leave without taking a minute to tell you how much I admire what you accomplished here. Your parents are very proud."

Miranda goggled before she could control it. "My parents?"

"Yes, Elizabeth was just saying—"

"Annie." Andrew said the name, almost like a prayer, and Elise broke off to stare up at him. "Excuse me."

He moved away, making his way toward her. She looked lost, he thought, in a sea of people. And so lovely with her shining hair. Her red dress glowed like a flame, throwing off heat and life among all the sober and conservative black.

"I'm so glad you came." He caught her hands like lifelines.

"I don't know why I did. I already feel ridiculous." The dress was too short, she thought. It was too red. It was too everything. Her department store earrings looked like cheap chandeliers—and what had possessed her to buy shoes with rhinestone buckles? She must look like a slutty Pilgrim.

"I'm so glad you're here," he said again, and ignoring the raised eyebrows, kissed her.

"Why don't I just grab a tray, pass drinks? I'd fit in better that way."

"You fit in fine. Come over and talk to Miranda." But when he turned, his eyes locked with Elise's.

She stood exactly where he'd left her. He saw Miranda touch her arm, murmur something, but Elise only shook her head, then hurried away.

"Your wife looked upset," Annie commented as acid churned in her stomach.

"Ex-wife," Andrew reminded her, grateful to see Miranda making her way toward them.

"Annie, it's so good to see you. Now I know who Andrew's been looking for all evening."

"I wasn't going to come."

"I'm glad you changed your mind." It was rare for Miranda to follow impulse, but she did so now, bending down to press her cheek to Annie's. "He needs you," she whispered, then straightened with a smile. "I see some people I think you'd enjoy meeting. Andrew, why don't you introduce Annie to Mr. and Mrs. Boldari."

He followed the direction of her nod and grinned. "Yeah, thanks. Come on, Annie, you're going to love these people."

It lifted Miranda's heart, that warm glow she'd seen in Andrew's eyes. Her spirits rose, so much so that she allowed Ryan to pull her into a dance.

When she caught a glimpse of Richard, his nose all but pressed to a painting of the Holy Family, his eyes intent behind his glasses, she simply turned away.

She'd take Ryan's advice—this time—and live in the moment.

She was considering another glass of champagne and another dance, when Elizabeth found her. "Miranda, you're neglecting your duties. I've spoken with several people who said they've yet to have a word with you. The exhibition isn't enough, you have to follow through."

"Of course, you're right." She handed the champagne she hadn't yet sipped to her mother and their gazes held for one long moment. "I'll do my duty. I'll do what has to be done, for the Institute." She stepped back.

No, she realized, she was also going to do what needed to be done, for herself. "You might have said—just once tonight you might have said to me that I'd done a good job. But I suppose it would have stuck in your throat."

She turned, walked up the stairs to mingle with the guests on the second level.

"Is there a problem, Elizabeth?"

She flicked a glance over at her husband as he came to her side, then looked back up at Miranda. "I don't know. I suppose I'll have to find out."

"Senator Lamb would like to see you. He's a big supporter of the NEA."

"Yes, I know who he is." Her voice was a shade too sharp. Deliberately she smoothed it out. "I'll be happy to speak with him."

And then, she thought, she was going to deal with Miranda.

She lost track of Ryan, assumed that Andrew was making Annie comfortable with the Boldaris. For an hour, Miranda concentrated on her role as hostess. When she finally slipped off into the ladies' room, she was desperately relieved to find it empty.

Too many people, she thought, leaning against the counter a moment. She just wasn't good with so many people. Conversations, small talk, weak jokes. Her face was stiff from holding a smile in place.

Then she shook herself. She had nothing to whine about. Everything was perfect. The exhibit, the gala, the press, the response. It would all go a long way to repairing the recent chinks in her reputation.

She should be grateful for it. She would be grateful for it if she knew what to do next.

Decisions were for tomorrow, she reminded herself. Tomorrow, after she'd confronted her mother. That was the only answer, she decided. The only logical step. It was time the two of them faced off.

And if her mother was guilty? Part of a conspiracy of theft and murder?

She shook her head. Tomorrow, she thought again, and reached in her bag for her lipstick.

The explosion of sound had her hand jerking. The slim gold tube clattered onto the counter. Her eyes, locked on their twins in the mirror, went wide with shock.

Gunshots? Impossible.

Even as the denial raced through her, she heard the high, horrified sound of a woman's scream.

She rushed to the door, knocking her bag off the counter and scattering its contents behind her.

Outside people were shouting, some were running. She shoved through, using hands and elbows. She broke free and ran for the steps just as Ryan rounded the lower landing.

"It— From upstairs. It came from upstairs."

"Stay here."

He might have saved his breath. She hiked up her skirt and was pounding up behind him. He knocked aside the velvet rope that blocked the third-floor office level from the party area.

"You check that way," she began. "I'll look down—"

"The hell you will. If you won't stay put, then you'll come with me." He took a firm hold of her hand, doing his best to block her body with his as he started down the hall.

More footsteps sounded on the stairs behind them. Andrew leaped the last three. "That was a gun. Miranda, go downstairs. Annie, go down with her."

"No."

Since neither woman was going to listen, Ryan gestured to the left. "You check that way. We'll go down here. Whoever fired the gun is probably long gone," he said as he cautiously nudged open a door. "But you stay behind me."

"What are you? Bulletproof?" She reached in under his arm and flicked on the light. He simply shoved her back and stepped into the room himself to do a quick sweep. Satisfied it was empty, he pulled her in.

"Use this office. Lock the door and call the police."

"I'll call them when I know what to tell them." She

elbowed him aside and strode down the hall to the next room.

He all but wrenched her arm out of its socket. "Try to be a little less of a target, Dr. Jones."

They worked their way down until he spotted a faint light pooling under the door leading to her office. "You changed for the party here. Did you leave your light on?"

"No. And the door should be locked. It's not quite closed."

"Take off your shoes."

"Excuse me?"

"Take off your shoes," he repeated. "I want you to be able to run if you have to, not break an ankle in those heels."

Saying nothing, she leaned against him long enough to remove them. It should have been funny, she thought, the way he took one, holding it spike out like a weapon as they approached the door.

But her hand was going damp in his, and she couldn't find the humor.

He eased to the side of the door, nudged it. It opened another two inches, then bumped into an obstruction. Once again, Miranda reached under his arm to turn on the overheads.

"Oh my God."

She recognized the lower half of the filmy white gown, the soft glitter of silver shoes. Dropping to her knees, she pushed at the door with her shoulder until she could squeeze inside.

Elise lay crumpled, facedown. Blood trickled

from a wound at the back of her head and slipped over her pale cheek. "She's alive," Miranda said quickly, when she pressed her fingers to Elise's throat and found a fluttery pulse. "She's alive. Call an ambulance. Hurry."

"Here." He shoved a handkerchief into her hand. "Press that against it. See if you can stop the bleeding."

"Just hurry." She folded it into a pad, wanting the thickness, and applied pressure. Her gaze skimmed over, rested on the bronze *Venus* she kept in her office. A copy of the Donatello Ryan coveted.

Another bronze, she thought dully. Another copy. Another victim.

"Miranda, what—" Andrew pushed in the door, then jerked to a stop. "Jesus. Oh Jesus, Elise." He was on his knees, fumbling at the wound, at her face. "Is she dead? Oh sweet God."

"No, she's alive. Ryan's calling for an ambulance. Give me your handkerchief. I don't think it's deep, but I need to stop the bleeding."

"She needs to be covered. Do you have a blanket, some towels?" Annie demanded. "You need to keep her warm in case she's in shock."

"In my office. There's a throw. Just through there."

Annie stepped quickly over Andrew.

"I think we need to turn her over." Miranda pressed the fresh cloth firmly. "To make sure there's no other injury. Can you do it, Andrew?"

"Yeah." His mind had gone stone cold. He

reached out carefully, supporting Elise's neck as he rolled her. Her eyelids fluttered. "I think she's coming around. I don't see any blood except for the head wound." He touched a finger gently to a bruise forming on her temple. "She must have hit her head there when she fell."

"Miranda." Annie stepped back into the room. Her eyes were dark, her voice dull. "Ryan wants you. Andrew and I will take care of her."

"All right. Try to keep her calm if she comes around." She got to her feet, stopping only when Annie squeezed her arm.

"Brace yourself," she murmured, then moved over to cover Elise with the throw. "She'll be all right, Andrew. The ambulance is on its way."

Miranda stepped into her office. One ambulance wasn't going to be enough, she thought dizzily. A couple of handkerchiefs weren't going to mop up all this blood.

It was pooling on her desk, dripping down to soak into her carpet. Splatters of it were on the window behind her desk like sticky red rain.

On her desk, flung onto his back with red spreading over his frilled white shirt, was Richard Hawthorne.

Security kept the press and the curious away from the third floor. By the time the homicide team arrived, the scene had been secured, and Elise was on her way to the hospital.

Miranda gave her statement again and again,

going back over every step. And lying. Lying, she thought dully, was becoming second nature.

No, she had no idea why either Richard or Elise would have been in her office. No, she didn't know why anyone would have killed him. When they finally told her she was free to leave, she walked downstairs on legs that felt as fragile as glass.

Annie sat on the bottom step, hugging her elbows.

"Won't they let you leave, Annie?"

"Yeah, they said they were finished with me for now."

Miranda glanced toward the guards flanking the archways, the scatter of police roaming the hall. And sat beside Annie. "I don't know what to do with myself either. I think they're still talking to Ryan. I didn't see Andrew."

"They let him go with Elise, to the hospital."

"Oh. He would have thought that was the right thing to do."

"He still loves her."

"I don't think so."

"He's still hung up on her, Miranda. Why wouldn't he be?" Then she pressed her hands to the sides of her head. "And I'm insane, ashamed, pitiful to be worrying about that when a man's been shot, and Elise is hurt."

"You can't always control your feelings. I didn't used to believe that, but now I know."

"And I used to have a good handle on mine. Well." She sniffled, rubbed her hands over her face, then rose. "I'd better go home."

"Wait for Ryan, Annie. We'll drive you."

"It's okay. I've got my heap out there. I'll be fine. You tell Andrew I hope Elise is okay, and . . . I'll see him around."

"Annie, I meant what I said earlier. He needs you."

Annie dragged off her party earrings, rubbed the blood back into her earlobes. "He needs to count on himself. He needs to know who he is and what he wants. I can't help him with that, Miranda, and neither can you."

She couldn't seem to help anyone, Miranda thought when she was alone and staring down at her hands. Nothing she'd touched, nothing she'd done over the last months had resulted in anything other than disaster.

She looked over her shoulder as she heard footsteps on the stairs. Ryan came down, skirted around her, then saying nothing, brought her to her feet and into his arms.

"Oh God, oh God, Ryan. How many more?"

"Ssh." He stroked her back. "It was his own gun," he murmured in her ear. "The same one I found in his room. Someone shot the poor bastard with his own gun. There was nothing you could have done."

"Nothing I could have done." She said it wearily, but pulled back to stand on her own. "I want to go to the hospital, check on Elise. Andrew's there. He shouldn't be alone."

* * *

He wasn't. It surprised Miranda to see her mother in the waiting lounge, staring out the window, a paper cup of coffee in her hand.

Andrew stopped pacing when she came in, then shook his head and began again.

"Is there any word?" Miranda asked him.

"They stabilized her down in emergency. X rays, tests—they haven't come in to tell us the results. The resident on duty downstairs thought concussion, but they want to do a CAT scan to rule out any brain damage. She was out a long time. She lost a lot of blood."

And some of it, he noted, stained the hem of Miranda's dress.

"You should go home," Andrew said. "Ryan, take her home."

"I'm going to stay with you, just the way you'd stay with me."

"Okay. Okay." He rested his brow against hers. They stood linked while Elizabeth turned from the window and studied them. When she caught Ryan watching her, her cheeks pinkened slightly.

"There's coffee. It's neither fresh nor palatable, but it's very strong and hot."

"No." Miranda moved away from Andrew, stepped forward. "Where's Father?"

"I—don't know. I believe he was going back to the hotel. There was nothing for him to do here."

"But you're here. We need to talk."

"Excuse me, Dr. Jones."

All three of them turned, made Cook's mouth twitch. "Guess that's pretty confusing."

"Detective Cook." Miranda's stomach was quickly sheathed in ice. "I hope you're not ill."

"Ill? Oh, oh, hospital, sick. No. I came down to talk to Dr. Warfield once the doctors clear it."

"To Elise?" Baffled, Andrew shook his head. "I thought you were with robbery. Nobody was robbed."

"Sometimes these things are connected. The homicide boys will talk to her. Going to be a long night. Maybe you can tell me what you know, give me a clearer picture before I talk to Dr. Warfield."

"Detective . . . Cook, is it?" Elizabeth moved forward. "Is it really necessary to hold an interrogation in a hospital waiting room while we're waiting with some degree of distress for test results?"

"I'm sorry for your distress, ma'am. Dr. Jones."

"Standford-Jones."

"Yes, Elizabeth Standford-Jones. You're the victims' employer."

"That's correct. Both Richard and Elise work for me in Florence. Worked for me," she amended with a faint change in color. "Richard worked for me."

"What did he do for you?"

"Research, primarily. Richard was a brilliant art historian. He was a fount of facts and data, but more, he understood the spirit of the work he researched. He was invaluable."

"And Dr. Warfield?"

"She is my lab director in Florence. She's a capable, efficient, and trustworthy scientist."

"She used to be your daughter-in-law."

Elizabeth's gaze didn't waver, nor did it flick toward her son. "Yes. We've retained a good relationship."

"That's good. Most times ex-mothers-in-law tend to blame their sons' wives for the trouble. You don't see many who can work together and . . . retain a good relationship."

"We're both professional women, Detective. And I don't allow family difficulties to interfere with work, or with my opinion of an individual. I'm quite fond of Elise."

"Anything going on between her and Hawthorne?"

"Going on?" It was said with such frigid disgust the temperature seemed to plummet. "What you're suggesting is insulting, demeaning, and inappropriate."

"My information is that they were both single adults. I don't mean any insult by asking if they were involved. They were in a third-floor office together. The party was downstairs."

"I have no idea why either of them was in Miranda's office, but obviously they weren't alone." She moved past him when a doctor in green scrubs came to the doorway. "Elise?"

"She's doing well," he told them. "She has a fairly serious concussion, some disorientation, but the CAT scan was clear and she's in stable condition."

Elizabeth closed her eyes, and the breath she released was shaky. "I'd like to see her."

"I cleared the police in. They wanted to question

her as soon as possible, and she agreed. She became agitated when I suggested she wait until tomorrow. It seemed to ease her mind to talk to them tonight."

"I'm going to want some time with her." Cook took out his badge, then nodded toward Elizabeth and Andrew. "I'll wait. I've got plenty of time."

He waited over an hour, and wouldn't have gotten in to see her then if once again she hadn't insisted on making her statement.

Cook saw a fragile woman with a livid bruise on her right temple that spread purple toward her eyes. The eyes themselves were exhausted and rimmed with red.

But the flaws only added to her beauty. Her dark hair was swathed in white bandages. He knew the blow had been to the back of her head, and had bled profusely. He imagined they'd shaved some of that glossy hair to sew her up. Seemed a shame.

"You're Detective . . . I'm sorry, I can't remember the name they gave me."

"Cook, ma'am. I appreciate you talking to me."

"I want to help." She winced as she shifted and the pain radiated through her head. "They're going to give me drugs in a little while. I won't be able to think clearly once they do."

"I'll try to make this fast. Mind if I sit here?"

"No, please." She looked up at the ceiling as if focusing on moving beyond the pain. "Every time I begin, I think it's a bad dream. It didn't really happen."

"Can you tell me what did happen? Everything you remember."

"Richard. He shot Richard."

"He?"

"I don't even know that, not for sure. I didn't see. I saw Richard." Her eyes filled, spilled over, trailed tears down her cheeks. "He's dead. They told me he was dead. I thought maybe . . . I don't know—but they said he's dead. Poor Richard."

"What were you doing upstairs with him?"

"I wasn't with him—I was looking for him." She lifted her free hand to brush at the tears. "He said he'd go back to the hotel whenever I wanted to leave. Richard's not much on parties. We were going to share a cab. I wanted to leave."

"Dull party?"

"No." She smiled a little. "It was a wonderful exhibit, beautifully presented. But I . . . I'm sure you know the background by now. Andrew and I used to be married, and it was awkward. He had a date there."

"Excuse me, Dr. Warfield, but my information was that you divorced him."

"Yes, I did, and it was final over a year ago, but that doesn't stop you from feeling . . . from feeling," she ended. "It was awkward and depressing for me. I felt obliged to stay for at least two hours. Elizabeth's been very good to me, and this was important to her. Miranda and I have remained somewhat cautious friends, and I didn't want to leave the impression that her work didn't matter.

But I wanted to go and I didn't think anyone would notice by that time."

"So you went looking for Hawthorne."

"Yes. He only knew a handful of people there, and he's not a very social man. We'd agreed to leave around ten-thirty, so I tried to find him. I expected to find him huddled in a corner, or with his nose up against some map. Then I thought he might have gone upstairs, to the library. He wasn't there. Ah . . . I'm sorry, I keep losing my train of thought."

"That's okay. You take your time."

She closed her eyes. "I wandered around for a while, and I saw the light in Miranda's office. I started to go back down, but then I heard his voice. I heard him shout something, something like, 'I've had enough.' "

Her fingers began to tug at the sheet in agitated little plucks. "I walked over. There were voices. But I couldn't hear what they were saying."

"Was it a man's voice, or a woman's?"

"I don't know." Wearily, she rubbed at the center of her forehead. "I just don't know. It was very low, only a murmur really. I stood there a minute, not quite sure what to do. I suppose I thought he and Miranda might have come up to discuss something, and I didn't want to interrupt."

"Miranda?"

"It was her office, so I just assumed. I thought maybe I'd just go back alone, and then . . . I heard the shots. They were so loud, so sudden. I was so shocked I didn't think. I ran inside. I think I called out. I—It's just not clear."

"That's all right. Just tell me what you remember."

"I saw Richard, lying over the desk. The blood everywhere. The smell of it and what must have been gunpowder. Like a burn on the air. I think I screamed. I must have screamed, then I turned. I was going to run. I'm so ashamed, I was going to run and leave him there. Someone—something hit me."

Gingerly, she reached around to press at the bandage on the back of her head. "I just remember this flash of light inside my head, then nothing at all. Nothing until I woke up in the ambulance."

She was crying openly now and tried to reach the box of tissues on the table next to the bed. Cook handed it to her, waited until she'd wiped her face.

"Do you remember how long you looked for him?"

"Ten or fifteen minutes, I think. I don't really know."

"When you went into the office, you didn't see anyone?"

"Only Richard—" She closed her eyes so that tears squeezed through her lashes. "Only Richard, and now he's dead."

CHAPTER TWENTY-NINE

IT WAS NEARLY DAWN WHEN ANNIE OPENED THE DOOR and found Andrew in the hall. He was sheet-pale, his eyes heavy with shadows. He was still in his tux, the tie loose around his neck, the first stud missing. The snowy shirt was marred by creases and blood.

"Elise?"

"She's going to be all right. They'll keep her for observation, but she was lucky. Concussion, a few stitches. There's no sign of intracranial bleeding."

"Come inside, Andrew. Sit down."

"I needed to come, to tell you."

"I know. Come on in. I've already made coffee."

She was bundled in a robe, and had washed the makeup from her face, but he saw how tired her eyes were. "Have you been to bed?"

"I gave it a shot. It didn't work. I'll make us some breakfast."

He closed the door, watched her walk the short distance to the kitchen and open the undersized refrigerator. She took out eggs, bacon, a frying pan. She poured coffee into two thick blue mugs.

The early light played through the narrow windows, made patterns on the floor. The room smelled of coffee and carnations.

Her feet were bare.

She laid bacon in the black iron skillet and soon the room was full of its scent and sound. Solid, Sunday morning sounds, he thought. Easy homey scents.

"Annie."

"Sit down, Andrew. You're asleep on your feet."

"Annie." He took her by the shoulders, turned her around. "I needed to go with Elise tonight."

"Of course you did."

"Don't interrupt. I needed to go, to make sure she was all right. She was my wife once, so I owed her that. I didn't handle the marriage well, and handled the divorce less well. I thought about that while I was waiting for the doctor to come out and tell us how she was. I thought about that and what I might have done differently to make it work between us. The answer is nothing."

He let out a short laugh, running his hands up and down her arms. "Nothing. It used to be realizing that made me feel like a failure. Now it just makes me understand the marriage failed. I didn't, she didn't. It did."

Almost absently, he bent to kiss the top of her head. "I waited until I was sure she was going to be all right, then I came here because I had to tell you."

"I know that, Andrew." In support, and with mild impatience, she patted his arm. "The bacon's going to burn."

"I haven't finished telling you. I haven't started to tell you."

"Tell me what?"

"My name is Andrew, and I'm an alcoholic." He seemed to quiver once, then steady. "I've been sober for thirty days. I'm going to be sober for thirty one. I sat in the hospital tonight and I thought about drinking. It just didn't seem to be the answer. Then I thought about you. You're the answer. I love you."

Her eyes went damp, but she shook her head. "I'm not your answer, Andrew. I can't be." She pulled away, started to turn the bacon, but he reached over and snapped off the flame.

"I love you." He cupped his hands over her face to hold her still. "Part of me always has. The rest of me had to grow up enough to see it. I know what I feel and I know what I want. If you don't have those same feelings for me, and don't want what I want, then you tell me. You tell me straight. It's not going to send me out looking for a bottle. But I need to know."

"What do you want me to say?" She rapped one frustrated fist against his chest. "You're a Ph.D. I'm GED. You're Andrew Jones of the Maine Joneses, and I'm Annie McLean from nowhere." She put her hands over his, but couldn't quite make herself draw his away from her face. "I run a bar, you run the Institute. Get a grip on yourself, Andrew."

"I'm not interested in your snobbery right now."

"Snobbery?" Her voice cracked with insult. "For God's sake—"

"You didn't answer my question." He tugged until she was on her toes. "What do you feel for me, and what do you want?"

"I'm in love with you, and I want a miracle."

His smile spread slowly, dimples deep in his cheeks. She was quivering under his hands, and his world had just gone rock steady. "I don't know if it'll qualify as a miracle. But I'll do my best." He picked her up.

"What are you doing?"

"Taking you to bed."

Panic fluttered in her throat and curled all the way down to her toes. "I didn't say I'd go to bed with you."

"You didn't say you wouldn't. I'm taking a big chance here."

She grabbed the doorjamb and clung for dear life. "Really? Is that so?"

"Damn right. You may not like my moves this time around. If not, you'll probably turn me down when I ask you to marry me."

Her fingers went limp as wax and slid off the wood. "You—you could ask me now and save yourself the suspense."

"No." His eyes on hers, he laid her on the bed. "After. After, Annie," he murmured, and sank into her.

It was coming home, it was finding treasure. It was simple, and it was extraordinary.

They weren't innocent this time, weren't fumbling children, eager and curious. And all the years between then and now had given what was between them time to ripen.

Now was like decanting wine of a fine vintage.

Her arms came around him. He was so gentle, so careful, so gloriously thorough. His big hands smoothed over her, tracing her throat, her shoulders, paving the way for his lips.

He murmured to her, wonderful foolishness, as he stripped out of his jacket, let her help him out of his shirt. Then his flesh cruised along hers and made them both sigh.

Dawn was breaking in the rosy red light that heralded storms. But there in the narrow bed was peace and patience. Each touch, each taste was taken, was given with quiet joy.

Even when she trembled, when the need began to build to an ache inside her, she smiled and brought his mouth to hers again.

He took his time, stroking her body to life, his own pacing it. And the first time she crested, arching up and up with a moan of delight, he rolled with her for the sheer joy of it.

He traced kisses down her back, over her shoulder blades, down to her hips, then shifted her over to nuzzle at her breasts. Her hands moved over him, exploring, testing, arousing. As breath thickened and the sun grew strong, he slipped inside her.

A slow and steady rhythm, savoring, prolonging. Belonging. She rose and fell with him, making the climb, twined with him as they reached the top, holding tight when they trembled there. Falling with him was like drifting out of the clouds.

Then he shifted his weight, drew her against his side, buried his face in her hair.

"I still like your moves, Andrew." She sighed against his shoulder. "I really like your moves."

He felt whole again, healed. "I like your tattoo, Annie. I really like your tattoo."

She winced. "Oh God, I forgot about it."

"I'm never going to look at a butterfly in quite the same way again." When she laughed and lifted her face, he continued to smile. "It's taken me a long time to figure out what I need, what makes me happy. Give me a chance to make you happy. I want to build a life and a family with you."

"We both really screwed up the first time."

"We weren't ready."

"No." She touched his face. "It feels like we are now."

"Belong to me." He pressed a kiss into her palm. "Let me belong to you. Will you, Annie?"

"Yes." She laid her hand over his heart. "Yes, Andrew. I will."

Ryan stood in Miranda's office, trying to picture it. Oh, he could still imagine clearly enough the way it had looked the night before. Such things plant themselves on the brain and are rarely rooted out even with great effort.

There was a nasty stain on the carpet, the windows were smeared, and the dust from the crime scene investigation coated every surface.

How far would the bullet have propelled Richard's body? he wondered. How close to each other had he and his killer been standing? Close enough, he thought, for the bullets to have left powder burns on the tuxedo shirt. Close enough for Hawthorne to have looked into his murderer's eyes and have seen his death there.

Ryan was damn sure of that.

He stepped back, moved to the doorway, scanned the room.

Desk, chairs, window, the lamp that had been switched on. Counter, file cabinets. He could see it all.

"You shouldn't be in here, Mr. Boldari."

"They've taken the tape down," Ryan said without turning. "It seems the investigators got all they could from this area."

"Better we keep it closed off a while yet." Cook waited until Ryan moved out of the doorway, then shut the door. "No need to have Dr. Jones see all that again, is there?"

"No, no need at all."

"But you wanted to see it again."

"I wanted to see if I could get it all clear in my mind."

"And have you?"

"Not entirely. There doesn't appear to be any sign of a struggle, does there, Detective?"

"No. Everything tidy—but for the desk."

"The victim and his killer would have been standing about as close as you and I are just now. Wouldn't you say?"

"Give or take a few inches. Yeah, he knew who pulled the trigger, Boldari. You'd met him, hadn't you?"

"Briefly, when he arrived Friday, and again on the night he died."

"Never met him before that?"

"No, I hadn't."

"I wondered about that, seeing as you're in art, he was in art."

"There are a great many people in various areas of the business I haven't met."

"Yeah, but you know, it's a small world. You move around this place pretty tame."

"As do you," Ryan murmured. "Do you think I came up here last night and put two bullets into Richard Hawthorne?"

"No, I don't. We've got several witnesses who put you downstairs when the shots were fired."

Ryan leaned back against the wall. His skin felt sticky, as if some of the nastiness in the next room had clung to him. "Lucky for me I'm a sociable guy."

"Yeah—of course a few of those people are related to you, but there were those who weren't. So I figure you're clear. Nobody can seem to say where Dr. Jones, Dr. Miranda Jones, was during the time in question."

Ryan came off the wall quickly, almost violently, before he controlled it. But the move had caused

Cook's eyes to flicker. "You two have gotten very friendly."

"Friendly enough that I know Miranda's the last person who could kill."

Idly, Cook took out a stick of gum, offered it, then unwrapped it for himself when Ryan only continued to stare at him. "It's funny what people can do with the right motivation."

"And hers would be?"

"I've done a lot of thinking about that. There's the bronze, the one from here, the one that got lifted out of a display case very slick, very professional. I tracked a number of burglaries with that pattern. Somebody knows what they're doing, somebody's damn good at their job, somebody has connections."

"So now Miranda's a thief—an expert art burglar?"

"Or she knows one, is friendly enough with one," he added with a thin smile. "Funny how the paperwork on that piece went away too. Even funnier how I did some checking with a foundry this place uses, found out somebody else was doing some checking there. Somebody who claimed he was a student here at the Institute, gave a song and dance about checking on a bronze figure that was cast there about three years ago."

"And that would have exactly what to do with this?"

"The name he gave at the foundry doesn't check with the records here. And the bronze he was so interested in was a statue of David with sling. Seems he even had a sketch of it."

"Then that might have something to do with your burglary." Ryan inclined his head. "I'm delighted to know you're making some progress there."

"Oh, I plod right along. Seems Dr. Jones—Miranda Jones taught a class on Renaissance bronze figures."

"Being an expert in the field, I'm sure she's taught several on the subject, or related ones."

"One of her students used the foundry to cast a bronze *David* long after the missing bronze arrived for her to test."

"That's fascinating."

Cook ignored the mild sarcasm in Ryan's tone. "Yeah, it means there's lots of little dangles wanting to be tied up. The student, he dropped out right after that bronze was cast. And you know, somebody checked with his mother, said they were from here, wanted to get in touch with him. Kid moved to San Francisco. A couple nights ago, they fished him out of the bay."

"I'm sorry to hear that."

"You've got family in San Francisco."

This time Ryan's eyes narrowed and sparked. "Be careful, Detective."

"Just making a comment. Kid was an artist, you got an art gallery out there. I figured you might have known him. Name was Mathers, Harrison Mathers."

"No, I don't know a Harrison Mathers, but I can

check easily enough to see if we display any of his work."

"Might not be a bad idea."

"Is this Mathers what you'd call another dangle?"

"Oh yeah, just one of those things that make you scratch your head. Then I start thinking about that big-deal bronze in Florence, the one that turned out not to be such a big deal. I'd think Dr. Jones would be pretty upset about that, pretty pissed off at her mother too, for kicking her off the project. I found out somebody stole that piece, went right into the storage area at the National Museum over there and took it, slick as spit. Now why would somebody want to take something, risk that kind of theft for something that isn't worth more than the price of the metal?"

"Art's a subjective mystery, Detective. Maybe someone took a liking to it."

"Could be, but whoever did was a pro, not some half-ass thief. Pros don't waste their time, unless they've got good reason. You'd agree with that, wouldn't you, Mr. Boldari? Being a professional yourself."

"Certainly." Damned if he didn't like this cop, Ryan mused. "I detest wasting time."

"Exactly. Makes me wonder what that bronze is worth to somebody."

"If I see it, Detective, I'll do an appraisal and let you know. But I can tell you, if that bronze was real, if it was worth millions, Miranda wouldn't kill for it. And I think you agree," Ryan added. "Being a professional yourself."

Cook chuckled. Something wasn't square about the guy, he thought. But you had to like him. "No, I don't think she killed anybody, and I can't picture her dancing all over the world pinching pictures and statues. Woman's got integrity pasted on her forehead. That's why I know, in my gut, she's hiding something. She knows more than she's saying. And if you're friendly enough with her, Boldari, you'll convince her to tell me just what that is before somebody decides she's expendable."

She was asking herself just how much she could tell, how much she could risk telling. In the South Gallery, surrounded by the art of the masters, she sat with her hands over her face. And suffered.

She knew Cook was upstairs. She'd seen him come in, and like a child avoiding a lecture, had slipped behind a doorway until he'd passed by.

When her mother came in, she let her hands fall into her lap.

"I thought I might find you here."

"Oh yes." Miranda rose and picked up one of the champagne flutes from a huddle of them on a table. "Reliving past glories. Where else would I be? Where else would I go?"

"I haven't been able to find your brother."

"I hope he's sleeping. It was a difficult night." She didn't add that he hadn't been sleeping, at least not in his own bed, when she left the house that morning.

"Yes, for all of us. I'm going to the hospital. Your father's meeting me there. Hopefully Elise is up to visitors, and she'd hoped they would release her by this afternoon."

"Give her my best. I'll try to stop by later this evening, either the hospital, or the hotel if they've let her go. Please tell her she's welcome to stay at the house for as long as she likes."

"It would be awkward."

"Yes, but I'll make the offer nonetheless."

"It's generous of you. She—It was fortunate she wasn't hurt more seriously. It could have been . . . We might have found her like Richard."

"I know you're very fond of her." Miranda set down the glass in the precise spot where it had been. She was careful to make certain the stem of the glass fit exactly on the outline it had left on the cloth. "Fonder, I think, than you ever were of your own children."

"This is hardly the occasion for pettiness, Miranda."

She looked up then. "Do you hate me?"

"What a ridiculous thing to say, and what an inappropriate time to say it."

"When would be an appropriate time for me to ask my mother if she hates me?"

"If this stems from the business in Florence—"

"Oh, it goes back much farther, in much deeper than what happened in Florence, but that'll do for now. You didn't stand by me. You never have. All of my life I've waited for it, that moment when you'd finally be there. Why the hell weren't you ever there for me?"

"I refuse to indulge you in this behavior." With an icy stare, Elizabeth turned and started out.

She'd never know what prompted her to ignore a lifetime of training, but Miranda was across the room, grabbing Elizabeth's arm, whirling her around with a violence that stunned both of them. "You will not walk out on me until I have an answer. I'm sick to death of having you walk literally and figuratively away from me. Why couldn't you ever be a mother to me?"

"Because you're not my daughter." Elizabeth snapped it out, her eyes flaring to a blue burn. "You were never mine." She wrenched her arm free, her breath coming fast and hard as control frayed. "Don't you dare stand there and demand from me after all I've sacrificed, all I've endured because your father elected to pass his bastard off as mine."

"Bastard?" Her world, already shaky, tilted away under her feet. "I'm not your daughter?"

"No, you are not. I gave my word that I would never tell you." Infuriated that she'd allowed temper and fatigue to undermine her control, Elizabeth strode to the window, stared out. "Well, you're a grown woman, and perhaps you have a right to know."

"I—" Miranda pressed a hand to her heart because she wasn't sure it continued to beat. She could only stare at the rigid back of the woman who'd so suddenly become a stranger. "Who is my mother? Where is she?"

"She died several years ago. She was no one," Elizabeth added, turning back. The sun wasn't kind to women of a certain age. In its glare Miranda saw that Elizabeth looked haggard, almost ill. Then a cloud rolled over the sun and the moment was gone. "One of your father's . . . short-term interests."

"He had an affair."

"His name is Jones, isn't it?" Elizabeth said bitterly, then waved a hand as if annoyed. "In this case, he was careless and the woman became pregnant. She was not, apparently, as easily shaken off as most. Charles had no intention of marrying her, of course, and when she realized that, she insisted he deal with the child. It was a difficult situation."

A quick, nasty stab of pain lanced through the shock. "She didn't want me either."

With the faintest of shrugs, Elizabeth walked back and sat. "I have no idea what the woman wanted. But what she chose to do was demand that Charles raise you. He came to me and outlined the problem. My choices were to divorce him, live with the scandal, lose what I had begun to build here at the Institute, and give up my plans for my own facility. Or—"

"You stayed with him." Beneath the shock, the hot edge of hurt, was a simmering outrage. "After a betrayal like that, you stayed with him."

"I had a choice. I made the one that was best for me. It was not without sacrifice. I had to go into seclusion, lose months while I waited for you to be born." The memory of that could still swim to the surface like acid. "When you were, I had to present you as mine. I resented the fact of you, Miranda," she said evenly. "Perhaps that's unfair, but it's accurate."

"Yes, let's be accurate." Unable to bear it, she turned away. "Let's stick with the facts."

"I'm not a maternal woman nor do I pretend to be." Elizabeth gestured again, with some impatience in her voice. "After Andrew was born, I had no intention of having another child. Ever. Then through circumstances that were none of my doing, I was given the responsibility of raising my husband's child as my own. You were a reminder of his carelessness to me, of his lack of marital integrity. For Charles you were a reminder of a serious miscalculation."

"Miscalculation," Miranda said quietly. "Yes, I suppose that's accurate too. It's hardly a mystery now why neither one of you could ever love me—love at all if it comes to that. You don't have it inside you."

"You were well taken care of, given a good home, a fine education."

"And never a moment of true affection," Miranda finished, turning back. What she saw was a woman of rigid control, towering ambition, who had traded emotion for advancement. "I beat myself up all of my life to be worthy of your affection. I was wasting my time."

Elizabeth sighed, got to her feet. "I'm not a monster. You were never harmed, never neglected."

"Never held."

"I did my best by you, and gave you every opportunity to prove yourself in your field. Up to and including the Fiesole Bronze." She hesitated, then rose to open one of the bottles of water the cleaning staff had yet to clear.

"I took your reports, the X rays, the documents home. After I'd calmed down, after the worst of the embarrassment faded, I wasn't quite sure you could have made such blatant mistakes, or that you would skew test results. Honesty has never been something I doubted in you."

"Oh, thank you very much," Miranda said dryly.

"The reports, the documents were stolen out of my home safe. I might not have known, but I wanted something before I left to come here. And I saw they were gone."

She poured water into a glass, recapped the bottle, then sipped. "I wanted to get your grandmother's pearls, to bring them here and put them in the safe deposit box I keep at the local bank. I was going to give them to you before I left."

"Why?"

"Perhaps because while you were never mine, you were always hers." She set the glass aside. "I won't apologize for what I've done or the choices I've made. I don't ask you to understand me, any more than I have ever been able to understand you."

"So, I just live with it?" Miranda demanded, and Elizabeth lifted a brow.

"I have. I will ask you to keep what we've spoken of in this room. You are a Jones, and as such have a responsibility to uphold the family name."

"Oh yes, one hell of a name it is." But she shook her head. "I know my duties."

"Yes, I'm sure you do. I have to meet your father." She picked up her bag. "I will discuss this with him if you like."

"For what purpose?" Suddenly Miranda was weary, too weary to worry, to wonder, or to care. "Nothing's really changed at all, has it?"

"No."

When she was gone, Miranda let out a half-laugh and walked to the window. The storm that had been threatening all day was rolling in on a blistered sky.

"You okay?"

She leaned back as Ryan laid his hands on her shoulder. "How much did you hear?"

"Most of it."

"Eavesdropping again," she murmured, "sneaking in on little cat's paws. I don't know how to feel."

"Whatever you feel, it's right. You're your own woman, Miranda. You always have been."

"I guess I have to be."

"Will you talk to your father about this?"

"What would be the point? He's never seen me. He's never heard me. And now I know why." She closed her eyes, turned her cheek into his hand. "What kind of people are they, Ryan, that I come from? My father, Elizabeth, the woman who gave me to them?"

"I don't know them." Gently, he turned her until they were face-to-face. "But I know you."

"I feel . . ." She drew a long breath, and let it

come. "Relieved. For as long as I can remember, I've been afraid I was like her, had no real choice about being like her. But I'm not. I'm not."

Shuddering once, she laid her head on his shoulder. "I don't ever have to worry about that again."

"I'm sorry for her," he murmured. "For closing herself off to you. To love."

Miranda knew what love was now, the terror and thrill of it. Whatever happened, she was grateful that part of herself had been opened. Even if the lock had been picked by a thief.

"Yes, so am I." She held on, one last moment, then drew away to stand on her own. "I'm going to go to Cook with Richard's book."

"Give me time to get to Florence. I didn't want to leave today, not when you had all this on your mind. I'll leave tonight if I can manage it, or first thing in the morning. We'll cut it back to thirty-six hours. That should do it."

"I can't give you more than that. I need this to be over."

"It will be."

She smiled, found it easier than she'd imagined. "And no sneaking into bedrooms, no riffling through jewelry boxes or safes."

"Absolutely not. As soon as I'm finished with the Carters."

"Oh, for God's sake."

"I won't steal a thing. Didn't I resist those pearls of your grandmother's? All that lovely Italian gold of Elise's? Even the pretty little locket I could have given one of my nieces? I'd have been a hero."

"Your nieces are too young for lockets." She let out a sigh and leaned her head on his shoulder again. "I didn't get mine until I was sixteen. My grandmother gave me a very pretty heart-shaped one that her mother had given to her."

"And you put a lock of your boyfriend's hair in it."

"Hardly. I didn't have boyfriends. She'd already put her picture in it anyway, and my grandfather's. It was to help me remember my roots."

"Did it?"

"Of course. Good New England stock always remembers roots. I'm a Jones," she said quietly. "And Elizabeth was right. I might never have been hers, but I was always my grandmother's."

"You'll have her pearls now."

"Yes, and I'll treasure them. I lost the locket a few years ago. Broke my heart." Feeling better, she straightened. "I need to get maintenance in here. We have to put this place back in order. I'm hoping we can open the exhibit to the public tomorrow."

"You do that," he murmured. "I'll meet you back at the house later. Go straight there, will you, so I don't have to search you out."

"Where else would I go?"

CHAPTER THIRTY

ANDREW WHISTLED AS HE WALKED INTO THE HOUSE. He knew a grin was plastered on his face. It had been there all day. It wasn't just the sex—well, he thought, jogging up the stairs, the sex hadn't hurt. It had been a long dry spell for old Andrew J. Jones.

But he was in love. And Annie loved him back. Spending the day with her had been the most exciting, the most peaceful, the most amazing experience he'd ever known. It had been almost spiritual, he decided with a chuckle.

They'd cooked breakfast together, and had eaten it in bed. They'd talked until his throat was raw. So many words, so many thoughts and feelings bursting to get out. He'd never been able to talk to anyone the way he could talk to Annie.

Except Miranda. He couldn't wait to tell Miranda. They were going to be married in June.

Not a big, formal wedding, nothing like what he and Elise had done. Something simple and sweet, that's what Annie wanted. Right in the backyard with friends and music. He was going to ask Miranda to be his best man. She'd get such a kick out of that.

He stepped into his bedroom. He wanted to get out of the wrinkled mess of the tuxedo. He was taking Annie out to dinner, and tomorrow, he was buying her a ring. She said she didn't need one, but on that one issue he was going into override.

He wanted to see his ring on her finger.

He shrugged out of his jacket, tossed it aside. He vowed to shovel out his room sometime that week. He and Annie wouldn't be moving in after they were married. The house was Miranda's now. The new Dr. and Mrs. Jones were going house hunting as soon as they got back from their honeymoon.

He was going to take her to Venice.

He was still grinning as he struggled to tug out his studs. Out of the corner of his eye he caught a blur of motion. Pain exploded in his head, a burst of red light behind his eyes. His knees buckled as he tried to turn, tried to strike out. The second blow had him crashing into a table and falling into the black.

The storm broke. Miranda was still a mile from home when the rain flooded over her windshield. Lightning slashed so close that its companion burst of thunder shook the car. It was going to be a mean one. She forced herself to slow her speed though she wanted nothing more at that moment than to be home, to be dry and warm and inside.

Fog was sneaking along the ground, masking the shoulder of the road. To narrow her concentration, she switched off the radio, shifted forward in her seat.

But her mind played it all back.

The call from Florence, then the mugging. John Carter flying out while she was delayed. The bronze had been in the safe in her mother's office. Who had access to the safe? Only Elizabeth.

But if Miranda's association with Ryan had taught her anything, it was that locks were made to be picked.

Richard had run tests; therefore, he had gained access to the bronze. Who had worked with him? Who had brought the gun to the Institute and used it?

John? She tried to imagine it but kept seeing his homely, concerned face. Vincente? Loud, friendly, avuncular Vincente? Could either of them have pumped two bullets into Richard, have struck Elise?

And why in her office, why at an event with hundreds of people wandering the lower levels? Why take such a risk?

Because it had impact, Miranda realized. Because it once again put her name in the paper in a scandal. Because it had ruined the opening of the exhibit and overshadowed all the effort she'd put into it.

It was personal, it had to be. But what had she done to create that kind of animosity and obsession? Who had she harmed? John, she thought. If she was disgraced beyond repair, if she was forced to resign from the Institute, he would be the logical choice for her replacement. It would mean a promotion, a larger salary, more power and prestige.

Could it be that simple?

Or Vincente. He'd known her the longest, been the closest to her. Was there something she'd done to cause resentment, envy? Was it a matter of money to buy the jewels, the clothes, the big, splashy trips that made his young wife happy?

Who else was left? Giovanni and Richard were dead, Elise was in the hospital. Elizabeth . . .

Could that lifetime of resentment have bloomed into this kind of hate?

Leave it for the police, she told herself, and rolled the worst of the tension out of her shoulders when she pulled the car to the front of the house. In less than thirty-six hours she would pass this nasty ball over to Cook.

It meant spending most of her evening working out every step she could tell him. And all the steps she couldn't.

She picked up her briefcase. Richard's book was inside it, and she intended to read it cover to cover tonight. Maybe she'd missed something on the one quick skim she'd had time for.

The fact that her umbrella was in the trunk rather than on the seat beside her only proved her thoughts were too scattered and distracted for logical reasoning. She used the briefcase as a shield, holding it over her head as she made a dash to the porch.

She was soaked through anyway.

Inside, she dragged a hand through her hair to scatter the rain, and called out for Andrew. She hadn't seen him since she left the hospital the night before, but his car was parked in its usual spot. It was time, she'd decided, they too had a talk.

It was time she told him everything, trusted him enough for that.

She called out again as she started upstairs. Damn it, she wanted to get out of her wet clothes, take a hot bath. Why wouldn't he at least answer?

Probably sleeping, she thought. The man slept like the dead. Well, he was going to have to do a Lazarus, because she wanted to tell him everything she could before their mother arrived.

"Andrew?" His door wasn't quite closed, but she gave it a perfunctory knock before nudging it open. The room was pitch-dark, and though she imagined he would curse viciously, she reached for the light switch that would turn on the floor lamp. She muttered an oath of her own when the lamp stayed dark.

The power was still on. Damn it, he hadn't replaced the bulb again. She started forward, intending to give him a good shake, and tripped over him.

"Andrew, for God's sake!" In a brilliant flash of lightning she saw him at her feet, still wearing the tux he'd put on the night before.

It wasn't the first time she'd come across him

passed out in his clothes, sprawled on the floor and stinking of liquor.

The anger came first, one hot spurt of it that pushed her to just turn around, just walk out and leave him where he'd fallen. Then the disappointment, the grief flooded in.

"How could you do this to yourself again?" she murmured. She crouched down, hoping he wasn't so far gone that she couldn't rouse him and get him into bed.

It struck her suddenly that she didn't smell whiskey, or the sick sweat that carried it. She reached down, shook him, then with a sigh laid a hand on his head.

And felt the sticky warmth. Blood.

"Oh God. Andrew. No, oh please." Her smeared and trembling fingers probed for a pulse. And the bedside lamp switched on.

"He's not dead. Yet." The voice was soft, with a light laugh at the edges. "Would you like to keep him alive, Miranda?"

Normally Ryan hated to repeat himself, but he let himself into Elizabeth's suite exactly as he'd done before. It wasn't the time for fancywork. The rooms were silent and empty, but that didn't matter to him.

He'd have found a way around, or through, any occupant.

In the bedroom, he took out the jewelry case precisely as he had two nights ago. And removed the locket.

It was only a hunch, just a kernel of ice in his

gut, but he'd learned to follow his instincts. He studied the old photographs, saw no particular resemblance. Then again, perhaps around the eyes. Maybe there was something around the woman's eyes.

Using a small probe, he popped the elegant little oval out. She'd had it inscribed under her photo, not her husband's. He'd thought she would.

And his blood was cool and steady as he read it: *Miranda, on the occasion of your sixteenth birthday. Never forget where you come from or where you wish to go. Gran*

"We've got you," he said quietly, and slipped the locket into his pocket. He was already pulling his phone out as he hurried back out to the corridor.

"Elise." Miranda forced herself to speak calmly, to keep her eyes on Elise's face and not on the gun that was pointed dead-center at her chest. "He's badly hurt. I need to call an ambulance."

"He'll keep for a while." With her free hand, she tapped the neat bandage on the back of her own head. "I did. It's amazing how quickly you can bounce back from a good bash on the head. You thought he was drunk, didn't you?" Her eyes glittered with delight at the thought. "That's really perfect. If I'd thought of it and had time, I'd have gotten a bottle and poured it over him. Just to set the scene. Don't worry, I only hit him twice—not nearly as often, or as hard, as I hit Giovanni. But then Andrew didn't see me. Giovanni did."

Terrified Andrew would bleed to death while she

did nothing, Miranda snatched up a T-shirt from the littered floor, balled it, and pressed it to the wound.

"Giovanni was your friend. How could you have killed him?"

"I wouldn't have had to if you'd left him out of it. His blood's on your hands, just like Andrew's is right now."

Miranda curled her fingers into her palm. "And Richard."

"Oh, Richard. He killed himself." A faint line of irritation dug between her eyebrows. "He started falling apart right after Giovanni. Falling apart, piece by piece. Cried like a baby, told me it had to stop. No one was supposed to die, he said. Well." She moved her shoulders. "Plans changed. The minute he sent you that ridiculous e-mail, he was dead."

"But you sent the others, the faxes."

"Oh yes." With her free hand, Elise twisted the delicate gold chain draped around her neck. "Did they frighten you, Miranda? Confuse you? Make you wonder?"

"Yes." Keeping her movements slow, she tugged a blanket from the foot of the bed and settled it over her brother. "You killed Rinaldi too."

"That man was a constant annoyance. He kept insisting the bronze was real—as if a plumber would know anything about it. He even stormed into Elizabeth's office, babbling, rambling. But it made her start thinking. I could tell."

"You have the bronze, but you'll never be able to sell it."

"Sell it? Why should I want to sell it? Do you think this is about money?" She pressed a hand to her stomach as she laughed. "It's never been about money. It's you. It's you and me, Miranda, like it's always been."

Lightning shimmered against the glass of the window behind Elise, ragged forks of it digging into the sky. "I've never done anything to you."

"You were born! You were born with everything right at your fingertips. The prized daughter of the house. The eminent Dr. Jones of the Maine Joneses, with your highly respected parents, your fucking bloodline, your servants, your snooty grandmother in her big house on the hill."

She gestured wildly, turning Miranda's stomach to a greasy wave as the gun swung in every direction. "You know where I was born? In a charity ward, and I lived in a lousy two-room apartment because my father wouldn't acknowledge me, wouldn't accept the responsibility. I deserved everything you had, and I got it. But I had to work for it, to beg for scholarships. I made sure I went to the same colleges as you did. I watched you, Miranda. You never even knew I was there."

"No." Miranda removed the cloth from Andrew's head. She thought the flow of blood was slowing. She prayed it wasn't wishful thinking.

"Then again, you didn't do much socializing, did you? Amazing how all this money made you so boring. And I had to scrimp and save while all the time you were living in a nice house, being waited on, reaping in glory."

"Let me call an ambulance for Andrew."

"Shut up! Shut the hell up. I'm not finished." She stepped forward, jabbing with the gun. "You shut the hell up and listen to me or I'll shoot the sorry son of a bitch here and now."

"Don't!" Instinctively, Miranda shifted her body between the gun and Andrew. "Don't hurt him, Elise. I'll listen."

"And keep your mouth shut. Jesus, I hate that mouth of yours. You talk and everybody listens. Like you spit gold coins." She kicked a discarded shoe across the floor until it rapped solidly into the wall. "It should have been me, it should always have been me, and it would have been if the son of a bitch who got my mother pregnant, who promised her everything hadn't been married to your grandmother."

"My grandmother?" Miranda shook her head even as her fingers slid slowly down to check Andrew's pulse. "You're trying to tell me my grandfather was your father?"

"The old bastard just couldn't keep his zipper up, even into his sixties. My mother was young and stupid and she thought he'd ditch his ice bitch of a wife and marry her. Stupid, stupid, stupid."

To punctuate her feelings, she snatched up an agate paperweight from the occasional table and winged it over Miranda's head. It boomed against the wall like a cannonball.

"She let herself be used. Let him get away without paying, never did one goddamn thing to make him pay, so we lived hand to mouth." Her eyes glittered with fury as she shoved the table over.

Another Jones, Miranda thought frantically, another careless liaison and inconvenient pregnancy. She shifted to the balls of her feet, braced. But the gun swung back, its barrel aimed toward the center of her body. And Elise smiled beautifully.

"I watched you. I watched you for years. I planned for years. You were my goal as long as I can remember. I went into the same field. I was every bit as good as you. Better. I went to work for you. I married your useless brother, I made myself invaluable to your mother. I'm more of a daughter to her than you've ever been."

"Oh yes," Miranda said with perfect sincerity. "You are. Believe me, I mean nothing to her."

"You're the centerpiece. I'd have had your position sooner or later. You'd have been the one scrambling for scraps. Remember the *David?* That was quite a coup for you, wasn't it?"

"So you stole it, had Harry copy it."

"Harry was very enthusiastic. It's so pitifully easy to manipulate men. They look at me and they think, She's so delicate, so lovely. And all they want to do is fuck and protect."

She laughed again, sliding her gaze down to Andrew. "I'll say this for your brother. He had some good moves in bed. It was a nice side benefit, but breaking his heart was better. Watching him slide into the bottle because he couldn't figure out what he'd done to turn me away. Poor, poor Andrew."

Then her expression changed again, as capricious as the lightning outside and just as volatile. "I was going to reel him back eventually, after I'd finished everything. Finished you. What a beautiful irony that would be. I still will," she added, with a smile blooming again. "That cheap little number he's screwing now won't even be a memory when I move back to Maine. That is, if I let him live."

"There's no need to hurt him. It's not him, Elise. Let me call an ambulance. You can keep the gun on me. I won't try to get away. Just let me call an ambulance for him."

"Not used to begging, are you? But you do it well. You do everything so well, Miranda. I'll think about it." She cocked her head in warning as Miranda rose. "Careful. I wouldn't kill you, not at first, but I'd cripple you."

"What do you want?" Miranda demanded. "What the hell do you want?"

"I want you to listen!" She shouted it, waving the gun so that the barrel jumped from Miranda's heart to her head and back again. "I want you to stand there and listen to what I say, to do what I tell you, to crawl when I'm finished. I want it all."

"All right." How much time? Miranda thought frantically. How much time was left before Elise snapped, before the gun went off? "I'm listening. The *David* was really only practice, wasn't it?"

"Oh, you're smart. Always so smart. It was backup. I knew I could put a chink in your reputation with it. But I'm patient. There was bound to be something bigger—with the way your star was rising, there was going to be something more important. Then there was *The Dark Lady.* I knew, as soon as Elizabeth told me she was sending for you, that there was an important piece coming in, I knew this would be the one. She trusted me. I made certain she trusted me. Kowtowing to her every whim for years.

"Standjo's going to be mine too," she added matter-of-factly. "I'll be in the director's chair by the time I'm forty."

Miranda slid her gaze to the side, scanning for a weapon.

"You look at me! You look at me when I talk to you."

"I'm looking at you, Elise. I'm listening. It was *The Dark Lady.*"

"Have you ever seen a more magnificent piece? Anything quite so powerful?"

"No." The rain was pounding like battle drums against the window. "No, I haven't. You wanted her. I can't blame you. But you couldn't do it alone. So you had Richard."

"Richard was in love with me. I was very fond of Richard," she said almost dreamily. "I might have married him, for a while at least. He was useful, he could have continued to be very useful. We ran the tests at night. I had the combination to Elizabeth's safe. It was ridiculously easy. All I had to do was arrange for you to be delayed. I did specify that you weren't to be seriously hurt. I wanted to keep you healthy until I could ruin you."

"Richard made the copy."

"As I said, he was very useful. I did some of the

work myself. We wanted it to pass basic tests, even to fool some of the more involved ones. You were perfect, Miranda. You knew when you saw it, just as I did. It was unmistakable. You could feel it, couldn't you? The power of that piece, the glory in it."

"Yes, I could feel it." She thought she heard Andrew stir, but couldn't be sure. "You leaked the project to the press."

"Elizabeth is so strict about such things. Rules and regulations, proper channels, integrity. She reacted exactly as expected—it didn't hurt that I gave her subtle little nudges, all the while claiming that I was sure you didn't mean it. You'd just gotten caught up. You were so enthusiastic. I was your champion, Miranda. I was brilliant."

The phone rang while they stared at each other. And Elise smiled slowly. "We'll just let the machine pick that up, shall we. We have so much more to talk about."

Why the hell didn't she answer? Ryan fought his way through the storm, tires skidding on wet pavement as he pushed for speed. She'd left the Institute to go home. She wasn't picking up her cell phone, or the phone at the house. Steering one-handed, he punched in information and got the number for the hospital.

"Elise Warfield," he demanded. "She's a patient."

"Dr. Warfield was released this evening."

Ice gathered in his gut again. He punched the

accelerator, sending the car into a violent fishtail. Going against a lifetime of habit, he called the police. "Get me Detective Cook."

"I'm going to need the copies, Miranda. Where are they?"

"I don't have them."

"Now you know that's a lie and you lie so poorly. I really need those copies." This time Elise stepped forward. "We want this all tidy in the end, don't we?"

"Why should I give them to you? You're going to kill me either way."

"Of course I am. It's the only logical step, isn't it? But . . ." She shifted the gun and stopped Miranda's heart. "I wouldn't have to kill Andrew."

"Don't." Quickly, Miranda held up her hands, a gesture of surrender. "Please."

"Give me the copies, and I won't."

"They're hidden, out in the lighthouse." Away from Andrew, she thought.

"Oh, perfect. Can you guess where I was conceived?" Elise laughed until tears swam in her eyes. "My mother told me how he took her there—to paint her—then seduced her. How wonderful that it all ends where it really began." Elise gestured with the gun. "After you, Niece Miranda."

With one last glance at her brother, she turned. She knew the gun was aimed at her back. At her spine, she imagined. In a larger space she might have a chance. If she could distract Elise for just an instant, she could try. She was bigger, stronger, and she was sane.

"The police are closing in," she told Elise, keeping her eyes straight ahead. "Cook's determined to close this case. He won't give up."

"After tonight, the case will be closed. Keep moving. You always walk with such a purposeful stride, Miranda—let's be consistent."

"If you shoot me, how will you explain it?"

"I'm hoping that won't be necessary. But if it is, I'll put the gun in Andrew's hand, his finger on the trigger, and fire it again. It'll be messy, but in the end the logical conclusion would be you argued over this business. You struck him, he shot you. It's your gun, after all."

"Yes, I know. It couldn't have been easy for you to hit yourself, give yourself a concussion after you killed Richard."

"A bump on the head, a few stitches. I got a lot of sympathy out of it, and it goes a long way to putting me in the clear. How could a fragile little thing like me work up the guts to fake an attack like that?"

She jabbed the gun into the base of Miranda's spine. "But you and I know I can do a lot more."

"Yes, we do. We'll need a flashlight."

"Get it. You still keep it in the second drawer on the left, I imagine. Such a creature of habit."

Miranda removed the flashlight, flicking it on while testing its weight. It could be a weapon. All she needed was the opportunity.

She opened the back door and stepped out into

the driving rain. She thought of running, of taking a leap into the gathering fog. But the gun was still pressed into her back. She'd be dead before she took the first step.

"Looks like we're about to get very wet. Keep going."

Hunched against wind and rain, she walked steadily toward the point. Distance was imperative now. She could hear the waves crashing wildly, stirred by the storm. Every slash of lightning threw the cliffs into sharp relief.

"Your plan won't work out here, Elise."

"Keep going, keep going."

"It won't work. If you use that gun on me now, they'll know there was someone else here. They'll know it couldn't have been Andrew. And they'll find you."

"Shut up. What do you care? You'll be dead anyway."

"You'll never have everything I have. That's really what you want, isn't it? The name, the pedigree, the position. It'll never be yours."

"You're wrong. I'll have it all. Instead of just being ruined, you'll be dead."

"Richard kept a book." She used the circling stream of light from the tower on the point to guide her now, shifting her grip on the flashlight. "He wrote it all down. Everything he did."

"Liar!"

"Everything, Elise. It's all recorded. They'll know I was right. Dead or alive, I'll still have the glory. So everything you've done is for nothing."

"Bitch. You lying bitch."

"But I lie so poorly." Teeth gritted, she swung around. The force of the blow struck Elise on an upflung arm and sent her sprawling. Miranda leaped on her, grabbing for the gun.

She'd been wrong, she realized. Sanity wasn't an advantage. Elise fought like an animal, teeth snapping, nails gouging. She felt hot pain on her throat, a spurt and trickle of blood as they rolled over the rocky ground toward the edge of the cliffs.

Ryan shouted her name as he ran into the house, shouting it again and again as he pounded up the stairs. When he found Andrew terror squeezed his heart into a hot ball.

He heard the crash of thunder, then the echoing blast of gunshots. With fear drenching his skin, he shoved through the terrace doors.

There, silhouetted by the fire flash of lightning, he saw two figures tangled on the cliffs. Even as he offered up the first prayer, as he climbed over the rail to leap down, he saw them go off.

Her breath was sobbing, burning her throat. There was pain everywhere, the stench of blood and fear. She gripped the slippery butt of the gun, tried to twist it away. It bucked in her hand, once, twice, and the fury of sound punched pain in her ears.

Someone was screaming, screaming, screaming. She tried to dig her heels in for purchase and found her legs dangling in space. In the blasts and jolts of light, she could see Elise's face over hers, contorted, mouth wide, teeth bared, eyes blind with madness. In them, for one horrified second, she saw herself.

From somewhere she heard her name, a desperate call. As if in answer, she twisted, shoved viciously. With Elise clawing at her, they tumbled over the edge.

She could hear a woman laughing, or perhaps it was weeping as she tore at rock and dirt with her fingers, felt herself dragged down.

A thousand prayers babbled in her mind, a thousand jumbled images. Rock bit at her skin as her body fought to cling to the wall of the cliff. Panting, wild with fear, she looked over her shoulder, saw Elise's white face, dark eyes, saw her even now release her hold on rock to aim the gun—and then she fell.

Trembling, sobbing, Miranda pressed her cheek against the cold face of the cliff. Her muscles were screaming, her fingers burning. Below her, the sea she had always loved crashed impatiently and waited.

Her stomach shuddered, spewing a dizzying nausea into her throat. Fighting it back, she lifted her face to the pounding rain again, stared at the edge just a foot above her head, watched the shaft of light from the old tower slice through the dark as if to guide her.

She would not die this way. She would not lose this way. She kept her eyes focused on the goal and fought to find some small purchase with her feet. She clawed her way up one sweaty inch, then another before her feet slid free.

She was dangling by bloody fingertips when Ryan bellied over the edge.

"Jesus. Sweet Jesus, Miranda, hang on. Look at me. Miranda, look at me, take my hand."

"I'm slipping."

"Take my hand. You have to reach up, just a little." He braced himself on the slick rocks and held both hands down to her.

"I can't let go. My fingers are frozen. I can't let go. I'll fall."

"No you won't." Sweat slid down his face along with the rain. "Take my hand, Miranda." While his head screamed with panic, he grinned at her. "Come on, Dr. Jones. Trust me."

Her breath came out on a wild, broken sob. She pried her numb fingers from the rock and reached for his. For a gut-wrenching instant, she felt herself hang, a fingertip away from death. Then his hand clamped firm over hers.

"Now the other one. I need both your hands."

"Oh God, Ryan." Blind now, she let go.

When her full weight locked his arms, he thought they might both go over. He inched back, cursing the rain that made their hands slip, that seemed to turn the rock into sheer glass. But she was helping him, boosting herself with her feet, her breath hissing with the effort as they worked.

She used her elbows on the ledge, pressing down, scraping them raw as he dragged her the last few inches over the top.

When she collapsed on him, he wrapped her in his arms, cradled her on his lap and rocked them both in the rain.

"I saw you go over. I thought you were dead."

"I would have been." Her face was buried against his chest where his heart beat in hard, jerky pulses. From somewhere in the distance came the high pitched whine of sirens. "If you hadn't come. I couldn't have held on much longer."

"You'd have held on." He tipped her head back, looked into her eyes. There was blood on her face. "You'd have held on," he repeated. "Now you can hold on to me." He picked her up to carry her into the house.

"Don't let go for a while."

"I won't."

EPILOGUE

BUT HE DID. SHE SHOULD HAVE KNOWN HE WOULD. The thieving son of a bitch.

Trust me, he said. And she had. He'd saved her life, only to carelessly leave it in shambles.

Oh, he'd waited, Miranda thought as she paced her bedroom. He'd stuck by her until her cuts and bruises were treated. He'd stayed by her side until they were sure Andrew was out of danger.

His arms had been around her, protective, supportive, when she related the nightmare she'd been through with Elise.

He'd even held her hand while they gave Cook Ryan's slightly edited version of events. And she'd let him. She corroborated everything he said, amended pertinent details to keep him out of a prison cell.

He'd saved her life after all. The worm.

Then he'd vanished, without a word, without a warning. He'd packed up and left.

She knew just where he'd gone. He was the only other person who knew about the storage garage. He'd gone after *The Dark Lady.* She didn't doubt he had it by now, that and the *David.* He'd probably already passed them along to one of his clients for a fat fee and was basking on some beach in the tropics, sipping rum punch and oiling some blonde's butt.

If she ever saw him again . . . but of course, she wouldn't. All the business they had—the legal end of business—was being handled by his gallery manager. The exhibit was a raging success. He'd benefited from that, and from his involvement in helping to solve several murders.

She had her reputation. The international press was raving about her. The brave and brilliant Dr. Jones.

Elise had wanted to destroy her, and in the end had made her.

But she didn't have the bronze, and she didn't have Ryan.

She had to accept she would never have either.

Now she was alone in a big, empty house, with Andrew being fussed over by his fiancée as he recovered. He was happy and healing, and she was glad of it. And she was miserably envious.

She had her reputation all right, she thought. She had the Institute, and perhaps finally, the full knowledge of her parents' respect if not their love.

She had no life whatsoever.

So, she would make a new one. She dragged an impatient hand through her hair. She would take the advice everyone was peppering her with and go on a long, well-deserved vacation. She'd buy a bikini, get a tan, and have a fling.

Oh yes, that's going to happen, she thought with a scowl, and shoved open her terrace doors to step out into the warm spring night.

The flowers she'd planted in big stone urns filled the air with scent. The sweetness of stock, the spice of dianthus, the charm of verbena. Yes, she was learning about some small and lovely things, taking the time to learn. To enjoy.

To fall into the moment.

White and full, the moon rose over the sea, cruised among the stars, and gave the seascape she loved a mystic, intimate glow. The sea sang its rough song with an arrogance that made her yearn.

He'd been gone for two weeks. She knew he wasn't coming back. In the end it was as it had always been. There was something more important than Miranda.

Still, she'd get over it. She was already on her way. She would take that vacation, but she'd use the time right here. It was here she needed to be. Home, making the home she had never been given. She'd finish the garden, she'd have the house painted. She'd buy new curtains.

And while she would never trust another man in this lifetime, at least she knew she could trust herself.

"This moment would be more atmospheric if you were wearing a long, flowing robe."

She didn't whirl. She still had enough control for that. She turned slowly.

He was grinning at her. Dressed in thief's black and standing in her bedroom grinning.

"Jeans and a T-shirt," he continued. "Though you fill them out nicely, they lack the romance of a silk robe the breeze could flutter around you." He stepped out on the terrace. "Hello, Dr. Jones."

She stared, felt his fingertips brush her cheek where a bruise had yet to fade. "You son of a bitch," she said, and rammed her fist full out into his face.

It knocked him back several steps, had his vision wavering. But his balance was good. He shifted his jaw gingerly, dabbed at the blood on his mouth. "Well, that's one way to say hello. Obviously, you're not entirely pleased to see me."

"The only way I'd be pleased to see you is through steel bars, you bastard. You used me, you lied to me. Trust me, you said, and all the time you were after the bronze."

He worked his tongue over his gums, tasted blood. Damn, the woman had a straight-on right jab. "That's not entirely accurate."

She balled her fist, more than ready to use it again. "You went to Florence, didn't you? You walked out of here, got on a plane, and went to Florence for the statues."

"Of course. I told you I was going to."

"Miserable thief."

"I'm an excellent thief. Even Cook thought so—though he'll never prove it." He smiled again, combed his fingers through the thick, dark hair the breeze blew into sexy disorder. "Now I'm a retired thief."

She folded her arms. Her left shoulder was still sore from the night on the cliffs, and the ache eased when she supported it. "I imagine you can live very well in retirement for what you sold the bronzes for."

"A man wouldn't have to work again, in several lifetimes, for what the Michelangelo is worth." While she clenched her fists, he watched her warily as he took out a cigar. "She's the most exquisite thing I've ever seen. The copy was good, it hinted at the power of her. But it couldn't capture her heart, her mind, her essence. I'm amazed anyone who'd seen both could mistake one for the other. *The Dark Lady* sings, Miranda. She is incomparable."

"She belongs to the Italian people. She belongs in a museum where she can be seen and studied."

"You know, that's the first time you've referred to her that way. Before you always said 'it,' or 'the bronze,' but never *'her.'* "

She turned to look out over the lawn, where the garden—hers now—was glowing in the moonlight. "I'm not going to discuss pronouns."

"It's more than that, and you know it. You've learned something you neglected all these years in your quest for knowledge. Art lives."

He blew out a stream of smoke. "How's Andrew?"

"Now you want to discuss my family. Fine. He's doing very well. So are Elizabeth and Charles." It was how she thought of them now. "They're back to their separate lives, and though Elizabeth mourns the loss of *The Dark Lady,* she's well enough. Elise hurt her more. The breach of trust and affection." She turned away. "I know how she feels. I know exactly what it is to be used and discarded like that."

He started to step forward, then changed his mind and leaned back against the wall. Seductions, apologies, cooing words weren't the way with Miranda in her current mood.

"We used each other," he corrected. "And did a damn good job of it."

"And now we're done," she said flatly. "What do you want here?"

"I came to offer you a deal."

"Did you really? Why would I deal with you?"

"Several reasons come to mind. Tell me this first. Why haven't you given me up to the police?"

"Because I keep my word."

"Is that it?" When she didn't answer he shrugged, but it bothered him. "Okay then, on to business. I have something you'd like to see."

After tossing the cigar high over the rail, he turned back into the bedroom. He brought out his bag, took out the carefully wrapped contents. Even before he uncovered it, she knew, and was too stunned to speak.

"Gorgeous, isn't she?" He held the figure as a man holds a lover, with great care and possessiveness. "It was love at first sight for me. She's a woman who brings men to their knees, and knows it. She isn't always kind, but she fascinates. It's no wonder murder was done for her."

He looked over at Miranda, studied the way she looked with the moonlight sprinkling over her hair and shoulders. "Do you know, when I found her, stored in a metal box, locked into a chest in that dusty garage—where Elise's car was hidden, by the way—when I took her out and held her like this for the first time, I would have sworn I heard harpsong. Do you believe in such things, Dr. Jones?"

She could almost hear it herself, as she had in her dreams. "Why did you bring her here?"

"I imagined you'd want to see her again. You'd want to be sure I had her."

"I knew you had her." She couldn't help herself. Moving closer, she ran a fingertip over the smiling face. "I've known for two weeks. As soon as I realized you'd gone, I knew." She lifted her gaze from the bronze to his face. His beautiful, treacherous face. "I didn't expect you to come back."

"Actually, to be honest, neither did I." He set the bronze on the stone table. "We'd both gotten what we'd wanted. You've got your reputation. You're quite a celebrity these days. You've been vindicated. More than vindicated, you've been lauded. I imagine you've had offers from book publishers and Hollywood to sell your story."

She had, and it continued to embarrass her. "You haven't answered the question."

"I'm getting to it," he muttered. "I kept the deal. I never agreed to give the *David* back, and as to her—I never agreed to anything but to find her. I found her, and now she's mine, so there's a new deal on the table. How bad do you want her?"

It took all her willpower not to gape. "You mean to sell her to me? You want me to buy stolen property?"

"Actually, I was thinking of a trade."

"A trade?" She thought of the Cellini he coveted. And the Donatello. Her palms began to itch. "What do you want for her?"

"You."

Her rapid thoughts screeched to a halt. "Excuse me?"

"A lady for a lady. It seems fair."

She paced to the end of the terrace, back again. Oh, he was worse than a worm, she decided. "You expect me to have sex with you in exchange for a Michelangelo."

"Don't be stupid. You're good, but nobody's that good. I want the whole package. She's mine, Miranda. I might even be able to claim finder's privilege, though it's dicey. But I have her, and you don't. In the past few days it occurred to me, much to my discomfort, that I want you more than I want her."

"I'm not following you."

"Yes, you are. You're too bright not to. You can have her. You can put her on the mantel or give her back to Florence. You can use her for a doorstop, I won't give a damn. But you'll have to give me what I want for her. I've got a yen to live in this house."

There was such a terrible pressure in her chest. "You want to live here?"

He narrowed his eyes. "You know, Dr. Jones, I don't think you're pretending to be thick. You just don't get it. Yes, I want to live in this house. It's a good spot to raise children. Look at that, you went white as a ghost. God, that's one of the things I love about you. You're always so shocked when someone interrupts the logic. And I love you, Miranda, beyond sense."

She made some sound, it couldn't be construed as words, as her heart staggered in her chest. Stumbled. Fell.

He crossed to her, amused now rather than panicked. She hadn't moved a muscle. "I really have to insist on children, Miranda. I'm Irish and Italian. What else would you expect?"

"You're asking me to marry you?"

"I'm working my way up to it. It might surprise you that it's not any easier for me than it is for you. I said I love you."

"I heard you."

"Damn, stubborn—" He cut himself off, inhaled sharply. "You want the bronze, don't you?" Before she could answer he caught her chin in his hand. "You're in love with me." When her brows came together, he grinned. "Don't bother to deny it. If you weren't you'd have turned me over in a heartbeat when you realized I'd gone after her for myself."

"I've gotten over it."

"Liar." He lowered his mouth, just to nibble at hers. "Take the deal, Miranda. You won't regret it."

"You're a thief."

"Retired." He molded her hip with one hand, reached into his pocket with the other. "Here, let's make it official."

She struggled out of the kiss and jerked her hand free when he started to slip the ring onto it. The ring, she noted with surprise and delight, he'd given her once before.

"Don't be so pigheaded." He took her hand, uncurled her fingers and pushed the ring into place. "Take the deal."

Now she recognized the pressure in her chest. It was her heart beating again. "Did you pay for the ring?"

"Jesus. Yes, I paid for the ring."

She let herself consider it, watched it wink and sparkle. And let him sweat, she thought. She hoped. "I'll give her back to Italy. Explanations of how I came by her might be awkward."

"We'll think of something. Take the deal, damn it."

"How many children?"

His smile spread slowly. "Five."

She snorted out a laugh. "Please. Two."

"Three, with an option."

"Three, final."

"Done." He started to lower his head, but she slapped a hand on his chest. "I'm not finished."

"You would be, honey, if I kissed you," he said, with just enough arrogance to make her fight back a grin.

"No side work," she said primly. "Whatsoever, for any reason."

He winced. "For *any* reason? There might be a good one."

"For any reason."

"I'm retired," he muttered, but had to rub the ache in his chest. "No side work."

"You hand over to me any and all fake identification you've accumulated over your checkered career."

"All? But—" He caught himself. "Fine." He could always get more, should circumstances call for it. "Next?"

"That should do it." She touched his cheek, then framed his face. "I love you beyond sense," she murmured, cherishing his words enough to give them back to him. "I'll take the deal. I'll take you, but that means you're taking me. The Jones curse. I'm bad luck."

"Dr. Jones." He turned his lips into her palm. "Your luck's about to change. Trust me."